英 漢 對 照
天 方 夜 談
STORIES FROM
THE ARABIAN NIGHTS

英　漢　對　照

天　方　夜　談

目　　次

頁數

一．　這故事怎樣發生的 …………………………………… 2

二．　漁翁和妖魔 …………………………………………… 10

三．　魔馬的故事 …………………………………………… 20

四．　王子阿米德故事 ……………………………………… 46

五．　致富奇談 ……………………………………………… 84

六．　阿萊廷的故事 ………………………………………… 118

七．　橄欖案 ………………………………………………… 188

八．　智婢殺盜的故事 ……………………………………… 210

九．　阿保哈生的故事 ……………………………………… 258

十．　三姊妹的故事 ………………………………………… 304

十一．　航海家孫柏達的故事 ……………………………… 352

十二．　理髮匠第六兄弟的故事 …………………………… 430

十三．　王子陳亞拉生與魔王的故事 ……………………… 442

How The Stories Came To Be Told

It is well known that in former days the Sultan of the East were great *tyrants*[1], and knew no law but their own will. Now one of them had a wife who did not obey him, and he was so angry that he had her put to death; and because he no longer had any faith in women, he *caused it to be known*[2] that he meant to have a new wife every day, he would be married at night, and in the morning his wife was to have her head *cut off*[3]. This threw all the women in the *kingdom*[4] into a great *fright*[5]; for the Sultan would have only a beautiful woman for his wife, and no one knew when her turn would come.

It was the duty of the Grand Vizier to find a new wife for the Sultan each day, and you may be sure that he had to *drag*[6] these poor girls to the palace, for no one wanted the honor of being the Sultan's wife for one night if she was to have her head cut off the next day. What was the *terror*[7], then, of the Grand Vizier, when his own daughter, Schehera-zade, came forward and *begged*[8] to be the Sultan's wife!

"Do you know, my daughter," he asked, "what that means? Though you are the daughter of the Grand Vizier, that will not *save*[9] your life." Now

---

【註】 1. 暴君. 2. 佈告國內. 3. 斬(首). 4. 王國. 5. 恐怖. 6. 拉.
7. 驚嚇. 8. 請求. 9. 救.

這故事怎樣發生的

誰都知道，從前東方的蘇丹是一個非常暴虐的君主，他們不知道甚麽是法律，只要心裏想要怎樣做便怎樣做。卻說有一個蘇丹，因爲他的妻子對他不忠實，心中非常惱怒，立刻把她殺死，從此他便再也不信愛女子了。他佈告國內，每一天，要娶一個新的妻子；當天晚上和這女人結了婚，第二天早上這女人就要拿去斬首。這佈告宣佈出來，端的把全國婦女都嚇壞了。因爲那蘇丹每天要娶一個美女做妻子，全國女郎，誰都害怕自己要臨到這命運哩。

承辦這事的，乃是蘇丹的宰相。他的職務，每天須物色一個美人獻進宮去。你想他每天是何等地煩惱，強拉着這些可憐的女孩們進宮裏去；因爲誰都不願做一夜蘇丹的妻子，第二天早上，她的頭就給砍掉了。這宰相是何等吃驚着，當他看見自己的女兒西哈薩德，竟願意要求做蘇丹的妻子了！

他問道：『我的女兒，你知道那是怎麼一囘事？你雖是宰相的女兒，但也救不得你的性命呀。』西哈薩德是一個十

5

Schehera-zade was as brave as she was beautiful, and she said:

"I know it well, but I have thought of a plan by which, I may put an end, to this *dreadful state*[1] of things. If you do not take me to the Sultan, I shall go by myself." So the Grand Vizier went to the Sultan and told him that his own daughter begged for the honor of being the Sultan's wife for one night. The Sultan was *filled*[2] with *wonder*[3].

"Do not *err*[4]," he said to the Grand Vizier. "Though she is your daughter, her head must be cut off in the morning."

"I know it well," said the Grand Vizier, sadly; "but you know how it is with daughters, It is hard to say 'no' to them."

Now when Schehera-zade, was led into the presence of the Sultan, her *veil*[5] was lifted, and the Sultan saw that she was very *fair*[6]. But he saw also that there were tears in her eyes.

"Why do you *weep*[7]?" said he.

"I weep," she said, "because of my sister. I have the honor to be the wife of the Sultan; but I love my sister, and I cannot *bear*[8] the thought of saying good-by to her now. *Grant*[9] me one favor. Let her pass this one night, on a *couch*[10] near me."

【註】 1. 可怕的情形. 2. 充滿. 3. 驚愕. 4. 錯誤. 5. 面罩. 6. 美麗的. 7. 哭. 8. 忍. 9. 賜與. 10. 坑.

分勇敢的女孩子，她的勇敢和她的美色，是一般的卓絕。她便說：

『我十分知道的，我卻想得一個妙計，或許可以挽救那件可怕的事情。您倘不願意帶女兒進宮去，那末女兒可以自己走去。』那宰相只得走到蘇丹那裏，啓奏自己女兒要求這榮幸，做一夜蘇丹的妻子。蘇丹聽了，暗暗納罕。

他對宰相說：『你沒有弄錯吧！她雖是你的女兒，不過早上仍要斬首的呵。』

那宰相愁苦地說道：『陛下聖諭宣佈，臣非常清楚的，臣敢說臣的女兒得有例外嗎？』

西哈薩德帶到蘇丹的面前，當把面罩去掉的時候，蘇丹看見她生得非常美麗；卻又瞧見她兩眼滿是熱淚。

他說：『你爲什麼哭呢？』

她答道：『爲的是我的妹子，我雖有做蘇丹妻子的榮幸，但我愛我的妹妹，現在我以不能和她話別，因此悲痛得很。請皇上賜我一個恩典。讓她這晚睡在靠近我的一張坑上罷！』

The Sultan had already been won by the beauty of Schehera-zade, and he found it easy to grant the favor. So the younger sister, Dinar-zade, was brought in. Now Schehera-zade had told her sister how she was to act, and about an hour before *dawn*[1] Dinar-zade, who was wide awake, spoke and said:—

"Sister, if you are not asleep, I wish you would tell me one of those *delightful*[2] stories you know so well. It will soon be light." Schehera-zade turned to the Sultan and said:—

"Will *Your Highness*[3] *suffer*[4] me to tell my sister a story?"

"Freely," said the Sultan, who liked stories himself; and Schehera-zade began to tell a story, and she told it in such a way that, when *daylight*[5] came, s e had reached the *most interesting point.*[6] But at daylight the Sultan must needs rise and go to his *council.*[7]

"That is a most interesting story," said Dinar-zade, "but how does it end?"

"The end is more strange than the beginning," said her sister. "If Your Highness," she said, turning to the Sultan, "will let me live one more day, I can then finish the story."

The Sultan wanted very much to hear the end, so he gave Schehera-zade one more day to live.

【註】　1. 天明.　2. 有趣的.　3. 吾王.　4. 容許.　5. 日光.　6. 最有趣的地方.　7. 國務會議.

蘇丹見西哈薩德這般豔麗，早就傾倒了，如今對於她這個要求，自然容易允准。因此，那妹子狄娜薩德，帶進宮中來了。西哈薩德遂教她怎樣行事，在天未明的一點鐘前，狄娜薩德醒了過來，說道：

『姐姐，若你睡不着，請給我講個有趣的故事吧！那些故事，你知道得很多的。天快亮了。』西哈薩德乃轉向蘇丹說：

『高貴的王，能允許我給我妹妹講一個故事嗎？』

蘇丹說：『聽便。』他自己原來也很喜聽故事的；西哈薩德乃講着一個故事，她講的方法，是早已安排好的，一到天明，恰是談到最吃緊的地方。因為天色一明，蘇丹卽須起身早朝去了。

狄娜薩德說：『那是個最有趣的故事啦！但結局怎樣呢？』

他的姊姊向蘇丹說：『啊！結局比起首更離奇，更有趣啦！要是高貴的王肯饒恕我多活一天，那末我可講完這個故事。』

蘇丹要聽到這故事的結局，因此允許她這個要求，

meaning to have her head cut off after that. But when the next morning came, and Dinar-zade asked for the rest of the story, Schehera-zade told it in such a way that it carried her into the middle of another story; and daylight came, and that story was not done. The Sultan *put off*[1] her death one day more.

Thus it *went on and on*;[2] a story was never done, and for a thousand and one nights Schehera-zade told her stories to the Sultan. By that time, though she had not told nearly all her stories, the Sultan had grown so *fond of*[3] her, and had come to have such faith in her, that he forgot the wife who once did not obey, and made it known throughout the kingdom that Schehera-zade was to be the one Sultaness so long as he lived. The Grand Vizier and all the people had great joy at this; all the girls in the kingdom once more *breathed*[4] freely, and Schehera-zade kept on telling her stories.

Now these are some of the tales of the Thousand and One Nights.

【註】 1. 移後. 2. 日復一日. 3. 寵愛. 4. 呼吸.

但是談完了仍將她斬首。到了第二天早上，當狄娜薩德教她續談這故事後段的時候，她卻又引起另外一段的故事來，正在吃緊的當兒，天色又發白了；故事不能不暫停。蘇丹只得再許她多活一天。

這樣，一天一天的過着，每個故事從未在一夜中談完，西哈薩德不知不覺就給蘇丹講了一千零一夜故事。那時，她雖然還沒把所有的故事談完，那蘇丹卻變得這般寵幸她，信愛她了。把從前妻子違抗他的事，一古腦兒都忘掉了。他重諭全國，他永立西哈薩德為國后，當他在日的時候，他當盡力愛她保護她。宰相和人民都歡喜的了不得，全國女孩們到現在方始吐一口氣來，重吸自由空氣，西哈薩德在宮中仍繼續講她的故事。

現在這些故事，就是那一千零一夜中所談的幾個。

The Fisherman[1] And The Genie[2]

There was once an old Fisherman who was very poor. He could hardly keep himself, his wife, and his three children from *starving*[3]. Every morning he went out early to fish, but he had made it a rule, never to *cast his net*[4] more than four times a day.

One day he went to the *seashore*[5] before it was light. He cast his net, and then, when he thought it time, he drew it in to the shore. It was very heavy, and he was sure he had a good *draught*[6] of fishes. But no! he pulled hard, and when he had his net on the *beach*[7], he found he had *dragged* in a dead *ass*.[9]

He cast it a second time, and again he waited. Then he slowly drew it in, for it was very heavy. This time his hopes rose, but when the net came *ashore*[10] he found it held only an old *basket*[11] filled with *sand*[12] and *mud*[13].

Once more he threw his net. The third time never fails, he thought. Again the net came slowly ashore. But when he opened it, there was nothing in it but stones, *shells*[14], and *seaweed*[15]. The poor man

---

【註】 1. 漁夫. 2. 魔神. 3. 飢餓. 4. 撒網. 5. 海濱. 6. 一網. 7. 海灘. 8. 拉. 9. 驢. 10. 向岸地. 11. 籃. 12. 沙. 13. 泥. 14. 貝殼. 15. 海藻.

漁　翁　和　妖　魔

從前有個老漁翁，家中很是窮苦。他有一個妻子，三個孩子，因爲太窮了，差不多常常要使他的妻子和孩子們挨餓的。每天很早的時候，他就出去捕魚；但他有個習慣：天天只肯放下四次網便歇手不捉了。

有一天，他走到海邊，那時天尚未明。他放下了網，他將想收網的時候，可是非常沉重，他以爲網了一網大魚，歡喜得了不得。但是不！等他用死力地，把網拉上沙灘來一瞧，原來是一隻很大的死驢。

第二次他又下網，等了一囘，再很慢的拉起，漁網仍是很重。這次他想很有希望了，但拉到岸上一瞧，卻是一隻破籃，籃中盛滿了石子和沙土。

他又放下網。暗暗地想着，第三次決不會再落空了。等他把網很慢地拉將起來，打開來看時，還是沒有什麼，仍是石子，貝殼，和海藻等一類東西。那可憐的漢子

was *sore distressed*[1]. It looked as if he should have nothing to take home to his wife and children.

. It was now *dawn*,[2] and he stopped, to say his *prayers*,[3] for in the East *pious*[4] men say their prayers five times a day. And after he had said his prayers he cast his net for the fourth and last time. When he had waited long enough, he drew the net in, and saw that it was very heavy.

There was not a fish in the net. Instead, the Fisherman drew out a *copper jar*.[5] He set it up, and the mouth of the jar was covered with a *lid*[6] which was *sealed*[7] with *lead*.[8] He shook the jar, but could hear nothing.

"*At any rate*,"[9] he said to himself, "I can sell this to a *coppersmith*[10] and get some money for it." But first, though it seemed empty, he thought he would open it. So he took his knife and cut away the lead. Then he took the lid off. But he could see nothing inside. He turned the jar upside down, and *tapped*[11] it on the *bottom*,[12] but nothing came out. He set the jar upright again, and sat and looked at it. X

Soon he saw a light *smoke*[13] come slowly forth. The smoke grew heavier, and thicker, so that he had to step back a few *paces*[14]. It rose and spread till it

---

【註】 1. 大感痛苦. 2. 天明. 3. 禱告. 4. 虔敬的. 5. 銅瓶. 6. 蓋. 7. 封. 8. 鉛. 9. 無論怎樣. 10. 銅匠. 11. 輕敲. 12. 底. 13. 煙霧. 14. 步.

可憂愁死了，看來今天是沒有甚麼東西，可以帶給妻兒們了。

　　現在天已黎明，他便誠懇的祈禱，因爲照東方信教徒的習慣，每天是有五次的祈禱。祈禱完畢，便下着第四次的網，也是最後一次的網，他有意多等一回，纔收起網來，卻又是很重的一網。

　　不過網裏仍是沒有魚兒。但網到了一個銅瓶兒來了，他將瓶子豎起，瓶口上蓋着一個鉛鑄的蓋兒。他便把瓶子搖了發搖，但也聽不出什麼來。

　　漁翁自言自語道：『無論怎樣，我可以把這瓶兒賣給銅匠去，總可以弄得一點錢來。』不過瞧上去雖然好像空瓶兒似的，但總要想看個究竟，所以他便拿了把小刀，把那鉛鑄的蓋兒割開。他將蓋兒取下，向瓶裏望去，可是什麼也瞧不出來。他又把瓶倒覆過來，在瓶底輕輕地拍了幾下兒，也沒有什麼東西落下。於是他仍將瓶放好，呆呆地坐在地下看它。

　　但是一忽兒，那瓶裏驀地有陣輕淡的煙霧升起。那煙霧愈起愈濃，使他不能不向後退了幾步。煙霧升了起來，發展

shut everything out, like a great *fog*[1]. At last it had wholly left the jar, and had risen into the sky. Then it gathered itself together, into a *solid. mass*[2]. and there, before the Fisherman, stood a *great giant, of*[3] a Genie.

"Get down on your *knees*[4]," said the Genie, to the Fisherman, "for I am going to kill you."

"And why do you kill me? Did I not set you free from the jar?"

"That is the very reason I mean to kill you; but I will grant you one favor."

"And what is that?" asked the Fisherman.

"I will let you choose the manner of your death. Listen, and I will tell you my story. I was one of the *spirits, of heaven*.[5] The great and wise Solomon bade me obey his laws. I was angry and would not. So, to punish me, he shut me up in a copper jar, and sealed, it with lead. Then he gave the jar, to a Genie who obeyed him, and bade him *cast*[6] it into the sea.

"During the first hundred years that I lay on the *floor*[7] of the sea, I made a promise that if any one set me free, I would make him very rich. But no one came to set me, free. During the second hundred years, I made a promise that if any one set

---

開去，好像大霧的樣子，什麼東西也看不見。到後來那煙霧完全離開瓶兒，一直向上升去，卻凝成一個實體，眨眼間落在漁翁的面前，乃是個巨大的妖魔啊。

這怪物向漁翁說道：『快給我跪下！我要來殺掉你啦！』

『你爲什麼要殺死我呢；不是把你從瓶兒裏放出來，給你自由的嗎？』

『就因爲這個理由，所以我要殺掉你呀！不過我得給你一點恩情。』

漁翁說：『什麼恩情呢？』

『我可以允許你自揀一條死的方法。聽好！我告訴你這故事罷。我原是天上的一個妖神，那大智的沙羅門，要我服從他的法旨；我怒了，沒有遵從他，他就懲罰我，把我禁錮在一個銅瓶裏，用鉛鑄封了口。他喚另外一個服從他的妖神，把我丟在這海裏來。

『在起初的一百年內，我躺在海底下，自己曾經立過約言：有誰給我自由，將我放出，我要給他成爲巨富。但沒有誰給我自由啦。當第二個一百年裏，我又有過一個約言：誰能給

me free, I would show him all the *treasures*[1] of the earth. But no one came to set me free. During the third hundred years, I made a promise, that if any one came to set me free, I would make him king over all the earth, and grant him every day any three things he might ask.

"Still no one came. Then I became very angry, and as hundreds of years went by, and I still lay in the jar at the bottom of the sea, I *swore*[2] a great *oath*[3] that now, if any one should set me free, I would at once kill him, and that the only favor I would grant him, would be to let him choose his manner of death. So now you have come, and have set me free. You must die, but I will let you say how you shall die."

The Fisherman was in great *grief*[4]. He did not care so much for himself, for he was old and poor, but he thought of his wife and children, who would be left to starve.

"*Alas!*[5]" he cried. "Have pity on me. If it had not been for me you would not be free."

"*Make haste!*[6]" said the Genie. "Tell me how you wish to die."

When one is in such great *peril*[7], his *wits*[8] fly fast, and sometimes they fly into safety. The Fisherman said:—

【註】 1. 寶藏. 2. 立誓. 3. 誓. 4. 悲傷. 5. 天呀. 6. 趕快. 7. 危險. 8. 急智.

18

我自由，我要告訴他地上所有的一切寶藏，但沒有誰給我自由啦。到第三個一百年裏，我又有一個約言，有誰給我自由，我要使他成爲全世界上王中之王，而且允許他，每天替他做任何的三椿事情。

『但是還沒有誰來放我。於是我可十分怨恨了，一百年，一百年地過去着，我始終躺在瓶子裏，在海的底下。我就賭了一個重咒，現在若有人來給我自由，我當立時把他殺死，但是我可以給他一個恩情，是讓他自己選擇一條死法。你現在來給我自由。所以你必須被我殺死，但我讓你說怎樣的死着罷。』

漁翁大爲悲傷。他並不是憐恤着自己，他自己是又窮又老了；不過一想到他死後，妻兒們無衣，無食，就忍不住悲從中來。

他大聲喊着：『天呀！請你慈悲吧。要是沒有我，你不是還不能出險嗎？』

巨魔說：『你快說！你要怎樣的死法呀！』

當一個人到最危險的時候，常會發生急智，有時會履險爲夷。當時漁翁說道：

"Since I must die, I must. But before I die, answer me one question."

"Ask what you will, but make haste."

"Dare[1] you, then, swear, that you *really*[2] were in the jar? It is so small, and you are so *vast*,[3] that the great *toe*[4], of one of your feet could. not be held in it."

"*Verily*[5] I was in the jar. I swear it. Do you not believe it?"

"No, not until I see you in the jar."

At that, the Genie, to *prove*[6] it, changed again into smoke. The great cloud hung over the earth, and one end of it entered the jar. Slowly the cloud *descended*[7], until the sky was clear, and the last tip, of the cloud was in the jar. As soon as this was done, the Fisherman clapped, the lid on again, and the Genie, was shut up inside.

【註】 1. 敢. 2. 眞正地. 3. 巨大. 4. 足趾. 5. 確實地. 6. 證明. 7. 下降.

『既然一定要我死，我只好死。但在我死前，請你囘答我一句問題！』

『你問什麽呢？須趕快地說來。』

『你敢給我賭咒說，你是眞的在這瓶子裏嗎？這瓶是這麽小，你是那麽大，便是你的一隻大足趾也不能踏進瓶裏去呀。』

『我可以賭咒那眞是在瓶裏的！你不信嗎？ 』

『不，除非我親眼看見你在瓶裏。』

[3] 這時，巨魔爲證實起見，重行化做一陣煙霧。那濃厚的煙雲籠罩着地面，漸漸縮向瓶中去。當煙霧完全縮向瓶中去，天色立刻晴明了。這時候，漁翁忙把瓶蓋蓋起，那巨魔遂重被幽閉在瓶子裏面了。

The Story of The Enchanted Horse

I

New Year's Day[1], is a *great feast day*[2], in Persia. On one of these feast days the *Emperor*[3] of Persia, was seated on his throne, in the midst of his people, when a Hindu, appeared, leading a strange horse. *At first sight*[4], the horse looked, like any other horse, except that it was very handsome, and bore a very costly saddle, and bridle. But, on looking more *closely*,[5] one saw that it was not a live horse, but one that had been, very *artfully*[6], made by man. The Hindu *knelt*[7] before the throne and pointed to the horse.

"This horse," he said to the Emperor, "is *a great wonder*,[8] If I *mount*[9] him I can make him go through the air, to any place I choose, and he will go in a very short time. No one has ever seen such a wonder, and I have brought him here to show to you. If you wish, I will show you what he can do."

The Emperor was very *fond of*[10] strange things, and he was much pleased at such a sight. So he told the Hindu to mount his horse. The Hindu did so, and asked where he was to ride.

"Do you see that *far-off*[11] mountain?" said the Emperor. "Ride your horse there, and bring me a

---

【註】 1. 元旦. 2. 佳節. 3. 皇帝. 4. 初看見. 5. 仔細地. 6. 巧妙地. 7. 跪下. 8. 異馬. 9. 騎. 10. 喜歡. 11. 悠遠的.

魔　馬　的　故　事

一

元旦，是波斯最熱鬧的一個佳節。有一次，在這個佳節的日子，波斯皇帝坐在他的寶座上，擁在羣臣和人民中間，這時候，有一印度人帶着一匹異馬進來。那馬兒，初看去，和別的馬兒，沒有兩樣，不過樣子很神俊，那韁兒，鞍兒，覺得很貴重罷了。但仔細看起來，誰都覺得那馬兒並不是眞馬，乃是一匹由人工巧妙地造成的假馬。印度人伏在寶座前叩首，同時指着此馬。

他啓奏道：『這是一匹異馬。倘若我騎上了，就能平白地飛上天去，要到那兒，就到那兒，來囘是片刻間的事。沒有一個人看見過這罕見的奇物。我如今帶來給王一瞧。如果王願意，我可以當面試演，牠所能做的一切給你看。』

皇帝素向嗜好奇異的東西，見這般說來，非常歡喜，卽傳旨着令印度人試演。印度人騎上了馬於是問王到那兒去。

皇帝說：『你瞧見那座遠山嗎？你可以騎往那山，在那山脚下，有棵櫻樹長着，你便折下一束櫻枝兒帶囘來給我。』

branch of a *palmtree*[1] that grows at the foot of it." No
sooner had the Emperor said this than the Hindu
turned a *peg*[2] which was in the horse's *neck*[3], near the
saddle, and away went the horse, into the air and
straight toward the mountain. The Emperor and
all the people *gazed*[4] after him till the horse was a
mere *speck*.[5] Then he was *out of sight*.[6] But in a
quarter of an hour the horse had come back. The
Hindu *got off*[7] his back, and came to the throne, with
the palmbranch in his hand.

The Emperor had a great wish to *own*[8] the horse,
and he offered to buy him of the Hindu.

"I will sell him," said the Hindu, "if you will
pay me my price."

"And what is your price?" asked the Emperor.

"If you will give me your daughter, for a wife,
you may have my horse." At this all the people
laughed aloud, but the son of the Emperor was very
angry.

"Do not listen to the *wretch*,[9]" said the Prince.
"This *juggler*[10] to come into the family of the greatest
of kings!"

"I will not *grant*[11] him what he asked," said the
Emperor. "Perhaps he does not mean really to ask
such a price, and I have another *bargain*[12] to propose.

【註】 1. 櫻樹. 2. 木栓. 3. 頸. 4. 凝視. 5. 小點. 6. 不見了.
7. 下馬. 8. 主有. 9. 惡人. 10. 魔術家. 11. 允許. 12. 商議

皇帝話纔說完，印度人便轉動了一下那個馬頸下的木栓，那馬就平空的騰上天空，直向那山。風馳電掣般駛去。皇帝和朝臣們都望着天看得呆了，直望到那人馬在空中變成黑點般大小，終於看不見了纔罷。過了片刻，那馬囘來了。印度人下了馬，囘到殿上，手裏拿着一束青葱葱的櫻枝兒。

皇帝十分想得此馬，他吩咐印度人把那馬賣給他。

印度人說：『我願意賣的，不過要有相當的代價。』

皇帝問：『你要什麼代價呢？』

『陛下若肯把公主嫁給我，就可以得有此馬了。』許多臣子們都發笑，但是皇帝的兒子很是忿怒。

王子說：『不要聽這光棍的話！這光棍是要來騙取世界最尊嚴皇帝的公主哩！』

皇帝說：『我一定不允許他的要求。假如他眞心不想這個要求時，我可以和他再作別的商議。但是在我未作商議

But before I say anything more I should like to have you try the horse yourself."

The Hindu was quite *willing*[1] and ran forward, to help the Prince, mount, and to show him, how to manage the horse. But the Prince was too quick, for him, and sprang into the saddle, without aid, turned the peg, and away they flew. In a few moments neither, Prince nor Enchanted, Horse was to be seen.

The Hindu *flung*[2] himself at the foot of the throne and *begged*[3] the Emperor not to be angry with him.

"Why did you not call to him, when you saw him going?" said the Emperor.

"*Sire*[4]," said he, "you yourself saw how quickly he went. I was so taken by surprise, that I lost my *wits*;[5] and when I came to, my *senses*[6] he was out of sight, and hearing. But, sire, let us hope, that the Prince, may find the other peg. If he turns that the horse will come back, to earth again."

"Even if my son does find, the other peg," said the Emperor, "how do we know that the horse may not come down in the middle of the sea?"

"Be at *ease*[7] about that," said the Hindu. "The horse crosses, seas, without ever falling into them, and he will obey the rider, who turns the peg."

"That may be," said the Emperor. "But know that *unless*[8] my son does come home safe, or I hear that he is *alive*,[9] and well, you shall lose your head." And so he *bade*[10] the officers *shut up*[11] the Hindu in prison.

【註】 1. 情願的. 2. 伏. 3. 請求. 4. 陛下. 5. 神志. 6. 知覺. 7. 安心. 8. 除非. 9. 活著的. 10. 吩咐. 11. 關閉. 。

之前，我命你再試一趟罷。』

印度人十分願意，便想走上前來攙扶王子上馬，並叫他怎樣控御馬的方法。但是王子來得非常快，早已跳上馬鞍，撥動木栓，呼的一聲和馬騰空而去了。一忽兒，王子和魔馬已無影無蹤。

印度人伏在金殿下，叩首謝罪不已。

皇帝問：『你為什麼不阻止，當你看見他要騰空的當兒？』

他說：『陛下！你難道還不見他快得令人措手不及嗎？我真驚得呆了。等我覺得的時候，人和馬早已聽不見看不見了。但是我們只望王子能尋得着那第二木栓，將那木栓一轉動，這馬兒就會降落地面來的。』

皇帝說：『就使我的兒子尋着這木栓，我們怎知道，那馬兒不落到海中去呢？』

印度人說：『這倒不必憂慮。那馬兒經行在海面上時從不會降下，他是服從騎者轉動木栓的意思。』

皇帝說：『果真這樣，倒也罷了！不過我的兒子若是不能平安回來，或得不到確實平安的消息，定取下你的頭顱。』於是，他便命左右把印度人關在牢裏。

II

Now when the Prince turned the key on the neck of the Enchanted Horse, horse and rider flew through the air, like the wind. Up and up they went, and, *as*[1] the horse was not a real horse, it did not get tired, and stop. The Prince did not know what to do. He turned the peg *backward*[2], but that did not stop the horse. Then he began to *search*[3] for another peg, and at last he found a small peg, *behind*[4] the ear. He turned that, and *at once*[5] the horse began to move toward the earth.

They did not go back as swiftly, as they went up. It *grew dark*[6] and the Prince did not know where they would *alight*[7]. He could do nothing, so he let the *reins*[8] lie on the neck of the horse and sat still.

At last he felt the earth beneath the horse's feet. The horse stopped, and the Prince got off, cold and *stiff* [9] and very hungry. He looked about him as well as he could in the middle of the night, and saw that they were before the door of a palace.

The door stood *ajar*[10], and the Prince went in He found himself in a hall lighted by a dim lamp. There, fast asleep, were some soldiers, with swords by their side. They were there to guard some one, and, as another door stood open, the Prince passed through

【註】 1. 因為. 2. 向後方地. 3. 搜尋. 4. 在後. 5. 立即. 6. 天黑了. 7. 降下. 8. 韁繩. 9. 疲乏的. 10. 半開地.

二

　　且說王子轉動那魔馬頸上的木栓，　馬和騎者在天空風也似的向前馳去。他們前進，前進，一直前進，因為馬兒不是眞馬，所以不覺得困乏停止下來。王子不知怎樣辦才好。他將木栓旋向後面，但馬兒並不停歇。他無法，乃又搜尋另一木栓，終於發見一個小小的，隱在耳朵後邊。他轉動了那個木栓，馬纔開始向地面降下。

　　慢慢地降下來，並不像上升時的那麼快。天色已黑了，王子不知道到那兒纔得到地。不過實在沒有辦法，只得握着韁繩，安坐馬上。

　　後來他終於發見馬足下的實地，馬已停止下來了；王子下了鞍，卽感到又冷，又疲乏，又餓。他四處張望，在半夜的黑暗裏，發見自己是落在一所宮院的門前。

　　宮門是半開半掩着，　王子走了進去。他知道走到一個大廳上，點着一盞半明不滅的燈火。有幾個睡熟的兵士在那兒，腰裏都掛着劍。從他們的情形看來，似乎守護一個什麼人。對面有一門也是開着，直通內室，王子走進去，瞧見

into the *inner room*[1]. There he saw lying on a *couch*[2] a most beautiful woman, asleep, and about her, also asleep, were her *maids*[3].

The Prince knelt by the side of the couch and gazed at the *fair creature*[4]. Then he gently *twitched*[5] her *sleeve*[6], and she awoke. Her eyes fell on the Prince kneeling there, but she showed no fear, for, as soon as her eyes opened, he said:—

"Beautiful Princess, I am the Prince of Persia. I have come here by a very strange way, and I ask you to *protect*[7] me. I do not know where I am, but I know no *harm*[8] can come to me when I see before me so fair a Princess."

"You are in the kingdom of Bengal," she replied. "and I am the daughter of the King. I am living in my own palace in the country. You may be sure that no harm will come to you. If you have come from Persia, you have come a long way, and must be hungry and tired. I am very *curious*[9] to know how you came, but first you shall have food and sleep."

Then the Princess called her maids, and they awoke and *wondered*[10] much at what they saw. At the command of the Princess, they led the Prince into a *hall*[11], where they gave him food and drink. Then they led him to a room where he could sleep and left him.

【註】 1. 內室. 2. 坑. 3. 婢女. 4. 美人. 5. 扯. 6. 袖. 7. 保護. 8. 傷害. 9. 好奇的. 10. 驚愕. 11. 會室.

一個十分美麗的女子，熟睡在一張坑上，有許多婢女圍着她，但也都睡着了。

王子跪在坑的邊上，定睛看了這美麗的女子一回。後來輕輕地拉着她的衣袖，她醒了。她眼光落在跪倒面前的王子身上，並沒有顯出驚惶的面色，因爲在她一睜開眼的時候，他便說：

『美麗的公主啊，我是波斯王子。我是由一條很奇的路程到這裏來的。我求你保護。雖然我不曉得這兒是什麼地方，但瞧見眼前有這般艷麗的一位公主，諒來是不會加害我的。』

她囘答道：『你已經在孟加拉國了。我是本國皇帝的公主。這是我住的宮院。你可放心，沒有誰來敢加害你的。若你眞從波斯國來的，你是行了很遠的路程了，你一定飢餓與疲倦不堪。我很想急於知道，你是怎樣來的，但是我先讓你吃飽睡醒再說罷。』

公主便喚起她的婢女。婢女們醒了，忽然看見王子吃了一驚。她們奉了公主的命令，領王子走到餐室，備了豐美的西食，給他吃喝，後來便帶他到一間臥室裏，讓他安息。

As soon as it was *light*[1] the Princess of Bengal arose and dressed herself in the most *splendid*[2] *robes*[3] she had. She *put on*[4] her finest things and wore her most *precious*[5] rings and *bracelets*[6]. Indeed, she quite tired out her maids, making them bring her one beautiful thing after another, before she could make up her mind what to wear. When she was at last ready, she sent word to the Prince that she would *receive*[7] him.

Now the Prince had slept well, and had risen and dressed himself. So when the Princess sent for him he went at once into her presence, and made a low *bow*[8] and thanked her for the honor she had done him. He then gave an *account*[9] of the strange way in which he had come, and said that he would now mount his horse and go back to Persia; for his royal father must be in great pain, not knowing where his son might be.

"*Nay*,[10]" said the Princess, "you must not go so soon. I wish to show you the *glories*[11] of Bengal, that you may tell something of what you have seen in the *court*[12] of Persia." The Prince could not *refuse*[13] such a *request*,[14] and thus he became the *guest*[15] of the Princess.

Each day some new sport or feast was had. They hunted; they had music; they saw games and *plays*;[16] and the time went swiftly by.

【註】 1. 天明. 2. 華美的. 3. 衣服. 4. 穿起. 5. 珍異的. 6. 手鐲. 7. 接見. 8. 敬禮. 9. 說明. 10. 不. 11. 光榮. 12. 宮庭. 13. 拒絕. 14. 要求. 15. 賓客. 16. 戲劇.

　　當天明的時候，孟加拉公主就起牀，穿了一身最鮮豔
悅目的衣服。戴着極珍貴的飾品，套着精美的手鐲和戒指。
她因要打扮整齊，挑選種種美麗的衣飾，端的把婢女們
都鬧厭了。直到自己裝扮得如花如玉，纔命令去請王子
來。

　　那王子很舒適的睡了一夜，第二天一早就起身，穿着
整齊。恰好公主的僕人已奉命來請。他立即來到公主面前，
向公主行了個禮，謝她昨夜盛意的款待。道謝畢，就訴說
從怎樣的奇路來的，他說如今要騎馬回波斯了；免得他父
王不知兒子的下落，要大大憂慮哩。

　　公主說：『且慢！你不要去得如此忽促。我願意把孟
拉加的一切光榮顯示給你看，但你能夠先把波斯宮裏的事
情，告訴我一點嗎？』王子對這要求，難以拒絕，於是便
做了公主的賓客。

　　每天，必有新的遊戲或宴會，他們倆盡情地快樂，行獵
聽音樂，觀戲劇，光陰就此迅速地消磨過去了。

III

But when two months had thus been spent, the Prince could put off his return *no longer*[1], and said as much to the Princess. It was indeed much harder for him now to go, for each had come to care greatly for the other. The Prince had often ridden the Enchanted Horse to show the Princess what he could do, and now, when the time was come for him to take leave, he said boldly:

"You see, dear Princess, what a wonderful horse this is, and how perfectly I can *manage*[2] him. Will you not *trust*[3] yourself to me? We will ride together to my home. My father will be rejoiced to see me, and will welcome you. We will be married at the Court of Persia, and all will be well."

The Princess of Bengal was not *loath*[4] to go, and so in the early morning, when no one was awake, she made herself ready. The Prince and the Princess got up on the Enchanted Horse; the Prince placed the horse with his head toward Persia, and turned the peg. Off they went, and in two hours they *reached*[5] the *capital*.[6]

They stopped outside of the town at a country house, belonging to the Prince. There the Prince bade his servants care for the Princess, and he himself went on to the palace. His father was *overjoyed*[7] to see him,

---

【註】 1. 不再． 2. 駕御． 3. 信任． 4. 不顧意． 5. 達到． 6. 京城． 7. 大喜．

三

　　兩個月很快的消磨過去，王子思家心切，他接連對公主說他要囘國，不能再住下去，現在他們倆已經互相深深地戀慕着了，他們實在是難捨難分。有時候王子常騎着魔馬給公主瞧，但如今要分別的當兒，他再也忍不住說：

　　『你瞧，親愛的公主，這是一匹多麼奇異的馬兒，我駕御牠是這樣的純熟，你不相信嗎？倘我們能一塊兒騎囘家，我父王看見我們，定然很歡喜的。他必定也十分歡迎你。我倆就在波斯宮裏結婚，一切必能十分圓滿。』

　　孟加拉公主並沒有反對，所以在一天早上，很早的時候，誰都沒有起身，她便自行收拾整齊。王子和公主跨上魔馬，把馬頭朝着波斯，轉了轉木栓。他們就騰空飛行，約莫兩點鐘光景，飛到波斯京城。

　　他們將馬落在城外的一所莊院，這是王子的別墅。王子吩咐僕役們，好好地當心侍候公主，他自己一人先進宮

and, after he had gazed his fill at his son's face, he wished to know, all about the Hindu's horse, and what had happened.

The <u>Prince</u> told him all, and *dwelt*[1] upon the great kindness which had been shown him in Bengal. He ended, by telling the king, how he had brought the Princess on the Enchanted Horse with him, and begged that he might be *permitted*[2] to marry her, for the kingdom of Persia was more *powerful*[3] than Bengal, and the Princess was not equal to him in *rank*.[4]

The King gladly gave his *consent*,[5] and bade the Prince go at once and *fetch*[6] the Princess. He sent for the Hindu also out of prison and said to him:—

"I put you in prison while my son was in danger. Now he has returned, and I set you free. Take your horse and *begone*.[7] Never let me see your face again."

Now the Hindu had heard of what had happened, and how the Prince had gone to fetch the Princess. He mounted his horse at once, and went straight to the country house. He reached the place before the Prince, and told the *captain*[8] of the *guard*[9] that he had been sent by the King, to fetch the Princess on the Enchanted Horse. The captain of the guard *readily*[10] believed him, as did the Princess, who got up on the horse behind the Hindu.

【註】 1. 居住. 2. 允許. 3. 强大的. 4. 身分. 5. 允許. 6. 接來. 7. 滾蛋. 8. 隊長. 9. 衛隊. 10. 欣然地.

去。他父親瞧見了他，喜出望外，先看一看兒子的面色，就命他講述關於印度人的馬，並他一切經過的情形。

王子把一切事情訴說了，又詳說孟加拉公主的好意，慇懃招待他。末了，他告訴怎樣把公主帶着同來，他懇求國王允許和她結婚，照例波斯國遠比孟加拉國強大，那公主是不能相配的。

國王很快活地允許了，便吩咐王子將公主趕快接來。同時命把印度人從牢裏放出，對他說道：

『我因爲我兒子在危險的時候，所以將你囚在牢裏，現在他已經囘來了，我放你出獄吧。取你的馬兒去，我永遠不願再瞧見你。』

這時印度人，早已把王子取得一位公主囘來以及其他的詳情，都打聽得明白了。他便騎上魔馬，直向別墅飛去。他到的時候王子還沒有趕到，他便下馬告訴衞隊長，說國王有旨，着他迎接公主囘宮，駕着魔馬同去。隊長自然認以爲眞，公主也沒有疑惑，她逐同着印度人騎着馬起行飛去。

The Hindu did indeed ride through the air to the palace, but he did not alight. He *stayed*[1] too high up to be reached by any *bow*[2] and *arrow*[3], but where the King and his *court*[4] could see them. The King was beside himself with *rage*,[5] but he could do nothing. The Hindu *mocked*[6] at him and then rode off with the Princess, no one knew where.

The Prince was far more beside himself than the King, for he knew how lovely the Princess was, and here was she *snatched*[7] away from him in this cruel way. He went to the country house, *borne down with grief*,[8] that he might be where the Princess last had been. The captain of the guard fell at his feet and *besought*[9] him to pardon him.

"Rise," said the Prince, "and do not let us waste our time in vain *reproaches*.[10] I must at once *set forth*[11] to seek my Princess. Do you *obtain*[12] for me the dress of a *pilgrim*,[13] and do not let any one know what I am to do."

The captain did as he was bid, and the Prince pulled off his own dress and put on the disguise. He took a box of jewels with him and set off in search of the Princess.

IV

Now the Hindu had ridden with the Princess until he come to the *Vale*[14] of Cashmere. Here he let the

---

【註】 1. 停駐. 2. 弓. 3. 箭. 4. 朝臣們. 5. 忿怒. 6. 嘲弄. 7. 攫取. 8. 不勝憤悶. 9. 懇求. 10. 比責. 11. 出發. 12. 獲得. 13. 香客. 14. 山谷

　　印度人眞的先駕到宮裏去，不過他不降落地面，而停駐在天空，這停駐的所在，爲弓矢所不及，但爲皇帝和他的朝臣們都能夠看見。皇帝惱怒異常，卻是沒有辦法。印度人乃將他嘲弄一番，於是將公主載去，誰也不知道他的去處了。

　　王子比國王更是忿怒，因爲他覺得公主是多麼可愛，但是她被別人用這般惡計盜去。他走到他的別墅裏，視物思人，恨不得立時便死，那衞隊長跪在他的面前，只管叩頭求饒。

　　王子說：『你且站起來！我不要浪費時間，來作無益咨責。我要立刻去尋公主。你替我辦一套香客的衣服，我的事情，無論何人不要讓他知道。』

　　隊長遵照他的吩咐，辦妥一切，於是王子脫去原衣，打扮香客的模樣兒。他又帶着一盒珠寶，便上路尋訪公主去。

四

　　印度人帶着公主，一直駛到嘎什密爾山谷，纔讓魔馬

39

Enchanted Horse come to the ground, but he did not at once *enter*[1] the city. He told the Princess he *meant* to have her for wife, and when she would not consent he began to *beat*[3] her. She cried out for help, and, as good *luck*[4] would have it, the Sultan of Cashmere was near *at hand*[5] with some of the people of his court. He saw the Hindu raise his hand to beat the Princess, and he stopped him and asked:—

"Why do you beat this woman?"

"Because she is my wife and will not obey me. May a man not beat his own wife?"

"I am not his wife," cried the Princess. "Sir, I do not know who you are, but I am a Princess of Bengal. This man is a *wicked*[6] *magician*[7] who stole me away just as I was to marry the Prince of Persia, and this is the Enchanted Horse on which he brought me."

The Sultan *could not help believing*[8] so beautiful a woman, and he at once bade his officers cut off the Hindu's head, and led the Princess back with him to the palace. She was overjoyed, and thought he would now *re tore*[9] her to the Prince of Persia. The Sultan said nothing, but placed her in the hands of the women of the palace and had her beautifully dressed.

The Princess heard the *trumpets*[10] sounding and the *drums*[11] beating. She thought this was a *notice*[12] of her return; but soon the Sultan entered and told her to make ready to marry him; that they should be

---

【註】 1. 進入. 2. 想. 3. 打. 4. 運氣. 5. 近處. 6. 兇暴的. 7. 魔術家. 8. 不得不相信. 9. 交還. 10. 喇叭. 11. 鼓. 12. 通知.

落地，但他並不立刻進城去。他告訴公主，要她嫁給他，公主不肯答應，他就發怒舉手便打。公主乃高聲呼叫。恰巧這時這嘎什密爾、蘇丹正和幾個從臣在近處散步。蘇丹瞧見印度人舉手要打公主，便大聲喝住他，問道：

『你為什麼打這女子？』

『她是我的妻子，因為她不肯服從我，所以打她。一個男子不能打自己的妻子嗎？』

公主大聲說：『先生，我並不是他的妻子。我不知道你是誰，但我是孟加拉國的公主啊。這是一個兇暴的魔術家，在我和波斯王子結婚的時候，他把我搶了來，這匹馬就是他的魔馬，他把我坐在上面，將我帶了來的。』

這蘇丹見公主生得這般的美麗，她的話，自不得不信，他立刻命左右把印度人斬首，將公主領到自己的宮裏去。公主大喜，暗想蘇丹必定送她回去，和波斯王子結婚了。但蘇丹把她交給宮女們，吩咐將最美麗的衣服給她穿著起來。

公主聽得嗚嗚的喇叭聲，和鼕鼕的鼓聲，她想定是蘇丹歡送她回波斯去了。但是一轉眼間，蘇丹來了，告訴她準備和他結婚並立即舉行婚禮，因為這樣的美人他從沒有

married at once, for he had never before seen any one so beautiful, and he was *sure*[1] he never should again.

The Princess was in *despair*[2] at this, and threw herself down in her grief. She *fainted*[3] and when she came to herself, and saw how she was in the power of the Sultan, she made believe that she had lost her mind, and began to talk, in a *wild*[4] *crazy*[5] *manner*.[6] The Sultan could do nothing with her, so he left her in the care of the women.

V

Day after day[7] went by, and the Princess was *no better*.[8] The Sultan sent far and wide for wise men and doctors, but no one could cure the Princess. All Cashmere heard of this strange *affair*,[9] and so the news came to the ears of a Pilgrim who one day came to the capital. The Pilgrim was no other than the Prince of Persia, and he went straight to the Sultan.

"I am come," he said, "because I have heard of the sad *fate*[10] that has *befallen*[11] the Princess of Bengal whom you were to *wed*.[12] I am a wise man, and I know of a *cure*.[13]"

"It cannot be," said the Sultan. "The Princess loses her wits still more when a wise man comes into her presence."

【註】　1. 確信．　2. 失望．　3. 昏暈．　4. 狂妄的．　5. 瘋狂的．　6. 樣子．　7. 逐日．　8. 不見好．　9. 事件．　10. 命運．　11. 遭遇．　12. 成婚．　13. 治擬．

瞧見過，也不會再能瞧到的。

這使公主大大的失望，她非常的悲傷，竟然昏暈過去。待她蘇醒的時候，見自己已落在蘇丹強暴勢力之中，反抗也是無用，她就假裝發瘋的樣兒；手足亂舞，口中亂說。蘇丹無法，只好命宮女們當心看守着她。

五

一天一天的過去，公主的病仍無起色。蘇丹召了許多術士和醫生們來診治，但是沒有一點效驗。全嘠什密爾的人民，都聽到這件奇事，後來這消息傳到一個繩進城的香客耳朵裏。這香客原來就是波斯王子。他聽了這消息立即走到蘇丹那裏。

他說：『我是特地來的，因爲我聽到孟加拉公主有不幸的疾病，我是術士，我能夠治愈她。』

蘇丹說：『恐你不能罷！公主的病沉重得很，很多名醫術士，都不能醫好她。』

"I must see her, and see her *alone*,[1]" said the Pilgrim. "I am sure I can cure." So the Sultan, who was glad of one more hope, led the Pilgrim to the door of the room where the Princess was, and *stood back*.[2] The Princess did not know the Prince in his *disguise*,[3] and *flew at*[4] him. But the Prince, when he was near her, said in a *low*[5] voice:—

"I am not a Pilgrim. I am the Prince of Persia, come to set you free. Do as I tell you." At once the Princess became quiet, and the Sultan was overjoyed at the sign, of better health. The Pilgrim stayed a short time in the room, and then went away, Each day he visited the Princess, and each day she grew a little better. The Sultan thought nothing too good for the Pilgrim. *At last*[6] the Pilgrim said to the Sultan:—

"Only one thing *remains*[7] to *complete*[8] the cure, of the Princess. She came here, on the Enchanted Horse. Now the *charm*[9] of the horse has *passed over into*[10] the Princess, and we must rid her of it, in the presence, of the horse. I have a strange *incense*[11] which I will burn, and that will *dispel*[12] the last *remnant*[13] of disease. Let the Enchanted Horse be brought to-morrow into the great court, of the city, and let the Princess, *clad*[14] in her most costly *raiment*,[15] stand by the side of the horse."

香客說：『我要一定獨自看她，我自有靈法療治她。』蘇丹見多了一個希望，心中很喜，親自引導香客到公主的臥房前，自己退後站着。公主不知是王子假裝了來的，一見有人，便飛身撲來打他。但王子等她近身時，低聲說道：

『我不是一個香客，是波斯王子，我來救你。請你照我的吩咐行事。』 當時公主忽然變得安靜起來了，那蘇丹看見公主這種情形，十分快活。香客在屋子裏，不一囘便自走出。從此以後，他每天進宮，給公主治病，他看了一次，公主便好一些。蘇丹十分歡喜，不知怎樣酬報這香客才好。最後香客對蘇丹說道：

『只是還有一點病根子，不能給公主治得。她騎了魔馬到這裏來。如今必定是馬作怪，纏着公主作祟，倘能將這魔馬，放在當前，我便可以治愈了。我有一種奇異的香料，當馬前一燒，病可立刻消失。明天請將魔馬帶到野外，同時公主須裝扮好了，站在馬旁。』

The Sultan bade his servants do as the Pilgrim, gave orders, and all the people in the city, were met to see the strange, cure, of the Princess.　As they all stood watching, the Pilgrim *lighted*[1] the incense, and a great *smoke*[2] arose, which *shut out*[3] the Enchanted Horse, the Princess, and the Pilgrim.

In a little while the smoke *cleared away.*[4]　There on the ground, lay. the dress of a Pilgrim; high up in the air, was the Enchanted Horse, and on it, the Princess and a Prince. The head of the　horse, was turned towards Persia.

【註】 1. 點火. 2. 煙. 3. 掩罩. 4. 消滅了.

蘇丹傳命，照香客所說的一切，要立刻辦安，奇事哄動全城，大家爭着去看奇異的治病法。在眾人環看的時候，香客把香料燒着，濃烟大發，魔馬，公主，和香客，都掩罩在裏面。

一忽兒烟消霧散。地上但留著一套香客的衣服，那魔馬卻高飛上雲霄去了。馬上端坐一位王子和公主。那馬頭是向波斯去的。

The Story Of Prince[1] Ahmed

I

There was a Sultan of India who, after a long *reign*[2], had reached a good old age. He had three sons: the eldest was named Houssain, the second Ali, the youngest Ahmed. He had also a beautiful *niece*[3] who had grown up with his sons.

Now, when his niece was old enough to marry, the Sultan sought for a husband among the princes of the country. But no sooner did he make this known than he found that each of his sons was in love with the girl. This made him most unhappy, for he saw that if one married her the others would *quarrel*[4] with him. He called his three sons to him and said:

"My sons, I see that it will go hard with you. Your *cousin*[5] loves each of you, but she can marry one only. We must find some way by which you can agree. Let each go on a journey to a *separate*[6] country, and return here twelve months from to-day. I will give you each a large sum of money, that you may travel as *befits*[7] your rank. Then let each bring back some *rare gift*[8], and he who brings the rarest shall have the Princess, my niece."

They *agreed*[9] to this, and set forth a day's journey together. At the end of the day they slept at an *inn*[10],

---

【註】 1. 王子. 2. 統治. 3. 甥女. 4. 爭吵. 5. 表妹. 6. 各別的.
7. 適合. 8. 奇異的禮物. 9 同意. 10. 旅舍.

48

王 子 阿 米 德 故 事

一

　　從前<u>印度</u>有個蘇丹，在位很久，年紀已經很老了。他有三個兒子：長子名叫<u>霍桑</u>，次子名叫<u>阿里</u>，最小的一個兒子名<u>阿米德</u>。他又有一個美麗的甥女兒，自幼是跟他兒子們一起長大的。

　　如今那位甥女已到結婚的年齡了，<u>蘇丹</u>想在本國王子中，替他挑選出一個丈夫來。當他纔把意見宣佈的時候，他便發現他的三個兒子，個個戀愛着此女。這着實使他煩悶，因爲他知道，要如有一個兒子和她結婚，那另外兩個必定和他爭吵。他便喚三個兒子到跟前，說道：

　　『孩兒們，我看這件事對於你們太爲難了。你表妹同樣的愛着你們，但她只能嫁給一人。我們定須想一種大家同意的辦法，來解決一下才好。我想你們每人可以到一個不同的國度去游歷，從今天起，滿十二月回來。我給你們各人多量的錢財，以便途中應用。不過在游畢回國的時候，每人須帶回一種奇罕的禮物，誰的禮物最出奇，誰便和我的甥女結婚。』

　　他們都允應了，第一天的路途，是同走的。天色晚了的時候，他們便歇腳在一個旅舍裏，次早起來，大家各自

49

and when the morning came they parted, agreeing to meet at the same place in a year *lacking*[1] two days.

Prince Houssain went to the *seacoast*[2], to a town where merchants came together from all parts of the world.　Here he saw shops filled with wonderful goods. Indeed, as he walked on and on, he became very tired, and was glad when a merchant asked him to sit down *in front of*[3] his shop.　As he rested, a man passed by with a *carpet*[4] about six feet square, and cried with a loud voice that its price was forty *purses*[5].　The Prince called him to him, and looked at the carpet.

"This is a good darpet," said he, "but why should it cost so much?　I see nothing wonderful about it."

"It is true," said the crier, "you can see nothing wonderful, and yet this carpet is well worth forty purses; for if you *own*[6] the carpet and sit on it, you will be carried to any place you wish in the *twinkle*[7] of an eye."

"If that be so," said the Prince, "it is well worth its price."

"I speak the truth," said the crier, "and, to prove it to you, take your seat on it with me, and I will wish us back in the inn you have just left."　No sooner said than done.　They sat on the carpet, and at once were in the room where the Prince *lodged*[8].　The Prince

【註】 1. 缺少.　2. 海邊.　3. 在 . . . 之前.　4. 地毯.　5. 土耳其錢幣之名.　6. 主有.　7. 霎眼.　8. 下宿.

分途上路，　並約定滿一年的期前兩天，　三個人再在此會集。

大王子霍桑向海邊走去，　走到一個城市，這城市是萬國商人雲集的商埠。　每一處鋪子裏，　都充滿著奇異貨物。他在街上踱來踱去，　十分疲倦。　後來有一個商人招呼他，他就快活地在他鋪子前坐下。正當這個時候，他忽然看見一人，手拿著一塊地毯，約莫六尺見方，高聲唱賣，索價四十金。王子即叫住他，看那地毯。說道：

『地毯果然很好,不過為什麼要賣得這樣貴?我瞧不出這地毯出奇的地方。』

那賣客說：『眞的，你瞧不出；　但是這地毯卻足值四十金呢！　倘若你買了它。　坐在上面，你願意到什麼地方，眨眼間就可到了。』

王子說：『倘使眞的這樣，這就值得了。』

賣客說：『我說的是實話。可以當面試驗給你看，你且同我坐在毯上，我們回到你的客棧裏去。』　說後。他們就坐在那方地毯上，一霎時光，便落在王子的客棧裏。王

gladly gave forty purses for the carpet, and it was now his.　But as he needed no time for returning home, he *remained*[1] in the town the rest of the year, enjoying its *wonders*[2].　He was sure there could be no greater gift than the carpet.

Prince Ali, the second brother, made his way to Persia.　When he reached the capital, he walked about the streets and heard the criers calling out their goods.　There was one who had in his hand an *ivory tube*[3] about a foot long and an inch *thick*.[4]　He cried out that he would sell this to any one for forty purses.

"This is a very simple tube," said the Prince. "Why do you ask such a high price for it?　I see nothing wonderful about it."

"It is true," said the crier.　"You can see nothing wonderful, and yet this tube is well worth forty purses; for if you own the tube you have but to look through it and you can see *whatever*[5] you wish to see.　Indeed, you may now try it, and see if I am not right."

So Prince Ali wished to see his father, the Sultan, and he looked through the tube and saw him on his *throne*[6], looking well and happy.　Then he looked for the Princess, and saw her, too, laughing among her *maids*[7].　At that he gladly paid his forty purses, for he was sure there could be no greater gift.

Now Prince Ahmed, the youngest, made his way to Arabia, and as he walked through a *bazaar*[8] he heard

---

【註】　1. 居留．　2. 奇事．　3. 象牙管兒．　4. 厚．　5. 不論什麼．　6. 座．　7. 婢女．　8. 市場．

子快活地，把四十金，將地毯買了。因為他有了地毯囘家路上毋須躭擱，他便留在城市中，快樂地度過一年中其餘的日子。他想決定沒有比這地毯更寶貴的禮物了。

✎　且說二王子阿里，取路向波斯去。當他到了波斯京城，在大街上閒逛的時候，他聽得許多叫賣者，兜售他們的貨物。內中有一人，手拿一支象牙管兒，約莫一尺長一寸厚的光景。他大聲叫賣，誰出價四十金，就賣給誰。

王子說道：『這是個十分簡單的管兒，你為什麼要賣得這樣貴呢？我瞧不出這管兒有甚出奇之處。』

這賣客說：『眞的，你實在瞧不出這管兒奇異之處，可是這管兒卻很值得四十金呢；因為你若買了這管兒，從中望去，你想望什麼，就給你望什麼。這是眞的，我你可以面試，就知道我不是欺騙你了。』

王子聽說，他想望一望他的父親，便從管中瞧去，看見父親坐在殿上，很康健而快樂的樣子，他又望一望公主，見公主和羣婢嬉笑着。如此，他快活地付給了四十金，因為他想決沒有比這更寶貴的禮物了。

現在小王子阿米德，取路向亞利伯進行，當他經過一個市場的時候，他聽得一個叫賣者，手中拿一隻蘋果，高

a crier, with an apple in his hand, calling out that he would sell it for thirty-five purses.

"Thirty-five purses!" he said. "An apple for thirty-five purses? Why do you ask such a high price for it? I see nothing wonderful about it."

"It is true," said the crier. You can see nothing wonderful, and yet this apple is well worth the price I ask. For it will *cure*[1] any sick person, even if he is at the point of death. He has but to smell of it, and he will be made well at once."

"If that be so," said Prince Ahmed, "the apple is well worth the price. But how can I know if it really works this great cure?"

"Every one here knows it to be true;" said the crier; and one after another came up and said he knew the apple would thus cure the sick. One man said he had a friend who lay very ill, and he was very sure the apple would make him well.

"Let us try it," said the Prince; "and if you prove what you say, I will give you forty purses for the apple." So they went to see the sick man, who *smelled*[2] of the apple and was at once cured. Prince Ahmed made *haste*[3] to buy the apple, for he was sure there could be no greater gift.

II

When the year drew near its end, Prince Houssain got on his carpet, and wished himself back at the inn

---

【註】 1. 治療. 2. 嗅. 3. 趕急.

聲喊着，要賣三十五金。

他說：『要賣三十五金？一隻蘋果那有這麼高的價錢呢？我瞧不出這蘋果有甚出奇之處。』

賣客說：『果然，你是瞧不出奇異之處，但這蘋果卻足值這個價錢呢。因爲牠能穀治愈百病，雖病人垂死的時候，也可治活。只要他嗅一嗅，病就霍然全愈哩。』

王子阿米德說：『倘是這樣，這蘋果果然值得；不過我怎能知道這些話是眞實的呢？』

叫賣者說：『這裏誰都知道是眞的，』　果然，一個一個的路人走來，都說這個蘋菓兒，確能治病的。又有一個人說，他的朋友病得很重，只有這隻蘋果可以治得好。

王子說：『讓我們去試一試，要眞的能證明你的說話不虛，我可給你四十金。』　他們因此就去看那病人，那人嗅到這隻蘋果，病果然立刻好了。王子阿米德急忙把這蘋果買下，因爲他想，這是再沒有比這更偉大寶貴的禮物了。

二

一年之期將滿，大王子霍桑坐在他的地毯上，要囘到

where he was to meet his brothers, and in the twinkle of an eye he was there. Not long afterwards Prince Ali came, and *last of all*[1] Prince Ahmed. They met one another *joyfully*[2], for each was sure he had the greatest gift.

"We shall have time enough to talk about our travels," said the eldest brother. "Let us at once show what we have brought. Do you see this *lain*[3] carpet? Yet I paid forty purses for it, and it is worth it, for I came here from the *seacoast*[4] on it in a moment of time. What can you show equal to this?"

Prince Ali said:

"Your carpet is truly wonderful. Yet see this simple tube. I paid forty purses for it. Look through it. You can see whatever you wish. Tell me if it is not worth more than your carpet." Prince Houssain took the tube and turned it toward the palace of the Sultan, and looked through it. At once he turned *pale*.[5]

"Alas, my brothers!" he said. "Of what *avail*[6] is it that we should bring our gifts? I see the Princess lying on her bed, with all her   ids about her, and she is about to die."

"Say you so?" said Prince Ahmed, and he looked through the tube also. "If we can but reach her in time I can *save*[7] her by this apple. See! it looks like a common apple. Yet I paid forty purses for it, and

---

【註】1. 最後. 2. 喜悅地. 3. 摸索的. 4. 海邊. 5. 蒼白的. 6. 效 用. 7. 救授.

先前和他兄弟約會的客棧中去，一霎時，他就到了。隨後二王子阿里趕到，末後是小王子阿米德。他們哥兒三個，見面很是歡喜，因為各人想着自己已經是得到最大的禮物了。

大哥說：『時光尚早，我們何不大家談談旅途的經過情形，我們取出各人的禮物來瞧瞧。你們曾且這樣素的地毯嗎？可是我卻用四十金買來的，這價錢也確實值得，因為我從海邊到此，是坐在這上面來的。真的只要一霎時光。你們得到什麼，能和這地毯相比嗎？』

王子阿里說：

『你的地毯果然希奇；但是你瞧這個簡單的管兒罷。我用四十金買來的。從管兒裏面望着。你想看什麼，就可看到什麼。告訴我，這難道比不過你的地毯嗎？』大王子霍桑便取過這管兒，向蘇丹的宮裏望去。他忽然面上失色。

『啊呀，我的兄弟們啲！這些禮物，我們帶了去有什麼用呢？我看見公主已臥病在牀，羣婢圍着她的牀前，她差不多就要死啦！』

王子阿米德接過管兒瞧着。說道：『你說的不差，要如我們能立刻趕到她那裏，我得用這隻蘋果治好她。瞧！這看來　像一隻平常的蘋果。但是我用四十金買來的，這是

it is well worth the price; for if one smells of it, *no matter*[1] how sick one is, there will be an *instant cure*.²"

"Then let us get at once on my carpet," said Prince Houssain. "There is *room*[3] for us all three, and we will wish ourselves in the Princess's room." This they did, and no sooner were they there amongst the weeping maids than Prince Ahmed held the apple to the face of the Princess. With her last breath she drew in the *odor*[4] of the apple. She opened her eyes and looked about her.

"Why do I lie here?" she asked, "and why are you weeping? I am perfectly well." The three Princes now left the room and came to the Sultan, their father. He was *overjoyed*[5] to see them once more, and they told their tales, and gave their gifts, and bade him say which of them should have the Princess. He took long to think it over, and then said:—

"It is not possible to say with perfect *justice*[6]. It is true, Ahmed, that you cured the Princess with your apple. But you could not have known she was sick if she had not been seen through Ali's tube; and you could not have reached her in time if you had not *ridden*[7] on Houssain's carpet. It is true, Ali, that your tube showed you the Princess sick; but that would have done no good if you had not Houssain's

很值得這價錢；因爲不論是誰，病得怎樣，只要一嗅，立刻就能治好的。』

　　大王子霍桑說：『那末我們同坐在這地毯上罷，這地毯幸喜可坐三人，我們就到公主的房裏去。』 不多時他們就到了，立在環泣的羣婢中，王子阿米德早就擎着蘋果到公主的臉上去。當她最後的一次呼吸，嗅到那蘋果的香味。她睜開眼來，四面瞧着。問道：

　　『我睡在這裏做什麼？你們爲什麼哭呢？我覺得十分舒服呢！』 於是哥兒三個離開病室，走到他們的父親蘇丹那裏去了。他瞧見他們囘來，大喜，他們告訴了他們的故事，取出各自的禮物呈上，請他說，誰該有着公主。他凝思了一回，說道：

　　『要十分公正的道理來說， 這實是不容易的一件事。阿米德，你是用蘋果治好公主的；但是若沒有阿里的管兒，卻不能知道她病着；而且如果沒有霍桑的地毯，準時趕到，雖有蘋果也是無用。阿里雖然用管兒瞧見公主的臥病；但是如果沒有霍桑的地毯坐了來，阿米德的蘋果給她嗅，便

carpet to ride on, and Ahmed's apple for her to smell of. It is true, Houssain, that your carpet brought all three here in time, but you would not have come at once before the Princess died if you had not seen her through Ali's tube; and if you had come, it would have done no good if Ahmed had not brought his apple. No. You have all brought wonderful gifts, but it would not be right to give the Princess to one more than to another　We must try another way."

So he bade[1] them go out to the plain, each with a bow[2] and an arrow[3]; he who shot his arrow the farthest should have the Princess. They were followed by the Sultan and all the people, and the three brothers shot in turn. Houssain drew his bow and shot his arrow a great distance. Then Ali, seeing where that arrow had flown, pulled his bow with all his might, and his arrow flew still farther. Last came Ahmed, who drew his bow. Away sped[4] the arrow, far, far away. They looked for it, but could not find it. And so, *in spite of*[5] all Ahmed could say, the Sultan gave the Princess to Ali, and there was a great *wedding*.[6]

III

Prince Houssain would not stay to the wedding. He got on his carpet and went off to a far country, and sat by himself and thought. Prince Ahmed, also, was too sad to stay at court. He left before the

---

【註】 1. 吩咐． 2. 弓． 3. 箭． 4. 前進． 5. 不管． 6. 婚禮．

是瞧見她病着，也是徒然。霍桑雖然有地毯，能把你們三個人，立時帶到這兒的，但是如果沒有阿里的管兒瞧着，決不會便到公主的跟前，就是來了，若沒有阿米德的蘋果，也是無用。但是你們都帶着奇物囘來了，至講到公主這一層，誰都該娶她，但又誰都不能娶她。我們必須另找方法來解決。』

他便吩咐他們到郊外去，每人帶一張弓和一枝箭；誰把箭射得頂遠的，誰就得有公主。他們去後，蘇丹和衆朝臣都隨了去，弟兄三人逐行比箭。霍桑彎弓發箭，一箭射得很遠。阿里瞧見這箭的去處竭盡平生之力，拉弓射去，卻比霍桑射得更遠。最後阿米德，把弓彎着，呼的一聲，那箭一直前去，射得無影無蹤，找來找去，不能找着。因此，雖經阿米德一切的辯白，但蘇丹斷定將公主配給阿里，盛大的婚禮，不日舉行了。

三

王子霍桑不願參觀這婚禮。便坐在地毯上，遠飛到異國去，他終日靜坐凝思。王子阿米德覺得在宮中，心中太難過了。就在舉行婚禮之前，獨自離開，因爲他不知道他

wedding, and, as he was very *curious*[1] to know what had become of his arrow, he went in search of it.

He went to the spot where he had shot his arrow, and then walked on and on; he looked on one side and the other, but he did not see it, but still went on. At last he came to a *steep*[2] *pile*[3] of *rocks*[4], and there, at the foot of the rocks, was the arrow. He was *amazed*[5]. He knew he could not have shot so far, that no man could; but there it was.

As he stood in front of the rock he saw an *iron*[6] door. He *pushed*[7] it and it opened. With his arrow in his hand he *pressed*[8] in. At first he stood in a dark cave. Then it became very bright, and he found himself in a great palace, and before him stood a lady with the *air*[9] of a queen. She came forward and said:—

"Welcome, Prince Ahmed. I have been waiting for you. I am a Peri, the daughter of one of the *mightiest*[10] of the *genies*[11]. I know all about you and your brothers, and the Princess whom you did not marry. It was I who caused the carpet to be mabe, and the tube, and the apple. I also caused your arrow to fly out of sight, for I wished to *draw*[12] you to this place. If you will live with me and be my husband, I will make you happy as long as you live."

Prince Ahmed let himself be *led*[13] through the palace. He saw all the wonders of the place.

【註】 1. 欲探知的. 2. 峻險的. 3. 堆. 4. 岩石. 5. 驚愕. 6. 鐵.
7. 推. 8. 擠入. 9. 態度. 10. 最有勢力. 11. 魔神. 12. 誘引. 13. 領導.

的箭究竟射到何處，決意要尋出箭的蹤跡來。

　　他到發箭的地點，一步一步的向前走去，他不停地這邊，那邊，瞧着，但一點蹤跡也沒有看到，他只得再走向前去。到後來，他走到一堆峻險的大岩石邊，在那岩石脚下發現到他的箭在那裏。他驚訝着，他知道自己決不能射得這麼遠，別人也沒有這樣的本領，不過這枝箭確在這兒哩。

　　他正在那山前發呆的時候，眼前却瞧見了一扇鐵門。他上前去一推，門呀的一聲地開了。他手裏拿着箭，便走了進去。起初山洞裏黑暗異常。接着便忽然明亮起來，他走到一所大宮院。在他面前，立着一個貴婦，態度莊嚴華麗，好像一個皇后的樣子，那位貴婦，迎前說道：

　　『歡迎，王子阿米德。我等你好久了。我是一位神女，一個最有勢力的神人的女兒。你和你們兄弟間的事，以及你那不曾娶得公主的事，我都知道的。地毯啦，管兒啦，蘋果啦，都是我做成的。使你的箭尋覓不得，也就是我，因爲我要你到這裏來呢。倘你願意和我住在這裏，做我的丈夫，我可使你一生快活不盡。』

　　王子阿米德走進宮裏去。他瞧見宮中盡是奇異的東西。

He saw the *fairies*[1] and genies who lived there, and he sat down at a great feast. Every day the Peri planned some surprise, some new and strange thing, and for six months Prince Ahmed lived happily with her.

IV

At the end of that time, Prince Ahmed had a great longing to go to his father; for he knew that his father must think him dead. So he told his wish to the Peri. She was in great fear lest he would go and never come back to her and Prince Ahmed loved her dearly, and said he would not go at all if it *troubled*[2] her.

Now the Sultan *mourned*[3] the loss of his son, Prince Ahmed. He sent his servants to every place, but they could not find him; and as time went on the Sultan grew more and more sad. At last a Wise Woman was brought before him, and the Sultan asked her to find out if Ahmed were alive, and where he was.

"If you will give me time till to-morrow," she said, "I think I can find out." When the next day came she said: "Prince Ahmed is alive, but I cannot yet tell where he is"; and the Sultan could learn no more, but this was much.

Prince Ahmed said nothing more to the Peri of his wish to see his father; but she knew that he still

---

【註】 1. 仙女. 2. 困惱. 3 悲哀.

有許多仙子們和神女們，同住在那裏，他坐上一席極精美盛大的筵席，任情吃了個飽。那神女每天陪着他玩，做各種新奇古怪的事物給他看，王子阿米德於不知不覺之間，同她快樂地住了六個月。

四

六個月以後，王子阿米德想起他的父親，渴欲囘家一望，因爲他知道，父親定然料他已死。他把這心事告訴神女。但她怕他一去不返，大爲驚慌；王子阿米德已是熱烈地愛她了，看她不願意，他也不願再談了。

蘇丹自從兒子阿米德失縱以後，十分悲痛。他命僕人們四處尋找，但始終沒有誰能找到。蘇丹愈覺得悲傷。後來，他召了一個女巫入宮，命她查看阿米德在那裏，是否活在世上。

她說：『你如容我到明日，我想我能夠尋出的。』 次日她來說道：『王子阿米德是活着，不過住處，我無法知道，不能夠告訴你。』 蘇丹除了這點消息外，也不能得到什麼。

王子阿米德雖不再向仙子要求去看父親；但仙子卻知道他仍要去的，因爲　　　是悲鬱着，悄悄地不言不語，有

wished to go, for he was sad, and often *silent*.[1] So one day she said to him:

"I know you still wish to see your father, but I know also that you are true to me and to your word. You shall go, but let me tell you must and what you must not do. Do not tell your father where you have been all this time, not tell him of me. Tell him only that you are happy, and that the *sole*[2] reason for going back was to make him at ease in his mind."

Prince Ahmed *promised*,[3] and *set off*[4] for the palace, riding a most *splendid*[5] horse, and with twenty men on horses to ride with him. It was not very far to the Sultan's palace, and the Sultan was filled with great joy when he saw his son once more. True to his word, Prince Ahmed told nothing of what had *happened*[6] to him, and on the third day he rode back to the Peri.

·received him gladly, and she was so sure now of his love for her that she said nothing about keeping him always by her. *Rather*,[7] she sent him again to his father at the end of the month. Thus it went on, and Prince Ahmed again and again went to see his father, the Sultan; and his father *forebore*[8] to ask him whence he came.

But the servants of the Sultan began to be *jealous*[9] of Prince Ahmed, and to fill the ears of his father, the Sultan, with *warnings*.[10] They said that he could not

---

【註】 1. 沈默的. 2. 唯一的. 3. 允許. 4. 出發. 5. 雄壯的. 6. 遭遇. 7. 寧願. 8. 忍住. 9. 嫉妒的. 10. 警告.

一日她對他說道：

『我知道你仍要囘家去看望父親，　我也知道你對我，和你的話，都是眞實的。你可以囘去，不過須牢記我言。千萬不要告訴你父親這許多時候在什麼地方，也切不要提到我。只說你是快樂地過活，現在囘家惟一目的，爲安慰親心就是了。』

王子阿米德應允，遂騎上最雄壯的馬，跟着二十個從者，向宮廷走去。這離蘇丹的宮廷很近，蘇丹瞧見他囘來，快活得眼中流淚。阿米德爲守信起見，關於他的奇遇並沒有告訴父親，到了第三天，他便囘到仙子處來了。

她欣然地迎接他，　如今她深信他是熱烈地在愛她了，遂不再以他的別離爲念。到月底，她願送他再囘家去走一遭。這樣，王子阿米德時時囘家省親；蘇丹卻也容忍到今，不再問他的來歷。

但是蘇丹的衆臣，開始懷疑和妒忌王子阿米德了。他們在蘇丹面前，說了阿米德許多壞話。他們又說，他來的地

come from *afar*,[1] for his horses were always fresh; and that he must have great riches; and finally that it was clear he meant to get the kingdom away from the Sultan. The Sultan thanked his servants, but said he did not believe his son would act thus.

Still, he did begin to have some fear. So he sent again for the Wise Woman and bade her find out where his son went to. She learned by her *art*[2] where Prince Ahmed found his arrow, and she also went to the foot of the rocks. There she hid herself and saw the Prince come with his men. Then she saw them no more, and she knew they must have gone through some *fairy gate*.[3]

V

When it was time, a few days later, for the Prince to make another *visit*[4] to the Sultan, the Wise Woman had laid a plan which she now carried out. She went again to the rocks and lay as if nearly dead. So when the Prince came out through the gate he saw a poor sick woman, not able to speak, and he was filled with *pity*.[5] He bade his men place her on a horse, and then rode back through the gate into the Palace of the Peri.

The Peri knew at once that all was not right, and warned the Prince that some one was trying to do him *harm*.[6] But he said this could not be, for he knew no

---

【註】 1. 從遠處地. 2. 魔術. 3. 仙洞. 4. 拜訪. 5. 憐憫. 6. 損害.

方並不遠，因爲那些馬兒並不疲倦；他定然異常豪富的；他不肯說出他的所在，這是很顯明的，他要謀奪蘇丹的江山。蘇丹謝了他們的好意；他說他不信兒子會幹出這樣的事情。

話雖如此，　他卻不無一點驚懼。　因此他再召了那女巫，命她務須找出他兒子的地方。她用蠱術，算出王子阿米德尋得他箭的去處。遂走到那裏，暗伏在岩石邊。他看見王子同他的從者行到這裏，驀地不見了，她知道他們定是走進什麼仙洞去了。

五

過了幾天，是王子要去看望蘇丹的時候，那女巫便想得一個妙計。　她再走到那岩石脚下，　睡下裝做要死的樣子。　當王子從洞門裏走出，　一眼看見洞邊躺着一個病婦，病勢很重，話都不能說了，他覺得十分可憐。遂囑從者把她扶上馬，送她到仙子的宮裏。

那仙子立刻覺得事情不妙，警告王子，說有人在暗算他。但他說，決沒有這回事，因爲他知道自己不曾得罪過

had *wronged*[1] no one; and so he set forth again to see his father, the Sultan.　The Peri took care of the woman, who soon revived and looked about her.　She was amazed at the splendor of all she saw, and the Peri had her led through all the halls.

At last she was sent on her way through the fairy gate, but when she turned to see where it was, that she might find it again, it was not to be seen.　So now she went back to the Sultan, and told him all she had found out.　At the end of her tale she said:

"You see, O Sultan, what great riches the Peri has.　What if she should now *urge*[2] your son to *seize*[3] your throne and *add*[4] the wealth you have to her own?"

The Sultan was much moved, and called on his councilors to advise him.　They were for laying hold at once of the Prince and his men, and of *clapping*[5] them into prison, even if they did not put them to death.　The Wise Woman asked leave to be heard.

"Would that be best?" she asked.　"The Prince's men are genies.　You cannot hold them.　If they chose they could at once *escape*[6] through the air to the Peri, and she would come and take your kingdom by force. No.　Rather set your son some great task.　If he does it, well and good.　You will then have *gained*[7] something.　If not, you will have a *charge*[8] to bring against him."

【註】 1. 得罪. 　2. 催迫. 　3. 篡奪. 　4. 增加. 　5. 幽閉. 　6. 逃避. 7 得到. 　8. 罪名.

誰；所以，他又坦然地探望父親蘇丹去了。仙子看護着病
婦，不多時蘇甦過來，女巫張目四處偷望。宮中的一種華
貴富麗的景象，使她看了，暗暗驚奇不止。仙子見她蘇甦，
便引她穿過幾個房間，把她送將出來。

　　末後，她被送出了仙門，她囘頭急望，仙門已經不見
了，就是再尋時，也沒絲毫影蹤。她回到蘇丹那裏，把經過
的事情，都告訴了。末後她說道：

　　『呵！蘇丹啦，你瞧，那仙子多麼豪富呵！倘若她
現在要逼你兒子篡位，其實也無非爲增加她自己的財產罷
了。』

　　蘇丹大爲心動，卽召衆臣商議對付的方法。他們主張，
立刻把王子和從者們拘拿，卽不殺死，也須幽閉牢中。女
巫不以爲然，請允許她發表意見。

　　她說：『這樣就能妥當嗎？王子的從者們都是妖魔哩。
你們無法捉拿他們的。他們見事情不妙，便會立刻飛報仙
子，她便有所藉口，來用強力奪取蘇丹的天下。依我想來，
還是令你的兒子做些難做的事兒。要是他遵命，顯見他還沒
有惡意；而且你反可得利。要是他拒絕，那時你也可以名
正言順將他問罪了。』

"What would you ask of him?" said the Sultan.

"Ask him to bring you a *tent*[1] small enough to be carried in a man's hand, yet large enough to *shelter*[2] your whole army." They all agreed that this was a wise plan to follow, and the next day, when the Prince came to *pay his respects*,[3] the Sultan said:—

"My son, I have learned that you have married a Peri. It is only right that she should show her power for you, and that you should prove the honor you *profess*[4] for me. You see how much it costs me whenever I go to war. I have to *provide*[5] *mules*,[6] *camels*,[7] and other beasts of *burden*[8] to carry the tents of the army. Now I am sure the Peri could easily give you for me a tent which a man could carry in his hand, but which would shelter my whole army. Ask her for it." The Prince was much troubled at this.

"You are right," said he, "when you say that I have married a Peri. How you found it out I do not know. And I dare not say if she will do this thing. But you are my father, and I obey your *commands*.[9]"

"Son," said the Sultan, "your wife must have little love for you if she is not willing to do so simple a thing. Go ask her." The Prince was greatly *vexed*,[10] and he left the court at once, though he had not stayed his usual time. The Peri met him on his return, and saw that his face was sad. She asked him his trouble.

【註】 1. 帳幕. 2. 遮蔽. 3. 問候. 4. 承認. 5. 預備. 6. 騾. 7. 駱駝. 8. 負重. 9. 命令. 10. 煩惱.

蘇丹說：『你想命他做怎樣的難事呢？』

『命他給你帶一個帳幕，縮小起來可以拿在手中，擴大起來卻能容納你全隊的軍馬。』 他們都稱贊這是個好主張，次日，王子來探問他父親的時候，蘇丹對他說道：

『我的兒子，我曉得你跟着一個仙子結了婚。這是十分充足的理由，她必定將她的仙術顯示給你看，同時你又足以顯出你對老父的忠實。你知道我行軍時，是多麼糜費。我須備許多騾，駱駝以及各種負重的獸類，來載着軍士所需用的帳幕。現在我想那仙子爲你的緣故，定能很容易的爲我造成一個帳幕來，其小須一人可握在掌中，其大要足以遮蔽得我全部的軍馬。你便煩她做一個來罷。』 王子聽了，異常煩悶。

他說： 『你說我跟着一個仙子結了婚， 這是實在的。但我不知道你是怎樣知道的。我也不敢說，這枳東西，她定然能做。 不過你是我的父親， 我必須服從你的命令。』

蘇丹說： 『孩子，這樣簡單的東西，倘你妻不願意爲你效力， 這是表明她對你很薄情了。 趕快去問她要吧。』王子立即辭別出宮，非常煩惱。仙子見他囘來，出來迎接，卻見他愁容滿面。便問他爲甚事不快。

"I do not know how it was found out," said he, "but the Sultan, my father, has learned of our marriage." The Peri had a ready answer to give him. She told him that the woman he had helped was a *spy*.[1]

"But there is something more," said she; "what is it?" Then he told her what his father had bade him ask of her. "Be at rest," she said smiling. "I will soon prove to your father my love to you." And so she called a maid and bade her bring the largest tent she had. The maid came back shortly with a small *case*[2] in her hand, and the Peri gave this to the Prince.

He was *puzzled*[3]. He had heard the order given for the largest tent, and here was nothing but a small case that might hold a finger ring. The Peri smiled.

"Do you think I jest with you?" she asked. "Go," said she to one of her servants, "and set up the tent." And then the tent was set up in a field, and the Prince saw that it was large enough to cover two armies such as his father had.

"You see," said the Peri, "that the tent is larger than you need. But you must know that it can be large or small, as you choose; and when it is set up for an army, it will be just right for that army."

【註】 1. 間諜　2. 匣．　3. 迷惑.

他說：『我不知道，這件事怎樣會被父親知道的，我父親蘇丹已知道我們倆結婚了。』仙子毫不躊躇的告訴他前天他所救的那個病婦，就是一個間諜。

『現在定然出有事故了，是怎樣的呢？』於是他便把他父親要求的事情，一一訴說。她笑着道：『我立刻可以給你父親，證明我確是愛你的。』她叫了一個仙女來，吩咐她把那最大的帳幕取了來。仙女走去，不一囘，手中拿着一隻小匣，仙子接了過來，交給王子。

他迷惑着。他原要一頂最大的帳幕，這裏卻是一隻小匣兒，只僅僅容下一隻戒指罷了。仙子微笑着說道：

『你想我和你開玩笑嗎？去吧。』她隨對一個僕人說：『去把這帳幕張開來！』那帳幕是張設在一塊荒地上，王子瞧了，果然很大，像他父親那樣的軍馬數目，足殼容納兩隊。

仙子說：『你看，這帳幕比你所要求的還大呢。但你要知道，這帳幕是能大能小，隨你歡喜；你軍隊有多少，牠便可給你遮蔽多少。』

VI

So the tent was placed again in its little case, and the Prince rode off with it to the palace of his father, the Sultan. The Sultan wondered at so *speedy*[1] a return, and when he saw the tent, and it was set up, and it covered his whole army, his wonder knew *no bounds*[2]. But now he was filled with secret *envy*[3] of his son; and the more he thought of it, the more he feared the power he had through the Peri.

The Sultan called the Wise Woman again, and she told him to ask for water from the Fountain of Lions. Now it was well known that this was a most *perilous*[4] thing to do; and when the prince heard the Sultan ask for water from the Fountain of Lions he was very angry. But he said again that he would lay the matter before the Peri. He did so in these words, after telling her of his father's pleasure over the tent:

"My father asks now an even greater gift. He asks for water from the Fountain of Lions. I have always done, when I could, what my father asked. But this shall be as you please, for he has no right to ask such a gift from you."

"Be at rest," said the Peri. "I know who has put this into your father's mind; but he shall not find *fault*[5] with you or with me The Fountain of

------

【註】 1. 迅速的. 2. 無限制. 3. 嫉妒. 4. 危險的. 5. 過失.

六

把帳幕重行收入原來的小匣裏，王子騎着馬，帶給他父親蘇丹。蘇丹見他這樣快的回來，很覺驚訝，及瞧見那帳幕，當張開眞的能殼容下他所有的軍馬，更覺得駭異。不過同時他卻愈加疑忌兒子了，他愈想愈慌，他想他兒子得到有這般奇術的仙子難道說不會謀奪他的江山嗎。

蘇丹遂召女巫商量，她教他命兒子取獅子泉的泉水進獻。話說取這獅子泉是一件極危險的事情。王子聽蘇丹說命取獅子泉時，異常驚怒，但他只得說，且回去和仙子商量再爲取來。他囘到仙子那裏，先將他父親見帳幕很喜悅的話說了，隨後說道：

『我父親現在又要求一件更大的禮物呢。他要獅子泉的泉水，在我能力所及的地方。我當然要服從父親的命令，但對於你卻隨你的便，他原沒有權利，向你要求這樣的禮物。』

仙子說：『你可放心，我已知道這是誰挑唆你父親的，話雖如此，他並不能難倒你我。那獅子泉是在一個大宮廷

Lions is in the middle of the court of a great *castle*[1]. Four fierce lions guard the gate; two sleep while the other two are awake. I will show you how you can pass them safely."

The Peri had a *needle*[2] and *thread*[3] in her hand as she spoke, and by her side lay other balls of thread. She gave one to the Prince and said:—

"Take this ball of thread. Take also two horses. You will ride one and lead the other; the second is to carry a *sheep*[4] killed to-day, and cut into four quarters. You must also take a *bottle*[5] which I will give you. You will need it for the water you are to bring back.

"Set out early to-morrow. When you reach an iron gate throw the ball of thread before you, but hold the end of the thread. The ball will *roll*[6] toward the castle. Follow it and you will come to the four lions. They will awake and *roar*[7]. Throw a quarter of the sheep to each, then *clap*[8] *spurs*[9] to your horse and ride to the fountain. Fill your bottle with water and ride back. The lions will be busy in eating and will not touch you."

The Prince did as he was bid. He threw the ball; he reached the lions; they roared; he *tossed*[10] a quarter of the sheep to each; he rode to the fountain and rode back with the water. But when he had passed the lions again, he saw that two of them left their food and began to follow him.

【註】1. 候宮. 2. 針. 3. 線. 4. 羊. 5. 瓶. 6. 滾. 7. 吼. 8. 擊 — 刺距. 10. 拋.

旁邊，有四隻兇猛的獅子守門；照例兩隻睡，兩隻醒。我且教你一個方法，你便可安然進去了。』

　　仙子說這些話的當兒，手裏拿着一針一線，她的旁邊又有好幾個線團。她便拿個線團兒給王子道：

　　『拿着這線團，再取兩匹馬兒。你騎上一匹，牽帶一匹。把一隻新宰的肥羊割成四塊，載在牽着的馬上。此外我再給你一個瓶兒帶去。你可將這瓶兒盛水帶囘來。

　　『明天一清早就去。你趕到鐵門那裏，可拋下線團在你的面前，但握緊線的一端。這球兒自會滾到那宅子裏去。你便跟着走。到那四隻獅子的時候，他們驚醒，便大聲咆哮着。你可給牠們每隻拋下一塊羊肉，即趕馬速向那泉井奔去。盛滿一瓶，立刻奔囘。這些獅子爲忙於吃食，便不會來襲擊你了。』

　　王子依着她話做去。他把那線團拋下，果見有四隻猛獅；牠們大聲咆哮着；他給每隻獅子丟下一塊羊肉；立刻趕到泉井，取着泉水囘來。不過當他重行經過獅子面前的時候，卻有兩隻獅子，棄了食，向他跟來。

At first he drew his sword, for he thought he should have to fight for his life; but soon he saw they meant him no harm. One went before, the other followed behind, and so they came at last to the palace of the Sultan. Then the lions turned back and left the Prince, who went forward to his father.

"Here, *sire*[1]" he said, as he bowed low, "is water from the Fountain of Lions. I wish you so much health that you never will need it." The Sultan was well pleased; then he said:

"Son, you have done well. I have but one thing more to ask of you and your fairy wife. I wish you to bring me a man not above a foot and a half high, whose *beard*[2] is thirty feet long, who carries upon his shoulder a *bar*[3] of iron weighing five hundred pounds, which he uses as a *club*[4], and who can speak."

VII

The Prince was in *dismay*[5]. He knew not where such a *creature*[6] could be found; but he went back to the Peri and told his tale.

"I know by this," he said, "that my father means to harm me forever".

"Be not cast down," said she. "I know the man. He is my brother. He is very *violent*[7], but he is also very kind to those who wish him well. Do not fear when you see him."

【註】 1. 陛下. 2. 鬚. 3. 棒. 4. 棍. 5. 氣餒. 6. 人. 7. 兇暴的.

其初，他就拔出劍來，因為他想，當為自己的生命而鬥；不過他立刻看見，牠們並不來傷害他，一隻獅子在前，一隻獅子在後，一直護送王子到蘇丹宮前。牠們卽離開王子走了，他進去見他父親。

他行禮說道：『萬歲！這是獅子泉的泉水啦。我願你福體永康，永遠不喝着此泉！』蘇丹心裏甚是喜悅，但他過了一會卻說：

『孩子，你做得眞不差。我現在只有一件事，再要你和你美麗的妻子爲我辦一辦。我要你帶着一個人來，高不過一尺半，鬍鬚須有三十尺長，臂膀帶上一根鐵棒，有五百磅的重量，這棒原是他用作手杖。而且又要會說話。』

七

王子悶悶不樂。他不知道，在那裏方可以找到這樣一個人。他囘到仙子處，便把這事情告訴她。

他說：『我是知道，我父親不過借此殺害我罷咧。』

她說：『不要憂愁。我知道那人的。他原來就是我的哥哥。他卻十分兇暴，但對於好意待他的人也甚和善，你見他時，且不必害怕。』

At that she bade a servant make a fire in a *pan*[1] on the *porch*[2] of her palace. She took some *incense*[3] and threw it into the fire. There was a thick cloud of smoke. When it cleared away the Peri's brother stood before them.

When the Prince looked on him, a *chill*[4] ran down his back. The man was a foot and a half high; he had a beard thirty feet long, and he carried on his shoulder a club of iron five hundred pounds in weight. He looked fiercely at the Prince.

"Who is this man?" he asked.

"It is my husband," said the Peri. "He is Ahmed, son of the Sultan of India." Then the Peri's brother looked more kindly on him.

"His father, the Sultan," said the Peri, "has a great *desire*[5] to see you, and, as a favor to us both, I wish you would let him take you to the palace."

"He need but lead the way; I will follow him."

So the next day Prince Ahmed took the Peri's brother to the palace. As they drew near, the people were so *alarmed*[6] they fled into their houses, and the streets were empty. At the palace gates, the guards, too, ran away, and so the two went in and there sat the Sultan on his throne with his councilors about him.

"Thou hast sent for me," said the Peri's brother, going straight up to the throne. "What dost thou wish?"

【註】 1. 鍋. 2. 走廊. 3. 香料. 4. 寒顫. 5. 欲望. 6. 儆恐.

　　她說了，遂命一個僕人到廊下鍋中，點起一把火來。她又取些香料，放在火上。一陣濃煙過去，卻見那仙子的哥哥，站在他們的面前。

　　王子瞧見他的時候，嚇得毛骨聳然。這人高僅一尺半，鬍鬚卻有三十尺長，肩膀上掮着一根鐵棒，足足有五百磅重，他狠狠地盯着王子。

　　『此人是誰？』他問。

　　仙子說：『他是我的丈夫，名叫阿米德，印度蘇丹的王子。』仙子的哥哥見如此說時，面色便和平了。

　　仙子說道：『他父親蘇丹，很渴望的想和你會見，這是你對我們共同的恩惠，我希望你便讓他引你到宮中去走一遭罷。』

　　『只要他引路，我便跟他走。』

　　次日，王子阿米德便領着仙子的哥哥向王宮走去。當他們走到離宮殿不遠，衆百姓見了，都害怕，拚命向屋子裏避逃，街上頓時奔逃一空。到宮門的時候，衞兵也嚇得飛奔，他們便這樣地走進王宮去，但見那蘇丹端坐在他的殿上，朝臣們兩邊站定。

　　仙子的哥哥便直奔到殿上說：『你命人喚我來，所爲何事？』

The Sultan did not dare speak. He put his hands before his eyes to shut out so fearful a sight.

"Wilt thou not speak?" asked the little man in a *rage*[1]; and, before Ahmed could stop him, he let his bar of iron fall on the Sultan's head and *crushed*[2] him to the earth. Then he *slew*[3] all the enemies of Ahmed, and *strode*[4] out into the court.

"There is one other," said he,—"the woman who *stirred*[5] up the envy of the Sultan. Let her be brought."

When the woman was brought, he crushed her also to the earth.

"Learn," said he, "what it means to give *wicked*[6] advice and to *pretend*[7] sickness. Now," he went on, "let Prince Ahmed, my *brother-in-law*[8], be Sultan of India." Then all the people shouted:

"Long live Sultan Ahmed!" The Sultan's *robes*[9] were put upon him, and the little man at once sent for his sister and caused her to be *crowned*[10] the Sultana of India.

Prince Ahmed gave to Prince Ali a great *province*[11] to rule over. He sent also for Houssain, and told him he, too, should have a province. But Houssain sent back word he was quite content to live where he was. He wanted no province or riches. He wanted only to live in quiet.

【註】 1. 忿忿.　2. 擊碎.　3. 打死.　4. 大步.　5. 挑唆　6. 刁惡的.
7. 假裝.　8. 妹丈.　9. 袍.　10. 加以冠.　11. 省.

這時候，蘇丹眞是嚇壞了，他再也說不出甚麼話來。但以手掩面，閃避不及。

『你爲什麽不說話啦？』那個矮人狂怒了；就舉起他的鐵棒兒，在王子來不及阻止的時候，便向蘇丹頭上打去，已把他從殿上打倒在地，變成肉醬了。他又輕揮鐵棒把阿米德的所有仇人，一齊打死，然後大步兒走出。

他說：『還有一個人，那個挑唆蘇丹的女巫，把她拿來。』

當這婦人拿到的時候，他也將她一棒兒，打成肉醬。

他說：『好女子，這就是你挑唆和裝病人的結果。』他又嚷着說：『如今，當讓我妹丈，王子阿米德，承繼印度的蘇丹。』衆百姓歡呼：

『蘇丹，阿米德萬歲！』蘇丹的袍加上阿米德的身上，這矮人便立刻送他的妹妹到宮，立做印度的皇后。

王子阿米德給一省的地方，與王子阿里統治着。他又差人告訴霍桑，他也和阿里一樣，應當有一省統治。但王子霍桑囘說，他卻十分滿足現在所住的地方。不願受封，也不願富貴，但願清靜地度日。

5. The History of Cogia Hassan Alhabbal

I

It was the habit of Haroun Al Raschid, the Caliph of Bagdad, to go about his city in *disguise*[1], that he might learn the true condition of his people. On one *occasion*[2] he was surprised at seeing a new building, fit for the palace of a great lord, in a street he had not passed through for a long time. At the Caliph's request the Grand Vizier found out, from one who lived near by, that the house belonged to one Cogia Hassan, *surnamed*[3] Alhabbal, *on account of*[4] his trade of *rope-making*,[5] at which the neighbour had seen him working when poor. By whatever means he had grown rich, he was certainly poor no longer, for he lived in a manner befitting his palace.

"I must see this fortunate rope-maker," said the Caliph, and on the next day the Grand Vizier brought him to the court, where he told his own story *after the following fashion*[6]:—

Commander of the Faithful, my name is Hassan, but from my trade I am commonly known by the name of Hassan Alhabbal. I owe the good fortune I now enjoy to two dear friends, whose names are Saad and Saadi. Saadi is very rich, and always *maintained*[7] that wealth was necessary to happiness, since without

【註】 1. 喬裝. 2. 場合. 3. 外號. 4. 因為. 5. 打繩. 6. 如下情形. 7. 主張.

五　致　富　奇　談

一

話說巴革達德有個凱立夫（卽囘教教皇），名叫哈龍亞爾‧拉西德，他有一種習慣，專喜喬裝，在城子裏私訪，考察民情。有一次，他打從一條街上經過，這條街好久沒有走了，他突然瞧見一座新建高大巨宅，莊麗巍峨，好像一個巨公的府第一樣，不覺十分驚異。在凱立夫查問之後，宰相卽從一個隣居，探出消息，這巨宅的主人名叫郭奇亞‧亨生，因他以打繩爲業，一般人都稱他外號做亞爾亨白爾，這打繩的，在他窮苦做工的時候，一般鄰里都親眼瞧見他。但現在卻暴富起來，他的種種生活情形，居然和他的華屋相配。

凱立夫說：『我必定要見見這位幸運的繩匠，』第二天宰相果然把打繩匠帶往宮中。那打繩匠便談他經過的故事，和發財由來，如下列的情形：——

教主嚩，我名叫做亨生，但因爲我的職業，一般人通常都稱我做亨生‧亞爾亨白爾的。我現在所享受的好運，全靠我兩個好朋友，他們的名字是捨德和捨提。捨提十分有錢，他常說幸福全由金錢來的，因爲沒有錢，誰都不能

it no one could be independent. Most *poverty*,[1] he said, came from a man's not having enough to begin with, and he thought that any man who made a right use even of small means would surely grow rich. Saad, on the other hand, *contented*[2] that a poor man might gain wealth by other means, sometimes indeed by mere chance.

"Well," said Saadi, "we will not *dispute*[3] it any longer, but to test our *opinions*[4] I will give a sum of money to some honest but poor workman; if he does not obtain wealth and ease with it, then you shall try if you can succeed better by any means you may *employ*.[5]"

Soon afterwards Saad and Saadi passed my house one day while I was at work at my rope making. They expressed surprise that, with all my industry, I could not do better and save some money. I told them that, work as I might, I could *barely*[6] keep my family alive, to say nothing of buying materials for larger *ventures*.[7] We talked a while longer and then Saadi pulled a purse out of his bosom and said:

"Here, take this purse; it contains two hundred pieces of gold. God bless you, and give you *grace*[8] to make the good use of them I desire, and be sure my friend Saad and I will both have great pleasure if they help towards making you any more *prosperous*[9]."

【註】 1. 貧窮. 2. 贊成. 3. 辯論. 4. 理論. 5. 使用. 6. 僅僅地. 7. 事業. 8. 恩惠. 9. 興旺的.

過活啦。他說，多數的貧窮，由於沒有錢，不能發展，他想，倘若有錢，雖是很小數目，若能正當地經營起來，不論是誰，定能做成富翁。捨德的意見卻極端相反，他以爲一個窮人，得到財富，或許靠另外的途徑，有時，眞是從一種絕無僅有的僥倖。

捨提說：『我們且不必徒口空辯，且去實地把我們的理論去實驗一下，我給一注錢與一個誠實的苦工，看他能否由此致富，你倘有妙法兒，也可同樣地去試着的。』

過了不多時，有一天，捨德和捨提兩人同走過我的門前，那時我正在忙碌地打着繩。他們看我做工做得這般辛勤還是一貧如洗，沒有一點兒餘蓄，他們覺得甚是驚訝。我告訴他們，無論我怎樣地辛苦做活，一家仍難得到溫飽，莫說買原料謀發展了。我們再談一囘兒，捨提便從懷裏摸出一個錢袋來，說：

『這裏有個錢袋，袋裏有金洋二百圓，你拿去吧。上帝保佑你，我希望你好好兒應用牠們，牠們果能使你興旺起來，我的朋友捨德和我，都很快樂的。』

Commander of the Faithful, Hassan went on, my joy was so great that my speech failed me, and I could only thank my *benefactor*[1] by laying hold of the *hem*[2] of his garment and kissing it; but he drew it from me hastily, and the two friends walked on.

I returned to my work thinking, how shall I keep this purse safe? for there is neither box nor *cupboard*[3] in my poor house to lock it up. It seemed best on the whole to lay aside ten pieces for present use, and to *wrap*[4] the rest in the *folds*[5] of the *linen*[6] which went about my cap. Out of the ten pieces I bought a good stock of *hemp*[7], and, as my family had eaten no meat for a long time, got some for supper.

As I walked home, a *famished*[8] *vulture*[9] flew upon me, and would have borne the meat away if I had not held it very fast; but in the struggle my *turban*[10] fell on the ground. The vulture at once let go his hold on the meat, and, seizing my turban, flew away with it. I cried out so loud that all the men, women, and children near by joined me; but our cries had no effect on the vulture, and soon he and turban were both lost to sight.

This made me very sad, and as I had to buy a new turban my ten pieces of gold did not last long. While they lasted, my little family and I lived better than usual, but when they are gone our poverty was

---

【註】 1. 恩人. 2. 衣邊. 3. 廚. 4. 裹. 5. 摺縫. 6. 竹布. 7. 大麻. 8. 餓的. 9. 鷹. 10. 頭巾.

享生又道，教主啦！我這時候的快活，眞是到了十二萬分，連話都喜得說不出來了，我不知怎樣感謝他，只知抓住他衣邊狂吻以表示我對我恩主的謝意，但他急拖了衣服，兩個朋友掉頭不顧的去了。

我重行再做我的工，但一壁思忖：我怎樣地設法得保這錢袋安穩呢？因爲在我那可憐的屋子裏，旣沒有箱，又沒有樹，可把這錢鎖在裏邊。我從各方面仔細想過，最穩妥的辦法，只有取出十塊金洋，放在一邊作爲現用外，其餘都緊縈在我裹頭的竹布頭巾摺縫裏。我將取出來的十塊金洋，帶到市上買了許多的大蔴，因我家裏好久不曾吃肉了，我又買了些肉，作爲晚餐。

當我囘家的當兒，有隻餓鷹猛向我撲地飛來，他看我的肉未曾拿緊，本想一啄擺去的；但我正在與鷹格鬪，卻把我的頭巾兒脫落到地上去了。那鷹見我頭巾落地，立時便給了肉，將頭巾抓了飛去。我失聲狂叫，許多男女孩子們，都驚動走近我身邊來，助我呟喝；但我們的呼叫聲，對於那鷹毫無用處，一忽兒，牠和頭巾都不見蹤跡了。

這事使我很覺難堪，我必須再買一方新的頭巾來，但我那十塊金洋不是永久用不完的。有着這些金洋的時候，我的一家大小和我，當然過得很舒適，可是當錢都用完了，

as hopeless as ever.   Yet I did not *murmur*[1] or *repine.*[2]
"God," said I, "was pleased to give me riches when I
least expected them.   He has thought fit to take them
away again.   I will praise his name for all the bene-
fits I have received, and submit myself, as ever, to
his will."

My poor wife did not bear the loss so calmly, and
when I told the neighbors that the vulture had carried
away a hundred and ninety pieces of gold, besides my
turban, they did not believe a word of it, and only
laughed.

About six months after this misfortune, the two
friends came to me again.   "Well," said Saad, "we do
not ask you how *affairs*[3] go, since we saw you last;
without doubt they are better."

"Gentlemen," I answered, "I deeply *grieve*[4] to
tell you that your good wishes and my hopes have not
had the success we expected."

Then I told them exactly what had happened,
scarcely thinking they would believe it.   Nor did they
at first, but they knew me for an honest man, and Saad
recalled[5] other strange true stories of vultures, so that
Saadi himself seemed almost *convinced*[6].   Bidding me
be more careful in future, he pulled a purse out of his
waistband[7], and counted out into my hand two hundred
pieces of gold, which I put into my bosom for want of
a purse.   Before I could half express my thanks for
this second kindness the two friends walked away.

【註】 1. 怨恨. 2. 不平. 3. 事務. 4. 心痛. 5. 憶起. 6. 相信. 7. 腰帶.

我仍舊一貧如洗。但我也並不怨恨。我說：『上帝，當我並不希望錢財的時候，你賜給我財富了。你想，這錢財應該再拿回去，可是我爲了所受的一切恩惠，將仍頌讚着，將仍如平日一般地，恪從上帝的聖意。』

我可憐的妻子，對於這金洋和頭巾的喪失，卻沒有像我一樣的達觀。當我告訴隣人們，說那鷹除衘掉我的頭巾，卻還衘我百九十塊金洋去，但他們並不見信，只是大笑。

這件不幸事件的發生約莫六個月光景，那兩位朋友來了。捨德說，『恭賀你，我們且不必問你的事情如何，但看樣兒，你比從前好得多啦。』

我答說：『先生，慚愧得很，我白辜負了你倆的好意，和我自己的希望了。』

我確細細地訴說一遍當時所出的亂子，心裏自想這種事也難教人見信的。在起初，他們果然不信，不過他們看我確是個非常誠實的人，捨德又憶起蒼鷹的許多奇事來，因此捨提居然也就見信了。囑我以後，務須十分小心，他便又從腰帶裏取出一個錢袋，親數二百塊金洋，放在我的手裏，我因爲沒有錢袋，當下就揣在懷裏，在我還沒有說完半句的感謝話兒，那兩位朋友就拔腳走了。

I did not take up my work again that day, but hastened home Finding neither wife nor children within, I pulled out my money, put ten pieces on one side for present use, and wrapped up the rest in a clean linen cloth, *tying*[1] it fast with a *knot*[2], and placing it for safety in an *earthen vessel*[3] full of *bran*[4] which stood in a corner. Into this I thought no one would look; and when my wife came in soon afterwards I went out to buy some hemp, without saying anything to her about this second gift from Saadi.

While I was absent a *sandman*[5], who sells washing balls which women use in the baths, passed through our street. My wife, who had no money, asked him if he would exchange his washing balls for some bran. The sandman *consented*[6], and the *bargain*[7] was made.

I soon came home with my hemp, and saw at once that the pot of bran was gone. I asked my wife, in great fear, what had become of it, and she told me of her bargain with the sandman.

"Ah, unfortunate woman!" I cried, "you know not what you have done. With the bran, you have given the sandman a hundred and ninety pieces of gold, a second gift from Saadi."

At this my wife became like one *distracted*[8], beating her breast and tearing her hair and clothes. "Where shall I find the sandman?" she cried; "O husband why did you not tell me in time?"

【註】 1. 縛. 2. 結. 3. 瓦罐. 4. 糠. 5. 賣肥皂者. 6. 同意. 7. 買賣. 8. 使狂.

那天我沒有做工，急忙奔囘家去。妻子和孩子們都不在家，我一個人把金子從懷裏取出，拿出十塊金洋，作爲現用，將餘下的金洋，都包裹在一件清潔竹布小衫裏面緊緊地打了一個結。在我的屋隅有一隻儲着糠的罐兒，我把布衫塞在那糠罐兒裏，上面用糠罩好，放在屋的壁角處，自忖這再穩妥沒有了。我妻不久囘來，我因爲要急於出去買蔴，未曾告訴她捨提第二次的餽贈。

當我不在家的時候，有個賣肥皂人，這肥皂是婦人們洗澡用的，走過街上。我妻想買一塊肥皂使用，可是沒有錢，問他有點兒糠肯不肯掉換。那商人說可以的，於是交易遂成功了。

我買了蔴，急忙地囘來，一眼便看那個糠罐兒，不見了。我大大地驚慌，問我妻糠罐兒到那兒去了，她告訴我說，這罐兒早已和賣肥皂人掉換了貨物了。

我大聲說：『啊！不幸的婦人！你定然不知道你幹的是什麼事。你想那是粗糠嗎，你已給一百九十塊金洋與那個賣肥皂人，這糠裏是捨提第二次的贈金藏放在裏面呢。』

我妻聽了這話，頓像發了瘋一般，鎚着胸，把她的頭髮和衣裳，都撕去了。她哭着說：『我從那兒去追尋賣肥皂的人呢？啊，丈夫，爲甚，你不先告訴我一聲呢？』

"We must bear our loss patiently," I said. "After, all, what have the rich which we, have not? We breathe the same air, and are warmed by the same sun. They die as well as we. In short, while we live in the fear of God, there is no advantage which we ought to *covet*[1]."

Thus we comforted ourselves, and I worked on at my trade as if nothing had happened, only I *dreaded*[2] to look Saadi in the face when he should come and ask me how I had improved his two hundred pieces of gold.

II

After some time, Saad and Saadi again called to see how I had *prospered*[3]. Each still held his first opinion about the best way of helping me. I made believe that I did not see them, and never lifted up my eyes until they spoke. Then I told them with shame of my second misfortune. "Could I guess that a sandman would come by that day," I said, "and that my wife would give him our pot of bran? Perhaps I should have been more *prudent*[4]; but ah, sir," I added as I turned to Saadi, "I see that it has pleased God that I should not be *enriched*[5] at your hand, but that I must remain poor. Yet I owe you as many thanks as if I had gained great wealth."

【註】 1. 轉變. 2. 畏懼. 3. 成功. 4. 謹慎. 5. 使富.

　　我說：『我們必須忍受我們的喪失罷，總之，我們生就窮命，又那得有財富來呢？ 我們一樣也有空氣呼吸着，一樣也受陽光照耀着。他們有錢的人死了，也和我們一樣。我們一生，只爲敬愛上帝而生活，貪婪有甚益處。』

　　我們這樣地自己安慰自己，我仍舊做我的業務，好像不曾有過這囘事的樣子，不過但怕再見捨提的面，當他再來問我，把那二百金洋經營得怎樣了。

二

　　過了不久，捨德和捨提又來訪問我，看我有沒有發達起來。每人仍懷着不同的意見，和先前一樣的情形。我假做不曾瞧見他們，沒有擡起頭來，直等他們說起話來。我很難爲情地， 把那第二次的不幸事件告訴給他們。 我說：『我怎能知道，偏是那天賣肥皂人要來，偏是我妻要把我們那樣罐兒，給她掉換呢？大概我太謹愼了罷；但是，先生！』 當我掉頭向捨提時，我又說：『我知道上帝是不歡喜我從你手裏，變成富有，我一生是窮定了，話雖如此，但我對你卻仍是感激，好像得了大財富一樣。』

"I do not *regret*[1] the four hundred pieces of gold," answered Saadi, "I gave them in duty to God, and *for the sake of*[2] testing my opinion. Now Saad," he said to his friend, "you may try your way, and see if something besides money will make a poor man rich. Let Hassan be the man."

Saad had a piece of *lead*[3] in his hand which he showed Saadi. "You saw me," said he, "take up this piece of lead which I found on the ground; I will give it to Hassan, and you shall see what it comes to be worth."

Saadi *burst*[4] out laughing. "What is that bit of lead worth?" said he; "a *farthing*[5]! What can Hassan do with that?"

"Take it, Hassan," said Saad; "let Saadi laugh; you will tell us some news of the good *luck*[6] it has brought you one time or another."

I thought him in *jest*[7], but took the lead and thanked him and the two friends walked away.

That night, when I pulled off my clothes, the piece of lead, of which I had not thought again, *tumbled*[8] out of my pocket. I took it up, and laid it on the place nearest me. That same night it happened that a fisherman who lived hard by was *mending*[9] his nets and found a piece of lead wanting. It was too late to buy any, and if he did not fish that night his family must go hungry the next day. Therefore

---

【註】 1. 懊喪. 2. 因為. 3. 鉛. 4. 破口. 5. 小錢. 6. 幸運. 7. 戲謔. 8. 跌落. 9. 修理.

　　捨提答道：『我並不懊喪我那四百金洋，我是爲了上帝而贈你　爲了試驗我的意見而贈你。』現在捨德，他又向他的朋友說：『你可試驗你的主張罷，瞧，除掉金錢外，有什麼東西，能夠使一個窮人變做富有。就把這個亨生當做被試的人罷。』

　　捨德手裏拿着一小片兒鉛，他給捨提看了一看。『你瞧我的罷！這一小片兒鉛，是我方纔從地上拾來的；我要把牠來贈給亨生　你當見日後，這點鉛能變做一注洪運哩！』

　　捨提破口大笑，『這一些兒鉛卻值得什麼？』　他說；『一文錢啦！亨生要那個幹甚？』

　　捨德說：『亨生！你且拿去，讓捨提見笑去罷；你或許有一朝會告訴我們從這上面得到極大幸運呢。』

　　我想他是和我開玩笑了，但是我也就取了下來，謝過他後，那兩位朋友各自去了。

　　那天晚上，我脫下了我的衣服，這片兒鉛，早已不記得了，卻從我衣袋裏落下。我隨把它拾起，放在我靠近的地方。事有湊巧，那天晚上恰有個漁夫，需要一片兒鉛，作爲修網之用。夜已深了，沒有買處，倘若他晚上不去打魚呢，第二天全家卽無食物可吃，所以他喚了妻子，吩咐向

he called his wife, and bade her ask among the neighbors for a piece of lead. When she had been to every door but ours, she told her husband that none was to be had. "There is no use of going to Hassan's house," she said; "they never have anything when one wants it."

"*No matter*[1]," said the fisherman, "you must go there. This may be the lucky time."

We were *roused*[2] by her knocking, and when I heard what she wanted, I told my wife just where I had put the piece of lead Saad had given me. *Groping*[3] about in the dark she found it, and handed it out to the fisherman's wife, who was so *delighted*[4] that she promised us at once the first cast of her husband's nets, whatever it might prove to be.

The fisherman was so pleased to get the lead that he made the promise good by coming to me the next day with a fish about a yard long, and thick in *proportion*[5].

"Neighbor," he said, "it pleased God to send me no more than this one fish for you. Such as it is, I desire you to accept it. Had He sent me my net full, as He did in other casts, they should all have been yours."

"Neighbor," I answered, "the bit of lead was such a *trifle*[6] that it should not be valued at so high a rate. Neighbors should help each other in their

---

【註】 1. 不妨. 2 驚起. 3. 摸索 4. 喜悅. 5. 相稱. 6. 無價值的東西.

各鄰家去討一片鉛來。她除卻我家，全都去問過，她回家告訴丈夫，說沒有一家有這東西。她說：『亨生家是不必去的，他從沒有甚麼東西，可以給人家的。』

漁夫說：『不妨，你也應該向他家去走一遭。說不定會有僥倖的時候哩。』

她在外邊敲門，把我們驚起，聽她說出需要的東西時，我告訴我妻，捨德曾給我一片兒鉛，遂教她暗中摸給漁夫的妻子，漁夫的妻子大喜過望，她一口允許我們，要把她丈夫的第一網兒，不論所得是什麼，都拿來送給我們。

漁夫得了鉛，好生歡喜，第二天他照約送了一尾大魚來，足足有一碼長。

他說：『鄰人，我把這尾魚送給你，是上帝所喜悅的。這一些兒微禮，望你收下。上帝賜我網網不空，網網得手，都出於你的所賜。』

我答說：『你太客氣了，那一些兒鉛，值得什麼呢，那能受你這樣貴重的酬報。在小有需要的地方，做鄰居的原

little wánts.　You would have done the same for me. Yet, since you offer the fish so freely, I take it and return you my hearty thanks."

When I took it home my wife thought it too big either to *broil*[1] or to *boil*[2], with our small *gridiron*[3] and pot; but I told her I should like it cooked in any way, and returned to my work.

In cleaning the fish, my wife found a hard, clear *substance*[4] which she took for a piece of glass. She gave it to our youngest child for a plaything, and his brothers and sisters handed it about, admiring its brightness and beauty. At night, when the lamp was lighted, the children saw that it gave out a light when their mother stood between the lamp and them; and the younger children cried because the elder would not let them have it all time to play with in the dark.

Upon hearing the cause of their dispute when I came home, I called for the piece of glass, and bade my wife put out the lamp, when we found that the glass gave out so bright a light that we could see to go to bed by it.　I placed it on the *chimney*[5] and said: "Look! this is the great adventage that Saad's bit of lead brings us; it will spare us the expense of oil."

When the children saw that the lamp was out and the piece of glass supplied its place, they made so great a noise in their surprise that it *alarmed*[6] the neighborhood.

【註】 1. 炙. 2. 煮. 3. 焙器. 4. 實物. 5. 燈罩. 6. 驚動.

該互助。你也許有時候要這樣給我幫忙罷。不過，旣承你這般盛情送了來，我不能不收，我是十分激感你。』

當我提了魚囘家，我妻看見到爲難了。我家沒有這般大的焙器和鍋兒，能夠炙焙這樣大魚；我卻告訴她，不論怎樣燒法，能夠吃便算了。說畢，我就做工去。

我妻把魚洗淨，卻見魚肚裏有塊又堅硬又透明的東西，我妻當做是玻璃球，便拿給我們最小的一個孩子玩耍，他的哥哥，姐姐們，瞧見這東西亮晶晶地好看得很，也就取着同玩了一陣。但到晚間上燈的時候，孩子們瞧見這球兒卻發起光來，能夠照着他們的母親，這光比燈光還要亮，小的孩子見大的一個孩子，獨自搶了在黑暗中玩，不肯讓給他們，便哇哇的哭了。

我囘家的時候，他們正在爭吵，我查明了原因，便命取玻璃球來，並吩咐妻子熄去燈，但見那個玻璃球晶晶地光彩耀目，這光彩，可照見我們的一切。我便把它放在燈罩裏，說道：『瞧！這是捨德的一小片兒鉛，給我們帶來的利益啦；它能夠使我們一輩子省卻燈油了。』

孩子們看見，這玻璃球能替代燈，他們又驚又喜，大聲呼叫起來，終於驚動了我們的隣家。

Now there was but a very thin wall between my house and that of my next neighbor, who was a very rich Jew and a jeweler; and the chamber in which he and his wife slept was next to ours. The noise my children made awakened them.

In the morning the jeweler's wife came to mine, and *complained*[1] of being *disturbed*[2] in the first sleep. "Good neighbor Rachel," said my wife. "I am very sorry; but you know the children will laugh and cry for a trifle. See here! It was this piece of glass, which I took out of a fish, that caused all the noise."

"Indeed," said the jeweler's wife, "I believe, as you do, it is a piece of glass; but I will buy it if you will sell it."

Here the children broke in, crying and *begging*[3] that their mother would not part with their *plaything*[4], and, to quiet them, she promised she would not. But as the Jewess went out, she asked my wife in a *whisper*[5] to sell it to nobody without first letting her know. Then she hurried to her husband's shop to tell him what she had seen, and on her way home came in to ask my wife privately if she would take twenty pieces of gold for the piece of glass.

This seemed so great a sum to my wife that she said she would do nothing with the glass till she had spoken to me about it. Just then I came home for my

<hr>

【註】　1. 埋怨.　2. 驚擾.　3. 懇請.　4. 玩具.　5. 耳語

原來在我的隔壁一家人家，是個有錢的<u>猶太人</u>，他是做珠寶生意。他家和我家只壁一層很薄的牆壁，他和妻子睡的房間，卻巧又貼近我們喧鬧的地方。因此我孩子們的喧聲，將他們倆好夢驚醒了。

第二天一清早，那珠寶商的妻子就走到我家裏，埋怨昨晚我們驚動他們好睡。我妻說：『<u>立且爾</u>！我眞的對不起你們；你知道孩子們不過爲一點兒小事，就此笑鬧着。你瞧！便是爲這玻璃球兒，我從一尾魚肚裏取出，就引起他們吵鬧的聲音。』

那珠寶商的妻子說：『眞的，我也和你一樣，相信這是一個玻璃球兒；但是我要買它，如果你願意賣掉它。』

這裏孩子們都着慌了，一片聲似的，求他們的母親，千萬不要賣掉他們這玩意兒，她爲安慰他們，便允許他們不賣。但那<u>猶太</u>女人走出去的時候，喚着我妻耳語，叮囑她切勿賣給他人。她說了，便慌忙地趕到她丈夫的鋪子裏，告訴她丈夫，所見的一切情形。便又奔了回來。祕密地喚了我妻，問她二十塊金洋，她肯把這玻璃球兒賣掉嗎？

偌大的數目，倒使我妻躊躇起來了。她說沒有給我知道之前，不敢自做主張。恰好這時候，我囘家午餐，我妻

dinner, and my wife stopped me at the door to ask if
I would take twenty pieces of gold, offered by our
neighbour, for the piece of glass. I made no answer,
but called to mind the *confidence*[1] with which Saad
had said that the bit of lead would make my fortune.
The Jewess, thinking I was silent because the price
was too low, said: "I will give you fifty, neighbor, if
that will do."

So soon as I saw how *eager*[2] she was, I told her
that I expected a great deal more. "Well, neighbor,"
said she, "I will give you a hundred, and that is so
much that I know not whether my husband will
approve my offering it."

Then I told her plainly I would have a hundred
thousand pieces of gold for it; that I saw plainly that
the *diamond*[3] — for such I now guessed it to be — was
worth a great deal more; but, to *oblige*[4] her and her
husband as neighbors, I would limit myself to that
price; and if they refused to give it, other jewellers
would give much more.

By several biddings she came up to fifty thousand
pieces of gold, and when the Jew came home at night,
he went still higher, *haggling*[5] at every advance, but
paying me in the end the one hundred thousand pieces
which I demanded.

Having thus sold my diamond, I was rich beyond
my fondest hopes, and thanked God for his *bounty*[6].
If I had known where Saad and Saadi lived, I would

【註】 1. 信任. 2. 切望的. 3. 鑽石. 4. 施恩于. 5. 爭執. 6. 恩惠.

在我未進門的時候，便對我說，問我二十塊金洋，肯把那玻璃球兒，賣給我們高鄰嗎？　我猛可想起捨德對我說的，這一片兒鉛可使我得到極大幸運的那句話來，便默默地沒有作聲。那猶太女人見我默不作聲，以爲我嫌價錢太少，說道：『鄰人我便給你五十塊，怎樣？』

我看她這般心切地求買，當下便告訴她，我所希望的數目較這差得遠哩，他說：『好隣人，就給你一百金洋罷！這數目恐怕我的丈夫還不肯哩。』

我老實告訴她，非十萬塊金洋不賣；我說，我顯見這是鑽石——因爲我此時料定這必是塊鑽石了——這價錢並不算多；不過因爲我們是隔壁近隣，纔肯克己到這樣賤價；要如他們不買，自有別的珠寶商肯出更高的價值．

多次的商量，她把價錢添加到五萬塊金洋。晚上那個猶太人囘來，他又將價錢增高些，每次增價，必經一番爭執，結果他終出了我所要求的那十萬塊金洋的數目。

這樣地出賣了我的鑽石，我眞做夢也沒有想到，會得到這許多錢，我只有叩謝上帝的厚賜。我若知道捨德和捨

have gone and thrown myself at their feet in *gratitude*,[1] for each had intended an equal kindness.

Then I thought of the use to which I should put my great wealth. My wife was for buying rich clothes, house, and furniture; but my plan was different. I began at once going to the people of my own trade who worked as hard as I had done, and giving them money in advance to work for me at all sorts of rope making. By this means I *secured*[2] almost all the business in Bagdad, and every one was pleased with my exactness and *prompt*[3] payment. Soon I had to *hire*[4] *warehouses*[5] in several parts of the town to hold my goods. With clerks over each, selling at wholesale and *retail*,[6] the profits became large; and, to bring my business together, I built the house you saw yesterday. Though it makes so great a show, it consists, for the most part, of warehouses for my business, with rooms for myself and family,

III

Some time after I had removed to this house, Saad and Saadi called on me in my former place, where they learned, to their surprise, that I was become a great man of business, no longer plain Hassan, but Cogia Hassan Alhabbal. They set out at once to visit me in my new *abode*.[7] When I saw them coming I ran

【註】1. 感恩. 2. 獲得. 3. 迅速地. 4. 租. 5. 貨棧. 6. 零售. 7. 住所.

提的住處，我必定奔去跪在他們面前，要感謝得流淚．因爲他們都是一般地給我厚恩。

我既得了這筆大財，便想怎樣措用的方法。我妻主張買着高房美器，鮮衣華服，受用受用；但我的計劃，並不是這樣的。我立即走到那些刻苦耐勞同業那裏，給他們工錢，教他們替我做着各種繩子。我用這個方法，差不多把巴革達德的繩業都佔下了，我出的工錢比別人優厚，付給他們又迅速，因此每個工友沒有不歡迎我。不多時我在這城子裏，設立幾處分棧，以推廣我的營業。每棧僱用一個司帳。經營批發和另售等事，這利益愈加大了；我又打算使營業集中在一處，便造了你昨天所見的那座房屋，以爲總棧。這院子外相雖然壯麗，但是大部分卻都用以堆積貨物，就中有幾間，是我和我的家屬住着的。

三

我搬進新屋沒有好久，捨德和捨提仍到我那舊處去探望我，他們立即知道我，居然成了一個巨商，不再稱做亨生，已稱做郭奇亞·亨生了，他們又驚又喜，馬上到我的

to meet them, and would have kissed the hem of their garments; but they would not allow it, and embraced me. Yet I *protested*[1] that I had not forgotten the respect that was their due, or how much I owed them; and begged them to sit down in the place of honor, and seated myself opposite to them.

Then Saadi said to me: "Cogia Hassan, I cannot express my joy to see you. I am sure that those four hundred pieces I gave you have made this great change in your fortune."

Saad could not at all agree and said: "Saadi, I am *vexed*[2] that you still think the two *accidents*[3] of which Hassan has told us did not *befall*[4] him. Let him speak for himself, and say to which of us he owes most of his present good fortune."

"Gentlemen," said I, "I will *relate*[5] to you the whole matter with the same truth as before." I then told them the very history which I have now related to you, Commander of the Faithful.

Saadi could no more believe the story of the diamond and the fish than what I told him of the vulture and the sandman. "But," said he, "I am sure that now you are rich, as I intended you should be by my means and I rejoice sincerely."

When they rose to go I said: "There is one *favor*[6] I have to ask: I beg of you to stay with me to-night, and to-morrow I will carry you by water to a small

新屋裏來看我。我一見他們到來，急忙起迎，想親吻他們的衣邊；但是他們不許，都和我擁抱了。我再三陳說，對於他們的大德大恩，使我永遠感激不盡；我請他們高坐在客位上，自己在一傍陪坐。

於是捨提向我啓口道：『郭奇亞·享生，我瞧見你，不勝歡喜。我想定是我那四百塊金洋，使你這般順利的了。』

捨德見他這麼說了，好生不服，說道：『捨提，我眞惱你，還只管想着享生告訴我們的那兩件份兒的不眞實呢。敎他自己說，看是我們二人中，誰是最幫助他發展到如今的地位。』

我說：『先生，我仍舊用以前一樣的眞誠來給你倆訴說這件事。』我於是把方纔對你所說的事實，一一說給他們聽。

捨提對於這鑽石和魚的故事，正和以前我告訴他鷹和賣肥皂人的故事，一樣地難以見信。他說：『我決定你現在是富有了，因爲我的本意是想用我的方法，來富厚你的；我還是誠摯地祝賀着你。』

當他們將要起身作別，我說：『我求先生們當給我一點光榮。我求你倆今晚宿在敝舍，明天我邀你們到我的一

111

country house which I have bought, and we will return in the evening."

This they consented to do, and the evening passed most pleasantly, with supper and music and talk about my house and business and good fortune. I held them alike in my *esteem*,[1] for without Saadi, Saad would never have given me the piece of lead; and without Saad, Saadi would not have given me the four hundred pieces of gold.

The next morning, very early, we were *rowed*[2] by six *rowers*,[3] in a pleasure-boat well *carpeted*,[4] to my country-house. The friends could not say enough for the beauty of my gardens, and grove of orange and *lemon*[5] trees. The *fragrant*[6] air was full of the music of birds, and Saad and Saadi frequently stopped to thank me for bringing them to so beautiful a place.

At the end of the grove I pointed out a wood of large trees. Into this, two of my boys, whom I had sent into the country for the air, had just gone with a *tutor*[7] and a slave. Seeing a nest in the branches of a *lofty*[8] tree, they bade the slave climb for it. On reaching it he was greatly surprised to find it made of a turban, which he brought down, and, thinking I might like to see so strange a nest, sent it to me by the elder boy.

【註】 1. 尊敬. 2. 划. 3. 划夫. 4. 鋪地毯. 5. 檸檬. 6. 芬芳的. 7. 家庭教師. 8. 高的.

個新築的別墅中去逛一逛，那裏我們可乘船去，到晚上囘來。』

他們立刻答應，那晚上我們過的很快樂，在我的屋子中有豐盛的晚餐，音樂，我們無所不談，關於房子，生意，以及營業的前途。我對他們的禮貌，是一樣敬重的，因爲要如沒有<u>捨提</u>，<u>捨德</u>永不會贈給我那塊鉛片兒；要如沒有<u>捨德</u>，<u>捨提</u>也永不肯贈我那四百塊金洋。

第二天清早的時候，我們就坐在一隻很好的小船上，用六個划槳的人，划我們到我的別墅去。這兩位朋友見我的花園中，有名花無數，橘林，檸檬樹，風景幽雅美麗，一片聲的稱讚不絕。在花菓的香氣中，卻又聽到小鳥清脆的唱叫，<u>捨德</u>和<u>捨提</u>時時停步下來，頻謝我帶他們到這樣美麗的一個地方來。

在橘林的盡頭，我們同看一個大林子。原來我有兩個孩子因見別墅中空氣清新，所以送他們到這裏來住，這時候，他們正和一個師傅，一個僕人，到那林子裏去玩。卻瞧見一顆高樹上的極枝裏，做有一個鳥窠，他們便教僕人，爬上樹將那鳥窠取下來玩。僕人爬到了樹頂，大吃一驚，原來那鳥窠是用頭巾做成的哩，他取了下來，想我一定很喜歡瞧瞧這個奇怪的鳥窠，我的大兒子，便急忙地拿來給我瞧。

The two friends and I wondered at the nest, I most of all, because I *recognized*[1] the turban as the one with which the vulture had flown away. After I had examined it well, and turned it about, I said to my guests:

"Gentlemen, do you remember the turban I wore on the day you did me the honor first to speak to me?"

"I do not think," said Saad, "that either of us noticed it; but if the hundred and ninety pieces of gold are in it, there can be no doubt."

"Sir, this is the very turban," I answered; and, taking the young birds out of the nest, I bade them look closely while I *unwrapped*[2] it. Soon I took out the purse which Saadi knew to be the one he had given me. I emptied it before them and said: "There, gentlemen, there is the money; count it and see if it be right"; which Saad did; and found it to be a hundred and ninety pieces of gold.

Saadi could no longer *deny*[3] a truth which was so *plain*,[4] and said to me: "I agree, Cogia Hassan, that this money could not serve to enrich you; but what about the other hundred and ninety pieces, which you would make me believe you hid in a pot of bran?"

"Sir", I answered, "I have told you the truth in regard to both sums, and I shall hope yet to prove it to you."

【註】　1. 察覺.　2. 拆開.　3. 否認.　4. 明顯的.

　　我和兩個朋友，看了這鳥窠。都是一驚，我尤其驚訝得很，因爲我一眼發見那頭巾，正是我以前失去的那方頭巾，我又仔細地看了一遍，乃對我的客人們說：

　　『先生們，還記得我戴的那方頭巾嗎，當你們第一次向我說話的時候？』

　　捨德說：『我想我們中誰也不會留心到這個罷；不過這裏邊若有一百九十塊金洋存在，那是自然無疑的了。』

　　我答道：『先生，這正是那方頭巾呢，便把小鳥取出窠來，我一壁拆開這個鳥窠，一壁請他們留心細看。我很快就搜出那個錢袋來了，這錢袋捨德一看，正是他給我的那個。我當他們面前，把金洋倒了出來，說道：『這裏，先生們，是那些金洋啦，數數看，看數目對不對？』捨德果然數了，正是一百九十塊金洋。

　　捨德見事情這般眞確，再也不能說不信了，乃向我說：『我同意，郭奇亞・亨生，不是我這筆錢，使你富裕起來的；不過還有那一百九十圓金洋，你對我說是藏在糠罐兒裏的，那到底是怎樣？』

　　我答道：『先生，我告訴你關於這兩筆款子的事，那是實話，我希望那個也能給你證明着。』

We stayed in the country till sunset, and after a ride of two hours reached Bagdad by moonlight. It happened through the fault of my *grooms*[1] that we were then out of grain for our horses, and the store-houses were all shut. A slave was sent out to find what he could in the shops, and soon returned with a pot of bran. In emptying it he found a linen cloth, tied up, and very heavy. This he brought to me just as it was found. I saw at once what it was, and said to my two friends:—

"Gentlemen, it has pleased God that you should not part from me without knowing that I have told the truth. Here are the other hundred and ninety pieces of gold."

Then I counted out the money before them and called my wife, who declared the pot to be none other than the one she had given the sandman.

Saadi could doubt no longer, and, turning to his friend, said: "I *yield*[2] to you, Saad, and admit that money is not always the means of becoming rich."

When Saadi had spoken I said to him: "I dare not propose to return to you the three hundred and eighty pieces of gold, since I know that you gave them without a thought of return; but if you approve, I will give them to-morrow to the poor, that God may bless us both."

【註】　1. 馬夫.　2. 同意.

我們在鄉下一直玩到西方日落，乘著月光，騎著馬行了兩點鐘，回到巴革達德地面。這時候，我的馬夫沒有把我們的馬兒喂飽，那些馬兒肚飢都不能跑路，糧食店卻又關了門。我便遣一個僕人到幾爿鋪子裏去問，有沒有可供馬吃的東西。他拿了一罐兒糠來回來。將糠皮倒下，看見罐兒內有沉重一件東西，用竹布小衫緊緊地裹着突然落下。他覺得怪異，忙拿來給我。我一眼便望出這是什麽東西了，乃向我那兩位朋友說：

『先生們，蒙上帝的恩典，在和你倆未分別前，幸而兩件異事，一朝都水落石出。這兒，又是那一百九十塊金洋。』

我便在他們跟前，當面把錢點清，併喚我妻爲證，她指說這罐兒正是她交給賣肥皂人的那個。

撒提再也不能懷疑了，乃轉向他朋友說：『我信服你，撒德，承認金錢不是一定能夠使人致富。』

撒提說完了後，我對他說道：『我不敢提議，把這三百八十塊金洋還你，因爲我知道你贈金的時候，並不想償還的；但是假如你贊成，我明天把牠們都贈給窮人們罷，上帝必會祝福我們。』

The two friends lay at my house that night also. When we *parted*[1] the next day, I regarded their *permission*[2] to continue in their friendship, and to visit them, as a great honor.

The Caliph, at the *conclusion*[3] of this story, said: "Cogia Hassan, I have not for a long time heard anything that has given me so much pleasure. Thou oughtest constantly to return thanks to God, and to use well his *blessings*.[4] The same diamond which made thy fortune is now in my *treasury*,[5] and I am happy to learn how it came there. Because there may remain in Saadi some doubts about the singular beauty of this diamond, which I *esteem*[6] as my most precious jewel, I would have you carry him and Saad to my treasurer, who will show it to them."

Then Cogia Hassan *prostrated*[7] himself at the throne and *retired*.[8]

【註】 1. 分別. 2. 准許. 3. 結束. 4. 天惠. 5. 國庫. 6. 覩. 7. 俯伏. 8. 告辭.

　　那天晚上，這兩位朋友都留宿在我家裏。第二天，他們告別了，我懇求他們繼續我們的友誼而以看望他們，爲我無上榮幸。

　　那凱立夫在聽完了這故事，說道：『郭奇亞·亨生，我好久沒聽到這般有趣味的故事了，這故事眞使我快活啊！你應時時感謝上帝，並好好兒享用他的恩賜。那塊使你幸運的鑽石，如今卻收藏在我的庫房裏，我很快活地曉得牠是怎樣得來的。這鑽石我是視做無價之寶的，但在捨提還不知道這鑽石的珍貴，他們不無懷疑。我願你將他和捨德帶到我的庫房裏來，教掌庫人拿給他們瞧瞧罷。』

　　郭奇亞·亨生乃伏在金殿前謝恩，告辭出來。

6. The Story of Aladdin

I

In one of the large and rich cities of China there once lived a *tailor*[1] named Mustapha. He was so poor that by the hardest daily labor he could *barely*[2] support himself and his family, which *consisted only of*[3] his wife and a son.

This son, Aladdin, was a very careless, idle and *disobedient*[4] fellow. He would leave home early in the morning and play all day in the streets and public places. When he was old enough, his father tried to teach him the tailor's *trade*,[5] but Mustapha no sooner turned his back than the boy was gone for the day. He was frequently punished, but *in vain*;[6] and at last the father gave him up as a hopeless idler, and in a few months died of the *grief*[7] Aladdin caused him.

The boy, now free from *restraint*,[8] became worse than ever. Until he was fifteen, he spent all his time with idle *companions*,[9] never thinking how useless a man this would make of him. Playing thus with his *evil mates*[10] one day, a stranger passing by stood to observe him.

The stranger was a person known as the African *magician*.[11] Only two days before, he had arrived

---

【註】 1. 裁縫． 2. 僅當地． 3. 組合而成． 4. 不孝的． 5. 手藝． **6.** 徒然． 7. 憂愁． 8. 約束． **9.** 朋友． 10. 壞朋友． 11. 魔術家．

六　阿萊廷的故事

一

從前，在中國的一個大城裏，住着一個裁縫名叫莫大發。他很窮苦，他雖然祇有他的妻子和一個兒子，一家不過三口，但他每天最刻苦辛勤地賺來的錢，卻僅足供一家溫飽。

他兒子阿萊廷，是一個十分魯莽遊蕩和不肖的孩子。每天清早的時候，他便出去，在大街上或公衆娛樂的地方遊逛。到很晚的時候，方纔回家。他年紀已不小了，他父親要叫他學裁縫業。可是莫大發一轉身，離開他的時候，他早逃到不知那兒去了。他雖常常挨父親的打，不過完全無效；後來，他父親索性認定他是個不屑教誨的浪子，完全放任不管，自己氣了幾個月，就氣死了。

自父親死去，無人管束，那孩子更任意放縱了，一天壞似一天。到十五歲的時候，他竟整天和些壞朋友，勾搭在一起，全不想一個人生在世上，應該幹些兒事業。有一天，當他正和那班壞朋友玩耍的時候，卻有個不相熟的人走來，站在那裏看他。

原來那生人是個著名的非洲魔術家。他從本土非洲到

121

from Africa, his native country; and, seeing in Aladdin's face something that showed the boy to be well fitted for his purposes, he *had taken, pains*[1] to learn all that he could find out about him.

"Child," he said to Aladdin, calling him aside, "was not your father called Mustapha the tailor?"

"Yes, Sir," answered the boy; "but he has been died a long time."

Then the African magician *embraced*[2] Aladdin and kissed him, saying with tears in his eyes, "I am your uncle. I knew you at first sight; you are so like my dear brother." Then he gave the boy a *handful*[3] of money, and said: "Give my love to your mother, and tell her that I will visit her tomorrow, that I may see where my good brother lived and died."

"You have no uncle," said Aladdin's mother when she had heard his story. "Neither your father nor I ever had a brother."

Again the next day the magician found Aladdin playing in the streets, and embraced him as before, and put two pieces of gold into his hand, saying: "Carry this to your mother. Tell her I shall come to *sup*[4] with you to-night; but show me first where you live."

This done, Aladdin ran home with the money, and all day his mother made ready to receive their *guest.*[5] Just as they began to fear that he might not

【註】 1. 已經竭力. 2. 擁抱. 3. 一把. 4. 吃喝. 5. 賓客.

這城裏來，不過兩天光景；因瞧見阿萊廷的面貌，正是他所尋求的，可以幫助他所要做的事，他遂用心探訪，關於他的一切家世和現狀。

他喚了阿萊廷到一傍去：『孩子，你父親不是做裁縫的名叫莫大發嗎？』

孩子答道：『是的，不過他早已去世。』

於是那非洲魔術家抱住阿萊廷親吻，淚流滿面地說：『我是你的叔父。我一眼便認得出你的；你的面貌神情，活像我的哥哥。』他便給一大把錢與這孩子，說道：『請你替我向你母親問好，便說明天我來拜望她，順便瞧瞧我那已去世的哥哥，家境如何。』

阿萊廷的母親聽了這事，對阿萊廷說道：『你沒有叔父的，你父親沒有兄弟，我從來也沒有兄弟的哩。』

第二天阿萊廷在大街上玩耍的時候，那魔術家又來找他。和昨天同樣地擁抱了他，給兩塊金洋在他手裏，說道：『把這帶給你母親去。告訴她說，我今天晚上來同你們晚餐；請你先把住址告訴我罷！』

阿萊廷說了住址，拿着錢奔到家裏，他的母親爲預備款待新客，足足忙了一整天。當他母子二人着慌恐他找不

find the house, the African magician *knocked*[1] at the door, and came in, bringing wine and fruits of every sort. After words of greeting to them both, he asked only to be placed where he might *face*[2] the *sofa*[3] on which Mustapha used to sit.

"My poor brother!" he exclaimed. "How unhappy am I, not to have come soon enough, to give you one last embrace!"

Then he told Aladdin's mother, how he had left their native land of China forty years ago, had *travel'ed*[4] in many lands, and finally *settled*[5] in Africa. The *desire*[6], had seized him to see his brother, and his home once more, and therefore had come, alas! too late.

When the *widow*[7], wept at the thought of her husband, the African magician turned to Aladdin and asked: "What business do you follow? Are you of any trade?"

The boy hung his head, and his mother added to his shame, by saying: "Aladdin is an idle fellow. He would not learn his father's trade, and now will not *heed*[8] me, but spends his time, where you found him, in the streets. Unless you can *persuade*[9] him to mend his ways,[10] some day I must turn him out, to *shift*[11], for himself."

Again the widow wept, and the magician said:—

【註】 1. 敲.   2. 面對着.   3. 沙發.   4. 遊歷.   5. 定居.   6. 願望.
7. 寡婦.   8. 留心.   9. 勸誘.   10. 改善行為.   11. 設計.

到這家門的時候，那非洲魔術家已經在外邊敲門了，併帶了許多美酒鮮菓。他向他們倆道過幾句寒喧後，他要求坐的一處所在，要能瞧見莫大發常坐的那張椅子。

他大聲說：『可憐的哥哥，我多麼不幸，不克和你臨終一別！』

他告訴阿萊廷母親，四十年前他怎樣地離開中國，怎樣漫游各國，到後來又怎樣地住在非洲。因爲要想探望他的哥哥，和他的家屬，心中起了這樣的一個念頭，便萬里奔回，但是，天啦，我來得太遲了。

這寡婦當提起了亡夫，不禁兩淚交流，那非洲魔術家卻又掉頭問阿萊廷道：『你做什麼生意呢？現在有沒有職業？』

這孩子垂着頭，他母親又增加他的羞慚，說道：『阿萊廷是一個懶漢，他不學他父親的業務，現在又不受我的教束，每日在大街上，就是你看見他的那些處所遊蕩，除非你能教訓他改過，我終有一天，必把他驅逐出去，讓他在外自去生活。』

那寡婦又哭了，魔術家道：

"This is not well, *nephew*.[1] But there are many trades, besides your father's. *What say you*[2] to having a shop, which I will *furnish*[3] for you with fine *stuffs*[4] and *linens*[5]? Tell me freely."

This seemed an easy life, and Aladdin, who hated work, jumped at the plan. "Well, then," said the magician, "come with me tomorrow, and, after clothing you *handsomely*[6], we will open the shop."

Soon after supper, the stranger, *took his leave*[7]. On the next day, he bought the boy, his promised clothes, and, *ntertained*[8] him, with a company of merchants at his *inn*[9]. When he brought Aladdin home to his mother at night, she called down many *blessings*[10] on his head, for all his kindness.

Early the next morning the magician came for Aladdin, saying they would spend that day, in the country, and on the next, would buy the shop. So away they walked through the gardens and palaces outside of the city. Each palace seemed more beautiful than the last, and they had gone far before Aladdin thought the morning half gone. By the *brink*[11] of a fountain they rested, and ate the cakes and fruit which the magician took from his *girdle*[12]. At the same time he gave the boy good advice about the company, he should keep. On they went again, after their *repast*[13], still farther into the country, till

---

【註】 1. 姪兒. 2. 你可想. 3. 供給. 4. 織物. 5. 亞麻布. 6. 美地.
7. 告辭. 8. 款待. 9. 旅館. 10. 祝禱. 11. 緣. 12. 腰帶. 13. 餐.

『這個卻是不好，姪兒，不過職業有許多，不只是你
父親的一種業務。你可想開一月店嗎？我可以供給你許多
很好的緞料和布正。你儘管對我講啊。』

開店好像是快樂的生活，阿萊廷原來厭恨做工作，現
在對於這個提議，端的歡喜得直跳起來。『好，那末，就
這樣罷。』魔術家說：『明天我且先把你打扮齊整了，再
計議開店的事情。』

吃過晚飯，不多時客人告辭走了。第二天，他果然給
那孩子帶了一身很齊整的衣服來，併用一個伙伴，同他在
客棧裏作伴。晚上，他親自送他回家到他母親那裏。她見
他這般義氣，不知為他祝福了多少。

第二天早晨，那魔術家來邀阿萊廷，說他們今天到鄉
村去逛一天，再後一天就要料理開店了。他們這樣地走到
城外，經過無數的花園和宮院。卻是愈走風景愈佳，一座
宮院勝過一座宮院；在阿萊廷還沒想到有半個早上的辰光，
他們早走了許多路程了。到得一泉水旁邊，他們小憩一會
兒。魔術家從他的腰帶裏，拿出許多甜餅和鮮菓來，兩人
吃着。同時他又說了許多好話勸戒孩子，教他必須交好的
朋友。他們休息一回，起身再行，一直向鄉村走去，便到

they nearly reached the place, between two mountains, where the magician intended to do the work that had brought him from Africa to China.

"We will go no farther now," said he to Aladdin. "I will show you here some strange things. While I *strike*[1] a light, gather me all the loose, dry sticks you can see, to *kindle*[2] a fire with.

There was soon a great *heap*[3] of them, and when they were in a *blaze*[4] the magician threw in some *incense*[5] and spoke magical words, which Aladdin did not understand.

This was scarcely done, when the earth opened just before the magician, and they both saw a stone with a brass ring fixed in it. Aladdin was so frightened that he would have run away, but the magician seized him and gave him *a box on the ear*[6] that knocked him down.

"What have I done, to be treated so?" cried Aladdin, trembling.

"I am your uncle," was the answer; "I stand in your father's place; make no replies. But, child," he added softening, "do not be afraid. I shall ask nothing but that you obey me *promptly*[7], if you would have the good things I intend for you. Know, then, that under this stone there is a *treasure*[8] that will make you richer than the greatest *monarch*[9] on earth.

【註】 1. 生 (火). 2. 點火于. 3. 堆. 4. 火焰. 5. 香料. 6. 一個耳光. 7. 迅速地. 8. 財寶. 9. 君主.

一處所在，在兩山的中間，這所在正是那非洲魔術家到中國來想幹事的地方。

他向阿萊廷說：『我們如今不要再走了，這兒，我可給你瞧些新奇的事兒。我生着一個火，你給我四處收集點乾的亂柴，把火生起來。』

亂柴一忽兒積了一大堆，當他們站在火焰旁邊，那魔術家撒上一把香料，口中喃喃地念起咒來，阿萊廷聽了，一些兒都不能懂得。

這咒語還沒有念完，一聲響亮，地面忽然裂開，恰在魔術家的跟前，他們倆便見裂口中，有一個大石盤，石盤上扣着一個銅環。阿萊廷嚇得拔脚就跑，但這魔術家一把抓住他，又給他一掌，把他打倒了。

『我幹了甚事，你卻這般待我？』阿萊廷驚懼着，大聲喊說。

那人回答說：『我是你的叔父，就和你父母一般；是不許辯白的。卻又柔聲地說，「孩子啊！你可不要害怕。只要你聽我的話，就可得無盡的利益。你知道，這石盤下，有一種寶貝，你若取得了，雖天下最富足的皇帝，也

No one but yourself may lift this stone or enter the cave[1]; so you must do instantly, whatever I command, for this is a matter of great importance to both of us."

"Well, uncle, what is to be done?" said Aladdin losing his fear.

"Take hold of the ring and lift up that stone,"

"Indeed, uncle, I am not strong enough; you must help me."

"No," said the magician; "if I help you we can do nothing. Lift it yourself, and it will come easily." Aladdin obeyed, raised the stone, with ease, and laid it on one side.

When the stone was *pulled up*[2] there appeared a *staircase*[3] about three or four feet deep, *leading to*[4] a door. "Descend,[5] my son," said the magician, "and open that door. It will lead you into a palace, divided into three great *halls*[6]. Before you enter the first, *tuck up*[7] your robe with care. Pass through the three halls, but never touch the walls, even with your clothes. If you do, you will die, instantly. At the end of the third hall you will find a door, opening into a garden, planted with trees, *loaded*[8] with final fruit. Walk directly across the garden, to a *terrace*[9], where you will see a *niche*[10] before you, and in the niche a *lighted lamp*[11]. Take it down and *put it out*[12].

【註】1. 洞. 2. 拉起. 3. 樓梯. 4. 通到. 5. 下去. 6. 臨. 7. 攀起. 8. 結滿. 9. 台地. 10. 壁龕. 11. 明燈. 12. 把他吹熄.

比不上你呢。但是除卻你，卻沒有誰舉得起這石盤，進得這地洞的；所以，你必須好好兒服從我的命令，因爲這事對我們倆非常重要的。』』

『好的，叔父，該怎樣幹呢？』 阿萊廷說着；不再駭怕了。

『握住環兒，將這石盤舉起。』

『叔父！我怕沒有這樣力量，你得幫助我一下才行。』

魔術家說：『不，倘若我幫助你，便不行了。你且獨自去舉，一定十分容易的。』 阿萊廷照他的話去做果然很便當的，把石盤搬起放在一邊。

當這石盤拿起的時候，見有一道石梯，約莫三四尺深，通到門兒。魔術家說：『下去，兒啊！推開那門兒。內有一座宮院，有三間大廳。在你走進第一間廳的時候，須先小心地撩起你的衣服。走過這三間大廳，都不可以碰着牆壁的，便是衣角兒也不能碰着。倘若碰着，你立刻便沒有命了。走完了第三廳，又有一扇門通到一個園子，這園裏種着結滿新鮮果子的樹兒。直穿過園子走到一層臺，那裏你可見當前有個壁龕，龕子裏點着一盞明燈。吹熄了火，

Throw away the *wick*[1] and *pour out*[2] the *liquor*,[3] which is not oil, and will not hurt your clothes; then put the lamp into your *waistband*[4] and bring it to me."

The magician then took a ring from his finger and put it on Aladdin's, saying: "This is a *talisman* against all evil, *so long as*[6] you obey me. Go, therefore, **boldly**, and we shall both be rich all our lives."

Aladdin descended, found all to be as the magician had said, and carefully obeyed his orders. When he had put the lamp in his waistband, he wondered at the beauty of the fruit, in the garden, white, red, green, blue, *purple*[7], yellow, and of all other colors, and gathered some of every sort. The fruits were really *precious jewels*[8]; but Aladdin, *ignorant*[9] of their *immense*[10] value, would have *preferred*[11] *figs*[12] *grapes*[13], or *pomegranates*[14]. Nevertheless, he filled two *purses*[15], his uncle had given him, besides the *skirts*[16] of his *vest*[17], and *crammed*[18] his *bosom*[19] as full as it would hold.

Then he *returned* with *extreme*[20] care, and found the magician *anxiously*[21] waiting.

"Pray, uncle," he said, "lend me your hand to help me out."

【註】 1. 燈心. 2. 瀉去. 3. 液體. 4. 腰帶. 5. 護身符. 6. 在...的時候. 7. 紫色的. 8. 高貴的寶石. 9. 不知的. 10. 無限的 11. 揀著 12 無花果. 13 葡萄. 14. 石榴. 15. 袋. 16. 邊. 17. 馬甲. 18. 塞滿 19. 胸 20. 非常的. 21. 焦急地.

把燈拿出。丟掉燈蕊，瀉去液質，但這並非是油，不會汚穢你的衣服；就把燈繫在腰帶裏，給我帶來罷。』

　　魔術家說畢，從手指上脫下一隻戒指兒，戴在阿萊廷的手指上說：『這是辟邪物，於你服從我的時候，便能驅除一切邪魔。鼓起你的勇氣，快下去罷，我們倆馬上就可富貴啦。』

　　阿萊廷走下，所見一切，果如魔術家所說的一樣，便小心地服從他所吩咐的話。當他已經把燈取出繫在腰帶裏的時候，因驚訝着園果的美麗，白的，紅的，綠的，藍的，紫的，黃的，一切色彩都有，遂把每種都採取了一些。原來這些　兒實是最寶貴的珠寶；但阿萊廷並不曉得這樣珍貴。他僅揀着無花果，葡萄，或者石榴採下。話雖如此，他却盛滿叔父給他的兩口袋子以外，衣裳的胸襟內還塞得滿滿的。

　　他十分謹愼地走回，却見魔術家已等候得很焦灼了。

　　他說，『對不起，叔父！請伸一隻手來提我出來。』

"Give me the lamp first," replied the magician. "It will be *troublesome*[1] to you."

"Indeed, uncle, I cannot now, but I will as soon as I am up."

The magician *was bent on*[2] taking it at once from his hand, but the boy was so laden with his fruit, that he *flatly*[3] refused to give it over, before getting out of the cave. This drove the magician into such a *passion*[4] that he threw more incense into the fire, spoke two magical words, and instantly, the stone moved back into its place, with the earth above it, as it had been when they first reached the spot.

Aladdin now saw that he had been deceived, by one who was not his uncle, but a *cruel*[5] enemy. In truth, this man had learned from his magic books about the secret and value of the Wonderful Lamp, which would make him richer than *any earthly ruler*[6] if he could but receive it freely given into his hands by another person. He had chosen Aladdin, for this purpose, and when it failed he set out *immediately*[7] on his return to Africa, but *avoided*[8] the town, that none might ask him what had become of the boy.

II

Aladdin was indeed *in a sorry plight*[9]. He called for his uncle, but in vain. The earth was closed above him, and the palace door at the foot of the

---

【註】1. 困累的. 2. 堅欲. 3. 斷然地. 4. 忿怒. 5. 殘酷的. 6. 人間任何君主. 7. 立刻地. 8. 避去. 9. 在困境中.

魔術家答說：『先將燈拿給我，這燈壓住你，使你很難上來的。』

他說：『眞的，叔父，我現在實在不能夠，但我馬上就爬上來。』

魔術家立刻伸下手去取燈，但是那孩子卻見果兒這般沉重，他惟恐給了燈，仍不能爬上，那時反爲不妙，所以便不肯先把燈交出。這使魔術家非常忿怒起來。他撒了一把香料在火上，喃喃地念了一回咒，立時把那石盤飛回原處，地也合攏了，恰像未舉火時一樣。

阿萊廷如今纔恍然大悟，他是受騙了，他知那人不是他叔父，是一個兇惡的讎人，果然，這人從魔術書上，知道這寶燈的祕密和價值，倘他能使另一個人自願地，把這燈獻給他，他可使自己比一切帝王都富。他揀選阿萊廷就是爲此目的，當他一見事情不妙，乃立卽囘非洲去，他又繞道避去那城子不走，因爲怕有人盤問那孩子的消息。

二

阿萊廷嬬的十分悲愁。他叫叔父，但是無益。他頂上的地面已經合攏了，宮院的門在樓梯脚下封閉了。他狂聲

steps). His cries and tears brought him no help. At last he said: "There is no strength or power but in the great and high God;" and in *joining his hands to pray*[2] he rubbed the ring which the magician had put on his finger. Instantly a *genie*[3] of frightful *aspect*[4] appeared and said: "What *woulds't thou*[5] have? I am ready to obey *thee*[6] I serve him who possesses the ring on *thy*[7] finger,—I, and the other slaves of that ring."

At another time, Aladdin would have been frightened at the sight of such a figure: but his danger gave him courage to say: "Whoever thou art, *deliver*[8] me from his place."

He had no sooner spoken these words than he found himself outside the cave, of which no sign was to be seen on the *surface*[9] of the earth. He lost no time in making his way home, where he *fainted*[10] from weakness and afterwards, told his mother of his strange adventure. They were both very *bitter*[11] against the cruel magician, but this did not prevent Aladdin from sleeping soundly until late the next morning. As there was nothing for *breakfast*[12], he *bethought*[13] him of selling the lamp, *in order to*[14] buy food. "Here it is," said his mother, "but it is very *dirty*[15]. If I *rub*[16] it clean I believe it will bring more."

【註】 1. 樓梯. 2. 合掌祈禱. 3. 妖神. 4. 容貌. 5. ＝will you.
6. ＝you. 7. ＝your. 8. 救出. 9. 表面. 10. 乏力. 11. 痛恨.
12. 早餐. 13. 想起. 14. 爲…起見. 15. 銹汚的. 16. 擦.

痛哭，竭力呼叫，卻是沒效。後來，他說：『沒用了，祇得求告上帝罷；』　在合掌禱告的時候，他偶然把一隻手摩擦到魔術家給他的那戒指兒。立刻見一個容貌可怕的妖神發現在他面前說道：『　請示有何法旨？　我服從你的命令。我自己，還有那些別的僕人，都供你驅遣，因爲你的指上戴有那隻戒指。』

倘不在這種危險的時候，阿萊廷瞧見這般兇惡的妖魔，一定要嚇得魂不附體，可是他眼前的危險卻鼓起他勇氣來說：『不管你是誰，救我離開這地方罷！』

他話的尚未說完，便已好端端地站在洞外，說也奇怪，那地面一點痕跡兒都沒有。他立刻奔家去，到得家中，已氣盡力竭，息一會兒，纔能把這危險奇遇的事告訴給母親。他母子兩個深切地恨着那兇惡的魔術家；不過夜晚阿萊廷仍是睡覺得很好，直睡到第二天早上纔起身，因爲太窮沒有早餐吃，他卽想把那盞燈掉換點食物。母親說：『燈是在這兒，不過很銹污，要如我擦得亮淨些，我想總可多換得些東西。』

No sooner had she begun to rub it than a *hideous*[1] genie of *gigantic*[2] size appeared before her, and said in a voice of *thunder*[3]. "What wouldst thou have? I am ready to obey thee as thy slave, and the slave of all those who have the lamp in their hands,—I, and the other slaves of the lamp."

In terror at the sight, Aladdin's mother fainted; but the boy, who had already seen a genie, said boldly: "I am *hundgry*[4]; bring me something to eat."

The genie disappeared, and returned in *an instant*[5] with a large silver *tray*,[6] holding twelve covered silver dishes filled with *tempting viands*,[7] six large white bread cakes on two plates, two *flagons*[8] of wine, and two silver cups. All these he placed upon a *carpet*[9], and disappeared before Aladdin's mother had come out of her *swoon*.[10]

When she was herself again, they satisfied their hunger, and still there was enough food for the rest of that day and two meals on the next. This they put aside, and Aladdin's mother made him tell of all that had passed between him and the genie during her swoon. The simple woman thought it all a dangerous and *wicked business*[11], and begged Aladdin to sell both the lamp and ring; but he persuaded her to let him keep them both, *on the condition that*[12] she should have nothing to do with genies again.

【註】 1. 可怕的. 2. 巨大的. 3. 雷. 4. 飢餓的. 5. 忽然. 6. 盤. 7. 美味的食品. 8. 壜. 9. 拭毯. 10. 暈倒. 11. 不祥的事兒. 12. 在…條件之下.

　　她繞擦着燈，立時就有一個巨人似的兇神在她面前，聲如響雷設說道：『請示有何法旨？我是預備供你驅遣的，是你的奴僕。還有這燈的別些僕人，都是供那有燈在手的人們驅遣。』

　　阿萊廷的母親瞧見這樣的兇神，嚇得昏了過去；但那孩子，已經看過一位妖神，便大膽說：『我餓啦；給我辦點吃的東西來。』

　　那妖神忽然不見了，立時就拿來一個大銀盤兒，盤裏盛着十二個銀碟子，都有蓋兒蓋着的，碟子裏盛都是珍饈異味，另外有兩個盤子，裏面放着六個很大白麵做成的糕餅，又有兩細罐美酒，和兩隻銀杯兒。這些東西他都安排在絨毯上，在阿萊廷母親沒蘇醒以前，他又忽然隱去。

　　她醒來的時候，他們吃得十分快活，又剩下許多，足供當日兩餐和次日兩餐的食料。吃完收拾清楚，阿萊廷母親，乃敎他告訴當她嚇暈的時候，他和那妖神間的一切經過情形。這個腦筋簡單的女子，心想這一切都是危險和不祥的事兒，主張阿萊廷把燈和戒指速行賣去；但是他極力反對，他要留下這兩件寶物，不過他允許她以後可不再瞧見妖神的。

When they had eaten all the food left from the feast the genie brought, Aladdin sold the silver plates, one by one to a Jew, who *cheated*[1] him by paying but a small part of their value, and yet made the boy think himself rich. The tray he sold last, and when the money it brought was spent, he rubbed the lamp again, and again the genie appeared, and provided the mother and son with another *feast*[2] and other silver dishes. These kept them *in funds*[3] for some time longer, especially as Aladdin had the good fortune to meet with an honest *goldsmith*[4], who paid him the full value of the metal. Aladdin, all the while, by visiting the shops of merchants, was gaining knowledge of the world and a desire to improve himself. From the jewelers he came to know that the fruits he had gathered when he got the lamp were not merely colored glass, but stones of untold value, the rarest in the city. This, however, he had the *prudence*[5] not to tell to any one, even his mother.

III

One day, as Aladdin was walking about the town, he heard an order *proclaimed*[6] that the people should close their shops and houses, and keep within doors while the Princess Buddir al Buddoor, the Sultan's daughter, should go to the bath and return. Aladdin

---

【註】 1. 詐欺. 2. 饗宴. 3. 有錢的. 4. 金匠. 5. 謹慎. 6. 布告.

當他們把妖神帶來的飯菜都吃完了，阿萊廷又把這些銀碟兒，一隻一隻的賣給一個猶太人，這猶太人欺他不識貨，出很便宜的價錢買下，但阿萊廷卻心滿意足了。末後他總賣掉這銀盤兒。當得來的錢都用完了，他再擦那燈，那妖神便再顯現出來，卻又給這母子倆一席酒筵和若干銀碟兒。這次他們把賣款卻使用得久長些，因為阿萊廷碰到了一個誠實的金匠，付給他十足的價錢。阿萊廷這時候，為增加他經驗起見，時常到各商店裏去走動。從珠寶商方面，他知道先前取燈的時候，所採集的果兒，並不是些著色的玻璃，原來都是無價之寶，希世之珍呢。不過這個他卻非常謹慎，嚴守祕密，不讓外人知道，便是對他母親也不肯漏出一些兒消息。

三

有一天，阿萊廷正在大街上閒逛，忽聽得皇上有令佈告，命市上各店各戶均須閉門迴避，因為皇帝女兒步褔，阿步獨，公主要來出浴，打這裏經過。阿萊廷很想瞧瞧公主

was filled with an *eager*[1] desire to see the face of the Princess, and *contrived*[2] to place himself behind the door of the bath. When she was a few *paces*[3] away from it she removed her *veil*[4], and Aladdin saw for a moment one of the most beautiful faces in the world. When she passed by him he quitted[5] his hiding place; and went home thoughtful and grave.

"Are you ill?" asked his mother.

"No," he answered, "but I love the Princess more than I can *express*[6], and am resolved that I will ask her in marriage of the Sultan."

His mother thought him mad, but Aladdin said: "I have the slaves of the lamp and the ring to help me," and then told her for the first time what riches he possessed in the jewels brought from the *underground*[7] palace. "These," he said, "will *secure*[8] the favor of the Sultan. You have a large *porcelain*[9] dish fit to hold them; *fetch*[10] it, and let us see how they will look when we have arranged them *according to*[11] their different colors."

Their eyes were *dazzled*[12] by the splendor of the jewels when they were arranged in the dish, and Aladdin's mother consented at once to take them to the Sultan, and ask his daughter's hand for her son.

Early the next morning she wrapped the dish in two fine *napkins*[13] and set out for the palace. Though the crowd was great, she made her way into the

---

【註】 1. 切望的. 2. 設法. 3. 步. 4. 面罩. 5. 離去. 6. 陳述. 7. 地下的. 8. 獲得. 9. 委. 10. 拿來. 11. 按照. 12. 眩惑. 13. 巾.

的容貌。設法躱藏在浴室門後。她走近只距離數步的當兒，便把面罩揭下，阿萊廷一時看得呆了，原來是世界上一個頂美麗的女子哩。待她經過他身邊的時候，他離開了隱處。囘家後戀戀思念不止，憂愁成疾。

母親問：『你不是病嗎？』

他答道：『不，我因愛慕公主，弄得神魂不定；我決定去向蘇丹，要求把公主招我爲駙馬。』

他母親想他發瘋了，但阿萊廷又說：『我有燈和戒指的神僕相助。』乃又告訴她，他有明珠寶玉，都是些無價之寶，以前從那地下皇宮探來的，他說：『這些就可以得到蘇丹的歡心了。你有一大瓷鉢可以盛着牠們；拿來，讓咱們安排一下，怎樣可使牠們顏色配置得格外好看。』

當這些珠玉端整地排在盤兒裏，顆顆發光，鮮豔奪目，把他們眼睛都撩亂得睜不開了。阿萊廷母親立卽允許，把牠們獻給蘇丹，要求他的公主嫁給她的兒子。

第二天早上，她把珠盤兒包在兩匹細布，裏便直向皇宮走去。雖然人數擁擠不堪，她卻一直走到殿上，站立在

divan[1], or audience hall, and placed herself just before the Sultan, the Grand Vizier, and other lords, who sat beside him. But there were many *cases*[2] for him to hear and judge, and her turn did not come that day. She told Aladdin that she was sure the Sultan saw her, and that she would try again.

For six days more she carried the jewels to the divan, and stood in the same place. On the sixth the Sultan, as he was leaving the hall, said to the Grand Vizier: "For some time I have observed a *certain*[3] woman standing near me every day with something wrapped in a napkin. If she comes again, do not *fail*[4] to call her, that I may hear what she has to say."

On the next day, therefore, she was called forward. She bowed her head till it touched the carpet on the platform of the throne. Then the Sultan bade her rise and said:—

"Good woman, I have observed you many days. What *business*[5] brings you here?"

"*Monarch of monarchs*[6]," she replied, "I beg you to pardon the boldness of my *petition*[7]."

"Well," said the Sultan, "I will forgive you, *be it what it may*,[8] and no hurt shall come to you Speak boldly."

【註】 1 朝廷. 2. 案件. 3. 某的. 4. 忘記. 5. 事務. 6. 衆君之長.
7. 請願. 8. 無論如何.

144

蘇丹面前，宰相，和衆大臣，都兩邊分立站着。不過那日，聽理的案子，實在太多了，她卻沒有輪到。她告訴阿萊廷說，蘇丹一定看見了她的，她下次必須再走。

她帶着珠盤兒，一連去了六天，仍站在殿上那天原來站的地方。到了第六天，蘇丹將行退朝的時候，卻對宰相說：「這幾天我瞧見有個女人，不知拿了些什麽，包裹在匹布裏，每天佇立在殿上離我很近的地方。要如她明天再來，你不要忘掉喚她上來，我要聽她有無說話。」

第二天，因此，她被喚着了。她在金殿上，俯伏叩首，行禮既畢，蘇丹命她站起，說道：

「好女人，我看見你好多天了。你來這裏，有什麽事？」

她答道：「陛下，臣妾有事啓奏，必須陛下赦罪，臣妾纔敢。」

蘇丹說：「恕你無罪。無論怎樣，我們總不來傷害你。可直奏來好了。」

This gave her *heart*[1] to tell the *errand*[2] on which her son had sent her. The Sultan listened without anger till she was done, and then asked what she had brought tied up in the napkin. She took the china dish, which she had set down at the foot of the throne, *untied*[3] it, and *presented*[4] it to the Sultan.

His wonder knew *no bounds*[5] when he looked upon the jewels. Not until he received the gift from the woman's hands could he find words to say, "How rich! how beautiful!"

Then he turned to the Grand Vizier and said: "*Behold*[6], admire, wonder! and *confess*[7] that your eyes never beheld jewels so rich and beautiful before. What sayest thou to such a present? Is it not *worthy of*[8] the Princess, my daughter? Ought I not to *bestow*[9] her on one who values her at so great a price?"

"*I cannot but own*,"[10] replied the Grand Vizier, "that the present is worthy of the Princess. But wait for three months. Before that time I hope my son, whom you *regard with favor*,[11] will be able to make a nobler present than this Aladdin, of whom your majesty knows nothing."

The Sultan *granted this request*,[12] and said to Aladdin's mother:—

【註】 1. 勇氣. 2. 使命. 3. 解開. 4. 呈獻. 5. 無限制. 6. 瞧. 7. 承認. 8. 值得. 9. 授與. 10. 我只得承認. 11. 寵愛. 12. 准奏.

她聽了，乃把兒子要求婚的話，一一都奏明了。蘇丹聽着，毫無怒色，待她說畢，纔問她布裹裏的是什麼東西。當她朝見的時候，那瓷盤原放在金殿下邊的，現在她把布正打開，將瓷盤雙手獻給蘇丹。

蘇丹瞧見這些珠寶，十分驚訝。沒有等這禮物接到手時，便讚聲不絕地說：『多美呀！多珍貴呀！』

他於是掉頭向宰相道：『瞧！多珍貴呀！這樣珠兒，恐怕你從未見過。你想這聘禮怎樣？對我公主敬不敬？我配不配把她許給出這麼厚重的聘禮的人呢？』

宰相答說：『臣只得承認，這聘禮對公主很配。不過請再等三個月吧。在三月內，臣希望臣子能殼有比阿萊廷更貴重的一副聘禮；臣的兒子是素蒙陛下愛寵的，要比這不相識的阿萊廷，當更能蒙萬歲的寵厚。』

蘇丹准奏，乃對阿萊廷的母親說：

"Go d woman, go home, and tell your son, that I agree to what you have proposed, but I cannot marry t e Princess, my daughter, for three months. At the end of that time come again."

The *news*[1] which Aladdin's mother brought home filled him and her with joy. From that time forth he *counted*[2] every week, day, and hour as they passed. When two of the three months were gone, Aladdin's mother went out one evening to buy some oil, and found the streets full of joyful people, and officers busy with preparation for some *festival*.[3]

"What does it mean?" she asked the oil merchant.

"*Whence*[4] came you, good woman," said he, "that you do not know that the Grand Vizier's son is to marry the Princess Buddir al Buddoor, the Sultan's daughter, tonight?"

Home she ran to Aladdin and cried: "Child, *you are undone!*[5] the Sultan's fine promises *will come to nought*.[6] This night the Grand Vizier's son is to marry the Princess Buddir al Buddoor."

Aladdin was *thunderstruck*,[7] but wasted no time in idle words against the Sultan. He went at once to his chamber, took the lamp, rubbed it in the same place as before, when instantly the genie appeared, and said to him:—

【註】 1. 消息. 2. 計算. 3. 慶祝. 4. 從何處. 5. 你完了. 6. 歸子烏有. 7. 如雷擊頂.

『好女人，你且回去，對你兒子說，朕准你所請求的，但是在三月以內，朕卻不允把公主賜婚。到三個月後再來罷。』

阿萊廷的母親把這消息帶回家去，母子兩個快活非常。從這日起，他一刻不停地數着日子，每週每日每時，他無不念着日子。兩個月後，一天晚上，阿萊廷母親出去到市上買油，忽見街上許多人，都充滿著快樂。有許多司事人懸燈結彩，忙着預備一個盛大的筵會。

她問賣油商人，『今晚是什麼一回事？』

他說：『你這女人是那裏來的？你難道不知道？今晚蘇丹的公主，步福·阿步獨，招大丞相的兒子爲駙馬呢？』

她趕忙奔到阿萊廷那裏，大聲喊道：『孩子，完了。蘇丹允許我們的要求現在歸於烏有了。今晚步福·阿步獨公主與大丞相的兒子要舉行婚禮了。』

阿萊廷聽了，如雷擊頂；不過，他並不耗費時間空言咒咀蘇丹。他立刻走到他的寢室裏，拿了燈，在從前擦的所在，摩擦一下，立時一個妖神顯現出來，向他說道：

"What wouldst thou have? I am ready to obey thee as thy slave,—I, and the other slaves of the lamp."

"Hear me," said Aladdin; "thou hast *hitherto* obeyed me, but now I am about to *impose*[2] on thee a harder task. The Sultan's daughter, who was promised me as my bride, will this night be wed to the son of the Grand Vizier. Bring them both hither to me when they are married."

"Master," replied the genie, "I obey you."

Aladdin did not have to wait long after *supping*[3] with his mother and going to his chamber to be shown again that the genie was indeed his faithful slave. On this night and the next the Princess and the Grand Vizier's son *were borne away*[4] from the Sultan's palace in a *manner*[5] which none could understand, not even they themselves. The strange event was told to few, but the Sultan was one of them. He *consulted*[6] with the Grand Vizier, and, as both of these parents feared to *expose*[7] the young *couple*[8] to further dangers from *unseen foes*,[9] the marriage was *cancelled*,[10] and all the merrymaking *in honor of*[11] it was stopped. None but Aladdin knew *the cause of*[12] all the trouble, and he kept his secret to himself. Least of all did the Sultan and Grand Vizier, who had quite forgotten Aladdin, *suspect*[13] that he had a hand in the matter.

【註】 1. 迄今. 2. 辦. 3. 吃喝. 4. 失蹤. 5. 情形. 6. 磋商. 7. 遭受. 8. 夫妻. 9. 暗地仇人. 10. 取消. 11. 慶祝. 12. 起因. 13. 懷疑.

『請示有何法旨？我和這燈的別些僕人，都是預備供你驅遣的，爲你的奴僕。』

阿萊廷說：『聽着，你素來服從我命令的，我現在卻有件更難的事，要你去辦。蘇丹的公主原許我做新娘的，今晚她卻招大丞相的兒子做駙馬。在他們倆舉行結婚的當兒，你給我把這兩人帶到這裏來罷。』

妖神答道：『主人，我遵照你的命令。』

阿萊廷和母親用過晚餐，沒有多久，囘到他的房裏一瞧，果見那個妖神端的是他的忠僕。這天晚上，那公主和大丞相的兒子忽然在蘇丹的皇宮中失蹤，情形非常奇怪，非但旁人不懂，便是他們自己也是莫名其妙。這件異事除皇帝外，知道的人極少。他便和大丞相密商，因爲兩家父母都怕那對小夫妻生命發生危險，只得把這婚禮作罷，一切宴樂慶賀的儀式停止。這樣什麼人也猜不透裏面的原因，只有阿萊廷明明知道這亂子的原由，不過他嚴守祕密，不讓一個人知道。蘇丹和宰相早經忘掉阿萊廷了，所以也沒有一點疑及是阿萊廷作怪。

IV

Of course[1] Aladdin had not forgotten the Sultan's promise, and, on the very day which ended the three months, his mother came again to the divan, and stood in her old place. When the Sultan saw her she was called forward, and, having bowed to the floor, she said:—

"Sire, I come at the end of three months to ask you to *fulfill*[2] the promise you made to my son."

The Sultan could hardly believe the request had been made *in earnest,*[3] and, after a few words with the Grand Vizier, decided to *propose terms*[4], which one of Aladdin's humble position could not possibly fulfill.

"Good woman," he said, "it is true that sultans ought to *abide*[5] by their word, and I am ready to keep mine. But as I cannot marry my daughter without further *proof*[6] that your son will be able to support her in royal state, you may tell him that I will fulfill my promise, so soon as he shall send me forty *trays*[7] of *massy gold,*[8] full of the same sort of jewels you have already given me, and carried by forty black slaves, who shall be led by as many young and handsome white slaves, all dressed *magnificently.*[9] When this is done, I will bestow my

---

【註】 1. 當然. 2. 履行. 3. 有真意的. 4. 提出條件. 5. 保守.
6. 證明. 7. 盤子. 8. 重金. 9. 華麗地.

四

阿萊廷當然不會忘掉蘇丹的約言，在三個月的最後一天，他母親便又重到殿上，站在原來的處所。蘇丹瞧見她，便喚她上殿，行禮旣畢，她說：

『陛下，現在正是三個月的最後一天，臣妾前來，是請求陛下賜恩的，招臣妾的兒子爲駙馬，以見皇帝無戲言。』

皇帝對這件婚事，本來不大願意，現在見對方又來請求，逐和大丞相商議了一囘，決以公主爲金枝玉葉，不合招平民爲駙馬。

他說：『好女人，君無戲言，果然不錯，朕自當保守前言。不過你知道朕的女兒乃是金枝玉葉，不能下嫁平民爲妻。你去告訴你兒子，他當備下彩禮要四十個黃金大盤兒，個個盤兒裏要盛滿精美的珠玉，須用四十個黑人頂來，又須四十個年輕貌美的白人，率領着他們：這些人衣服都須華麗。倘這些你的兒子能夠備辦齊全，我准守前

daughter, the Princess, upon him. Go, good woman, and tell him so and I will wait till you bring me his answer."

As Aladdin's mother *hurried*[1] home, she laughed to think how far the Sultan's demand would be *beyond her son's power.*[2] "He awaits your answer," she said to Aladdin when she had told him all, and added, laughing, "I believe he may wait long."

"Not so long as you think," replied Aladdin. "This demand is a mere *trifle.*[3] I will prepare to answer it at once."

In his own chamber, he *summoned*[4] the genie of the lamp, who appeared without *delay,*[5] and promised to *carry out*[6] Aladdin's commands. Within a very short time, a train of forty black slaves, led by as many white slaves, appeared *opposite*[7] the house in which Aladdin lived. Each black slave carried on his head a *basin,*[8] of massy gold, full of pearls, *diamonds,*[9] *rubies,*[10] and *emeralds.*[11] Aladdin then said to his mother:—

"Madam, pray lose no time. Go to the Sultan before he leaves the divan, and make this gift to him, that he may see how *ardently*[12] I desire his daughter's hand."

With Aladdin's mother *at its head,*[13] the *procession*[14] began to move through the streets, which were soon

【註】 1. 急行. 2. 超出她的兒子的能力以外. 3. 小事. 4. 召喚. 5. 延滯. 6. 實行. 7. 向. 8. 盤. 9. 鑽石. 10. 紅玉. 11. 綠寶石. 12. 熱忱. 13. 引導. 14. 隊伍.

約，賜公主給他成婚。去罷，告訴你的兒子，朕等候你們的好消息！』

阿萊廷的母親急忙回家，卻暗暗好笑，心想皇帝的要求，是遠非她兒子的能力，所能措辦。她一一告訴給兒子後，說道：『他等候你的囘音呢！』又笑着說：『我想信他要永遠的等候呢！』

阿萊廷說：『並不需要像你所想這樣長。這種要求乃是小事。我立刻就能答應他。』

他在房中，召了燈的妖神，那妖神立卽現身出來，遵照阿萊廷的命令辦理。一囘兒，果有四十個白人，各領着一個黑人，顯身在阿萊廷的庭中。每一黑人頭上頂着一隻黃的金盤兒，盤裏盛滿珍珠，鑽石，紅玉，綠寶石。阿萊廷乃向母親說道：

『母親，不要耗費時候。趕快到蘇丹那裏去，在他還沒有退朝之前，便把這彩禮獻上，以表示兒要娶公主的誠意。』

阿萊廷的母親在前引導，這羣人開始從街上走過，個個衣服鮮麗，隊伍整齊，一白一黑，並肩前進；街上的人

filled with people *praising*[1], the beauty and bearing of the slaves, splendidly dressed, and walking at an equal distance from one another. At the palace nothing so *brilliant*[2] had ever been seen before. The richest robes of the court looked poor beside the dresses of these slaves. When they had all entered they formed a half circle around the Sultan's throne; the black slaves laid the golden trays on the *carpet*[3] touched it with their *foreheads*,[4] and at the same time the white slaves did likewise. When they rose the black slaves *uncovered*[5] the trays, and then all stood with their arms crossed over their *breasts*.[6]

This done, Aladdin's mother advanced to the throne, bowed to the floor, and said:—

"Sire, my son knows that this present is much below the notice of the Princess Buddir al Buddoor, but hopes that your majesty will *accept*[7] of it, and make it pleasing to the Princess. His hope is the greater because he has tried to carry out your own wish."

With *delight*[8] the Sultan replied:

"Go and tell your son that I wait with open arms to *embrace*[9] him; and the more haste he makes to come and receive the Princess, my daughter, from my hands, the greater pleasure he will give me."

While he showed the slaves, and the jewels, to the Princess, Aladdin's mother carried the good news to

---

【註】 1. 讚美. 　2. 華美的. 　3. 地毯. 　4. 額. 　5. 揭去. 　6. 胸.
7. 嘉納. 　8. 愉快. 　9. 歡迎.

見了，個個喝釆。到了殿上，這般華美整齊的隊伍，是從
來沒有見過。朝臣們最華美的服飾，來和這些僕人們的衣
服比較，都覺得灰黯失色了。當他們到了宮前，在金殿
上，排了半個圈子；黑的人各把金盤兒放在地毯上，以額
叩地；同時白的人也一樣地朝見。朝拜旣畢，他們站起，
黑的人逐揭開盤蓋，各用雙手在胸前托着這些金盤兒。

　　這樣，阿萊廷的母親向前走上金殿，叩首道：

　　『陛下，臣妾的兒子知道這些微禮，不足蒙步福・阿
步獨公主的一顧，但願陛下收下，勸公主將就。他本欲多
備彩金，不過陛下旣有御旨在先，他卻不敢不從。』

　　蘇丹快活地答說：

　　『去，告訴你兒子罷，說朕歡迎他；他愈早來接受公
主，朕心愈是快活。』

　　當蘇丹引這些僕人們，和珠寶，給公主去瞧，阿萊廷
母親便將這好消息，帶給她兒子去。她說：『你可快活，

her son. "My son," she said, "you may *rejoice*[1], for the Sultan has *declared*[2] that you shall marry the Princess Buddir al Buddoor. He waits for you with *impatience*[3]."

Aladdin was *overjoyed*,[4] but, saying little, *retired*[5] to his chamber. Here he rubbed the lamp, and, when its slave appeared, said:—

"Genie, *convey*[6] me at once to a bath, and give me the richest robe ever worn by a monarch."

This was soon done, and he found himself again in his own chamber, where the genie asked if he had any other commands.

"Yes," answered Aladdin, "bring me a *charger*[7] better than the best in the Sultan's *stables*[8]. Fihim with *trappings*[9], worthy of his value. Fuqish twenty slaves, clothed as richly as those who cried the presents to the Sultan, to walk by my sidand follow me, and twenty more to go before me i'two *ranks*[10]. Besides these, bring my mother six women slaves, as richly dressed ats any of the Prcess Buddir al Buddoor's, each carrying a completeross fit for a Sultan's wife. I want also ten thoand pieces of gold in ten *purses*[11]. go, and make hast'

The commands were instantly fulfilledand Aladdin gave the six women slaves to his mher, with the six dresses they had brought, wrapp in silver *tissue*[12]. Of the ten purses he gave four his

---

【註】 1. 欣喜. 2. 明言. 3. 切望. 4. 大喜. 5. 退. 6. 給. 戰馬. 8. 廐. 9. 馬飾. 10. 排. 11. 錢袋. 12. 織物.

蘇丹已把步福·阿步獨公主允許嫁給你了。他急着要見你呢。』

阿萊廷大喜，他不說什麼，便退到房裏。擦着燈，當燈神現身時，他說：

『請立刻給我身上洗一洗浴，再給我一件最華貴的皇服。』

這個不一囘就已辦好，當他重現身在房中的時候，妖神躬身唱喏，問可有別的事要辦。

阿萊廷說：『我要一匹千里龍駒，比蘇丹御廐裏的馬還要好。給牠裝飾起來。要二十個僕人，服飾和先前送禮去的僕人一般華麗，擁護着我，另外還要二十個，分做兩行，在前開道。以外，再給我母親六個宮女，卻要個個和步福·阿步獨公主的宮女，一般俏麗華貴，各帶一套服飾，合於皇后用的。我再要十千金幣，分成十袋裝着，趕快去辦！』

這個命令立刻辦好，阿萊廷把六個宮女給與母親，她們帶有六全套皇服，用銀絲織成的包裹包着。十個錢袋中，他分四個錢袋給母親，還有六個卻教僕人們提着，吩

mother, and the other six he left in the hands of the slaves who brought them, saying that they must march before him and throw the money by *handfuls* into the *crowd*[2] as the procession moved to the Sultan's palace. Mounted on his horse, Aladdin, though he had never *ridden*[3] before, appeared with a *grace* which the most practiced horseman might have *envied*[5]. It was no wonder that the people made the air *echo*[6] with their shouts, especially when the slaves threw out the handfuls of gold.)

The Sultan met him at the palace with joy and surprise that the son of so humble a mother as the woman he had seen should have such *dignity*[7] and good looks, and should be dressed more richly than he himself had ever been. He embraced Aladdin, held him by the hand, and made him sit near the throne. Then there was a great feast, and after it, the *contract of marriage*[8] between the Princess and Aladdin was drawn up. When the Sultan asked him if he would stay in the palace and complete the marriage that day, Aladdin answered:—

"Sire, though my impatience is great to enter on the honor your majesty has granted, yet I beg first to be *allowed*[9] to build a palace worthy of the Princess, your daughter. I pray you to give me ground enough near your own, and I will have it finished with the *utmost speed*.[10]"

【註】 1. 一把. 2. 羣衆. 3. 騎馬. 4. 美姿. 5. 羨慕. 6. 回聲. 7. 高貴. 8. 訂婚. 9. 許可. 10. 最快的速度.

咐他們．在隊伍出發進宮的當兒，他們當在馬前，一把一把的將金錢向羣衆散去。阿萊廷在先前雖沒有騎過馬，但現在他騎在馬上，一種瀟灑自然的姿態，雖慣於騎馬的人們，看見無不十分羨慕。因此所經過的地方，歡聲雷動；尤其是這些僕人們，在擲着大把的黃金當兒。

蘇丹在宮中迎接他，非常歡喜，他卻十分驚訝以前所見那樣一個微賤的女子，卻生得這樣一個羊脂白玉般的美少年。衣飾的精美，是他從來所不曾看見過的。當下擁抱着阿萊廷，用手握着他，教他坐在金殿一傍。隨後，便是大開筵席，不多時蘇丹公主和阿萊廷的婚約訂好了。蘇丹問他，要不要當天就在宮中舉行婚禮，這時候，阿萊廷答道：

『萬歲容稟，臣兒雖然十分願意早迎公主鸞駕，可是臣卻不敢草率從事。臣當另築一座富麗宮室給公主。即請萬歲在近宮處，劃一塊地方，臣立即趕造新屋。』

The requset was granted, and Aladdin took his leave with as much politeness as if he had always lived at court. Again, as he passed through the streets, the people shouted and *wished him joy*[1]. In his own chamber once more, he *took* the lamp, rubbed it, and there was the genie.

"Genie," said Aladdin, "build me a palace, *fit*[2] to receive the Princess Buddir al Buddoor. Let its *materia's*[3] be of the *rarest*[4]. Let its walls be of *massive*[5] gold and silver, *bricks*[6]. Let each front contain six windows, and let the *lattices*[7] of these (except one, which must be left unfinished) be *enriched*[8] with diamonds, rubies, and emerads, beyond anything of the kind ever seen in the world. Let there be courts and a *spacious*[9] garden, *kitchens*,[10] *storehouses*[11], *stables*,[12] — well *equipped*,[13] — offices, servants, and slaves. Above all, provide a safe treasure-house, and fill it with gold and silver. Go, and fulfill my wishes."

Early the next morning the genie returned, and bore Aladdin, to the place where the palace had been built. Everything was done, as Aladdin had commanded. The officers, slaves, and *grooms*[14] were at their work in hall, and stable. The hall, with the twenty-four windows, was beyond his *fondest hopes*.[15]

【註】 1. 祝他快樂. 2. 適合. 3. 材料. 4. 最希罕的. 5. 厚重的. 6. 磚. 7. 格子窗. 8. 裝飾. 9. 廣大的. 10. 廚房. 11. 儲藏室. 12. 馬廄. 13. 裝備. 14. 馬夫. 15. 最大的希望.

這個奏立即允准了，阿萊廷逐行告別，一切禮貌，好像素來居住在皇宮裏的。當他重經過街上時，百姓又是歡呼，祝他快樂。阿萊廷到了房中，取燈擦着，妖神顯現。

阿萊廷說：『你去建造一座皇宮，合於我迎致步福‧阿步獨公主的。材料必須精選世上希罕之物。須用黃金做牆壁，白銀做磚砌成。每面開着六扇窗子，這些窗櫺須用鑽石，碧玉，瑪瑙，和別些珍奇物品作裝飾，不過留有一個窗子空着。宮院裏要有朝房，廚房，儲藏室，馬廄；——和一所寬大的花園，都須整齊，而且要配着傢具，宮中須有司事奴婢，愈多愈好。更緊要的，還須有一個堅固的庫房，儲滿金子和銀子。你替我造着吧。』

第二天一早，那妖神囘來了，請阿萊廷到新造的皇宮裏去瞧，果然，一一如阿萊廷的吩咐。那些司事人等，和奴僕馬夫們，都在忙碌地辦事。大廳裏開有二十四扇明窗，阿萊廷看了，說不出的歡喜。

"Genie," he said, "there is but one thing wanting, — a fine carpet for the Princess to walk upon from the Sultan's palace to mine. Lay one down at once."

In an instant the desire was fulfilled. Then the genie carried Aladdin to his own home.

When the Sultan looked out of his windows in the morning, he was *amazed*[1] to see a shining building, where there had been but an empty garden. "It must be Aladdin's palace," he said, "which I gave him *leave*[2] to build for my daughter. He has wished to surprise us, and let us see what wonders can be done in a single night."

He was only a little less surprised, when Aladdin's mother, dressed more richly than even his own daughter had been, appeared at the palace. So good a son, he thought, must make a good husband. And soon the son himself appeared; and when in *royal pomp*[3] he left his humble house for the last time, he did not fail to take with him the Wonderful Lamp which had brought him all his good fortune, or to wear the ring he had received as a *talisman*[4]

V

His marriage to the Princess was *performed*[5] with the utmost splendor. There was feasting and music, and *dancing*[6], and when the Princess was

---

【註】 1. 驚愕. 2. 許可. 3. 壯麗一如王者. 4. 護身符. 5. 舖張.
6. 跳舞

他說：『不過還缺了一件東西——一件好地毯，從皇宮鋪到這兒，以便公主行走。立刻給我鋪下罷。』

地毯立時鋪好。妖神陪着阿萊廷重返他自己屋子裏去。

話說蘇丹在淸晨的時候推窗一望，驚得目瞪口呆，原來在那塊荒園地上，一夜來就造成一座瓊樓玉閣哩。他說：『這必是阿萊廷的宮院了，那裏正是我給他建築的所在。他眞是存心嚇我們，一夜就造成這樣的奇物。』

他瞧見阿萊廷的母親現身在院子裏的時候，徧體華服，比他自己的女兒，穿着更要富麗，他很是吃驚。他想，這樣孝順的兒子，定能做成溫良的丈夫。不多時那兒子來了，這時候，他完全用王者的儀仗了。他雖然最後一次離開茅舍，他卻不曾忘掉取那寶燈，和戴上那只魔術家給他的辟邪的戒指。

五

他和公主結婚的婚儀，鋪張得十分華富。有酒筵，音樂，和跳舞，當那公主一到她新皇宮的時候，大爲富麗堂

brought to her new palace she was so dazzled by its richness, that she said to Aladdin: "I thought, Prince, there was nothing so beautiful in the world as my father's palace, but now I know that I was deceived."

Then next day Aladdin with a troop of slaves went himself to the Sultan and asked him to come with the Grand Vizier, and lords of the court to a *repast*[1] in the palace of the Princess. The Sultan gladly consented, and the nearer he came to the building, the more he *marveled*[2] at its *grandeur*[3]. When he entered the hall of the twenty-four windows, he exclaimed:—

"This palace is one of the wonders of the world. Where else shall we find walls built of gold and silver, and windows of diamonds, rubies, and emeralds? But tell me this. Why, in a hall of such beauty, was one window left incomplete?"

"Sire," said Aladdin, "I left it so, that you should have the glory of finishing this hall."

"I take your wish kindly," said the Sultan, "and will give orders about it at once."

When the jewelers and goldsmiths were called they *undertook*[4] to finish the window, but needed all the jewels the Sultan could give, and the Grand Vizier lend for the work. Even the jewels of Aladdin's gift were used, and after working for a month the window

---

【註】　1. 飲宴.　2. 驚異.　3. 宏壯.　4. 着手.

皇所眩耀，她就向阿萊廷說道：『王子，我從前常想世界上的宮院，沒有更勝過我父王的了，但到現在，我纔知道，自己哄騙自己哩！』

第二天，阿萊廷隨着一大隊扈從，親到蘇丹那裏。請他率領宰相和衆朝臣，蒞臨公主的宮院裏飲宴。皇帝欣喜允諾，他向這所宮院，愈走近一步，愈驚訝着它的美麗輝煌。他到了大廳，見有二十四扇明窗，驚呼道。

『這宮院算得世界上奇物之一了。何處見有金銀砌成的牆壁兒，和鑽石，碧玉，瑪瑙裝成的窗子呢？但是你得告訴我，在這般富麗輝煌的宮殿上，剩下一扇窗子，沒有完成，是什麼理由呢？』

阿萊廷說：『我留下這扇窗子，沒有完成，是請陛下賜恩給牠完成。』

蘇丹說：『很好，謝你好意，朕當立刻傳旨動工。』

當玉工和金匠奉旨來完成這面窗壁，將用皇家國庫裏一切的珠寶用掉還不夠，卻還向宰相家借索若干，便是阿萊廷作爲聘禮的珠玉，也都用完了。做到一個月的工程，

was not half finished. Aladdin therefore *dismissen*
them all one day, bade them *undo*[2] what they had
done, and take the jewels back to the Sultan and
Vizier. Then he rubbed his lamp, and there was the
genie.

"Genie," he said, "I ordered thee to leave one
of the four and twenty windows *imperfect*[3], and thou
hast obeyed me. Now I would have thee make it
like the rest." And *in a moment*[4] the work was
done.

The Sultan was greatly surprised when the chief
jeweler brought back the stones and said that their
work had been stopped, he could not tell why. A
horse was brought, and the Sultan rode at once to
Aladdin's palace to ask what it all *meant*.[5] One of
the first things he saw there was the finished
window. He could hardly believe it to be true, and
looked very closely at all the four and twenty to see
if he was deceived. When he was *convinced*[6] he
embraced Aladdin and kissed him between the eyes,
and said:—

"My son, what a man you are to do such things
in the *twinkling of an eye*![7] There is not your fellow
in the world; the more I know the more I admire
you.

【註】 1. 解雇. 2. 拆卸 3 不完成的. 4. 一會兒. 5. 意指. 6. 相
信. 7. 霎眼間.

168

那窗壁卻祇砌得一半。阿萊廷因此辭去了他們，教他們將砌成的，都折卸下來，歸還皇帝和宰相。他乃擦着燈，妖神出現。說道：

『我以前命你建造那二十四扇窗子的明堂時，有一扇我教你剩下不完成的；現在我要命你去造成。』一會兒，這工作完成了。

蘇丹見玉工拿了珠寶金玉囘來，奏明他們的工程，現已罷歇，他不知什麼緣因，非常驚訝。因此立卽命令備馬，駕幸阿萊廷的宮院，問是什麼意思。他到了那裏，一眼就瞧見一扇完整的窗壁。他不信是眞的，親自去把這二十四扇窗牆，一一驗目過去，看他有沒有受騙。卻終於相信了，他便抱着阿萊廷，吻着他的前額，說道：

『孩子！你眞是奇人！霎眼間，卻造得這般奇巧的東西！你定是一位仙人；朕愈覺得愛羨你了。』

Aladdin won not only the love of the Sultan, but also of the people. As he went to one mosque[1] or another to prayers, or paid visits to the Grand Vizier and lords of the court, he caused[2] two slaves who walked by the side of his horse to throw handfuls of money to the people in the streets. Thus he lived for several years, making himself dear to all.

VI

About this time the African magician, who had supposed Aladdin to be dead in the cave where he had left him, learned by magic art that he had made his escape,[3] and, by the help of the genie of the Wonderful Lamp, was living in royal splendor.

On the very next day the magician set out for the capital of China, where on his arrival he took up his lodging[4] in an inn. There he quickly learned about Aladdin's wealth, and goodness and popularity[5]. As soon as he saw the palace, he knew that none but genies, the slaves of the lamp, could have built it; and he returned to his inn, all the more angry at Aladdin for having got what he wanted himself. When he learned by his magic that Aladdin did not carry the lamp about with him, but left it in the palace, he rubbed his hands with glee,[6] and said: "Well, I shall have it now; and I shall make Aladdin return to his low estate.[7]"

【註】 1. 回敎寺院. 2. 命令. 3. 逃避. 4. 投宿. 5. 聲望. 6. 歡喜. 7. 情況.

阿萊廷不但極受蘇丹的寵幸，且極受百姓們的愛戴。當他每次出行，或是上朝，或是上教堂或是去拜望宰相和衆朝臣們的時候，他必令兩個奴僕，跟在馬後，將滿把兒的金錢向街民拋去。這樣地，一連居住幾年，一般人無不熱烈地愛他。

六

在這時候那非洲魔術家，一向以爲他離開那地洞以來，阿萊廷早經死掉了，有一天，他用巫術一算，知道他已些得生命，而且得了這寶燈的妖神幫助，已住在仙宮一般的屋子裏了。

第二天他就向中國大城出發，等他到時，住在一個客棧裏。那裏，他又很快地探聽到阿萊廷的豪富，阿萊廷的仁德，和他厚結民心的事實。當他一見那座宮院時，他知道，除掉寶燈的妖神們，是決不能建造得這般瑰麗的，他囘到客棧裏，痛恨阿萊廷獲得了自己所要的寶物。他又用巫術算得阿萊廷並不曾把那燈隨身帶着，卻留藏在宮院裏，這時候，他眞歡善極了，拍掌說：『我必定可以得着燈，我必教阿萊廷仍囘到他的茅舍裏去。』

The next morning, he learned that Aladdin had gone with a hunting party, to be absent eight days, three of which had passed. He needed to know no more, and quickly formed his plans. He went to a shop and asked for a *dozen*[1] copper, lamps. The master of the shop had not so many then, but promised them the next day, and said he would have them, as the magician wished, handsome, and well *polished*.[2]

When the magician came back and paid for them, he put them in a *basket*[3] and started directly for Aladdin's palace. As he *drew near*[4] he began crying: "Who will change old lamps for new ones?" The children and people who crowded around *hooted*[5] and *scoffed*[6] at him as a madman or a fool, but he *heeded*[7] them not, and went on crying, "Who will change old lamps for new ones?"

The Princess was in the hall with the four and twenty windows, and, seeing a crowd outside, sent one of her women slaves to find out what the man was crying. The slave returned laughing, and told of the foolish offer. Another slave, hearing it said: "Now you speak of lamps, I know not whether the Princess may have observed it, but there is an old one upon a *shelf*[8] of the Prince Aladdin's *robingroom*[9]. Whoever owns it will not be sorry to find a new one in its stead. If the Princess chooses, she may have the

---

【註】 1. 一打. 2. 擦亮. 3. 籃. 4. 走近. 5. 喊叫. 6. 嘲笑. 7. 注意. 8. 架. 9. 更衣室.

　　第二天早上，他訪得阿萊廷出去行獵，要八天纔回家，現在三天已經過去了。他得此消息，不必再打聽了。立卽想成一個計策。到一家舖子裏，買一打白銅燈兒。店主人囘說此時貨不多，須明天方有，因爲魔術家要他把這些燈擦亮，弄得好看。他答應明天交貨。

　　第二天魔術家把燈買囘來，將它們放在一只籃子裏，遂向阿萊廷的宮院走去。當他走近時，他大聲叫唱：『誰要把舊燈掉換新燈嗎？』一羣孩子，一羣百姓，都圍着他，叫着笑着，以爲這人不是個瘋子定是個獃子，但他並不理會他們，一壁走，一壁喊：『誰要把舊燈掉換新燈嗎？』

　　公主閑坐在那二十四扇窗的大廳裏，看見一羣人擁擠在外邊，便遣一個宮女到那兒去瞧瞧，到底爲着什麼事？那宮女笑着囘來，告訴她會有這等傻事。另一個宮女，聽了說：『說到燈，我倒看見在王子阿萊廷的更衣室衣架上，有一盞舊燈，不知公主可曾看見了沒有？拿這樣的舊燈掉換一盞新燈，誰都不會着惱的。要如公主願意的，咱們何

pleasure of seeing whether this old man is *silly*[1] enough to make the exchange."

The Princess, who knew not the value of this lamp, thought it would be a good *joke*[2] to do as her slave *suggested*[3], and in a few moments it was done. The magician did not stop to cry "New lamps for old ones" again, but hurried to his inn and out of the town, setting down his basket of new lamps where nobody saw him.

When he reached a lonely spot he *pulled*[4] the old lamp out of his breast, and, to make sure that it was the one he wanted, rubbed it. Instantly the genie appeared and said: "What wouldst thou have? I am ready to obey thee as thy slave, and the slave of all those who have that lamp in their hands,—both I and the other slaves of the lamp."

"I command thee," replied the magician, "to *bear*[5] me and the palace which thou and the other slaves of the lamp have built in this city, with all the people in it, at once to Africa."

The genie made no reply, but in a moment he and the other slaves of the lamp had borne the magician and the palace *entire*[6] to the spot where he wished it to stand.

Early the next morning, when the Sultan went as usual to *gaze*[7] upon Aladdin's palace, it was no-

---

【註】　1. 愚的.　2. 笑話.　3. 提議.　4. 取.　5. 運.　6. 完全的.
7. 眺望.

不拿去和這呆子做筆交易。』

公主原不知道這是盞寶燈，心想這樣開一回玩笑也好，立時將交易做成。魔術家得了寶燈，口裏雖不住叫唱：『新燈掉舊燈呀！』　可是急急忙忙趕回客棧裏，馬上出城去，丟掉籃裏的新燈，沒有一個人看見他。

他到了荒郊的地方，把舊燈從胸懷取出來一瞧，決定這就是他所需要的一盞，他用手擦着。立刻現出妖神來，說道：『請示，有何法旨？我是預備供你驅遣的，尤如你的僕人。還有這燈的別些僕人，都是供那持有燈在手中的人們驅遣。』

魔術家答說：『我命令你把你和你的同伴在本城建造好的那座宮院，以及宮院裏的一切人口，給我都帶往非洲去。』

妖神不說什麼，不一刻，他和燈的別些僕人，已把魔術家和那座宮院，一齊攝往魔術家要去的地方去了。

第二天早上，蘇丹照常眺望着阿萊廷的宮院，可是已

where to be seen. How so large a building that had been standing for some years could disappear so completely, and leave no *trace*[1] behind, he could not understand. The Grand Vizier was *summoned*[2] to explain it. In secret he bore no good will to Aladdin, and was glad to suggest that the very building of the palace had been by magic, and that the hunting party had been merely an excuse for the *removal*[3] of the palace by the same means. The Sultan was persuaded, therefore, to send a body of his guards to *seize*[4] Aladdin as a prisoner of state. When he appeared the Sultan would hear no word from him, but ordered him put to death. This displeased the people so much that the Sultan, fearing a *riot*[5], granted him his life and let him speak.

"Sire," said Aladdin, "I pray you to let me know the *crime*[6] by which I have lost thy favor."

"Your crime!" answered the Sultan; "*wretched*[7] man! do you not know it? Follow me, and, I will show you."

Then he led Aladdin to a window and said: "You ought to know where your palace stood; look, and tell me what has become of it."

Aladdin was as much *amazed*[8] as the Sultan had been. "True, it is *vanished*,[9]" he said after a speechless *paus.*[10], "but I have had no *concern*[11] in its

---

【註】 1.痕跡. 2.召喚. 3.遷移. 4.捉. 5.暴亂. 6.罪. 7.卑賤的. 8.驚愕. 9.不見. 10.停頓. 11.關係.

一點兒沒有影蹤了。因想為什麼這樣一座大宮院，建造已有數年，竟一旦完全隱去，一點兒影蹤沒有，真使人莫明其妙。他便召宰相商議。那宰相暗地裏對阿萊廷原有惡感的，樂得乘機復讎，當下他就說這所宮院乃是妖術，他行獵去，也許是金蟬脫殼之計，避免這宮院移去的責任。蘇丹頓時信任了，遂點御林軍，把阿萊廷立時拘拿問罪。到來的時候，不問情由立刻推出斬首。這舉動使人民大為不服，蘇丹恐怕激動了民變，只得寬恕他性命，教他辯護。

阿萊廷說：『陛下！臣但願知道為什麼犯罪而斬？』

蘇丹怒喝道：『賊犯！你還不知罪嗎？跟我來，你瞧！』

他引阿萊廷到了窗口，說道：『看！你該知道，你的宮院那兒去了？快講來，這是怎麼一囘事？』

阿萊廷和蘇丹一樣地嚇得目瞪口呆。『真的，這宮院沒有了！』他息了一囘纔吐口氣說，『但是這件事與臣子完

removal. I beg you to give me forty days, and if in that time I cannot *restore*[1] it, I will offer my head to be *disposed*[2] of at your pleasure."

"I give you the time you ask," answered the Sultan, "but at the end of forty days forget not to present yourself before me."

The lords, who had *courted*[3] Aladdin in his better days, *paid him no heed*[4] as he left the palace in *extreme*[5] shame. For three days he wandered about the city, exciting the pity of all he met by asking if they had seen his palace, or could tell where it was. On the third day he wandered into the country. As he *approached*[3] a river he *slipped*[7] and fell down a bank. *Clutching*[8] at a rock to save himself, he rubbed his ring, and instantly the genie whom he had seen in the cave oppeared before him. "What wouldst thou have?" said the genie. "I am ready to obey thee as thy slave, and the slave of all those who have that ring on their finger,—both I and the other slaves of the ring."

Aladdin had never thought of help from this *quarter*,[9] and said with delight:—

"Genie, show me where the palace I caused to be built now stands, or bring it back where it first stood."

【註】 1. 恢復. 2. 處分. 3. 獻媚于. 4. 不理他 5. 極端的. 6. 行近. 7. 滑跌. 8. 緊握. 9. 方面.

全無干的。臣請求給四十天期限，我要把它恢復過來，要如到那時候不能，甘心憑陛下處罪。』

蘇丹說：『我許你這四十天的請求，不過你到期切勿忘卻。』

那些朝臣們，以前在阿萊廷得意的時候，均向他討好，現在當他失意出宮的時候，連正眼兒也不瞧他一眼了。他在城中一連跑了三天，逢人便問，他們曾瞧到他的宮院沒有？現在可知道它到兒去了？這種情形，傍人看了着實替他可憐。到了第三天，他走到鄉下去。在河邊的時候，一不小心，失足滑下河去。幸而握住一塊大石，不會跌落，他擦了他的戒指一下，立時有個以前他在地洞中見過的妖神，現身在他面前，說道：『請示有何法旨？我是預備供你驅遣的。還有這戒指的別些僕人，都供給戴這戒指在手上的人們驅遣。』

阿萊廷永沒有想到這方面的幫助，乃快活地說：

『請告訴我，那新造的宮院，到那兒去了，或者，你給我把它帶到原址來。』

"Your command," answered the genie, "is not wholly[1] in my power; I am only the slave of the ring, and not of the lamp."

"I command thee, then," replied Aladdin, "by the power of the ring, to bear me to the spot[2] where my palace stands, wherever it may be."

These words were no sooner out of his mouth than he found himself in the midst of a large plain,[3] where his palace stood, not far from a city, and directly above him was the window of his wife's chamber. Just then one of her household happened to look out and see him, and told the good news to the Princess Buddir al Buddoor. She could not believe it to be true, and, hastening[4] to the window, opened it herself with a noise which made Aladdin look up. Seeing the Princess, he saluted[5] her with an air that expressed his joy, and in a moment he had entered by a private door and was in her arms.[6]

After shedding[7] tears of joy, they sat down, and Aladdin said: "I beg of you, Princess, to tell me what had become of an old lamp which stood upon a shelf in my robing chamber."

"Alas!" answered the Princess, "I was afraid our misfortune[8] might be owing to that lamp; and what grieves[9] me most is that I have been the cause of it. I was foolish enough to change the old lamp for

---

【註】 1. 全.　2. 場所.　3. 原野.　4. 趕急.　5. 招呼.　6. 在她擁抱中
7. 流出.　8. 不幸.　9. 苦痛.

　　妖神說：『你的命令，卻不是完全在我權力之內的：我僅是戒指的奴僕，不是燈的奴僕啦！』

　　阿萊廷說：『那末，用你戒指的權力，將我帶到我的宮院那兒去罷，不管牠是天涯海角。』

　　這些話兒方才出口，他巳見自己站在一處荒郊，在他面前，矗立着他那金碧輝煌的宮院。這所在離城並不遠，他立的方向，正是朝着他妻子的房間。恰在這時，有個婢女外望，一眼就瞧見他，乃把這好消息告訴步福·阿步獨公主。她幾乎不信這是眞事，急忙奔到窗口，一陣響聲驚動了阿萊廷。他瞥見公主，歡喜得驚叫起來，不一會，他遂從角門裏走去，擁在公主的懷裏。

　　他們倆灑了幾行眼淚，一同坐下，阿萊廷說：『公主，請你告訴我，在我更衣室衣架上的一盞舊燈，怎樣了？』

　　公主答說：『啊唷！可不是就是那盞燈，引起我們的亂子嗎？這就是由於我的緣故嗎？我眞是可惱。我眞愚蠢，會把那舊燈掉換一盞新燈，到了第二天早上，我忽然發見

a new one, and the next morning I found myself in this unknown country, which I am told is Africa."

"Princess," said Aladdin, stopping her, "you have told me all by telling me we are in Africa. Now, only tell me where the old lamp is."

"The African magican," answered the Princess, "carries it carefully wrapped up in his *bosom*[1]. This I know, because one day he pulled it out before me, and showed it to me in *triumph*[2].

Aladdin quickly formed and carried out a plan to leave the palace, disguise himself, buy of a *druggist*[3] a certain *powder*[4] which he named, and return to the Princess. He told her what she must do to help his purpose. When the magician should come to the palace, she must *assume*[5] a friendly manner and ask him to sup with her. "Before he leaves," said Aladdin, "ask him to *exchange*[6] cups with you. This he will gladly do, and you must give him the cup *containing*[7] this powder. On drinking it he will instantly fall asleep, and we shall obtain the lamp, whose slaves will do our *bidding*[8], and bear us and the palace back to the capital of China."

It was not long before the magician came to the palace, and the Princess did exactly as Aladdin had bidden her. When, at the end of evening, she *offered*[9] her guest the drugged cup, he drank it, *out of*

【註】 1. 懷.　2. 得意.　3. 藥劑師.　4. 藥粉.　5. 假裝.　6. 交換.
7. 含有.　8. 命令.　9. 奉獻.

在這個陌生的處所，聽說是在非洲了。』

阿萊廷阻住她說：『公主！你已經告訴我，我們是在非洲的了。現在，單講燈在那兒呀？』

公主答說：『那燈給非洲魔術家，非常謹慎地把牠藏在懷中，我曉得這點，因爲他有一天，在我面前把這東西從懷裏摸出，樣子是非常得意似的。』

阿萊廷忽然想得一個妙計，連忙化裝了，離開宮院，到一個藥劑師那兒，買了他指明的某種藥，仍回到公主這裏。教她怎樣幫助他的法子。當那魔術家回來的時候，你必假作慇懃，勸他和你喝酒。『在他還沒有離開之前，』阿萊廷說：『你要求他和你換杯喝酒。他定然是高興的，你就乘便把這個藥放下。他喝了，立時便會昏倒，我們取得那燈，就可以命令燈的奴僕，把我們和這宮院，都攝往原處去了。』

沒有多久，那魔術家回宮來了，公主——遵照阿萊廷的吩咐行事。到了更深的時候，她把藥酒慇懃地遞給她的客人，他不能推辭她的盛情，接來喝得一個乾淨，一點餘

honor to her[1], to the last drop, and fell back lifeless on the sofa.

Aladdin was quickly called and said: "Princess, *retire*,[2] and let me be left alone while I try to take you back to China as *speedily*[3] as you were brought thence." On the dead body of the magician he found the lamp, carefully wrapped and *hidden*[4] in his *garments*.[5] Aladdin rubbed it and the genie stood before him.

"Genie," said Aladdin, "I command thee to bear this palace instantly back to the place whence it was brought *hither*."[6] The genie bowed his head and departed. In a moment the palace was again in China, and its *removal*[7] was felt only by two little *shocks*[8], the one when it was lifted up, the other when it was set down, and both in a very short *space of time*[9].

Early the next day the Sultan was looking from his window and *mourning*[10] his daughter's *fate*[11]. He could not believe his eyes when first he saw her palace standing in its old place. But as he looked more closely he was *convinced*[12], and joy came to his heart instead of the grief that had filled it. At once he ordered a horse and was on his way, when Aladdin, looking from the hall of twenty-four windows, saw him coming, and hastened to help him *dismount*[13]. He

---

【註】 1. 区為尊重她. 2. 退. 3. 迅速地. 4. 藏. 5. 衣服. 6. 在此處. 7. 遷移. 8. 震動. 9. 時間的長度. 10. 悲悼. 11. 命運. 12. 相信. 13. 下馬.

蘯都沒有，他立刻暈倒過去，在沙發椅上。

阿萊廷立刻趕到，他說：『公主，請退，讓我一個人在這兒，我可施法立卽把你攝囘中國。』 他便從魔術家屍體的胸前取得那盞燈，這燈緊緊地在衣服內，阿萊廷取出燈來一擦，妖神便顯現在面前。

阿萊廷說：『我命你立刻把這所宮院。攝往牠原來的處所。』妖神點了點頭去了。一忽兒，那宮院又重在中國，在這邊移中不過微微地震盪了兩下，一是在運起的時候，一是在落下的時候，震盪的時間都很短的。

第二天早上，蘇丹從他窗口望去，悲嘆她女兒的命運。忽然望見那座宮院，端正地矗立在原處。他初看時，疑是眼花 但再仔細一瞧，實是千眞萬確，一時悲去歡來，心裏說不出的喜悅。他立時備馬去看，阿萊廷正在二十四扇窗的大廳裏，看見蘇丹駕到。赶忙出迎，扶他下鞍。他立

was brought at once to the Princess, and both wept tears of joy. When the strange *events*[1] had been partly explained, he said to Aladdin:—

"My son, be not displeased at the *harshness*[2] I showed towards you. It rose from a father's love, and therefore you will forgive it."

"Sire," said Aladdin, "I have not the least reason to complain of your *conduct*[3], since you did nothing but what your duty required. This wicked magician, the basest of men, was the *sole*[4] cause of all."

VII

Only once again were Aladdin and his palace in danger from magic *arts*[5]. A younger brother of the African magician learned of what had happened, and, *in the guise of*[6] a *holy woman*,[7] Fatima, whom he killed that he might pretend to take her place, came to live in the palace. The Princess, thinking him really the holy woman, *heeded*[8] all that he said. One day, admiring the beauty of the hall, he told her that nothing could *surpass*[9] it if only a *roc's*[10] egg were hung from the middle of the *dome*[11]. "A roc," he said, "is a bird of *enormous*[12] size which lives at the *summit*[13] of Mount Caucasus. The *architect*[14] who built your palace can get you an egg."

【註】 1. 事件. 2. 苛刻. 3. 舉動. 4. 唯一的. 5. 奸計. 6. 喬裝爲. 7. 女尼. 8. 信任. 9. 勝過. 10. 大鵰. 11. 圓屋頂. 12. 巨大的. 13. 頂上. 14 建築家.

即去望公主，父女兩人喜極下淚。這奇事一部分給解釋淸楚的當兒，他對阿萊廷說：

『王兒，請你不要記着，我給你的一種殘暴。這是出於做父親的天性，你須得原諒才好。』

阿萊廷說：『這是陛下應當如此，臣兒怎敢懷恨。總之，這卑鄙狠惡的魔術家，是這一切的禍因罷了。』

七

自後，祇有一次阿萊廷和他的宮院，重陷在魔術的危險裏。那非洲魔術家有位兄弟，知道了這件事情，用計殺掉一個女尼叫做發鐵木，喬裝做她的樣子，混進這宮院裏來。公主當她是眞的女尼，便很信任着她。有一天，他們說到這廳子的美麗，便乘機告訴她，若能弄得一個大鵬鳥卵兒，懸挂在廳的圓頂中，這廳就可算是十分完全了。她說：『大鵬是一種無限般大的鳥兒，牠是宿在高加索的山頂上。那造宮院的建築師，定能弄到一個大鵬鳥卵的。』

When the Princess told Aladdin of her desire, he summoned the genie of the lamp and said to him:—

"Genie, I command thee in the name of this lamp, bring a roc's egg to be hung in the middle of the dome of the hall of the palace."

No sooner were these words spoken than the hall shook as if ready to fall, and the genie told Aladdin that he had asked him to bring his own master and hang him up in the midst of the hall; it was enough to *reduce*[1] Aladdin and the Princess and the palace all to *ashes*;[2] but he should be *spared*,[3] because the request had really come from another. Then he told Aladdin who was the true *author*[4] of it, and *warned*[5] him against the *pretended*[6] Fatima, whom till then he had not known as the brother of the African magician. Aladdin saw his danger, and on that very day killed his wicked enemy with the *dagger*[7] which was meant to be his own death.

Thus was Aladdin *delivered*[8] from the two brothers who were magicians. Within a few years the Sultan died at a good old age, and, as he left no *male*[9] children, the Princess Buddir al Buddoor came to the throne, and she and Aladdin *reigned*[10] together many years.

【註】 1. 使歸于　2. 灰燼.　3. 寬宥.　4. 主謀者.　5. 警告.　6. 假裝.
7. 短劍　8. 逃生.　9. 男的.　10. 統治.

公主便把這意思，告訴給阿萊廷，他乃召燈神前來說：

『我用這燈的權力，命你給我取一大鵬鳥的卵，掛在這廳子的圓頂正中。』

這話剛纔說完，那廳子已是亂幌起來，好像要倒下來的樣子，妖神告訴阿萊廷，說他已命他把妖神們的主子，拿來掛在廳的中心了；這能使阿萊廷，公主，和宮院，都立時化成灰燼；如果他放下就好，因爲這主見是由別人出的。他乃告訴阿萊廷，出這主見的是誰，教他快把這喬裝的發鐵木處死，他到現在纔被發見出來，原來是那個非洲魔術家的阿弟。阿萊廷一聽到這個毒計，當下就拔劍把他刺死了。

阿萊廷這樣的從兩魔術家手裏，出險逃生。不多幾年，那蘇丹年老駕崩，因他沒有王子，步福·阿步獨公主乃被立爲嗣君，繼承大統，她和阿萊廷共同管理中國好多年呢。

7. The Story of Ali Cogia, A Merchant of Bagdad

In the *reign*[1] of the Caliph Haroun al Raschid there lived at Bagdad a merchant who was neither rich nor poor, but lived in comfort in the house that had been his father's. For three successive nights he had a strange dream, which gave cause to the *events*[2] of this story. An old man appeared to him, and with a *severe*[3] look *reproached*[4] him for not having made a *pilgrimage*[5] to Mecca. The *vision*[6], seen three times, gave him much trouble. He knew that, as a good Mussulman, he ought to make the pilgrimage; but he had supposed that his *charities*[7] and other good works might excuse him. Yet the dream *pricked*[8] his conscience so *sorely*[9] that he made up his mind to go. Therefore he let his house, and sold all of his goods except a few which he thought he could turn to better profit at Mecca. After this was done, he had a thousand pieces of gold which he wanted to leave behind him in some place of safety.

This was the plan which, upon careful thought, he *adopted*[10]: he took a good large *jar*[11] and put the thousand pieces of gold into it, and covered them over with *olives*[12]. When he had closed the mouth of the jar he carried it to a merchant, one of his best friends, and said to him:

【註】 1. 朝代　2. 事件　3. 嚴厲的　4. 譴責　5. 朝山進香　6. 幻象　7. 慈善事業　8. 刺痛　9. 疼痛地　10. 採用　11. 罐　12. 橄欖

七　橄　欖　案

從前在哈龍、亞爾、拉西德凱立夫的時代，巴革達德有一個商人，家道小康，安樂地過着日子。他曾一連三夜，做着一個異夢。這個異夢，就是引起本故事的原因，他夢見有個老人，聲色俱厲地，責備他爲什麼不到米加聖地去朝謁進香去。這夢兒一連三夜，都是這樣，使他十分納悶。他原知道一個虔誠的回教徒，應該到聖地去朝謁的；不過一個人做善積德，上帝也許原宥，所以他一直因循未去。現在這夢使他甚是擔心，便決心去朝拜聖地。他租去他的房屋，賣掉他的貨物，只存下若干，在米加可獲厚利的東西，帶往去賣。在料理停當之後，尚剩一千金洋，他想得一穩妥保藏的地方。

他幾次考慮之後，便採用這樣的一個方法：他用一個堅實的大罐兒，把一千金洋安放在裏邊，上面再用橄欖蓋沒着。當他把罐口封好了，就帶往他的一個好朋友那裏，這朋友也是商人，對他說道：

"You know, brother, that in a few days I mean to *depart*[1] with the *caravan*[2] on my pilgrimage to Mecca. I beg the favor of you to take *charge*[3] of a jar of olives, and keep it for me till I return."

The merchant promised to do this, and in the kindest manner said: "Here, take the key of my *warehouse*[4] and set your jar where you please. You shall find it there when you return."

When the caravan started, Ali Cogia, riding a *camel*[5] loaded with the goods he thought fit to carry, started with it. He arrived safe at Mecca, performed all his religious duties at the *temple*,[6] to which the faithful go every year in throngs, and then exposed his goods for sale. Two merchants soon came by. They *purchased*[7] nothing, but as they walked away Ali Cogia heard one of them say to the other:—

"If this merchant knew what profit these goods would bring him at Cairo he would carry them *thither*[8] and not sell them here, though this is a good mart."

Ali Cogia had often heard of the beauties of Egypt, and *resolved*[9] to go to Cairo. This he did, and with the profits from his sales went to Damascus. Having once begun to travel it was an easy matter to keep on, and for seven years he went from place to place, even as far as Hindostan. Then he resolved to return to Bagdad.

【註】　1. 出行.　2. 隊商.　3. 保藏.　4. 棧房.　5. 駱駝.　6. 廟宇.
7. 購買.　8. 向彼方.　9. 決定.

『兄弟，你曉得我這幾天內要結伴到米加朝拜去。我懇求你一件事，就是這罐橄欖，請替我保藏着，等到我囘來。』

那商人允許了，和顏悅色地說：『這兒，是我棧房門的鑰匙，你隨便放在那兒吧。你囘來的時候，可仍往原處去取。』

旅行隊將要出發的當兒，亞里郭奇亞把要賣的貨物，都裝藏在一匹駱駝身上，自己也騎在上面，跟着同去。他平安地到了米加，隨着大隊的信徒們，在那廟宇裏朝拜旣畢，便從事售賣他的貨物。有兩個商人從他那處走，他們並不買什麽，但在去的時候，亞里，郭奇亞卻聽得他們中的一人對另一人說道：

『要如這人曉得這些貨物，在開羅怎樣奇貴，他一定要帶到那兒去賣，不在這兒賣了。』

亞里郭奇亞素來聽到埃及的美麗，所以決定向開羅去走一遭。他在開羅果然賣得好價，用生意上賺來的錢，又到大馬色去旅行。大凡遊歷的人，遊興一濃便不容易停止的，他這兒那兒，一共遊歷了七年，便遠如印度也去遊歷過了。他乃打定主意，囘到巴革達德去。

All this time his friend, with whom he had left the jar of olives, never thought of him nor of them. One evening the merchant was supping with his family when the talk happened to fall upon olives, and his wife, wishing to eat some, said she had not tasted any for a long while.

"Now you speak of olives," said the merchant, "you put me in mind of a jar which Ali Cogia left with me seven years ago, when he went to Mecca, putting it himself into my warehouse. What is become of him I know not. When the caravan came back, they told me he was gone for Egypt. Certainly he must be dead by this time, and we may eat the olives if they prove good. Give me a *plate*[1] and a *candle*[2]; I will go and *fetch*[3] some of them, that we may taste them."

"Pray, husband," said his wife, "do not *commit*[4] so *base*[5] a *deed*[6]. They were given to you in trust, and if Ali Cogia should return, as I am sure he will, what will he think of your honor? Besides, the olives must be *moldy*[7] after these seven years. I beg you to let them alone."

But the merchant would not listen. When he came to the warehouse and opened the jar, he found the olives moldy; but, to see if all were moldy to the bottom, he turned some of them upon the plate, and in shaking the jar some of the gold *tumbled*[8] out.

【註】 1. 盤. 2. 蠟燭. 3. 拿. 4. 幹. 5. 下品的. 6. 事. 7. 霉爛. 8. 滾出.

且說他的朋友，受了他橄欖罐兒的寄託，這幾年裏，早把他和橄欖的事情忘掉了。有一天晚上，那商人和他的家人們晚飯，偶然談話到橄欖，他妻子很想吃幾個，因爲她好久沒有嘗到這橄欖的美味。

那商人說：『你說到橄欖來，我倒想起七年前，亞里，郭奇亞到米加去的當兒，有一罐橄欖他自己寄放在我的棧房裏。我現在不知道他到底怎樣了。那個旅隊囘來，他們告訴我說，他獨自個兒到埃及去呢。現在我想，他定然死了，如果這些橄欖沒壞，我們倒可以受用一下。拿一個盤兒和一枝臟燭與我；我去拿一些來，大家嘗嘗。』

他妻子說：『丈夫，不要幹這樣卑鄙的事。我知道亞里，郭奇亞定會囘來的，他信任你，方將牠們交託給你，倘他囘來的時候瞧出了，你怎樣交待他？而且，橄欖到七年後，定然都霉爛了。我求你，隨牠去罷。』

那個商人不聽他妻子勸告。他到了棧房裏，把罐兒打開蓋兒來一看，這些橄欖果然都腐爛得不堪；但是他爲要看罐底裏有沒有幾隻好的，他倒點出來在盤子裏，當震動罐兒的時候，忽滾出好幾塊金子來。

Now the merchant loved gold dearly, and, looking deeper into the jar, he saw that only the top had been covered with olives, and that all below it was coin[1]. He put the olives directly back, covered the jar, and returned to his wife.

"Indeed, wife," said he, "you were right, the olives are all moldy; but I have left them just as I found them, and if Ali Cogia ever does return he will not see that they have been touched."

"I wish you had not *meddled*[2] with them at all," said his wife. "God grant that no *mischief*[3] may come of it."

The merchant spent most of that night thinking how he might take Ali Cogia's gold without any risk of being found out. In the morning he went and bought some olives of that year, and then, *secretly*[4] emptying the jar of the gold and the mouldy olives, filled it with the new ones, covered it up, and put it in the place where Ali Cogia had left it.

In about a month the traveler arrived at Bagdad. One of the first things he did there was to go to the merchant for his jar of olives, expressing his hope that it had not been in the way. The merchant *assured*[5] him that he had been glad to do this little service. "Here is the key of my warehouse," he said; "go and fetch your jar; you will find it where you left it."

[註] 1. 金錢. 2. 勁. 3. 禍. 4. 暗地. 5. 確說.

這商人原來愛財如命的，再向罐裏探看，知道原來在罐兒上面是些橄欖，底下都是金洋哩。他把橄欖重行放入，蓋好罐口，囘到妻子那裏。

他說：『妻子，你果然說得不錯，橄欖都已腐爛了；不過我已把牠們原封蓋上，卽使亞里郭奇亞囘來，也瞧不出已經動過了。』

他妻子說：『我但願你一點不要動牠，上帝便不會降禍的。』

那天晚上，這商人苦苦地想了一夜，他怎樣可以取得亞里郭奇亞的金子，不會有一點兒危險。早上他出去買了許多本年的橄欖，暗地裏把金子和爛橄欖取出，將新橄欖代替進去仍用爛的橄欖蓋着，上面封了口，放在亞里郭奇亞的原來地方。

約莫一個月光景，那旅行家囘到巴革達德來了。第一件事，就到這商人處取他的橄欖罐兒，說七年內，多多煩勞着他。商人說這些小事兒，又何必掛齒。『這是我棧房門的鑰匙啦，你自己去拿你的罐兒罷！那罐兒仍在原處呢。』

When Ali Cogia carried the jar to his inn and turned it over, nothing but olives *rolled*[1] out of it. He knew not what to think. For some time he neither spoke nor moved. Then, lifting up his hands and eyes to heaven, he exclaimed: "Is it possible that a man whom I took for my friend could be *guilty*[2] of such *baseness*?[3]"

Returning at once to the merchant, he told him that, besides the olives, he had left a thousand pieces of gold in the jar. If you had need of them, and have used them in trade, they are at your service till you wish to pay them back; only give me a written word to say that you will do so."

The merchant was ready with an angry answer: "You left a jar, found it in its place, and took it away. Now you come and ask me for a thousand pieces of gold. I wonder that you do not demand *diamonds*[4] or *pearls*[5]. Begone about your business."

The noise of their *quarrel*[6] drew other merchants to the spot, and Ali Cogia, seeing that he gained nothing by talk, left his unfaithful friend, telling him that he must appear for *trial*[7] before the *cauzee*,[8] an officer of the law whose *summons*[9] must be obeyed by every good Mussulman. "With all my heart," said the merchant; "we shall soon see who is in the wrong."

【註】 1. 滾. 2. 犯罪的. 3. 下賤. 4. 鑽石. 5. 珠寶. 6. 吵鬧. 7. 審問. 8. 回教國之高官. 9. 傳票.

亞里郭奇亞將罐兒取到了。囘到他的客棧裏，把罐兒倒下，只見橄欖接流地湊下來，以外什麼都沒有；他大驚失色。嚇得目瞪口呆，經過好久，他纔伸手向天，喊道：『天呀，我素來把那人當做好朋友看待的，不料他卻幹這樣卑鄙的事情！』

他立刻囘到那商人那裏，告訴他罐中除橄欖外，尚放有金洋一千元。『倘你因一時急需，把牠用掉在商業上，你不論何時償還我都可答應；現在只須寫一筆據，記明是借我的罷了。』

那商人早就滿面怒容的答道：『你留下的一隻罐兒，好好的在原地方拿去；如今你卻來問我一千金洋。我怪你爲什麼不來討一罐兒鑽石或珠寶呢。滾你的蛋罷！』

他們吵鬧的聲音，引攏大隊的商人來，亞里郭奇亞見和他好說是沒有什麼效力了。遂離開他那不忠實的朋友，一面聲言，他必向法官起訴。那商人說：『極願如此，我們倆正該辨一辨曲直。』

When the trial took place, the cauzee, after hearing the merchant's *defense*[1] of himself, asked if there were any witnesses, and, finding there were none, *dismissed*[2] the prisoner for want of *evidence*.[3] The merchant was in *triumph*[4] over the *verdict*[5], but Ali Cogia would not let the matter drop so easily. He lost no time in drawing up a petition to the Caliph that he should try the merchant himself, and received an answer that the trial would take place on the next day.

That same evening the Caliph, with his Grand Vizier Giafar and Mesroun, the chief of the *attendants*[6], went disguised through the town, as he was wont to do. Hearing a noise as he passed the entrance to a little court, he looked in and saw ten or twelve children at play in the moonlight. Curious to know what they were doing, he sat down on a stone bench near by, and heard one of the *foremost*[7] of the children say, "Let us play at the cauzee".

The affair of Ali Cogia and the merchant had made a great noise in Bagdad, and the children, who had heard of it, took to the game with eagerness, and agreed on the part each was to act. The boy who proposed the sport was to be the cauzee, and, when he had taken his seat with much *gravity*[8], another, as an officer of the court, presented two boys before

---

【註】 1. 辯護. 2. 駁下. 3. 證人. 4. 得意. 5. 判決. 6. 衛隊.
7. 為首的. 8. 莊嚴.

法庭開審的當兒，法官聽了商人的辯護，便問有沒有證明人，因為沒有誰作證，便認為證據不實，把控訴的案子殿下。那商人對於這判詞，十分快慰，但是亞里郭奇亞卻不甘心就此罷事。他立卽提起上訴，到凱立夫那兒，凱立夫親自承審這件案子，傳票發給原告被告兩造，定於明日開庭。

這凱立夫素來歡喜私行察訪，這天晚上他變換服裝，偕了宰相加佛和衞隊長墨郎，到街上去閑逛。當他走過一家院子的面前，聽得喧鬧的聲音，他向裏面望去，見有十來個孩子，正在月光下玩耍。這引起了他的好奇心，要想瞧瞧他們幹怎樣的玩意兒，便坐在附近的一張石橙上，只聽得一個為首的孩子說道：『我們假裝法官吧。』

原來亞里郭奇亞和那商人的案件，早經轟動巴革達德全城了。這些孩子們聽了這件事，乃很熱心地表演着，把原告被告兩造，分配停當。那提議這件玩意兒的孩子，充做法官，當他十分莊嚴地坐着的時候，另有個充做衞役的，

him, one as Ali Cogia and the other as the *accused* merchant.

The pretended cauzee then asked the pretended Ali Cogia what charge he had to bring against the merchant. After making a low bow, he told his story, and begged the cauzee to save him the loss of so much money. Then the pretended merchant was called, and made the same defense which the real merchant had made before the real cauzee. When he finished he offered to take his *oath*[2] that all he had said was true.

"Not so fast," replied the pretended cauzee; "before you come to your oath, I should be glad to see the jar of olives. Ali Cogia," said he to the boy who acted Ali's part, "have you brought the jar?"

"No," replied he.

"Then go and fetch it at once," said the other.

The pretended Ali Cogia went and soon returned with the jar, which he declared to be the one he had left with the merchant, and the merchant was called upon to say that it was the same. When the *cover*[3] was taken off the pretended cauzee said:—

"They are fine olives; let me taste them." Then, *pretending*[4] to eat some, he added: "they are *excellent*,[5] but I cannot think that olives will keep for seven years and be so good; therefore send for some olive merchants, and let me hear what is their opinion."

【註】 1. 被控的. 2. 宣誓. 3. 蓋. 4. 假裝. 5. 優良的.

把兩個孩子領到他面前來，一個扮做亞里，郭奇亞，另一個是被控的商人。

於是那假法官問那假亞里郭奇亞，為什麼事來控訴這商人。扮亞里，郭奇亞的孩子，先打了一個大躬，便訴說了他的案情，并懇求官法，判還他這麼多的金子的損失。其次，那假扮商人提上審問，他的辯白，卻和那眞商人在眞法官面前的辯護一樣。他說完了，他自願宣誓，證明他所說的話，句句是眞。

那假法官說：『慢來，在你宣誓之前我要看看那橄欖罐兒呢。』 他向那扮做亞里，郭奇亞的孩子說：『亞里，郭奇亞！你把那罐兒帶來了沒有。』

他說：『沒有。』

假法官說：『快去拿來。』

那假亞里，郭奇亞去了，說拿得一隻罐兒來，他稱說這罐兒，就是寄存在商人那裏的，那商人被問的時候，也說便是此罐，罐蓋兒拿去了後，假法官說道：

『這些倒是很好的橄欖；我來嘗嘗看吧。』 他裝做嘗了幾隻， 說道：『味道十分好， 不過我想橄欖存了七年，恐怕沒有這般好罷； 可喚幾位橄欖商人來，看他們怎樣說法。』

Two boys, as olive merchants, then appeared. "Are you olive merchants?" said the *sham*[1] cauzee. "Tell me how long olives will keep fit to eat?"

"Sir," replied the two merchants, "let us take what care we may, they will hardly be worth anything the third year; for then they have neither taste nor color."

"If that be so," answered the cauzee, "look into that jar and tell me how long it is since those olives were put into it."

The two merchants pretended to examine and taste the olives, and told the cauzee they were new and good. "You are mistaken," said the young cauzee; "Ali Cogia says he put them into the jar seven years ago."

"Sir," replied the merchants, "we can assure you they are of this year's growth, and we will *maintain*[2] there is not a merchant in Bagdad but will say the same."

The pretended merchant would have objected to this evidence, but the young cauzee would not hear him. *"Hold your tongue*[3]," said he, "you are a *rogue*.[4] Let him be *impaled*."[5] Then the children ended their play, clapping their hands with joy, and leading the feigned *criminal*[6] away to *execution*[7].

【註】 1. 假. 2. 担保. 3. 住嘴. 4. 光棍. 5. 刺死. 6. 罪犯. 7. 行刑.

有兩個孩子，充做橄欖商的，現身出來。那假法官問道:『你們都是橄欖商嗎?告訴我,橄欖可保到幾年不壞。』

兩商人答道：『大人，無論我們怎樣小心地保藏，到了第三年便沒有用；因為不是腐爛就要變色了。』

法官說:『要如眞的這樣，你們看看那罐裏的橄欖,告訴我，已藏有多少年呢?』

這兩個商人假意把橄欖考驗和嘗試，一會兒，乃告訴法官牠們都是又新鮮又好的。那年靑的法官說:『你錯了，亞里，郭奇亞說把牠們放在罐兒裏，是七年前呢?』

兩商人說:『我們決定牠們是今年的產物，我們可說，凡屬巴革達德的橄欖商，都要這樣說呢。』

那假商人對這證明，想要辯白，但這少年法官並不理他。說道：『住嘴，你這光棍。來，把他剌死。』孩子們演完這玩意兒，快活地拍手，大家擁這假罪犯出去行刑。

The Caliph Haroun al Raschid was perfectly delighted with the *shrewdness*[1] and good sense of the boy cauzee in an affair which was to be tried before himself the next day. As he rose from the bench he said to the Grand Vizier: "Could I possibly give a better sentence to-morrow?"

"I think not, Commander of the Faithful," replied Giafar, "if the case is as the children have played it."

"Take notice, then, of this house," said the Caliph, "and bring the boy to me to-morrow, that he may try this cause in my presence, and also order the cauzee who *acquitted*[2] the merchant to attend and learn his duty from a child. Take care, likewise, to bid Ali Cogia bring his jar of olives with him, and let two olive merchants attend."

The next day the Vizier went to the house where he thought the boy lived, and asked for the master, and as he was away from home his wife appeared, thickly veiled. The Vizier asked if she had any children; she answered that he had three, and called them. The eldest declared himself to be the one who had played the cauzee the night before.

"Then, my *lad*[3]," said the Vizier, "come along with me; the Commander of the Faithful wants to see you."

【註】 1. 幹練. 2. 宣告…無罪. 3. 少年.

凱立夫、哈龍、亞爾、拉西德對於那扮法官的孩子，在審理他明天將要審理的案子，卻有這般幹練和識見，十分狂喜。他從櫈上站起的時候，對宰相說道：『我明天可以審理得比這更好嗎？』

加佛答說：『教主，要如像這些孩子們玩耍的那樣，我想陛下是不能彀了。』

凱立夫說：『那末，記住這所屋子罷！明天你把那孩子帶來，我要教他在我面前審理此案，同時再把那寬恕奸商的法官，傳來聽審，可教他從這孩子學點兒知識。更須記着，命亞里，郭奇亞帶他的橄欖罐到案，準備兩個橄欖商伺候着。』

第二天，宰相親自到那孩子居住的屋子裏，問誰是家主，因為主人不在家，他妻子罩着面網出來應客。宰相問她可有孩子們嗎；她答說有三個，便喚了他們來。那最長的孩子直認昨晚扮做法官的，便是他。

宰相說：『好，我的少年！同我來；大教主要見你呢。』

This filled the mother with *alarm*[1], but the Vizier assured her that no harm was meant, and that he would bring the boy back within an hour. But before she let him go, she dressed him as she thought he should be dressed to appear before the Caliph.

When the Vizier and the boy reached the court, the Caliph saw that he was much *abashed*[2], and to set him at his ease said. "Come to me, child, and tell me if it was you that judged between Ali Cogia and the merchant. I heard the trial, and am very well pleased with you."

The boy answered *modestly*[3] that it was he.

"Well, my son," replied the Caliph, "come and sit down by me, and you shall see the true Ali Cogia and the true merchant."

The Caliph then took him by the hand and seated him on the throne by his side, and ask d for the two merchants. When they had come forward and bowed their heads to the carpet, he said to them:—

"*Plead*[4] each of you your cause before this child, who will hear and do you justice; and if he should be at a loss I will *assist*[5] him."

Ali Cogia and the merchant pleaded one after the other; but when the merchant proposed to take his oath, as before, the child said: "It is too soon; it is proper that we should see the jar of olives."

【註】　1. 驚異. 　2. 害羞. 　3. 恭敬地. 　4. 辯護. 　5. 幫助.

這母親大吃一驚，但宰相安慰她說，沒有事，一點鐘內就可以送回來的。母親方纔放心，她把他穿着齊整，纔教他跟去。

宰相和孩子到了朝堂，凱立夫瞧他很是害羞的樣子，教他坐在他的椅上，說道：『來，孩子。告訴我，審亞里，郭奇亞和商人案子的，是你嗎？我聽得這樣審理，很歡喜着你呢。』

這孩子恭敬地囘說，正是他。

凱立夫說：『好，我的孩子！過來坐在我的身傍吧，你就可看見這眞亞里，郭奇亞，和那眞商人呢。』

凱立夫親手牽着這孩子，教他坐在寶座的旁邊，審理那兩個商人。他們到來的時候，俯伏金階，叩首行禮，他對他們說道：

『我叫這孩子承審你們的事情，他必定會判斷得十分公正。你們可各把案情向他訴述；他若有不到處，我可以幫助他。』

亞里，郭奇亞和那商人，先後把情由各自訴述一遍；但當那商人想要宣誓的時候，這孩子說：『且慢；待我們看看那橄欖罐兒。』

When Ali Cogia had placed the jar at the Caliph's feet and opened it, the Caliph looked at the olives, tasted one and gave another to the boy. Then the merchants were called and reported the olives good, and of that year. The boy told them that Ali Cogia declared it was seven years since he had put them up, and they made the same answer as the children who had acted their parts the night before.

Though the *wretch*[1] who was accused saw that his *case*[2] was lost, he tried to say something more in his defense. But the child, instead of *ordering*[3] him to be impaled, looked at the Caliph and said: "Commander of the Faithful, this is no *jesting*[4] matter; it is your majesty that must condemn him to death, and not I, though I did it yesterday in play."

The Caliph, fully satisfied of the merchant's crime, handed him over to the ministers of justice to be impaled. Before the execution took place he confessed where he had *concealed*[5] the thousand pieces of gold, and they were restored to Ali Cogia,

The just *monarch*[6], then turning to the cauzee, bade him learn of the child how to do his duty more carefully, and, *embracing*[7] the boy, sent him home with a purse of a hundred pieces of gold.

【註】　1. 光棍.　2. 案件.　3. 命令.　4. 遊戲.　5. 藏匿.　6. 國王.
7. 抱.

亞里，郭奇亞乃把罐兒呈在凱立夫脚下，打開罐蓋來，凱立夫看着這些橄欖，取一隻自嘗，又給一隻與這孩子，於是召了橄欖商人來，均囘報說這些橄欖是當年的好橄欖。孩子告訴他們說，亞里，郭奇亞說他把橄欖放進罐兒裏，已有七年了，他們的囘答，和昨夜假扮他們的角色一樣的囘話。

那被控的光棍雖然明白他的案情要完全失敗，可是仍然要想詭辯。這孩子却不宣判他該拿去刺死，只向凱立夫道：「教主嘟，這並非是遊戲的事兒；把他正式宣判爲死罪的，該是陛下，不是我，雖然我昨天是做着玩的。」

凱立夫完全滿意於商人的犯罪，便把他付執法吏去執行死刑。行刑前，犯人把藏匿的一千金洋，供出所在，仍歸還亞里，郭奇亞。

這公正的國王向那法官，儆戒他從這孩子學習審判，以後須仔細留心他的職務，他親抱這孩子，賞他一百金洋，養送囘家去。

8.　Ali Baba and the Forty Thieves

I

There once lived in a town of Persia two brothers, one named Cassim and the other Ali Baba. Their father divided his small *property*[1] equally between them. Cassim married a very rich wife, and became a wealthy merchant. Ali Baba married a woman as poor as himself, and lived by *cutting wood*[2] and bringing it upon three *asses*[3] into the town to sell.

One day, when Ali Baba had cut just enough wood in the forest to *load*[4] his asses, he noticed far off a *great cloud of dust*[5]. As it *drew nearer*[6], he saw that it was made by *a body of horsemen*[7], whom he *suspected*[8] to be robbers. Leaving the asses, he *climbed*[9] a large tree which grew on a high *rock*[10], and had *branches*[11] *thick*[12] enough to hide him completely while he saw what passed beneath. The *troop*,[13] forty in number, all well mounted and *armed*[14], came to the foot of the rock on which the tree stood, and here *dismounted*[15]. Each man *unbridled*[16] his horse, *tied*[17] him to a *shrub*,[18] and hung about his neck *a bag of corn*.[19] Then each of them took off his *saddlebag*,[20] which from its weight seemed to Ali Baba full of gold and silver. One, whom he *took to be*[21] their captain, came under the tree in which Ali Baba was *concealed*[22];

【註】1. 資產. 2. 砍柴. 3. 驢. 4. 載于. 5. 飛塵障天. 6. 走近.
7. 一羣騎馬的人. 8. 推想. 9. 爬. 10. 岩石. 11. 枝. 12. 茂的. 13. 隊.
14. 武裝. 15. 下馬. 16. 放鬆韁繩. 17. 繫. 18. 灌木. 19. 一袋麥.
:20. 鞍囊. 21. 認爲. 22. 壓藏.

八　智 婢 殺 盜 的 故 事

一

有一次在波斯一個城子裏，住有兄弟兩個，哥哥叫做加新，弟弟叫做亞里巴巴。他們父親把一份薄薄的小資產，平均地分給他們哥兒兩個。後來加新娶得一個很有錢的妻子，頓時變做富商了。亞里巴巴娶的一個女子，卻和他一樣的貧窮，他們打柴度日，每日把砍的柴負在三匹驢子身上，趕到市上去賣。

有一天，亞里巴巴在林中砍柴，纔把柴在驢子背上載滿，忽見遠處，飛塵障天。近前一瞧，見有好多騎馬的人們。他想他們定是強盜了。就離開驢子，爬到山壁一棵大樹上，那樹的枝葉十分茂密，足以將他完全遮蔽，但他卻仍能瞧見下面。那隊騎馬的人兒，共有四十人，個個都是雄糾糾的武裝打扮，恰到樹下的山腳處，就下馬了。各人放鬆韁轡，把馬兒繫在一棵灌木上，拿一袋麥掛在頭頸裏。各人又都解開鞍囊。這些鞍囊，亞里巴巴照那重量看來，定然盛滿着金銀的。有一個隊長模樣的人，走到亞里巴巴

and, making his way through some shrubs, spoke the words, "Open, Sesame[1]." As soon as the captain of the robbers said this, a door opened in the rock, and after he had made all his troop enter before him, he followed them, when the door shut again of itself.

The robbers stayed some time within, and Ali Baba, fearful of being caught, remained in the tree. At last the door opened again, and the captain came out first, and stood to see all the troop pass by him. Then Ali Baba heard him make the door close by saying, "Shut, Sesame." Every man *at once*[2] *bridled*[3] his horses, fastened his *wallet*[4], and mounted again. When the captain saw them all ready, he put himself at their head, and they returned the way they had come.

Ali Baba watched them *out of sight*[5], and then waited some time before coming down. Wishing to see whether the captain's words would have the same effect if he should speak them, he found the door hidden in the shrubs, stood before it, and said: "Open, Sesame." Instantly the door flew *wide open.*[6]

Instead of[7] a dark, *dismal cavern*, Ali Baba was surprised to see a large chamber, well lighted from the top, and in it all sorts of provisions, rich *bales*[9] of silk, *stuff*[10], *brocade*[11] and *carpeting*[12], gold and silver *ingots*[13] in great heaps, and money in bags.

Ali Baba went boldly into the cave, and collected as much of the gold coin, which was in bags, as he

【註】 1. 胡麻. 2. 立刻. 3. 安上轡頭. 4. 行囊. 5. 看不見. 6. 大開. 7. 代替. 8. 悶人的山洞. 9. 捆. 10. 毛織物. 11. 花緞. 12. 地毯料. 13. 錠.

的樹下，穿過幾棵矮樹，口裏念着道：『開，胡麻。』那盜首這話兒纔說完，山壁裏有扇門兒，呀的一聲，自己開了，他指揮隊伍進去，自己跟着也進去，那門兒又復自己關上。

　　羣盜們在洞裏歇了許久，亞里巴巴因怕被他們看見，乃躱躱在樹上。後來，那扇門又重行開了，那隊長先走將出來，站定了，瞧着羣盜一齊出洞。亞里巴巴聽他教那門兒關上的訣兒，是『關，胡麻，』各人仍立即安上轡頭，緊好行李，跨上了馬。隊長見他們都預備整齊，便在前領着，向原路奔去。

　　亞里巴巴，看見他們，已去得遠了，卻又等一會兒，纔爬下了樹。想試一試那隊長的口訣，有沒有同樣效力，他便尋出隱藏在那矮樹叢中的門，站在門前，說道：『開，胡麻。』果然那門兒呀的開了。

　　亞里巴巴很驚訝的瞧見一所大房屋，並不是一個黑暗悶人的山洞，從頂上下來的光線，很是明亮，屋子裏有各式各樣的設備。很珍貴的絲織品、毛織物、花緞、地毯料，一綑一綑的，堆着不少，還有金元寶和銀元寶積了幾大堆；錢都用布包着。他見了大吃一驚。

　　亞里巴巴勇敢地走進洞去，拿了那盛在袋裏的許多金

thought his asses could carry. When he had loaded
them with the bags, he laid wood over them *so that*
they could not be seen, and, passing out of the door
for the last time, stood before it and said: "Shut,
Sesame." The door closed of itself, and he made the
best of his way to town.

When he reached home, he carefully closed the
gate of his little yard, threw off the wood, and
carried the bags into the house. They were emptied
before his wife, and the great heap of gold *dazzled*[2]
her eyes. Then he told her the whole *adventure*[3], and
warned her, *above all things*[4], to keep it secret.

Ali Baba would not let her take the time to count
it out as she wished, but said: "I will *dig* a *hole*
and *bury*[6] it."

"But let us know as nearly as may be," she said,
"how much we have. I will borrow a small *measure*,
and *measure*[8] it, while you dig a hole."

Away she ran to the wife of Cassim, who lived
near by, and asked for a measure. The *sister-in-law*[9],
knowing Ali Baba's *poverty*[10], was curious to learn
what sort of grain his wife wished to measure out,
and *artfully*[11] managed to put some *suet*[12] in the bottom of the measure before she handed it over. Ali
Baba's wife wanted to show how careful she was in
small matters and, after she had measured the gold,
hurried[13] back, even while her husband was burying

【註】 1. 以便. 2. 眩耀. 3. 奇遇. 4. 最重要的. 5. 掘一個洞.
6. 埋. 7. 斗. 8. 量. 9. 妯娌. 10. 貧窮. 11. 狡猾地. 12. 油脂. 13.
急促的.

洋，在金洋的袋上面，把木柴掩蓋，不致被人瞧見，出門的當兒，他站在門前說道：『關，胡麻。』那門兒便呀的自己關了，他趕緊囘到城裏去。

　他一到家裏，便小心地把他的小院門關了，搬下木柴，將袋子搬到房裏。在妻子面前，把袋子倒空，地上積下大堆的金子，他妻子的眼睛閃耀薄睜不開眼了。後來，他就把這奇遇告訴她，又叮囑她，千萬不可洩漏。

　亞里巴巴沒有時間再讓妻子去計數了，說道：『我掘下一個地洞，埋了牠們罷。』

　她說：『我們總要大約算一下看到底有多少金子。我去借一小斗來，計量一下，你一壁掘着地洞罷。』

　她奔到鄰近的，加新妻子那兒，問她要借一個斗。那嫂嫂素來曉得亞里巴巴貧窮的，心裏想要知道他家今天要量那種食糧，暗地裏狡猾地塗些兒油脂在斗下，纔把斗給她。亞里巴巴的妻子在小事情上，顯出她是怎樣不肯苟且的，一量好便急忙把斗送去，就是她丈夫還在埋金，也不

it, with the borrowed measure, never noticing that a coin had stuck to its bottom.

"What," said Cassim's wife, as soon as her sister-in-law had left her, "has Ali Baba gold in such plenty that he measures it? Whence has he all this wealth?" And envy possessed her breast.

When Cassim came home, she said to him: "Cassim, you think yourself rich, but Ali Baba is much richer. He does not count his money; he measures it." Then she explained to him how she had found it out, and they looked together at the piece of money, which was so old that they could not tell in what prince's *reign*[1] it was *coined*[2].

Cassim, since marrying the rich *widow*[3], had never treated Ali Baba as a brother, but *neglected*[4] him. Now, *instead*[5] of being pleased, he was filled with a *base envy*[6] Early in the morning, after a sleepless night, he went to him and said: "Ali Baba, you *pretend*[7] to be *wretchedly*[8] poor, and yet you measure gold. My wife found this at the bottom of the measure you borrowed yesterday."

Ali Baba saw that there was no use of trying to *conceal*[9] his good fortune, and told the whole story, offering his brother part of the treasure to keep the secret.

"I expect as much," replied Cassim *haughtily*[10]; "but I must know just where this treasure is and how to visit it myself when I choose. Otherwise I will

---

【註】 1. 朝代. 2. 鑄造. 3. 寡婦. 4. 輕視. 5. 代替. 6. 卑鄙的嫉妒. 7. 假裝. 8. 可憐地. 9. 匿藏. 10. 慢傲地.

顧着，更不曾留心斗盤下會膠着一塊金洋。

加新的妻子接到了斗後，心裏想道：『亞里巴巴卻有這許多金子，要用斗來量嗎？那裏來的這些財物呢？』妒嫉主宰了她的心胸。

當加新回家的時候，她向他說道：『加新，你想你自己已很富有，卻不知道亞里巴巴還比你富貴呢。他不點數他的金洋，卻用斗來量啦。』她乃告訴他，怎樣她發見出來的，他們同瞧着那塊金洋，卻見這是一個古幣，不知在什麼帝王時代鑄造的哩。

加新自娶了那有錢寡婦以來，從來不曾把亞里巴巴當做一個胞兄弟看待，常是瞧不起他的。如今聽了這消息，不但不歡喜，反而滿懷着一種卑鄙的嫉妒。一夜不曾入睡，第二天一清早，便趕到他兄弟那裏，說道：『亞里巴巴，你假裝做這般窮苦不堪的樣子，卻是用斗來量金子呢。我妻瞧見你昨天借的斗盤下，膠着金子哩！』

亞里巴巴想這種好運氣，無法隱藏，乃把這事都告訴給他了，並送一部分的金子給他，請保守秘密。

加新傲然地回答着：『我希望多得一點！我必須要知道這寶藏在那兒，我自己怎樣可以去取得。不如此，我定

inform against you[1], and you will lose even what you have now."

Ali Baba told him all he wished to know, even to the worns he must speak at the door of the cave.

Cassim rose before the sun the next morning, and *set out*[2] for the forest with ten *mules*[3] bearing great *chests*[4] which he meant to fill. *With little trouble*[5] he found the rock and the door, and, standing before it, spoke the words, "Open, Sesame." The door opened at once, and when he was within closed upon him. Here indeed were the riches of which his brother had told. He quickly brought as many bags of gold as he could carry to the door of the cavern; but his thoughts were so full of his new wealth, that he could not think of the word that should let him out. Instead of "Sesame," he said, "Open, *Barley*,"[6] and was much amazed to find that the door *remained fast shut*[7]. He named several sorts of *grain*[8], but still the door would not open.

Cassim had never expected such a *disaster*[9], and was so frightened that the more he tried to *recall*[10] the word "Sesame," the more confused his mind became. It was as if he had never heard the word *at all*.[11] He threw down the bags in his hands, and walked wildly up and down, without a thought of the riches lying round about him.

At noon the robbers visited their cave. From *afar*[12] they saw Cassim's mules *straggling*[13] about the

---

【註】 1. 告發你. 2. 出發. 3. 騾. 4. 箱. 5. 沒有多少困難. 6. 大麥. 7. 仍舊緊閉. 8. 穀物. 9. 不幸. 10. 想出. 11. 毫不. 12. 從遠遠地. 13. 彷徨.

去告發你，教你將所有的都失掉。』

　　亞里巴巴遂把他所要知道的，完全告訴了，就是那洞門開閉的方法，也都告訴給他。

　　第二天，太陽還沒有出來，加新便起身，牽十隻驢子負着大箱，向林子裏走去，他心想要裝滿了囘來。他尋那洞門，不一刻就尋着了，站在門前，說道：『開，胡麻。』那門兒立卽呀的開了，待他走進，那門又呀的關上了。這兒，果然像他兄弟所說，滿眼所見的盡是財寶，他竭盡氣力，一古腦兒搬着許多袋金子，到洞門口；因爲他一心想在新的財富上，倒把那開門的口訣兒忘記了。他不說：『胡麻，』却說，『開，大麥，』及見那門動也不動，才自着慌起來。他說了幾種穀名，可是那門還不見開着。

　　這個不幸運的事，加新永不曾想到的，他又慌又怕，愈想愈記不起這『胡麻』二個字兒來，他的心裏覺得紊亂不堪，不知怎樣，好像那個字兒，永不曾聽到過似的。他把手裏的袋子。丟下地來，昏亂地跑來跑去，再也想不到面前的金銀了。

　　正午時候，強盜們囘洞來。遠遠地，瞧見加新的驢子，

rock, and *galloped full speed*[1] to the cave. Driving
the mules out of sight, they went at once, with their
naked sabres[2] in their hands, to the door, which opened as the captain had spoken the proper words before
it.

Cassim had heard the noise of the horses' feet,
and guessed that the robbers had come. He resolved
to *make one effort for his life*[3]. As soon as the door
opened, he rushed out and threw the leader down,
but could not pass the other robbers, who with their
scimitars[4] soon put him to death.

The first care of the robbers was to examine the
cave. They found all the bags Cassim had brought
to the door, but did not miss what Ali Baba had
taken. As for Cassim himself, they guessed rightly
that, once within, he could not get out again; but
how he had *managed*[5] to learn their secret words that
let him in, they could not tell. One thing was
certain, — there he was; and to warn all others who
might know their secret and follow in Cassim's *foot-
steps*[6], they agreed to cut his body into four quarters
—to hang two on one side and two on the other,
within the door of the cave. This they did at once,
and leaving the place of their *hoards*[7] well closed,
mounted their horses and set out to attack the
caravans[8] they might meet.

【註】 1. 用最高速度跑. 2. 出鞘的刀. 3. 努力逃命. 4. 彎刀. 5. 設
法. 6. 足跡. 7. 蓄財. 8. 隊商.

在山邊徬徨，他們盡力奔回洞來。把驢兒驅散，各拔着刀，馬上衝到門前，那門兒被隊長說着適當的字兒，就呀的開了。

加新聽得橐橐的馬足聲，料想強盜們已到。他打定主意，拚着一死逃命。一到門兒開了的時候，他直衝出來，把隊長衝倒了，不過他不能逃過其餘的強盜，他們用着半月形式的刀，立刻把他砍死。

強盜們第一件事就是檢查山洞。他們發見加新帶到洞門口來的，一切袋子，但也並未漏掉亞里巴巴所取去的部分。對於加新自己他們是猜得很對的，說他是初次入內，但不知如何出去；不過他怎樣知道得那個祕密字兒，使他能夠進去，他們卻是不解。不過他是在這兒──這是他們能殼確定的。爲警戒別些人們，怕他們也知道個中祕密，而踏加新的覆轍，他們便把加新的死屍，割成四塊──將兩塊掛在洞門內的左邊。又將兩塊掛在洞門內的右邊，他們做好這個，乃把洞室關好，立卽離開這地方，騎上馬，又去伺候截劫過往的客商。

II

When night came, and Cassim did not return, his wife became very *uneasy*.[1] She ran to Ali Baba for comfort, and he told her that Cassim would cert- ainly think it unwise to enter the town till *night was well advanced*[2]. By midnight Cassim's wife was still more *alarmed*[3], and wept till morning, *cursing*[4] her desire to *pry*[5] into the affairs of her brother and sister-in-law. In the early day she went again, *in tears*[6], to Ali Baba.

He did not wait for her to ask him to go and see what had happened to Cassim, but set out at once for the forest with his three asses. Finding some *blood*[7] at the door of the cave, he took it for an *ill omen;*[8] but when he had spoken the words, and the door had opened, he was struck with *horror*[9] at the *dismal*[10] sight of his brother's body. He could not leave it there, and *hastened*[11] within to find something to *wrap*[12] around it. Laying the body on one of his asses, he covered it with wood. The other two asses he loaded with bags of gold, covering them also with wood as before. Then *bidding*[13] the door shut, he came away, but stopped some time at the edge of the forest, that he might not go into the town before night. When he reached home he left the two asses, laden with gold, in his little yard for his wife to *unload,*[14] and led the other to his sister-in-law's house.

【註】　1. 不安的. 　2. 夜已深. 　3. 驚慌. 　4. 呪詛. 　5. 窺探. 　6. 哭着.
7. 血. 　8. 凶兆. 　9. 戰慄. 　10. 恐怖的. 　11. 趕急. 　12. 包裹. 　13. 命令.
14. 卸下.

二

天色已晚，加新還不見囘家，他妻子感到十分不安。就走到亞里巴巴那裏去討信，他告訴她，想加新爲謹愼起見，日間不便進城，也許要等到午夜囘來，到了更深時候，加新妻子愈加着慌起來，咒咀自己不該偵探寂靜的事情，直自哭到天明，很早的時候，她含淚到亞里巴巴那裏去了。

她要求他去，瞧瞧加新到底是怎麼一囘事，亞里巴巴聽了，並不加以躊躇，立卽挽了三匹驢子，向林中走去。瞧見洞門口，有着血跡，便認爲不是好兆；當他說了那口訣，門呀的開了，他瞧見哥哥屍體的慘象，幾乎嚇昏，他不能不設法將屍體搬囘，趕緊奔到裏邊找些東西，把屍體包好。便將這屍體放在他的一匹驢子上，用柴掩在上面。又進去搬了幾袋金子，放在另外兩匹驢子上，一般的用柴掩着。他乃將門關上，走了出來，在林邊等了一囘，待天晚方始入城。到家的時候，他留下兩匹載有黃金的驢子，在小天井裏，敎他妻子解下自己牽着那另外一匹到嫂嫂的家裏。

Ali Baba knocked at the door, which was opened by Morgiana, a *clever*[1] slave, full of *devices*[2] to conquer difficulties. When he came into the *court*[3] and unloaded the ass, he took Morgiana aside, and said to her: —

"You must *observe*[4] a *strict secrecy*[5]. Your master's body is contained in these two *panniers*[6] We must bury him as if he had died a *natural death*[7] Go now and tell your *mistress*[8]. I leave the matter to your and *skillful devices*."[9]

They placed the body in Cassim's house, and, *charging*[10] Morgiana to act well her part, Ali Baba returned home with his ass.

Early the next morning, Morgiana went to a *druggist*,[11] and asked for a sort of *lozenge*[12] used in the most dangerous *illness*.[13] When he asked her for whom she wanted it, she answered with a *sigh*[14]: "My good master Cassim. He can neither eat nor speak." In the evening she went to the same druggist, and with tears in her eyes asked for an *essence*[15] given to sick persons for whose life there is little hope. "Alas!" said she, "I am afraid even this will not save my good master."

All that day Ali Baba and his wife were seen going sadly between their house and Cassim's and in the evening nobody was surprised to hear the *shrieks*[16] and cries of Cassim's wife and Morgiana, who told everybody that her master was dead.

【註】 1. 聰明伶俐的. 2. 策略. 3. 天井. 4. 注意. 5. 嚴密的祕密. 6. 駝籃. 7. 善終. 8. 主婦. 9. 奇謀妙計. 10. 囑託. 11. 藥鋪. 12. 錠劑. 13. 疾病. 14. 嘆氣. 15. 藥劑. 16. 痛哭.

　　亞里巴巴敲着門，開門的人乃是莫奇娜，她是一個聰明多智的婢女。他走到天井裏的時候，遂解下驢背上的東西，引莫奇娜到一傍，對她說道：

　　『你須嚴守祕密。你主人屍體是在這兩駝籃裏了。我們埋葬他，必須敎外人看來，好像是病死的樣子才好。現在你告訴一聲你主母知道。 此事我完全靠你的奇謀妙計了。』

　　他們把屍首放在加新的屋子裏，亞里巴巴囑託了莫奇娜後，牽着驢子囘家。

　　第二天淸早，莫奇娜走到一爿藥房裏，要買一種用來救急危險病症的藥品。藥師問她是誰服的，她嘆口氣答說道：『我的好主人加新。他不能吃，也不能說話了。』 到晚上，她又淚流滿面地，到那爿同一的藥房裏，要買一種病人差不多沒有挽囘希望的救急藥。並且說道：『我怕連這個都救不得我的主人了。』

　　那一天，亞里巴巴同他的妻子，整天的給人瞧見，滿面愁容地，忽而囘家，忽而到加新的屋子裏，忙個不了。所以一到晚上，人家聽得加新妻子同莫奇娜，號啕大哭的聲音，一點都不怪異，莫奇娜逢人便訴說他的主人已死了。

The next morning at daybreak she went to an old co*bler*[1], who was always early at work, and putting a piece of gold in his hand, said:—

"Baba Mustapha, you must bring your *sewing tackle*[2] and come with me; but I must tell you, I shall *blindfold*[3] you when we reach a *certain place*[4]."

"Oh! oh!" replied he, "you would have me do something *against my conscience*[5] or my *honor*.[6]

"*God forbid*[7]!" said Morgiana, putting another piece of gold in his hand; "only come along with me and fear nothing."

Baba Mustapha went with Morgiana, and at a certain place she bound his eyes with a *handkerchief*,[8] which she never unloosed till they had entered the room of her master's house, where she had put the *corpse*[9] together.

"Baba Mustapha," said she, "you must make haste, and sew the parts of this body together, and when you have done, I will give you another piece of gold."

After Baba Mustapha had finished his task, she blindfolded him again, gave him the third piece of gold she had promised, and, charging him with secrecy, took him back to the place where she had first found his eyes. Taking off the *bandage*,[10] she watched him till he was out of sight, lest he should return and *dog*[11] her; then she went home.

[註] 1. 皮匠.　2. 縫紉器具.　3. 遮目.　4. 某一個地方.　5. 違反良心.　6. 名譽.　7. 決不.　8. 手巾.　9. 屍體.　10. 布帶.　11. 追隨.

第二日天將黎明的時候，她走到一個老皮匠那里，那個皮匠每日均極早起來做工，她放一塊金洋在他手裏道：

『巴巴墨斯德發，請你帶了縫具隨我來；不過我須告訴你，我要遮住了你的眼睛同去的。』

他答道，『啊！啊！你教我做昧良心的事嗎！教我幹敗壞名譽的事嗎。』

莫奇娜說：『決不！你只管隨我來，不要害怕，』說着，又放一塊金洋在他的手裏。

巴巴墨斯德發隨莫奇娜走去，到了一處地方，她用手巾把他的眼睛遮住，直等到了她主人的家裏，纔把手巾解下，那裏她已把屍身端正地放好。

她說道：『巴巴墨斯德發！你且趕快把這些屍片縫合在一起，你縫好了，我再給你一塊金洋罷。』

在巴巴墨斯德發做好了這個工作後，她又把他遮沒了眼睛，給他所允許的那第三塊金洋，囑他務必保守祕密，送他到原來遮住他眼睛的地方。取下手巾，看他走得看不見了，纔行囘來。這樣，使他不能再囘身追隨她的蹤跡了。

229

At Cassim's house she made all things ready for the *funeral*[1], which was duly performed by the *imaum*[2] and other *ministers of the mosque*[3]. Morgiana, as a slave of the dead man, walked in the *procession*,[4] weeping, beating her breast, and tearing her hair. Cassim's wife stayed at home, *uttering doleful cries*[5] with the women of the neighborhood, who, according to custom, came to mourn with her. The whole *quarter*[6] was filled with sounds of sorrow.

Thus the manner of Cassim's death was *hushed up*,[7] and, besides his widow, Ali Baba, and Morgiana, the slave, nobody in the city *suspected*[8] the cause of it. Three or four days after the funeral, Ali Baba removed his few goods openly to his sister-in-law's house, in which he was to live in the future; but the money he had taken from the robbers was carried *thither*[9] by night. As for Cassim's *warehouse*[10], Ali Baba put it entirely under the charge of his eldest son.

III

While all this was going on, the forty robbers again visited their cave in the forest. Great was their surprise to find Cassim's body taken away, with some of their bags of gold.

"We are certainly found out," said the captain; "the body and the money have been taken by some

---

【註】 1. 葬禮. 2. 回教師. 3. 回教堂的教士們. 4. 行列. 5. 發出哀聲. 6. 地方. 7. 隱瞞起來. 8. 疑惑. 9. 向彼方. 10. 倉庫.

加新的家裏，把一切殯葬的儀節，都料理整齊。延着回教高僧，遵禮舉行。莫奇娜照着一個婢女的禮式，哭叫着，搥胸，撕髮，加新妻子留在家裏，放聲大哭，悲號的聲音，驚動四鄰，使一般鄰婦們都來依着習俗和她一同號哭。這一來，哭聲攘成一片。

加新慘死的情形，居然瞞過了，除開寡婦，亞里巴巴，和婢女莫奇娜，在城子裏再也沒有人疑惑他致死的原因了。在殯禮行過的三四天後，亞里巴巴公開地搬了一點東西，到他嫂子的家裏；但是他從強盜所取來的金子，卻在夜裏運住那裏去。加新的倉房，亞里巴巴完全給他的長子管理。

三

這且不表，話說那四十個強盜，重囘到他們林子裏的洞府看望，一見加新的屍體取去了，又不見了幾袋金子，他們大喫一驚。

那盜首說：『我們定須設法找出這屍體和金錢，定給

one else who knows our secret. For out own lives*
sake[1], we must try and find him. *What say you*[2], my
lads?"

The robbers all agreed that this must be done.

"Well," said the captain, "one of you, the boldest and most skillful, must go to the town, *disguised*[3]
as a stranger, and try if he can hear any talk of the
man we killed, and find out where he lived. This
matter is so important that the man who *under-
takes*[4] it and fails should suffer death. What say
you?"

One of the robbers, without waiting to know
what the rest might think, started up, and said, "I
submit[5] to this condition, and think it an honor to
expose[6] my life to serve the troop."

This *won great praise*[7] from the robber's comrades, and he disguised himself at once so that nobody
could take him for what he was. Just at daybreak
he entered the town, and walked up and down till he
came *by chance*[8] to Baba Mustapha's *stall,*[9] which was
always open before any of the shops.

The old cobbler was just going to work when the
robber bade him *good-morrow,*[10] and said:—

"Honest man, you begin to work very early;
how *can one of your age*[11] see so well? Even if it
were lighter, I question whether you could see to
stitch.[12]"

【註】 1. 緣故. 2. 你們的意見如何. 3. 假裝. 4. 從事. 5. 甘受
使遣. 7. 博得讚賞. 8. 偶然. 9. 舖子. 10. 早安. 11. 像你這樣歲
數的一個人. 12. 縫級.

232

另一個知道暗訣的人取去了，爲我們的生命計，我們必須要尋出他來。孩兒們，你們想是怎樣？』

諸盜對於這辦法，都同聲贊成。

盜首說：『好！但須得你們中的一人，要最勇敢，而且最精細的人，扮做一個客商，進城子裏去探聽有沒有被我們殺死的人，就去尋出他的住址。這事情十分重要，奉命的人若有違誤，幹不了這事，定當處死。你們意下如何？』

有一個強盜毫不思索，立刻站起身來，應命道：『我願奉命前去，便是死，爲全隊人的原故，也是很有光榮的。』

盜首大加獎許，他立刻改換裝束，使人瞧不出他是一個強盜，在天將發白的當兒他便入城去，到處暗訪。恰好走到巴巴墨斯德發的鋪子面前，那鋪子常是比人家早開門的。

老皮匠正在低頭工作着，強盜便進去問好，道：

『忠實的人，你做工眞早啦；倒虧你這樣大的年紀；便是天再亮些，也不容易縫針引線啦。』

"You do not know me," replied Baba Mustapha; "for old as I am I have *excellent*[1] eyes. You will not doubt me when I tell you that I sowed the body of a dead man together in a place where I had not so much light as I have now."

"A dead body!" exclaimed the robber, amazed.

"Yes, yes," answered Baba Mustapha; "I see you want to know more, but you shall not."

The robber felt sure that he was on the right *track*[2]. He put a piece of gold into Baba Mustapha's hand, and said to him:—

"I do not want to learn your secret, though you could safely trust me with it. The only thing I ask of you is to show me the house where you stitched up the dead body."

"I could not do that," replied Baba Mustapha, "if I *would*[3]. I was taken to a certain place, whence I was led blindfold to the house, and afterwards brought back again in the same manner."

"Well," replied the robber, "you may remember a little of the way that you were led blindfold. Come, let me blind your eyes at the same place. We will walk together, and perhaps you may *recall*[4] the way. Here is another piece of gold for you."

This was enough to bring Baba Mustapha to his feet. They soon reached the place where Morgiana had bandaged his eyes, and here he was blindfolded again. Baba Mustapha and the robber walked on till they came to Cassim's house, where Ali Baba

【註】 1. 優良的. 2. 門路. 3. 願意. 4. 憶起.

巴巴墨斯德發答說：『你不知道我的，我人雖老，眼睛卻仍很好，你若不信，我告訴你一件事，我曾在一家縫一具屍體在一塊兒的時候，那裏的光線，還遠不及現在的呢。』

強盜驚訝地叫着。『一具屍體！』

巴巴墨斯德發答說：『是呀，是呀。我看你像要仔細地知道這事情，但我勸你不要問牠吧。』

那強盜覺得這門路已對，便放一塊金洋在巴巴墨斯德發的手裏，對他說：

『我不要探聽你的祕密，雖然你便告訴我也不礙事。我所要求於你的，乃是你縫那屍體的住址在那裏？』

巴巴墨斯德發說：『便是我願意。我也是不能呢。我被引到一個地方，眼睛被遮沒了。後來囘家的時候，也是一樣的情形。』

強盜答說：『好，在你被遮沒了眼睛，走的一段路程，你總能記得起一點兒。來，讓我和你同到那地方，我把你的眼睛也遮住。我倆一塊兒走去，你大概便能記得這路途罷。這是另一塊金洋，給你的。』

這已殼使巴巴墨斯德發提起他的雙腿了。他們馬上就到了莫奇娜遮他眼睛的地方，這兒，他又重被遮沒了眼睛。巴巴墨斯德發同強盜，一直走到加新的屋前,纔停下步來,

now lived. Here the old man stopped, and when the *thief*[1] pulled off the *band*[2], and found that his guide could not tell him whose house it was, he let him go. But before he started back for the forest himself, *well pleased*[3] with what he had learned, he marked the door with a piece of chalk which he had remain his hand.

Soon after this Morgiana came out upon some *errand*[4], and when she returned she saw the mark the robber had made, and stopped to look at it.

"What can this mean?" she said to herself. "Somebody *intends my master harm*,[5] and *in any case*[6] it is best to guard against the *worst*.[7] Then she *fetched*[8] a piece of chalk, and marked two or three doors on each side in the same manner, saying nothing to her master or mistress.

When the robber *rejoined*[9] his troop in the forest, and told of his good fortune in meeting the one man that could have helped him, they were all delighted.

"*Comrades*,"[10] said the captain, "we have no time to lose. Let us set off at once, well armed and disguised, enter the town *by twos*,[11] and join at the great square. Meanwhile our comrade who has brought us the good news and I will go and find out the house, and decide what had best be done."

Two by two they entered the town. Last of all went the captain and the *spy*.[12] When they came to

---

【註】 1. 盜賊. 2. 帶. 3. 很歡喜. 4. 差使. 5. 意欲傷害我的主人. 6. 無論如何. 7. 禍事. 8. 拿來. 9. 復歸. 10. 伙伴們. 11. 兩個一夥. 12. 探子.

這屋子現在正是亞里巴巴住着的。那個老人一停下腳步，強盜便取下他束目的布帶，因見他的引導者，不知這是誰的屋子，他便讓他走了。強盜發見了這事情，很是歡喜，在他囘林子去以前，便取一支粉筆，上這門上做了一個暗記。

不一當兒，莫奇娜恰有事出去，當囘來的時候，忽見門上那強盜做的暗記，她站定瞧看。

她自言自語道：『這是什麼意思？定有人暗算我家主人了，無論怎樣，總該想一防備的方法才行。』她便取一支粉筆，就兩邊門上各畫了二三家，畫得一般樣子，卻不對她的主人主母提及這事。

當那強盜囘到林子裏，告訴他的同伴說是已經尋到了，他們都大喜。

盜首說：『伙伴們！我們不要失掉時間，讓我們立刻就去吧，各人假扮着。將軍器暗藏在身上，分做兩個人一班絡續進城，約會在一處場所集合。同時我和我們的探聽者，去尋出那家門戶，相機行事。』

兩個兩個地他們進了城。隊長和那探子走在最後。當

the first of the houses which Morgiana had marked, the spy pointed it out. But the captain noticed that the next door was *chalked*[1] in the same manner, and asked his guide which house it was, that or the first. The guide knew not what answer to make, and was still more *puzzled*[2] when he and the captain saw five or six houses marked after this same *fashion*[3]. He *assured*[4] the captain, with an *oath*[5], that he had marked but one, and could not tell who chalked the rest, nor could he say at which house the cobbler had stopped.

There was nothing to do but to join the other robbers, and tell them to go back to the cave. Here they were told why they had all returned, and the guide was declared by all to be worthy of death. Indeed, he *condemned*[6] himself, *owning*[7] that he ought to have been more careful, and prepared to receive the stroke which was to cut off his head.

The safety of the troop still demanded that the second comer to the cave should be found, and another of the *gang*[8] *offered*[9] to try it, with the same penalty if he should fail. Like the other robber, he found out Baba Mustapha, and, through him, the house, which he marked, in a place *remote*[10] from sight, with red chalk.

But nothing could escape Morgian's eyes, and when she went out, not long after, and saw the red chalk, she *argued*[2] with herself as before, and marked

---

【註】 1. 畫著. 2. 迷亂. 3. 式樣. 4. 保證. 5. 誓. 6. 定罪. 7. 承認. 8. 盜黨. 9. 企圖. 10. 不顯著的. 11. 證明.

238

他們到了莫奇娜做出暗記的那第一家時，探子指出了。但隊長卻見那第二家，也有粉筆畫的同樣的暗記，便問他到底是那一家，第一家呢，或第二家？探子莫知所對，當他和隊長瞧見一連五六家，都有這樣的粉筆暗記，更是弄得迷亂了。他對天發誓對盜首說，他畫的暗號僅是一家，不知是誰用粉筆畫了其餘諸家的，也不能指出，究竟是那一家門前，是那皮匠住步的。

盜黨見事不成，只得招集餘盜，使他們退囘山洞去。把探子宣佈了死刑。由他自己定罪，因爲辦事欠細心，有誤軍情，頭意受斬首的刑罰。

盜衆爲安全計，必須尋出那進洞的第二人，盜黨中又有一人，願去一試，要是遺誤，同樣受罰，他找到巴巴墨斯德發，由他指引出那家，用紅粉筆在很難看見的地方做了一個暗號。

不過這卻不能逃出莫奇娜的眼睛，當她出去不久的時候，看見了紅粉跡，她想是和先前一般的用意，遂就近處

the other houses near by in the same place and manner.

The robber, when he told his comrades what he had done, *prided*[1] himself on his carefulness, and the captain and all the troop thought they must succeed this time. Again they entered the town by twos; but when the robber and his captain come to the street, they found the same trouble. The captain was enraged, and the robber as much confused as the former guide had been. Thus the captain and his troop went back again to the cave, and the robber who had failed willingly gave himself up to death.

IV

The captain could not *afford*[2] to lose any more of his brave fellows, and decided to take upon himself the *task*[3] in which two had failed. Like the others, he went to Baba Mustapha, and was shown the house. *Unlike*[4] them he put no mark on it, but studied it carefully and passed it so often that he could not possibly mistake it.

When he returned to the troop, who were waiting for him in the cave, he said:—

"Now, comrades, nothing can *prevent*[5] our full *revenge,*[6] as I am certain of the house. As I returned I thought of a way to do our work, but if any one thinks of a better, let him speak."

【註】 1. 誇耀. 2. 堪. 3. 工作. 4. 不似. 5. 阻止. 6. 復讎.

同一地點，用同樣形狀，畫了許多家。

那強盜把他幹的事情，得意洋洋地告訴給他的伙伴們，自以爲十分細心了，盜首和全隊都想這次，定然可以成功了。我們又是雙雙兩兩地混進城去；但當那盜首和引路的強盜走到街上的時候，卻發見和先前一樣的困難，首領怒了，那強盜也一般的的惶惑無主。這樣，首領和盜衆只得重行退囘洞去，那誤事的強盜，甘心受斬。

四

盜首不願如此再失掉他勇敢的伙伴，決意親自去走一遭，以求成功。他和先前兩人一樣，也到巴巴墨斯德發那裏，請他指引出那家來。不過他卻不再用記號了，但仔細地察看，來往走了多次，直至將路走熟永不會再有錯誤。

當他囘洞的時候，見衆人都等候在那裏，他說：

『伙伴們，我們現在可以報讎了，我已決定那一家人家。我囘來的時候，路上想得一妙計，不過倘使誰有更妙的辦法，便請他說罷。』

He told them his plan, and, as they thought it good, he ordered them to go into the *villages about,*[1] and buy nineteen mules, with thirty-eight large *leather jars,*[2] one full of oil, and the others empty. Within two or three days they returned with the mules and the jars, and as the mouths of the jars were rather too narrow for the captain's purpose, he caused them to be widened. Having put one of his men into each jar, with the weapons which he thought fit, and having a *seam*[3] wide enough open for each man to *breathe,*[4] he rubbed the jars on the outside with oil from the full vessel.

Thus prepared they set out for the town, the nineteen mules loaded with the thirt-seven robbers in jars, and the jar of oil, with the captain as their *driver.*[5] When he reached Ali Baba's door, he found Ali Baba sitting there taking a little fresh air after his supper. The captain stopped his mules, and said:—

"I have brought some oil *a great way*[6] to sell at tomorrow's market; and it is now so late that I do not know where to *lodge.*[7] Will you do me the favor to let me pass the night with you?"

Though Ali Baba had seen the captain in the forest, and had heard him speak, he could not know him in the disguise of an oil-merchant, and bade him welcome. He opened his *gates*[8] for the mules to go into the yard, and ordered a slave to put them in a

---

【註】 1. 附近鄉村.　2. 皮簍.　3. 縫口.　4. 呼吸.　5. 驛夫.　6. 遠路.　7. 投宿.　8. 門.

　　他乃把他的計策告訴給他們，因為他們都想這是一條最好的方法，便命他們到四處村子裏去，買十九頭騾子，和三十八隻皮簍來，有一簍要盛滿了油，其餘都空着。二三天內，他們把騾子和皮簍都辦齊了，因為皮簍的口兒太狹，不合首領的用處，他命把牠們放開些。每隻簍裏，要足夠裝進一個人，和他的兵器在內，因為皮簍的縫口頗疏，足使簍中人，能彀呼吸着，他便在簍外滿塗了油跡。

　　這樣地結束停當，他們就出發進城，那十九頭騾子載着三十七盜在簍中，和一簍的油，盜首作為牠們的騾夫。當他到了亞里巴巴的家門，他瞧見亞里巴巴晚飯後，坐在門前閑眺。盜首停下了騾子，說道：

　　『我帶了點兒油，要趕明天早市去賣；現在天色晚了，我尋不得宿所。你肯方便我，宿一夜嗎？』

　　亞里巴巴雖然在林子裏，看見到盜首，和聽過他的說話聲音，但當他扮做一個油商來，便不認得了。當下便招呼他進來。開了門，將騾子趕進天井裏，着一個僕人牽

stable and *feed*[1] them when they were unloaded, and then called Morgiana to get a good supper for his *guest*.[2] After supper he charged her *afresh*[3] to take good care of the stranger, and said to her:—

"To-morrow morning I intend to go to the bath before day; take care to have my *bathing linen*[4] ready; give it to Abdalla" (which was his slave's name), "and make me some good *broth*[5] against my return." After this he went to bed.

In the meantime the captain of the robbers went into the yard, and took off the *lid*[6] of each jar. and told his people what they must do. To each, *in turn*,[7] he said:—

"As soon as I throw some stones out of the chamber window where, I lie, do not fail to come out, and I will join you at once."

Then he went into the house, and Morgiana showed him his chamber, where he soon *put out*[8] the light, and laid himself down in his clothes.

To *carry out*[9] Ali Baba's *orders*,[10] Morgiana got his bathing linen ready, and bade Abdalla to set on the *pot*[11] for the broth; but soon the lamp *went out*,[12] and there was no more oil in the house, nor any *candles*.[13] She knew not what to do, till the slave reminded her of the oil-jars in the yard. She thanked him for the thought, took the *oil-pot*,[14] and went out. When she came *nigh*[15] the first jar, the robber within said softly: "Is it time?"

【註】 1. 飼. 2. 客人. 3. 更. 4. 浴巾. 5. 肉湯. 6. 蓋. 7. 循序. 8. 關熄. 9. 實行. 10. 命令. 11. 鍋. 12. 熄滅. 13. 洋燭. 14. 油瓶. 15. 近.

他們到馬房裏去， 好好兒喂養着， 當貨物卸下來的時候，
又命莫奇娜辦飯款待客人。飯後，他又叮囑她一遍，教她
好好招待客人，又對她說道：

『明天天未亮， 我要洗浴的； 把我的浴巾收拾停當；
交給阿達拉，（一個僕人名，）我洗完了，預備一碗肉湯給
我。』吩咐畢，就去睡了。

這時候， 盜首走到天井裏， 揭開了每個皮簍的蓋兒，
教給他們行事機宜。一個個地對他們說道：

『我在臥房的窗前，一丟出石子的時候，你們就須跑
出簍來，接應我。』

他就進屋子裏去，莫奇娜將他引進臥房，他趕快地熄
滅了火，和衣躺下。

莫奇娜因受亞里巴巴的吩咐，便把他的浴巾預備好，命
阿達拉預備鍋去燉肉湯，不過火快要熄了，屋子裏卻沒有
一點油。又沒有一根洋燭，她一時失了主意，不知怎麼辦
才好，但那僕人告訴她，天井裏現有許多油簍放着。她謝
了他的指引便拿了油瓶走出去。當她走近第一油簍時，卻
聽見簍子裏的強盜，低聲問道：『是時候嗎？』

Of course she was surprised to find a man in the jar instead of the oil, but she saw at once that she must keep *silence*,[1] as Ali Baba, his family, and she herself were in great danger. Therefore she answered, without showing any fear: "Not yet, but presently." In this manner she went to all the jars and gave the same answers, till she came to the jar of oil.

By this means Morgiana found that her master had *admitted*[2] to his house thirty-eight robbers, of whom the *pretended*[3] oil-merchant, their captain, was one. She made what haste she could to fill her oil pot, and returned to her kitchen, lighted her lamp, and taking a great *kettle*[4] went back to the oil-jar and filled it. Then she set the kettle on a large wood fire, and as soon as it *boiled*[5] went and poured enough into every jar to *stifle* and destroy the robber within.

When this *deed*,[7] worthy of the courage of Morgiana, was done without any noise, as she had planned, she returned to the kitchen with the empty kettle, put out the lamp, and left just enough of the fire to make the broth. Then she sat silent, resolving not to go to *rest*[8] till she had seen through the window that opened on the yard whatever might happen there.

It was not long before the captain of the robbers got up, and, seeing that all was dark and quiet, gave the *appointed signal*[9] by throwing little stones some

【註】 1 鎖靜. 2. 許入. 3. 假裝. 4. 鍋. 5. 沸騰. 6. 窒息. 7. 事情. 8. 睡眠. 9. 約好了的暗號.

　　她見油簍裏，是人不是油，自然十分大駭，不過她立時便悟到亞里巴巴的全家，和她自己，都在大大的危險中，她立時鎮靜起來，不露一點驚慌，反囘答簍子裏的強盜，說：『還沒有，但是快了。』她對各簍說着同樣的囘話，最後才到得眞的油簍旁邊。

　　這樣一來，莫奇娜乃發見她主人，原來開門引進了三十八個強盜，而那個假油商，是他們的首領。莫奇娜就趕快盛滿了油瓶，囘到廚房裏，點亮了燈，又拿了一隻大鍋，到油簍去裝滿了油。卽把鍋架起大火來燒，把鍋中的油，燒得滾熱了，便向每只油簍裏灌進去，使簍裏的強盜立時喪命。

　　因爲這件事值得勇敢的莫奇娜幹的，她卻像她所計算的，做得一些兒響動都沒有，靜悄悄地，拿着空鍋，囘到廚房裏去，她吹息了燈，僅留一些兒火，足夠燉肉湯。她靜坐着不睡，從窗子裏定神向外望着，看天井裏有什麼動靜。

　　不多時，那盜首起來了，卻見裏外漆黑，四邊悄靜無聲，正是幹事的時候，他便向油簍投下幾塊小石子，很奇

of which hit the jars, as he doubted not by the sound they gave ' As there was no *response*,[1] he threw stones a second and a third time, and could not imagine why there was no answer to his signal.

Much *alarmed*,[2] he went softly down into the yard, and going to the first jar to ask the robber if he was ready, smelt the hot boiled oil, which sent forth a steam out of the jar. From this he suspected that his *plot*[3] was found out, and, looking into the jars *one by one*,[4] he found that all his gang were dead. *Enraged to despair*,[5] he forced the *lock*[6] of a door that led from the yard to the garden, and made his escap . When Morgiana saw him go, she went to bed, well pleased that she had saved her master and his family.

Ali Baba rose before day, and went to the baths without knowing of what had happened in the night. When he returned he was very much surprised to see the oil-jars in the yard and the mules in the stable.

"God *preserve*[7] you and all your family," said Morgiana when she was asked what it meant; "you will know better when you have seen what I have to show you."

So saying she led him to the first jar, and asked him to s e if there was any oil. When he saw a man instead, he *started back*[8] in alarm.

"Do not be afraid," said Morgiana; "he can do

【註】1. 反應. 2 驚駭. 3. 陰謀. 4. 一個一個的. 5. 失望欲狂. 6. 鎖. 7. 保護 8. 急急縮回.

靜，裏面一點聲音都沒有。他見一塊石子丟去，不見動靜，接連丟了第二，第三塊石子，他不懂爲什麼還沒有回音。

他很驚駭，便輕着腳步走到天井裏，向第一油簍，問那強盜預備了沒有，當他走近油簍時，卻聞得一陣熱油氣味，撲鼻冲來，猛喫一驚。他知道事情不妙，計謀敗露了，便向這些簍子一個一個瞧去，見他的羽黨都死了，他又悲又恨，卻是沒法，只得裂開天井裏一扇外門的鎖，從花園裏逃去。莫奇娜見他走了，便去睡覺，十分快活，她已救得她主人和他的一家性命。

天方黎明亞里巴巴卽起身入浴，夜裏的事一點都不知道。當他洗畢的時候，見天井裏這些油簍，和馬廐裏這些驘子，好生怪異。

莫奇娜在他詰問緣因的時候，說道：『上帝保全你一家的性命，我指給你看自然便會明白了。』

說畢，她引他到第一個油簍，問他裏面可有油。當他瞧見簍裏卻是一個人，嚇了一跳。

莫奇娜說：『不要害怕，他不能傷害你或任何人，他

neither you nor anybody else the least harm. He is dead. Now look into all the other jars."

Ali Baba was more and more amazed as he went on, and saw all the dead men and the *sunken*[1] oil-jar at the end. He stood looking from the jars to Morgiana, till he found words to ask: "And what is become of the merchant?"

"Merchant!" answered she; *"he is as much one as I am.*[2]"

Then she led him into the house, and told of all that she had done, from the first noticing of the chalk-mark to the death of the robbers and the *flight*[3] of their captain. On hearing of these brave deeds from Morgiana's own lips, Ali Baba said to her:—

"God, by your means, has *delivered*[4] me from death. For the first *token*[5] of what I *owe*[6] you, I give you your *liberty*[7] from this moment, till I can fully reward you as I intend."

Near the trees at the end of Ali Baba's long garden, he and Abdalla dug a *trench*[8] large enough to hold the bodies of the robbers. When they were buried there, Ali Baba hid the jars and weapons; and as the mules were of no use to him, he sent them at different times to be sold in the market by his slave.

V

The captain of the forty robbers had returned to his cave in the forest, but found himself so lonely

---

【註】 1. 空. 2. 他是商人同我是商人一樣——（我既不是商人，他也不是商人）. 3. 逃亡. 4. 救出. 5. 徵證. 6. 感. 7. 自由. 8. 坑.

是死了啦。現在再瞧別的油簍裏罷。』

亞里巴巴愈看愈驚，一直看到末一個空油簍。他站在那裏，瞧瞧油簍，瞧瞧莫奇娜，一句話都說不出來，好一會，纔問：『那末，那個油客人怎樣了？』

她答道：『油客人！他不是油客人，是和他們一樣的啊！』

她便引他到屋子裏，把她所幹的事情，從頭到尾都說了，怎樣她最初發見粉筆暗號，直至怎樣殺死這些盜衆，和他們的首領逃去。亞里巴巴聽了這些忠義勇敢的事情，從莫奇娜的口裏親自說出，乃對她說道：

『上帝從你的手裏，救我一死。第一件事我立刻要報答你，就是自現在起，我給你自由，以後我還要設法厚報你。』

亞里巴巴乃和阿達拉到花園的盡頭一棵樹根下，掘起一個大坑，把這些死屍都掩埋在裏邊。當他們埋好了，亞里巴巴藏起了油簍和軍器；因爲這些騾子對他沒有用處，便喚僕人，分頭賣掉牠們。

五

那四十個強盜的首領，囘到他的樹林洞裏，感到滿目

there that the place became *frig'tful*[1] to him. He resolved at the same time to *avenge*[2] the fate of his comrades, and to bring about the death of Ali Baba. For this purpose he returned to the town, disguised as a merchant of *silks*.[3]　By degrees he brought from his cavern many sorts of fine stuffs, and to *dispose*[4] of these he took a *warehouse*[5] that happened to be *opposite*[6] Cassim's which Ali Baba's son occupied since the death of his uncle.

He took the name of Cogia Houssain, and as a *newcomer*[7] was very *civil*[8] to the merchants near him. Ali Baba's son was one of the first to *converse*[9] with him, and the new merchant was most friendly. Within two or three days Ali Baba came to see his son, and the captain of the robbers knew him at once, and soon learned from his son who he was. From that time forth he was still more polite to Ali Baba's son, who soon felt bound to repay the many kindnesses of his new friend.

As his own house was small, he *arranged*[10] with his father that on a certain afternoon, when he and the merchant were passing by Ali Baba's house, they should stop, and he should ask them both to sup with him.　The plan was carried out, though at first the merchant, with whose own plans it agreed perfectly, made as if to *excuse himself*.[11]　He even gave it as a reason for not remaining that he could eat no salt in his *victuals*.[12]

【註】 1. 可怖的. 2. 復仇. 3. 絲織物. 4. 銷售. 5. 批發莊. 6. 對面. 7. 新來的. 8. 慇懃的. 9. 交好. 10. 商量. 11. 推辭. 12. 食物.

淒涼，差不多使他發抖起來。他想了多時，決定設計去結果亞里巴巴的性命，爲他的伙伴們報讎。他扮做一個絲商進城去。慢慢地絡續從洞裏運出許多上色綢緞到城，爲要銷售起見，找得一個批發莊，恰在加新貨店的對面，那貨店自加新死後，由亞里巴巴的長子管理。

他化名叫做郭奇亞亨生，正像一個新客人的樣子，他對附近的隣商都很客氣。亞里巴巴的兒子是第一個和他談話的人，那新商人和他非常親密，兩三天內，亞里巴巴來看他的兒子，盜首一見便認識他，亞里巴巴從他兒子的口裏，知道他是誰人。從此以後，他對於亞里巴巴的兒子，更其慇懃和悅，使他立時感到他新友的許多感情。

因爲他自己的屋子太窄小，一天午後，他同父親商量，要同客人到亞里巴巴的家裏去，他們留在那裏，一同晚餐。這個主意，恰中那個客商的心懷，不過他起首還假意客氣了一番。並且說出不能到席的緣因，因爲他是不吃合鹽的食物。

"If that is all," said Ali Baba, "it need not *deprive*[1] me of the honor of your company;" and he went to the kitchen and told Morgiana to put no salt into anything she was cooking that evening.

Thus Cogia Houssain was persuaded to stay, but to Morgiana it seemed very strange that any one should refuse to eat salt. She wished to see what manner of man it might be, and to this *end*,[2] when she had finished what she had to do in the kitchen, she helped Abdalla carry up the dishes. Looking at Cogia Houssain, she knew him at first sight, *in spite of*[3] his disguise, to be the captain of the robbers, and, *scanning*[4] him very closely, saw that he had a dagger under his garment.

"I see now why this greatest enemy of my master would eat no salt with him. He intends to kill him; but I will prevent him."

While they were at supper Morgiana *made up her mind*[5] to do one of the boldest deeds ever conceived. She dressed herself like a *dancer*,[6] *girded*[7] her waist with a *silver-gilt*[8] *girdle*,[9] from which hung a *poniard*,[10] and put a handsome *mask*[11] on her face. Then, when the supper was ended, she said to Abdalla:

"Take your *tabor*,[12] and let us go and *divert*[13] our master and his son's friend, as we sometimes do when he is alone."

【註】 1. 奪取. 2, 目的. 3. 不管. 4. 細察. 5. 打定主意. 6. 舞女. 7. 佩. 8. 鍍銀的. 9. 帶子. 10. 小刀. 11. 面具. 12. 花鼓. 13. 娛樂.

　　亞里巴巴說：『倘僅爲這一點兒，那倒不成問題的。』他便走到廚房裏，告訴莫奇娜說，燒煮晚餐，所有食物中都不要放鹽。

　　這樣郭奇亞亨生遂被勸留住了，不過有不吃鹽的客人，莫奇娜倒好生怪異了。她決意去瞧瞧，到底是怎樣的一位客人。當她烹煮已畢，便幫着阿達拉搬飯。不管客人怎樣喬裝，她一眼便認出郭奇亞亨生，是那強盜的首領假扮的，再仔細瞧一下，發見他內衣裏藏著一把利劍。

　　『現在我知道我主人的大讎人，爲什麼要不吃鹽的緣故了。他立意來殺害他。但我可以阻住他。』

　　當他們還在晚餐的時候，莫奇娜打定主意，要幹一件最勇敢的驚人事件。她扮成一個舞女，腰裏束着一條鍍銀的帶子，掛了一把小刀，戴着一個美麗的面具。當晚餐用畢，她向阿達拉說道：

　　『拿着你的花鼓，我們前去，使我們的主人和他兒子的朋友，娛樂一番，好像我們平日，在他一個人的時候，做的那樣。』

They presented themselves at the door with a low bow, and Morgiana was bidden to enter and show Cogia Houssain how well she danced. This, he knew, would *interrupt*[1] him in carrying out his wicked purpose, but he had to make the best of it, and to seem pleased with Morgiana's dancing. She was indeed a good dancer, and on this *occasion*[2] *outdid*[3] herself in graceful and surprising *motions*.[4] At the last, she took the tabor from Abdalla's hand, and held it out like those who dance for money.

Ali Baba put a piece of gold into it, and so did his son. When Cogia Houssain saw that she was coming to him, he pulled out his purse from his bosom to make her a *present*,[5] but while he was putting his hand into it, Morgiana, with courage worthy of herself, plunged[6] the poniard into his heart.

"Unhappy woman!" exclaimed Ali Baba, "what have you done to *ruin*[7] me and my family?"

"It was to preserve, not to ruin you," answered Morgiana. Then she showed the dagger in Cogia Houssain's garment, and said: "Look well at him, and you will see that he is both the pretended oil-merchant and the captain of the band of forty robbers. As soon as you told me that he would eat no salt with you, I *suspected*[8] who it was, and when I saw him, I knew."

Ali Baba embraced her, and said: "Morgiana, I

【註】 1. 妨害. 2. 場合. 3. 勝過. 4. 舉動. 5. 賞品. 6. 刺入. 7. 毀滅. 8. 猜想.

　　他們到了門口，深深地打了一躬，莫奇娜就被喚進去跳舞，在郭奇亞亨生眼裏看來，她的跳舞確是非常美妙。這個，他原知道足以阻止他的惡意，不過他竭力容忍着，似乎對於莫奇娜的跳舞，覺得很快活的樣子。她果然是個跳舞能手，這次她尤其賣弄她的技術，舞蹈得格外動人。後來，她從阿達拉手中取了鼓，高高地擊着，好像賣藝人討錢的樣子。

　　亞里巴巴投一塊金洋在鼓上，他的兒子也是一樣。當郭奇亞亨生瞧見她要來了，便向懷裏掏出他的錢袋，想給她一種賞品，但當他把手伸入懷中的時候，莫奇娜竭盡她平生之力，一刀向他胸前刺去，刺個正著。

　　亞里巴巴大聲說：『不幸的女子！你所幹的事壞了我和我的一家了。』

　　莫奇娜答說：『這是救你，不是損害你的呀，』便從郭奇亞亨生的衣內，取出他的劍來，說道：『我仔細看他正是那個假油商，也就是那四十個強盜的首領呢。當你對我說他不吃鹽，我就料定他是誰了，我一看便認識他。』

　　亞里巴巴親自抱了她，說道：『莫奇娜呀，我早就給

gave you your liberty before, and promised you more *in time;*[1] now I would make you my *daughter-in-law.*[2] Consider," he said, turning to his son, "that by marrying Morgiana, you marry the preserver of my family and yours."

The son was all the more ready to carry out his father's wishes, because they were the same as his own, and within a few days he and Morgiana were married, but before this, the captain of the robbers was buried with his comrades, and so secretly was it done, that their bones were not found till many years had passed, when no one had any concern in making this strange story known.

For a whole year Ali Baba did not visit the robbers' cave. At the end of that time, as nobody had tried to *disturb*[3] him he made another journey to the forest, and, standing before the *entrance*[4] to the cave, said: "Open, Sesame." The door opened at once and from the appearance of everything within the cavern, he *judged*[5] that nobody had been there since the captain had fetched the *goods*[6] for his shop. From this time forth, he took as much of the treasure as his needs demanded. Some years later he carried his son to the cave, and taught him the secret, which he *handed down in his family,*[7] who used their good fortune wisely, and lived in great *honor*[8] and *splendor.*[9]

【註】 1. 相當時間． 2. 媳婦． 3. 騷擾． 4. 門口． 5. 決定． 6. 貨品． 7. 傳家． 8. 光榮． 9. 蓄富．

你自由了，許你以後還有重酬；現在，我願你做我的媳婦。你想一想……』他轉向兒子說道：『你娶了莫奇娜，便是娶了我全家和你的救命恩人呢。』

父親一說，那兒子早就應允了。因爲他們意見正和他相同，不多幾天，他和莫奇娜結婚，但舉行結婚之前，那盜首和他的伙伴們埋葬在一起，這事情做得這般祕密，他們的骨頭過了許多年後，不曾見發見出來，也沒有誰把這件異事宣揚出去。

足有一年光景，亞里巴巴不曾去看望盜洞。到那時，因爲沒有誰騷擾他了，他便重行取路進林子去，站在洞門口，說道：『開，胡麻』那門兒蕎地呀的開了，從洞內種種情形看來，他決定自那盜首取貨開辦鋪子以來，沒有誰到過這兒。從此以後，那洞裏的錢財，便由他自由地取用。過了數年，他帶兒子到洞口，把那個祕密教給他，他們世代相傳。一家用財有道，成爲十分豪富和光榮的人家。

9.　The Story of Abou Hassan

I

In the *reign*[1] of the Caliph Haroun al Raschid there lived at Bagdad a very rich merchant. His only son, Abou Hassan, was educated with great *strictness*.[2] His youth was passed without any of those pleasures to which he thought his wealth *entitled*[3] him. When he was thirty, his father died and becoming sole *heir*[4] to the large property, he made up his mind that he would enjoy it. He divided his riches into two parts. With one half he bought houses in the city and farms in the country, *resolving*[5] to lay by all the *income*[6] they brought him. The other half, *consisting of*[7] *ready money*,[8] he *determined*[9] to spend for present *pleasures*.[10]

To this end he made the *acquaintance*[11] of wealthy youths of his own age and *rank*.[12] Every day he gave them splendid feasts at *lavish*[13] expense. At the end of the year his money was all gone, and the friends on whom he had spent it began to avoid and *desert*[14] him. This *grieved*[15] Abou Hassan more than the loss of his wealth. To be sure, he still had a good *estate*[16] in his lands and farms, and he resolved to find out if his friends were really as false as they seemed.

"I will go to them one after another," he said to his mother, "and when I have shown them what I

【註】 1. 朝代. 2. 嚴格. 3. 與以權利. 4. 承繼人. 5. 決定. 6. 收入. 7. 組合而成. 8. 現金. 7. 決定. 10. 享樂. 11. 相識. 12. 身分. 13. 揮霍的. 14. 捨棄. 15. 使悲. 16. 產業.

九　阿保哈生的故事

一

在哈龍亞爾拉西德凱立夫朝代的時候，巴革達德住有一個商人，十分豪富。他有一個獨子，叫做阿保哈生，受着嚴厲的教育。種種爲富家子弟所應有的享樂，在他少年時代，都沒有享用過。阿保哈生三十歲的時候，他的父親死了，他一個人承襲這宗巨產，遂決要把這財產盡量的享樂一下。他把產業，分做兩份。一份買市房與莊田，他打算將這項下每年所有的收入，都積蓄起來。另一份是現金，是預備眼前化用的。

主意旣定，他便廣結交遊，所結交的都是些富家公子。他每天備着精美酒饌請他們宴會。方過一年，他的現金都用完了，那些朋友們也就一天一天地疏遠他，冷淡他。這個使阿保哈生非常惱恨，比他的金錢喪失還要大。自然，他還有許多產業，不曾動得，此時他卻想到一個主意，要乘此機會試探他的朋友們，是不是都是那樣不忠實的。

他對他母親說道：『我且一個一個的到他們那兒去，先

have done on their account, will ask them to help me in my need, merely to see if there is any *gratitude*[1] in their hearts."

This he did at once, even promising to give *bonds*[2] for what they might lend him, and *tempting*[3] them with the hope of future feasts. But not one of his companions was moved by these *arguments*;[4] some even *pretended*[5] not to know him.

Full of *wrath*,[6] he went again to his mother, and told her of a new resolve he had made. Not only did he *renounce*[7] all his former companions, but he took an *oath*[8] never to *entertain*[9] again a *dweller*[10] in Bagdad. He further *vowed*[11] that he would not put in his purse more money than he should need for asking a single person to *sup*[12] with him, and that person must be a stranger just arrived in the city, and meaning to depart the next morning.

This plan he carefully carried out. Every morning he provided for a *repast*[13] for two, and at evening went to the end of the Bagadad bridge, where he invited a stranger to sup with him, and informed him of the law he had made for himself. The meal of which they partook was not costly, but well dressed. There was plenty of wine and cheerful talk. When he sent away his guest in the morning, he said: "God preserve you from all sorrow wherever you go. Do not take it ill if I tell you that we must

---

【註】 1. 感恩. 2. 證券. 3. 誘惑. 4. 言論. 5. 假裝. 6. 憤怒. 7. 斷絕. 8. 誓約. 9. 款待. 10. 住民. 11. 立誓. 12. 吃. 13. 食物.

把我爲他們所化掉的款子，告訴他們，然後懇求他們的幫助，不過這是要看看他們心裏有沒有感激罷。』

他就分頭去試，雖然他允許寫借據給他們，雖然他答應他們再用酒宴邀請他們。但是他的朋友中，沒有一個感動，答言幫助他，有幾個甚至假裝和他並不相識。

他十分憤怒，囘到他母親那裏，告訴她一種新的主見。他不但要完全斷絕以前的朋友們，而且立誓再也不接待巴革達德的一個住民，立願今後他款待賓客們的費用，決不超過款待一個客人以上，那個客人又必須是才到城的一個生客，意思就是那人只住一夜，第二天一早就離開的。

這個計劃，他很小心地實行了。每天早上，他辦下一席供兩人用的宴飲，晚上便走到巴革達德的橋塊下，請了一個生客來，同他夜餐，幷告訴他所立下的那條律例。他們所享用的肴饌，雖然不是珍羞異味，卻也治得極精美。賓主們淺斟互酌，談笑得非常快樂。當次早送客的時候，他說道：『上帝保佑你一路平安，請你不要見怪，我告訴

n'ver see each other again, either at home or anywhere else; so God *conduct*[1] you."

For a long time Abou Hassan had been exact in the *observance*[2] of his oath, when, one afternoon as he sat upon the bridge, the Caliph Haroun al Raschid came by, *disguised*[3] as a merchant of Moussul, and fol'owed by a tall, *stout*[4] slave. Abou Hassan, looking out for a guest, gave the stranger the usual *invitation*,[5] and told him what his custom was. The old *whim*[6] interested the Caliph, and he accepted the invitation, telling Abou Hassan only to lead the way, and he would follow.

So they came to the neatly furnished room, where the cloth was laid, and the supper served. They ate heartily, of what they liked best, without speaking or d'inking, according to the custom of the country. When they had done eating, the Caliph's slave brought water to wash their hands, and Abou Hassan's mother cleared the table and brought in a *dessert*[7] of various fruits. As soon as it was dark, w'x[8] *candles*[9] we'e lighted, and Abou Hassin, after requesting his mother to take care of the slave, set down bottles and glasses. The Caliph and Abou Hassan sat drinking and talking on many subjects till the night was far advanced, when the Caliph, well pleased with his *host's*[10] *treatment*[11] of him, said: "I beg of you to tell me how I may serve you, for though I am only a merchant, it may be in my power

---

【註】 1. 指導. 2. 遵守. 3. 假裝. 4. 強壯的. 5. 邀請. 6. 奇想. 7. 酒筵最後的食品. 8. 蠟的. 9. 蠟燭. 10. 主人. 11. 款待.

你，我們永不再相見，無論在家或在別處所在，因爲上帝會指導你一切。』

阿保哈生實行他的誓願，過了很久，有一天午後，當他坐在橋塊上的時候，那哈龍亞凱拉西德凱立夫，喬裝做一個孟索爾地方的商人樣子，背後跟着一個強壯的僕人，恰打那裏經過。阿保哈生瞧見有個客人來了，他照例去歡迎他，并告訴他的慣例怎樣。　這個奇想使凱立夫覺得有趣，便允許這邀請，告訴阿保哈生請在前引導他便在後面跟來。

他們到一間陳設精雅的屋子裏，桌上席布都已鋪好，夜餐已預備齊整了。他們各揀着自己最喜歡的肴饌，爽快地吃着，依照本國的習俗，不說話，也不喝酒。當他們食畢，凱立夫的僕人端着水，給他們洗手，阿保哈生母親抹淨桌子，便取上各種新鮮菓兒。天色黑了，點上蠟燭，阿保哈生求母親好生款待那僕人，便擺下酒瓶，杯兒，預備喝酒。凱立夫和阿保哈生面對面的坐下來，一壁喝着酒，一壁開談着各種的事件，一直喝到深夜。那凱立夫見阿保哈生招待慇懃，十分歡喜，便說道：『請你對我說，我怎樣可爲你效勞，因爲我雖然是個商人，但爲感謝你的盛情，准許

to oblige you myself or by some friend." To this Abou Hassan replied:—

"I can only thank you for your *offer*,[1] and for the honor you have done me in partaking of my *frugal fare*[3]. Yet I must tell you there is one thing I wish. I should like to be caliph for a single day, in the place of our *sovereign*[4] lord and master, Haroun al Raschid, Commander of the Faithful. The imam of the *mosque*[5] in the district where I live is a great *hypocrit*.[6] he and four of his friends try to lord it over me and the whole neighborhood. If I were caliph, I would punish the imam and his friends with a hundred strokes each on the soles of their feet, to teach them not to disturb and *abuse*[7] their neighbors in future."

The Caliph was much pleased with this thought of Abou Hassan's; and while his host was talking, he took the bottle and two glasses, and, filling his own first said: "Here is a cup of thanks to you." Then he filled the other, put carefully into it a little sleeping *powder*[8] which he had about him, and gave it to Abou Hassan, saying:—

"You have taken the pains to fill for me all night, and it is the least I can do to save you the trouble once. I beg you to take this glass, and drink to off for my *sake*.[9]"

Abou Hassan did as he was asked, and scarcely had he set the *glass*[10] upon the table, when he fell into a sound sleep. The Caliph commanded his slave to

---

【註】 1. 提議. 2. 摸索的. 3. 飲食. 4. 最上的. 5. 回敎寺院.
6. 僞君子. 7. 虐待. 8. 藥粉. 9. 緣故. 10. 酒杯.

我，或我的幾個朋友，報效你一下。』阿保哈生答說：

『我對你這番好意，只能心感，你不嫌菲酒薄菜，肯惠臨合下，實是我的榮幸。不過我可以告訴你，我有一件心願，就是想要做一天的凱立夫，以代替我們至尊的皇上，哈龍亞爾拉西德大教主。本教區寺院裏的主教，卻是外面慈善，內中陰險的一個偽君子；他和四個黨羽，無惡不作，百般魚肉鄉里和我，要如我做了凱立夫，定把他和他那四個羽黨，各打足掌一百，用以示警，使他知道隣里是不可欺負呢！』

凱立夫對阿保哈生這樣的思想，暗裏只有佩服；他當這主人談得起勁的時候，拿了酒壺和兩隻杯子，先給自己篩滿一杯，口裏說道：『這一杯酒，感謝你的盛意款待。』他說畢，又篩了一滿杯，偷着把身邊帶來的迷藥，放一些在酒裏，擎了酒杯兒，遞給阿保哈生道：

『感謝你陪我長夜喝酒，這一杯酒無非表示我的一點心意，請你為我乾了吧。』

阿保哈生舉杯就喝，還不曾把酒杯兒放在桌上，可就呼呼的睡着。凱立夫命他的僕人，把阿保哈生帶進皇宮去，

carry Abou Hassan directly to the palace, and put him into his own *state bed*.[1] This was done at once.

At the palace the Caliph *sent for*[2] the *Grand Vizier*.[3] "Giafar," he said, "do not be surprised tomorrow when you come to *audience*,[4] to see this man seated in my throne in the royal robes. **Pay** him the same respect that you would show to me. Do exactly as he bids you, even if his freedom in spending money should empty all my *coffers*.[5] Bid all the officers of the palace to *conduct*[6] themselves as if I were on the throne, and to carry on the whole matter so that nothing shall *spoil*[7] the pleasure I promise myself. Above all, fail not to awaken me before Abou Hassan; I wish to be present when he awakes."

II

Early in the morning the Caliph hid himself in a little raised *closet*[8] in the room where the *sleeper*[9] lay. All the officers of the court entered and took their usual places about the Caliph's bed. Just at daybreak, when it was time to make ready for the morning *prayer*[10] before sunrise, Abou Hassan was awakened by an officer who put a *sponge*[11] *steeped*[12] in *vinegar*[13] to his nose. His opening eyes saw the rich furnishing of a large room, vases of gold and silver, a silk *tapestry*[14] on the floor, a bed covering of cloth of gold *embossed*[15] with pearls and diamonds. Near

---

【註】 1. 御床. 2. 召見. 3. 首相. 4. 上朝. 5. 金庫. 6. 管理. 7. 敗壞. 8. 壁櫥. 9. 睡者. 10. 祈禱. 11. 海綿. 12. 浸漬. 13. 醋. 14. 花氈. 15. 製浮花於⋯⋯上.

安放在他的榻上。這事就立刻辦好。

　　凱立夫在宮裏，召了宰相。說道：『加佛！明天你朝見的時候，瞧這人穿了皇服，坐在我的寶座上，切不要驚訝。對他表示敬意，和對我一樣。他的命令，就是我的命令，必須遵照辦理，卽是耗盡我的庫幣都可以。你叮囑百官，須依照儀式進見，萬勿違誤，敗了我興趣。最緊要的，阿保哈生醒前，勿要忘記喚我；他醒的時候，我要瞧他呢。』

二

　　清早的時候，凱立夫躱在睡者臥房裏，一張小小的高壁橱裏。百官照例入宮，到凱立夫的榻前請安。在日出前要預備祈禱的時候了，一個宦官用浸透酵的海綿，送到睡者的鼻下，阿保哈生給驚醒了。他張開眼睛一望，見自己睡在一間廣大的屋子裏，這屋子鋪陳的富麗，眞是難以形容：有金銀做的花瓶兒，有絲織的地毯，牀被面是用金線織成的布帛，卻用珍珠，鑽石，作成繡花，靠近榻的一個

the bed on a *cushion*[1] were clothes of *tissue*[2] embroidered with pearls, and a caliph's *turban*.[3] Many slaves richly dressed were standing with *modesty*[4] and respect.

At the sight of this splendor, Abou Hassan was filled with amazement. But he told himself he was only dreaming about the wish he had made the night before. Yet this could hardly be, for the Grand Vizier, bowing to the ground, certainly said:—

' Commander of the Faithful, it is time for your majesty to rise to prayers; the morning begins to advance."

These words very much surprised Abou Hassan. *Clapping*[5] his hands before his eyes and lowering his head, he said to himself: "What means all this? Where am I? To whom does this palace belong? How is it possible for me to tell whether I am in my *right senses*[6] or in a dream?"

Lifting his head and opening his eyes, he saw the full morning sunshine, and there was Mesrour the chief of the officers, *prostrating*[7] himself before him, and saying:—

"Commander of the Faithful, your majesty will excuse me for saying that you used not to rise so late, and that the hour of prayer is over. It is time to *ascend*[8] your throne, and hold a council as usual; all the great officers of state await your presence in the council hall."

【註】 1. 坐褥. 2. 織物. 3. 頭巾 4. 謹慎. 5. 急置 6. 清醒. 7. 俯伏的. 8. 升上.

褥子上，放着一襲滿身鑲着珍珠的皇袍，和一頂凱立夫的頭巾。 地下站滿許多大臣， 都是朝服朝冠， 恭敬地侍立着。

瞧見這樣的華麗，阿保哈生充滿驚奇。他自想，莫非是昨夜心願的幻夢吧。不過他立刻覺得這不是幻夢，因爲他明見那宰相，打躬到地上，說道：

『至尊的教主，現在是陛下起身禱告的時候了；太陽就要出來啦。』

這話兒使阿保哈生更覺納罕。用手掩着自己的臉兒，俯下了頭，自言自語道：『這是怎麼一囘事？我在那兒呢？這是誰的宮院？我怎能知道是眞，或是夢呢？』

擡起頭睜開眼來，太陽已升得很高了。那個百官朝臣班首，麥西洛，又打躬奏道：

『教主，請恕臣直說，陛下素來起身，不是這麼遲的，如今早禱時候已過了。這是陛下升殿的時候了，朝臣都伺候在朝堂上，等着議事呢。』

By this time Abou Hassan was *persuaded*[1] that he was neither asleep nor in a dream. Looking earnestly at Mesrour, he said to him in a *serious tone*:[3] "Whom is it that you address as Commander of the Faithful? I do not know you, and you must mistake me for somebody else."

When Mesrour *assured*[4] him that he was Haroun all Raschid, he *burst out*[5] laughing, and fell backward on the *bolster*.[6] This pleased the Caliph so much that he would have laughed as loud himself, had he not feared to end the pleasant sport.

When Abou Hassan had tired himself with laughing, he called the nearest officer, and told him to *bite*[7] the end of his finger, that he might feel whether he was asleep or awake. The slave, knowing that the Cal ph was looking on, bit the finger so hard that Abou Hassan *snatched*[8] his hand quickly back again, saying:—

"I find I am awake; but by what *miracle*[9] am I become caliph in a night's time?"

No sooner had he risen from the bed and set his feet on the floor than he was greeted by the *salutations*[10] of all who were there: Commander of the Faithful, God give your majesty a good day." Then he was helped to dress, and was *escorted*[11] between rows of attendants to the council *chamber*,[12] no longer doubting that he was caliph, by whatever means the change had been wrought. Thus he was

---

【註】 1. 使信. 2. 莊嚴的. 3. 聲調. 4. 保證. 5. 不禁. 6. 枕. 7. 咬. 8. 縮. 9. 奇事. 10. 叩安. 11. 護送室.

這時候，阿保哈生自信，當不是睡着在夢中了。他仔細地看着麥西洛，用很莊嚴的聲調，說道：『你對誰稱教主？我並不認識你，你恐怕錯認着人吧。』

當麥西洛對他說他委實便是哈龍亞爾拉西德，這時候，他哈哈大笑，笑倒在枕上。這使凱立夫覺得十分有趣，倘他不怕撞破這玩意兒，他定要失聲大笑了。

阿保哈生自己笑倦的時候，他叫身邊一個官兒，教他咬他的指尖，看看到底是不是在夢裏。那官兒知道凱立夫親自看着，自不敢不服從，便用力一咬，阿保哈生縮手不及，說道：

『我的確是醒着，但這是怎樣的奇事，使我一夜變做凱立夫呢？』

他起了牀，把足才踏到地上，早有跟前的百官，上前叩安，口裏說道：『教主爺，萬歲，萬萬歲！』於是有人替他助穿皇服，有許多隨臣，擁護他進朝堂去，這時候，無論怎般不信，他卻是再不能疑惑自己不是凱立夫了。他端

seated upon the throne with all the *ceremonies*[1] of respect with which the true caliph was wont to be honored.

The Caliph himself in the meantime left the closet where he had been hiding, and went to another from which he could see all that happened in the council chamber. He could not but admire the *grace*[2] and *dignity*[3] with which Abou Hassan conducted himself in his *exalted staion,*[4] deciding promptly and wisely upon important matters.

While the Grand Vizier was making his report, Abou Hassan saw the *cadi,*[5] or judge of the police, whom he knew by sight, sitting in this place. "Stop," he said to the Grand Vizier; "I have an order of importance for the cadi."

The cadi came forward, and bowed to the ground. "Go at once," said Abou Hassan, "to such a *quarter,*[6] where you will find a *mosque;*[7] seize the imam and four old men, his friends, and give them each a hundred *strokes.*[8] After that, mount them all five, clothed in rags, on camels, with their faces to the tails, and lead them through the whole city, with a crier before them, who shall *proclaim*[9] with a loud voice: "This is the punishment of the those who *interfere*[10] in other people's affairs. Make them leave that quarter, and never set foot on it more." The cadi laid his hand upon his head, to show

---

【註】 1. 儀式. 2. 溫雅. 3. 威嚴. 4. 高位. 5. 下級法官. 6. 地方. 7. 囘教寺院. 8. 打. 9. 聲明. 10. 妨害.

坐在凱立夫的寶座上，受朝臣慶賀。

這時候，凱立夫也離開所躱着的高壁櫥，去躱在另一個高壁櫥裏，觀看那朝堂上的事情。他見阿保哈生端坐在他的殿上，決斷朝事，端的又敏捷，又伶俐，而且威儀和丰彩都好，祇有使他暗暗喝采。

當宰相報告的時候，阿保哈生一眼看見警長，這警長他原來認識的。他對宰相說：『且住，我還有重要的命令，遣警長上來。』

警長立時向前走上殿去，俯伏到地。阿保哈生說，『你去到某地方一所教院，那教院中一個主教，和他的四個羽黨，你捉了他們，各打他們一百下。打後，便把這五個人，各自綁好，掛在五匹駱駝的尾後，向街上遊行一遍，并用一個人，在駱駝面前，大聲呼着：「瞧，這是欺詐人民魚肉鄉鄰的奸賊所受的懲罰。」游過街後，即將他們，永遠

his obed e e· and, bowing again to the earth, retired,

Then addressing the Grand Vizier, Abou Hassan said: "Go to the *high treasure*[1] for a pause of a thousand pieces of gold, and carry it to the mother of one Abou Hassan; she lives in the same quarter to which I sent the judge of the police. Go, and return at once."

The Grand Vizier did as he was bid, and, followed by a slave bearing the money, searched out Abou Hassan's mother, to whom he said: "The Galiph makes you this *present*.[2]" The received it with the greatest surprise.

When the judge of the police and the Grand Vizier had returned and reported the *fulfilment*[3] of the commanders they had received, the business of the morning was brought to an end Abou Hassan made a sign to the officers that the council was over, and that they might all retire, which they did, bowing one by-one at the foot of the throne.

Abou Hassan was then conducted with much ceremony to a stately hall, where a table was set with gold plates and dishes, that *scented*[4] the air with the *spices*[5] and *amber*[6] with which the meats were seasoned. Seven young and beautiful ladies stood about to *fan*[7] him while he ate. *Charmed*[3] by their beauty, he paid them *witty*[9] *compliments*,[10] and

---

【註】 1. 財政大臣.　2. 禮物.　3. 成就.　4. 使香.　5. 香料.　6. 琥珀. .. 扇. 8. 迷惑. 9. 詼諧的. 10. 恭維.

逐出境。』警長舉手，表示服從，又復行禮，方始退出。

阿保哈生見警長出去，又對宰相說道：『你到庫房裏支一千金洋，裝做一袋，送給一個阿保哈生的母親去，她的住址，就是我恰命令警長去的那處所。速去速來。』

宰相奉命，令一個僕人負着錢袋跟着走。親自把這錢袋，交阿保哈生的母親，幷對她說道：『凱立夫贈送你這囘禮物。』她受了卻弄得莫名其妙。

當警長和宰相回來覆命，稱把差事辦完，這朝事乃畢。阿保哈生命朝臣散朝，衆朝臣聽說，又一個一個地到殿前致了敬禮，才退。

阿保哈生朝罷，於是又備極尊敬地，導入一間莊麗的廳子裏去，那兒桌子上都是金盤金碟，空氣中充滿着肉的香味，龍涎香的芬芳，和各種各樣的異香。當他進餐的時候，有七個絕色美女子替他打扇。他驚奇她們這般美麗，

said that he needed only one to fan him, and asked the other six to sit with him at the table and share his meal.

When the ladies perceived that he had done eating, they directed the slaves to bring water, and, rising from the table, one presented a gold *basin*,[1] another a gold *ewer*,[2] another a *towel*,[3] and, kneeling before him, they invited him to was his hands. He was then *escorted*[4] to another large hall, where there was a table, laid with several golden basins, holding *sweetmeats*[5] and the *choicest*[13] fruits; and seven other beautiful ladies were waiting to fan him. Finding it hard to decide to which of these ladies he should give the *preference*,[6] he asked them all to lay aside their fans, and sit down and eat with him. All this while the Caliph was watching him, more and more delighted that he had found a man who amused him so pleasantly.

When day began to close, Abou Hassan was conducted into still another hall, of greater *splendor*[7] than the others, brightly lighted and *superbly*[8] *furnished*.[9] Here *musicians*[10] were playing, and on a table by the wall, seven large silver *flagons*[11] were *set out*,[12] full of the choicest wines, and by them seven *crystal*[13] glasses of the finest *workmanship*.[14] In the other halls he had drunk nothing but water, according to the custom observed by all classes at

---

【註】 1. 水盆. 2. 水壺. 3. 毛巾. 4. 護送. 5. 糖果. 6. 最佳的. 7. 優待. 8. 華麗. 9. 華美地. 10. 陳設. 11. 樂師. 12. 壜. 13. 擺設. 14. 水晶. 15. 技巧.

便詼諧地給她們讚美了一遍，說只要一個來給他打扇，教餘下六個都同他在桌上共餐。

當這些女子們見他吃完了，她們指揮僕人取水，從桌子旁邊站起，一個托金盆兒，另一個托金鹽壺，又一個拿條手巾，都跪在他面前，請他洗手。有人扶他至另一大廳，那兒有一張桌子，放着七隻金碟兒，盛些甜餅和最鮮美的水果；另有七個美女侍候打扇。因爲這些女子都是一般姿色，一般秀麗，他簡直不能辨出誰好誰壞，他教她們一齊丟下扇子，陪他一同吃果兒。這一切那凱立夫都看得很仔細，見一個人這般有趣，使他愈看愈快活起來了。

將近黃昏時候，阿保哈生被人引到另一大廳裏，滿屋的燈光和華麗的設備，比前幾處，更加富麗堂皇。這兒有音樂嘹亮地奏着，靠壁的一張桌上，排列着七個大銀罐，盛滿最醇的美酒，旁邊放着七隻雕琢異工的水晶杯。原來在巴革達德有一個風俗，上至凱立夫，下至庶民，無論任

Bagdad, from the lowest to the highest, at the Caliph's court, never to drink wine till the evening.

Here, as in the other halls, he made *gallant* speeches to the beautiful ladies who were appointed to fan him, asking all their names, and drinking the health of each in turn. When this was done, one of them came forward with a glass of wine, into which she had secretly put a *pinch*[2] of the same powder which the Caliph had used the night before, and presented it to Abou Hassan, saying:—

"Commander of the Faithful, I beg your majesty to take this glass of wine, and before you drink it do me the favor to hear a song which I have *composed*[3] today. I *flatter*[4] myself it will not displease you."

When she had finished singing, he drank off the glass, but before he could give her the praises which he thought she *merited*,[5] his head dropped on the *cushions*,[6] and he slept as *profoundly*[7] as on the night before, when the Caliph had given him the powder. One of the ladies stood ready to catch the glass, which fell out of his hand; and then the Caliph, who had seen everything, came into the hall, in great joy at the success of his plan. He ordered Abou Hassan to be dressed in his own clothes, and carried back to his house, and to be put in his usual bed.

【註】 1. 獻媚的. 2. 一些. 3. 著作. 4. 自信. 5. 應得. 6. 椅子坐墊. 7. 酣熟的.

阿階級，白天祇准喝水，到晚上才能喝酒，所以阿保哈生，這一天在別些廳裏，喝的都是些白水。

這兒，他也像在別的廳子裏的時候一樣，對這些給他打扇的美女子們，說了一遍獻媚的話兒，一個個的問了她們的名字，給她們祝福，這時有一個女子走上前來，盛滿了一杯酒，她暗暗地把凱立夫昨夜用的蒙藥，滴一點在杯裏，敬給阿保哈生道：

『我請求陛下喝此一杯美酒，在陛下喝酒前，請聽我今天新譜的一隻曲兒如何？我並不自誇，這曲兒還不至使陛下污耳呢。』

當她唱着曲兒時，他舉杯一飲而盡，但不曾等到他說讚美她的話時，已是倒頭睡熟在椅上了，和昨夜凱立夫給他迷藥時一般的熟睡着。這時有一個女子，預備接他手中墜落的那隻杯子，那凱立夫原在旁看着他的，這時候，便走進宮裏來，見他的計策成功，十分快樂。他命把阿保哈生衣服換了，仍舊穿着他自己的衣服，送回到他的屋子裏去，放在他常睡的一張坑上。

III

Abou Hassan slept very late the next morning. When he awoke he could not believe that he was in his own room. He called aloud to the ladies of the palace by their names: "*Cluster*[1] of Pearls, Morning Star, *Coral*[2] Lips, where are you? Come *hither*."[3]

His mother heard him, and, running to his room, said: "What *ails*[4] you, my son? What has happened to you?"

He lifted his head and said *haughtily*[5]: "Good woman, who is it you call your son? I am not your son. I am the Commander of the Faithful, and you shall never persuade me to the contrary."

When she told him of the punishment that had fallen upon the imam and his friends, and of the present which the Caliph had sent to her, he was still more *convinced*[6] that he was the Caliph, for had he not ordered these things himself? She continued to tell him that he was not the Caliph, but her own son, Abou Hassan. At length this made him *furiously*[7] angry, and, rising from his bed, he began to beat her with a *cane*.[8]

The neighbors, hearing her cries for help, soon ran in, and, persuaded that he was *mad*,[9] seized him and bound him hand and *foot*,[10] and conducted him to a hospital for mad folk, where he was *lodged*[11] in a grated cell, and beaten every day with fifty strokes

【註】 1. 一球. 2. 珊瑚. 3. 至此處. 4. 苦惱. 5. 傲然地. 6. 使信.
7. 狂暴地. 8. 杖. 9. 瘋的. 10. 人. 11. 關鎖. 12. 密室.

三

第二天早上阿保哈生醒得很遲。當他睡醒的時候，再也不信他是在自己的屋子裏了。他大聲呼着那些宮女的名字：『眞珠呀，晨星呀，珊瑚唇呀，你們在那兒？快來。』

他母親聽他呼喊，奔到他的房間裏，說道：『你有什麼痛苦，我兒？你遇着怎麼一囘事呢？』

他擡起頭來，高傲地說道：『好女人，你是誰，呼你的兒子嗎？我不是你兒子。我乃是教主，你永不能教我不做教主了。』

當她告訴他，那教士和他的朋友們，都受着罰，她卻接到凱立夫給她的賞金，這時候，他更深信自己是凱立夫了，因爲這兩事不是他命令的嗎？她又告訴他，他並不是凱立夫，乃是他的兒子阿保哈生。這個終使他十分狂怒，他從牀上跳起，用手杖去打她。

鄰人們聽見她呼救的聲音，都跑了進來，相信他發瘋了，於是將他捉着，綑着手足，送到一所瘋人院，那兒他被關鎖在有鐵柵的牢房裏，每天在肩膀上鞭打五十下。天

across the shoulders. Each time he was advised to remember that he was not the Commander of the Faithful. '

His good mother visited him every day, and wept over his *hardships*.[1] It was not long before there practical *proofs*[2] that he was not the caliph had their effect. He admitted that he had been *deceived*[3] in some way that he could not understand. His mother was filled with joy at what she thought was the restoring of his mind, and told him her fears that the stranger whom he had brought home on the evening before his illness had been the cause of all the trouble.

"Give thanks to God, my son, for your *deliverance*,"[4] she said, "and pray that you may never fall again under the *spell*[5] of *magic*."[6]

Abou Hassan was at once *released*[7] and went home with his mother. He soon recovered his strength, and returned to his old habit of going to the Bagdad bridge, to invite a stranger to *sup*[8] with him. On the very first day, he had not been long at the bridge when he saw the Moussul merchan' coming toward him, followed by the same slave as before. He *shuddered*[9] at the sight, and with prayer, "God preserve me! *resolved*[10] to let the merchant pass as if unseen.

But the Caliph, who had *informed*[11] himself of what he happened to Abou Hassan, stopped, looked

---

【註】 1. 酷遇. 2. 證據. 3. 欺騙. 4. 援救. 5. 魅力. 6. 魔法. 7. 釋放. 8. 喝. 9. 懼怕. 10. 決意. 11. 告知.

天教他記牢，他不是教主。

　　他的慈愛的母親，天天去探望他，爲着他受苦和執迷
不悟哭泣着。不久他見這許多事實在眼前，證明他不是凱
立夫。他於是省悟，承認自己受着蠱迷，這原因連他自己也
不知道。他母親見他清醒了，非常歡喜，告訴他，她疑惑
在他病前那晚上，帶進來的生客，乃是這一切亂子的緣
因。

　　她說：『我兒，你須感謝上帝，使你得救，求他，使
你永不再墜入這個魔圈裏。』

　　阿保哈生立被釋放了，同母親回家。他很快的就恢復
了健康，依舊照他老例，每天到巴革達德橋塊，去邀請一
個生客同他晚餐。在第一天，他立在橋上不久的時候，便
瞧見那孟索爾商人徐徐走來，後邊跟着，仍是那個僕人。
他喫了一驚，祈禱說，『上帝保佑我！』他決定假裝沒有看
見的樣子，讓那商人過去。

　　但是凱立夫，這時候，他早就知道阿保哈生的事情了，

him in the face, and said: "Ho, brother Abou Hassan, I greet you! Give me leave to *embrace* you."

"Not I," replied Abou Hassan, "I do not greet you; I will have neither your greeting nor your embrace. Go about your business."

The Caliph was not to be put off by his *rude*[2] *behavior*;[3] and Abou Hassan, in spite of his law against supping twice with the same stranger, yielded at length to the Caliph's *caresses*,[4] and invited him to his house."

"You came," said Abou Hassan, "on one condition, that you neither make nor express any good wishes for me. All the *mischief*[5] that has happened to me came from that."

The Caliph agreed, and they went to the house of Abou Hassan, where the supper was served, the table cleared, and the wine and fruit put upon it by his mother. The ·talk turned upon the lonely life of Abou Hassan, and the Caliph expressed surprise that he was *content*[6] to live without a wife.

"I *warrant*[7] I can find you just the wife you need," said the Caliph; and taking Abou Hassan's glass he dropped a pinch of his sleeping powder into it as he filled it with wine, and handed it back, saying: "Come, let us drink to the fair lady's health."

Abou Hassan laughed as he took the glass. "Be it so, if you wish," he said; and again in a moment

---

【註】 1. 擁抱. 2. 無禮的. 3. 行為. 4. 熱誠. 5. 禍根. 6. 滿足. 7. 保證.

站定，瞧了瞧他的臉兒，說道：『噲，阿保哈生老哥，別來無恙！讓我吻抱你罷！』

阿保哈生說，『我不，我不願意問候你好；也不要你同好或吻抱，做你的生意去罷。』

那凱立夫對於他這粗暴的行爲，一點也不動怒；阿保哈生，雖然他立的約言是不肯請同一生客喫兩次晚餐的，終於凱立夫的熱誠，只好破例請他到家裏去了。

阿保哈生說：『你來不過有一條件，請再不要對我浅示你的好意。我所遭遇的一切不幸，都從這上面來的。』

凱立夫應允了，他們到阿保哈生的屋子裏去，那兒夜餐都已齊備，抹淨了桌子，酒和水菓是他母親親自擺上的。他們話題忽轉到阿保哈生的孤寂的生活上，凱立夫當時曙暗納罕，爲什麼他願意過這種獨身生活呢。

凱立夫說：『我保證我能夠爲你覓得一個如意夫人，』一壁便取了阿保哈生的杯子，盛滿了酒，放一點迷藥在杯子裏，擎囘來，說道：『來，讓我們喝這一杯，預祝你的美人兒健康。』

阿保哈生接着杯子大笑道：『但願如此！』一忽兒他額

he lay in a deep sleep, and was carried as before to the Caliph's palace.

IV

When they arrived at the palace, the Caliph ordered Abou Hassan to be put in the *very*[1] hall whence he had been carried home fast asleep a month before. He ordered all the officers, ladies, and musicians who were in the hall when he drank the last glass of wine to be there by *daybreak*,[2] and to act their parts well when he should awake. He himself must be *summoned*[3] in time, he told his chief attendant, to hide in the closet as before.

In the morning the effects of the powder wore off, and Abou Hassán began to awake. At that instant the musicians began an agreeable *concert*.[4] When the sleeper opened his eyes, he found himself in the gorgeous chamber of his first dream, and surrounded by the same persons. Here was a second wonder.

When the concert ceased and all the officers of the chamber stood in profound silence, Abou Hassan bit his finger, and cried out so loud that the Caliph could hear him.

"*Alas*,[5] I am fallen into the same dream as before, and must expect again the beatings and the cell at the *madhouse*.[6] He was a *wicked*[7] man that I

【註】 1. 同一的. 2. 黎明. 3. 召喚. 4. 合奏. 5. 啊呀. 6. 瘋人院. 7. 邪惡的.

然睡着，被帶進到皇宮裏去。

四

當他們到宮裏的時候，凱立夫命把阿保哈生，安放在他一個月前睡的那個廳子裏，給他睡下。他令他以前喝酒的，那廳裏的一切宦官，宮女，和樂隊都傳來，當他醒的時候，當心去服侍着他。他和以前一樣的躱在那高璧櫥中。

早上藥力過了，阿保哈生醒來。那時樂隊奏着一種動人的音調。他張開眼來一看，發見自己卻在初次夢裏來的那座華麗的宮裏，旁邊圍着，盡是頭一次所服侍他的人們，他又是吃了一驚。

當樂隊住了，宮室裏的執事人等，都屏絕無聲地站立着，阿保哈生咬着他手指，大聲呼叫起來，便是凱立夫也能聽到。

『唉，我墜入先前同樣的夢裏來了，定然又免不掉要進第二次的瘋人院和鞭打了。我昨夜帶進來的那人，原是

took home with me last night. He has done all this. Great God, I *commit*[1] myself into Thy hands; save me from the *temptation*[2] of *Satan*."[3]

Now he tried to go to sleep again, and to regard all he saw as a dream; but one officer took him by one arm, and a second by the other, and lifted him up, and carried him into the middle of the hall, where they seated him, and, all taking hands, danced and *slipped*[4] around him while the music sounded loudly in his ears.

Abou J'assan commanded silence, and in great doubt asked if he were indeed the caliph. When they told him he had never been out of the hall since the time he fell asleep in it, he *bared*[5] his shoulders, and bade the ladies look at the *livid*[6] marks of the strokes he had received.

"If I received these strokes in my sleep in this hall," he said, "it is the strangest thing in the world."

Then he called to an officer who stood near: "Come hither, and bite the *tip*[7] of my ear, that I may know whether I am asleep or awake."

The officer obeyed, and bit so hard that Abou Hassan cried aloud with the pain. At the same time the music struck up, and the officers and ladies all began to sing, dance and skip about him, and made such a noise that he was the more sure they were making him the subject of a *joke*.[8] Joining in the

---

【註】 1. 付託. 2. 誘惑. 3. 是魔鬼的王的名字, 他專門誘惑好人, 使他們背叛上帝. 4. 跳躍. 5. 露. 6. 青黑色的. 7. 尖頂. 8. 笑柄.

個惡人啊。這一切都是他幹的。偉大的上帝，我投在你的手裏：把我從這撒旦的誘惑中救出來罷。』

他要想再睡，視這一切作爲幻夢；但一個宮人走上扶了他一邊，另一個宮人又扶了他別一邊，把他扶立起來，攙他到廳中，叫他坐下，衆人就手攜着手，在他四周舞蹈，音樂又復奏着。

阿保哈生命她們靜下，心裏就大大的懷疑着，他不是眞的凱立夫嗎？她們告訴他，他自上次睡了以後，從沒有出過這宮門。他便露出他肩膀來叫這些女子前來，瞧看他的創痕。

他說：『要如我睡在這廳子裏，夢中受了這些鞭打，倒是世上最駭異的事情了。』

他喚靠近的一個人來，說道：『來，咬我的耳根，讓我知道，是眞的醒着呢？還是在做夢？』

那宦官從命，用力的咬了一下，阿保哈生果然大聲呼痛。同時，音樂大奏，衆宮女們又開始圍着她，唱歌，舞蹈，擾鬧的聲音，使他更信她們是把他開着玩笑。爲助興

spirit of it, he threw off his caliph's *habit*[1] and his *turban*,[2] jumped up in his *undergarments*[3] and danced with the rest, cutting such *capers*[4] that the Caliph could not contain himself, but burst into *violent laughter*,[5] and, putting his head into the room, cried: "Abou Hassan, Abou Hassan, have you a mind to kill me with laughing?"

As soon as the Caliph's voice was heard, everybody was silent, and Abou Hassan, turning to see whence it came, recognized the Moussul merchant, and knew him to be the Caliph. He was not in the least *daunted*,[6] but, seeing at once what had happened to him, entered into the Caliph's *humor*.[5]

"Ha! ha!" said Abou Hassan, looking into his face, "you pretend to be a merchant of Moussul, and *complain*[8] that I would kill you. You have made me beat my mother, and lose my senses, and have been the cause of all my troubles. I beg of you to tell me how you have done it; I would know, that I may get my senses back."

"You will remember," said the Caliph, "that when we first met, you said that your one wish was to be caliph for *four-and-twenty*[9] hours. I saw in this wish a *fruitful*[10] source of pleasure to me and my court, and I let you carry it out. By means of a strong sleeping powder which I put, without your knowledge, into the last glass of wine, I had you brought to my palace. You know the rest. I am

---

【註】 1. 衣服. 2. 頭巾. 3. 內衣. 4. 跳. 5. 狂笑. 6. 恐驚. 7. 脾氣. 8. 埋怨. 9. 二十四. 10. 豐富的.

起見，他脫下凱立夫衣服和頭巾，穿着內衣，便和她們一同跳舞起來，手舞足蹈，笑態百出，使凱立夫也忍不住，只得大聲狂笑了；探出頭來，呼道：『阿保哈生，阿保哈生，你難道要笑死我嗎？』

　　一聽到凱立夫的聲音，衆人都靜寂了，阿保哈生向發聲的地方望去，認出是那馬沙商人，乃知道他原來是凱立夫。他並無一點恐怖，但立卽看出是怎麼一囘事了，便順着凱立夫的意思，說道：

　　『哈！哈！』阿保哈生看了他一眼，說道：『你假裝是一個馬沙商人，還來埋怨我使你笑死。你曾使我打我母親，神智昏迷，造成我一切的亂子。我求你告訴我，你怎樣幹着的；我知道了，也敎我清醒一下。』

　　凱立夫說：『你當記得，在我們初次會面的時候，你說你有一種心願，要做二十四小時的凱立失。我見到你這心願，對我和我的朝廷，都是很好的玩意兒，我便讓你實現了。因要不讓你知道，我放下一種強性的迷藥，在你最後的一杯酒裏，後來把你迷倒帶進宮來。其餘部分，你是

sorry for the suffering that followed, and will do all I can to make *amends*.[1] *Thou art*[2] my brother; ask what thou *wilt*[3] and thou *shalt*[4] have it."

"Commander of the Faithful," replied Abou Hassan, "my *tortures*[5] are all forgotten, since my *sovereign*[6] lord and master had a share in them. The only *boon*[7] I would beg is that I may have access to your person, and enjoy, through my lifetime, the admiration of your *virtues*."[8]

The Caliph ordered a rich robe to be brought, gave Abou Hassan an office in the palace, with access at all times to his person, and directed the treasurer to give him a purse of a thousand pieces of gold. Abou Hassan bowed to the ground, and departed to tell his mother of his *good fortune*,[9] and how he had really been caliph, for the Caliph himself had told him so.

V

Admitted[10] thus to the court, and to the favor not only of the Caliph, but also of his Queen, Abou Hassan was soon married to her *favorite*[11] slave. No two persons could have been better suited to one another. It would have been better, indeed, if they had not been so much alike *in one respect*.[12] They *vied*[13] with each other in giving costly *entertainments*[14]

【註】 1. 報價. 2. you are. 3. will. 4. shall. 5. 苦痛. 6. 最高的. 7. 恩賜. 8. 懿德. 9. 好運. 10. 准許出入. 11. 寵愛的. 12. 在一方面. 13. 競爭. 14. 應酬.

知道的了。我很抱歉你後來受着痛苦，我願意盡我所能的來報償你。你好像是我的兄弟；隨你需要什麼，都可以。』

阿保哈生答說：『教主！我的痛苦都忘掉了，因爲這是我最高的皇上，幹這一部份的哩。我所求惟一的恩德，但願常能接近陛下，在我終生。隨時能夠讚仰你的懿德。』

凱立夫便命人取了一件華服來，贈賜阿保哈生一個官職，隨時得能接近他個人，又命司庫撥一千金洋給他。阿保哈生俯伏謝恩，辭別出來告訴他母親遇到這樣的好運，和怎樣他自己眞已做過凱立夫，因爲這是凱立夫親自告訴他。

五

這樣在宮中出入着，他不但得邀凱立夫的厚寵，且獲得皇后的歡心，不久他和皇后的一個寵婢結婚。他配那寵婢，是再也沒有更好的了。他們倆在性情上，是那樣酷肖的。眞的，若是他們倆不比賽着，把好東西來交結朋友們，

to their friends, and at the end of a single year had spent everything that was given them by the Caliph and Queen, besides the *portion*[1] of Abou Hassan's own fortune which he had saved. Being in great *straits,*[2] they took *counsel*[3] together, and Abou Hassan proposed[4] a pleasant *trick*[5] to be played upon the Caliph and his Queen.

"I will *feign*[6] myself to be dead," he said to his wife; "you shall lay me in the middle of my chamber with my feet towards *Mecca,*[7] as if I were ready for burial. Then you must weep and tear your hair and clothes, and go in all your tears to the Queen. When she is told the cause of your grief, she will give you money for my funeral, and a piece of gold *brocade*[8] in the place of the piece you will have torn. When you return to me, I will rise, lay you in my place, and act the same part with the Caliph, who will be as *generous*[9] as his Queen."

This they proceeded at once to do, with exactly the result that Abou Hassan had *predicted.*[10] Both the Queen and the Caliph were *distressed*[11] in turn to hear of the death of the *witty*[12] Abou Hassan and the favorite slave, and each made a generous gift to the pretended *survivor.*[13]

The Caliph, as soon as Abou Hassan had left him, *hastened*[14] to the Queen to *comfort*[15] her for

---

【註】 1. 部份. 2. 困窮. 3. 商議. 4. 提出. 5. 玩意兒. 6. 假裝. 7. 麥加——回教人的聖地，人死了足向麥加以示靈歸聖地之意. 8. 錦緞. 9. 慷慨的. 10. 預料. 11. 悲歎. 12. 詼諧的. 13. 生存者. 14. 趕急. 15. 安慰.

是很富有了。到一年終了的時候，除阿保哈生自己積存的一部份財產外，凱立夫和皇后賜給他們的東西，都一併化掉。在大大的窘迫中，夫婦倆共同商議着，阿保哈生乃提議一種快活的玩意兒，來戲弄凱立夫和皇后一番。

他對他妻子說：『我裝做假死，你把我放在室中，臉向着米加，好像我將預備埋葬的樣子。你哭着，撕亂你的頭髮和衣裳，哭到皇后那兒去。當她聽見你訴說因由和悲傷時，定會賞給你治喪費，一整匹的黃金布，作補償你所撕壞的衣服。當你回來的當兒，我可站起，把你放在我的地位上，去給凱立夫報告這同樣的情形，他定然也像皇后那麼慷慨的。』

他們議定，即刻便行，結果，果然不出阿保哈生所料。皇后和凱立夫先後聽得，那詼諧的阿保哈生和那寵婢的死耗，都很為歎悼，各贈一份豐富的禮金。

凱立夫等到阿保哈生出去了，便慌忙地到皇后那裏去

the loss of her favorite. He found her weeping, and said:—

"Madam, I grieve with you in the loss of your faithful slave."

"It is not she who is dead," replied the Queen, "but Abou Hassan, her husband."

"Madam," he answered, "you are *deceived*.[1] I have just seen him in perfect health."

"*Nay*,[2] but I have just seen her, weeping for his death."

Neither could believe the other, and at length the Caliph, in anger, bade the Vizier go and see if it were not Abou Hassan's wife who had died, and not he.

"I will *stake*[3] my garden of pleasures against your palace of the *paintings*[4] that I am right," said the Caliph.

"I accept the *wager*,[5]" said his Queen, "and will stand by it."

Meanwhile Abou Hassan, who knew that this question must arise, saw the Vizier coming towards his house, *guessed*[6] his *errand*,[7] and bade his wife make haste to act her part. He had *larely*[8] time to *wrap*[9] her up, and lay upon her the piece of brocade the Caliph had given him, when the Vizier entered.

When he returned and told the Caliph and his Queen what he had seen, she exclaimed:—

【註】 1. 欺騙. 2. No. 3. 賭. 4. 畫. 5. 賭. 6. 猜測. 7. 使命. 8. 恰好地. 9. 裹.

安慰她喪了寵婢。他見她正在哭泣，便道：

『皇后，我也爲你喪掉賢婢，很覺得悲哀。』

皇后說：『死的並非我的婢女，是她丈夫呵保哈生啊。』

他說：『后啊！你可受騙了。我方才看見他，是十分康健的。』

『不，我也方才見那婢女，爲丈夫死了，傷心地哭泣着哩。』

兩人都不相信。那凱立夫終於發怒了，遂命宰相去查，到底是阿保哈生妻子死，或是他自己死。

凱立夫說：『我可用我行樂的花園，同你宮裏的古畫，來賭着東道。』

皇后說：『我接受這個賭法，請大家不要反悔！』

話說阿保哈生早就知道，定會引起疑問的，當他看見那宰相走來，就料到他的使命，吩咐妻子趕快裝着死的樣子。他才手忙腳亂地，把她裹好，按放在凱立夫賞給他的金布裏，這時候，那宰相已進來了。

當他囘去，把所見的告訴給凱立夫和他的皇后時，她大聲說道：

"I am not blind[1] or mad. I know that it is Abou Hassan who has died. My *nurse*[2] in whom I have complete trust, shall go and see."

Watching from his window, Abou Hassan saw the nurse *hobbling*[3] as fast as she could towards his house. He called to his wife, who quickly wrapped him up, and, beating her breast, seated herself by his head. Thus the nurse found them, and hastened back to tell what she had seen.

"It is a strange series of *marvels*,"[4] said the Caliph, "and no one can be believed. Let us go ourselves, and learn the truth of the matter."

When Abou Hassan's wife saw them both coming, she cried out: "What shall we do! We are *ruined*."[5]

"*Not at all*,[6]" replied her husband. "At the rate they are walking, we shall be ready before they reach the door."

Then he and his wife laid themselves down side by side, in the middle of the chamber, as if dead, and covered themselves as well as they could, and waited till the Caliph and his Queen should come.

"*Alas*,"[7] said she, when they had opened the door, and looked in silence for some time at the sad sight, "it is true that my dear slave is dead, through grief, no doubt, at having lost her husband."

"Allow rather, madam," said the Caliph, "that

【註】 1. 瞎眼的. 2. 乳母. 3. 蹒跚而行. 4. 奇事. 5. 壞了. 6. 絕不. 7. 啊呀.

『我眼旣不瞎，又不癡。我知死的確是阿保哈生。我的乳母，你走去看一看眞實。』

話說阿保哈生從窗口瞧去，望見乳母蹣跚地走來。他便喚妻子，快把他裹了起來，坐在他頭邊，裝做搥胸撕髮的樣子。那乳母看見這種情形，急忙趕回去，把所見的報告，

凱立夫說：『這眞是異事，沒有誰相信的。讓我們自己去瞧，到底是怎麼一囘事情。』

阿保哈生妻子瞧見凱立夫夫婦一齊都來，驚惶得叫了起來：『我們怎麼辦好！我們可眞壞事了。』

丈夫說：『不要怕，隨他們奔得多快，我們可還趕得及呢。』

他和他妻子雙雙地躺了下去，在屋的中心，裝做死的樣子，自己拉金布罩裹着，以待凱立夫和皇后到來。

當他們打開了門，瞧見這種慘象，靜默了好一會兒，她說着，『啊！果眞我親愛的婢女死了，無疑，她爲悲悼她丈夫而死了罷！』

凱立夫說：『據我看，是她先死的，阿保哈生見她死

she died first, and that Abou Hassan could not live when she was dead."

"No," said the Queen, *unwilling*[1] to *yield*,[2] "Abou Hassan died first, because my nurse saw his wife alive, weeping for her husband's death."

The Caliph was *vexed*[3] that the truth was not yet clear, and tried to think of some plan that should *decide the wager in his favor*.[4]

"I will give," cried he, "a thousand pieces to the person who shall tell me which of the two died first."

He had scarcely spoken these words, when he heard a voice, under the brocade that covered Abou Hassan, say:——

"Commander of the Faithful, I died first; give me the thousand pieces of gold." At the same time Abou Hassan sprang up and threw himself at the Caliph's feet; and his wife in the same *manner*[5] ran to the Queen, who, after a moment of *fright*,[6] gave way to joy that her dear slave was still alive.

"So then, Abou Hassan," said the Caliph, laughing, "how came it into your head thus to *befool*[7] us both?"

Abou Hassan said, "I will tell you the whole truth," and *confessed*[8] for himself and his wife their folly and the debts it had caused, and humbly asked forgiveness for the trick they had practiced, if indeed

【註】 1. 不願的. 2. 屈意. 3. 煩惱. 4. 贏得他的東道. 5. 樣子. 6. 恐佈. 7. 愚弄. 8. 供認.

了，乃不能活着。』

皇后不服說：『不，確是阿保哈生先死啦，因爲我乳母還瞧見她妻子活着，痛哭她丈夫呢。』

這件事情弄不明白，凱立夫覺得煩惱，他想用計解決，贏得他的東道。

他大聲說：『我願出一千金賞格，徵求人告訴我，這兩個人究竟是誰先死。』

他把這話兒還沒說完口，這時候，便聽得蓋着阿保哈生的金布底下，有一種聲音說道：

『教主，是我先死啦，請給我一千金洋罷。』 同時候阿保哈生一躍起牀，跪在凱立夫的面前；他妻子也同樣地跪在皇后的面前。那皇后初時一怔，已而見她寵愛的婢女還是活着，又不禁大喜。

凱立夫笑着說：『原來是弄這一套玩意兒呀！怎地你想到愚弄我倆起來呢？』

阿保哈生說：『我照實告訴吧。』他便承認自己和妻子的愚笨，因迫於債務而想起這件玩耍，於是卑謙地求恕，

it had offended their highnesses who were so fond of pleasant jokes.

"Follow me," said the Caliph, "and I will give you the thousand pieces of gold that I promised you, for the joy I feel that you are both alive."

The Queen would not be *outdone*,[1] and gave another thousand pieces of gold to Abou Hassan's wife. Thus did they both *obtain*[2] favor, and *gain*[3] enough to supply all their wants.

【註】 1. 勝過. 2. 獲得. 3. 得利.

因爲皇上和皇后都這般地愛着玩笑，或許不至褻瀆尊嚴罷。

凱立夫說：『跟我來，我給你我所允許的一千塊賞金，爲我歡賀你們活着的禮物。』

那皇后也不肯示弱，賞了一千金給阿保哈生的妻子。他們倆這般得帝后的寵幸，所得賞賜，常足供他們的需用。

10. The Story Of The Three Sisters.

I

There was an Emperor of Persia who often walked in disguise through the city, attended by a trusty[1] minister, and meeting with many adventures. Once when he was passing through a street in which dwelt only humble folk,[2] he heard some people talking very loud within a certain house, and, looking in, saw three sisters sitting on a sofa.

"Since we have got upon wishes," said the eldest, "mine shall be to have the Sultan's baker[3] for my husband, for then I should eat my fill of that excellent bread called the Sultan's."

"For my part," said the second sister, " I wish I were wife to the Sultan's chief cook, for bread must be common in the palace, and I should eat of the choicest[4] dishes. You see that I have a better taste than you."

The youngest sister who was very beautiful and had more charms[5] and wit[6] than the others, spoke in her turn:

"For my part, since we are wishing, I wish to be the Emperor's queen consort,[7] and the mother of a lovely prince, whose hair shall be gold on one side of his head and silver on the other; when he cries, the tears from his eyes shall be pearl; and when he smiles,

---

【註】 1. 忠實的. 2. 人民. 3. 麵包師. 4. 最佳的. 5. 可愛. 6. 聰明. 7. 配偶者.

十　三　姊　妹　的　故　事

一

從前波斯有一個皇帝，他時常喜歡假扮着在城裏私訪，帶着一個忠實的臣子，遇到許多的奇事。有一次，他從一條街上走過，這條街住的都是貧民，他聽得有一家談話的聲音很響，向裏望去，見有三個姊妹坐在一張沙發上，閒談。

那大姐姐說：『我們何不談談各人的志願呢。我的志願，但願嫁給蘇丹的麵包師，因爲我可以盡量的享受那些做給蘇丹吃的最甜最香的麵包。』

二姐說：『我呢，我倒願嫁給蘇丹的廚師頭目。因爲麵包我想宮中一定到處很多，我該嘗嘗蘇丹最美味的菜，以飽口福。你瞧，我不是比你更會吃嗎？』

那最年幼的妹妹，卻長得十分美麗，比姊姊們更覺可愛，更見聰明，當下輪到了她，她說道：

『因爲我們談的不過是一種志願，依我的志願，我想做皇后，願做一個王子的母親，他的頭髮一半是金子的，另一半是銀子的；當他哭的時候，眼中拋的眼淚，點點都

307

his *vermilion*[1] lips shall look like a *rosebud*[2] fresh blown."

The Sultan resolved to *gratify*[3] these strange wishes, and bade his Vizier note the house, and bring him the three sisters on the next day. When they came before him, he asked them if they remembered the desires they expressed the night before. "Speak the truth," he said; "I must know what they were."

The sisters were so much *alashed*[4] that they could say nothing, and the Sultan told them that he knew their wishes.

"You," he said, "who wished to be my wife, shall have your desire this day; and you," he added, turning to the other two, "shall be married to my chief baker and cook."

The *nuptials*[5] all took place that day, the youngest sister's with all the *pomp*[6] that is usual at the marriages of the emperors of Persia, the others according to the rank of the Sultan's chief baker and head cook.

Though the older sisters had got their wishes, they were far from being content, and made many plans to *revenge*[7] themselves upon the Queen for having won a higher honor. Yet *outwardly*[8] they showed nothing but love and respect.

When the Queen gave birth to a young prince, as bright as the day, the child was given into the sisters' care; but they *wrapped*[9] it up in a basket,

---

【註】 1. 朱紅色的. 2. 玫瑰蕾. 3. 滿足. 4. 羞澀. 5. 婚禮. 6. 華麗. 7. 復仇. 8. 外表上. 9. 包裹.

成珍珠；當他笑的時候，他的紅唇如初放玫瑰一般的美麗。』

蘇丹決意想滿足她們這些奇願，便叮囑臣子記好這家人家，第二天須把這三姊妹，帶他進宮，當她們被帶到他跟前，他問她們，還記得昨天晚上所說的那些心願嗎？『照實說罷，我定要曉得牠們啦！』

三個姊妹都羞澀得一句話兒也沒有，蘇丹乃告訴她們，他所聽到的話。

他說：『你願做我妻子的，今天可了卻你心願了；』他又向另兩個說：『你們倆今天可嫁給我的總麵包師，和我的總廚師。』

三處婚禮都在那天一起舉行，那年幼的妹妹的婚儀，依照波斯皇帝的慣例，極盡人間的華麗，另兩個都照着麵包師和廚夫的等級舉行。

年長的兩姊妹，雖然達到她們的心願，卻遠不能滿足着，便施種種惡計，要想毒害皇后，因為她得了更高的榮幸。不過她們外表上，卻裝做非常敬愛她的樣子。

皇后不久誕生了一個王子，這孩子如太陽般的美麗，皇后卻交給兩個姐姐去當心看護；但是她們卻把這孩子，包

and floated it away on a canal that ran near the palace, and declared that the Queen had given birth to a little dog. This made the Emperor very angry.

In the meantime, the basket in which the little Prince was *exposed*[1] was carried by the stream towards the garden of the palace. By chance the keeper of the Emperor's gardens, one of the chief officers of the kingdom, was walking by the side of this canal, and, noticing the basket, called a gardener who was not far off, to pull it to shore with the *rake*[2] he had in his hand.

When this was done, the keeper of the gardens was greatly surprised to see in the basket a child, newly born, but with very fine *features*[3]. As he had no children of his own, he bore it with delight to his wife in their house at the entrance to the garden, and said:—

"God has sent us this child. Provide a nurse, and treat him as if he were our own son. From this moment, I hold him as such." The keeper's wife received the child with great joy.

The next year the Queen bore another prince, whom her sisters treated in the same cruel way, pretending this time that the child was a cat. Happily the same chance as before brought it into the hands of the keeper and his wife, both of whom received it with delight. The Emperor of Persia was even more *enraged*[4] than before, and would have made the Queen feel his anger, but for the *pleading*[5] of the Grand Vizier.

【註】 1. 遺棄. 2. 草耙. 3. 容貌. 4. 忿怒. 5. 諫阻.

繫好，放在一隻籃裏，丟在皇宮靠近的一條運河裏，由牠流去，口裏稱說皇后產生一隻小狗。皇帝聽到，十分惱怒。

這時候小王子坐着籃兒，給河流飄送到宮中的花園邊。恰巧有個園吏在河畔散步，他瞧見了籃兒，便喚附近的一個園丁，用他的草耙，把這籃兒撈起。

撈起的時候，園吏瞧見籃兒中，盛着一個新生的嬰孩，面貌很美，很是驚訝。因爲他自己正苦沒有孩子，便快活地把他帶到園門口自己的家裏，交給妻子道：

『上帝賜給我們這孩子，雇一個乳母，好生撫育他，尤如親生的一樣。我今後，便把他當做親生的孩子。』園吏的妻子更是歡天喜地，把這孩子接了過去。

第二年皇后又誕生了一個王子，她的姊姊們仍用同樣的殘暴手段，假稱這次產的是一隻小貓。這和先前一樣的機會，給帶到那園吏和他妻子手裏，他們倆又歡天喜地，把他撫養了。波斯皇帝這次更加忿怒，要想責罰皇后，後因宰相力諫才罷。

When a princess was born the next year, the two sisters exposed it to the same *fate*[1] as the Princes, her brothers, for they were *bent*[2] upon seeing the Queen cast off, turned out, and humbled. But the Princess, like her brothers, was saved by the keeper of the gardens.

The Emperor was told this time that his child was a *block*[3] of wood. He could no longer contain himself, but ordered a small *shed*[4] to be built near the chief *mosque*,[5] and the Queen to be *confined*[6] in it, subject to the scorn of those who passed by. This cruelty she bore with such *meekness*[7] that all who judged of things better than the *vulgar*[8] admired and pitied her.

II

In the meantime the keeper of the gardens and his wife brought up the Princes and the Princess as *tenderly*[9] as if they had been their own children. As they advanced in age, they all showed marks of superior *dignity*,[10] and a certain air which could belong only to *exalted*[11] birth. The keeper and his wife gave them names which had been borne by rulers of the kingdom,—to the eldest, Bahman, to the second, Perviz, and to the Princess, Perie-zadeh.

Both the Princes and the Princess were quick to learn all that their masters taught them, not only in books, but in exercises of the body, such as riding

---

【註】 1. 命運. 2. 決意. 3. 塊. 4. 小屋. 5. 教堂. 6. 囚禁. 7. 柔順. 8. 平民. 9. 慈愛地. 10. 威嚴. 11. 高貴的.

第三年皇后產的，乃是個公主，這公主的命運卻同兩個王子的命運一樣，因爲她們決心要瞧着皇后被廢，放逐出宮，成爲賤婦。但是這公主像她哥哥般地，又被園吏夫婦們救着。

皇帝這次聽她們告訴說。產的是塊木頭。他再也不能容忍了，乃命在大教堂邊，築一間草棚兒，把皇后關在裏邊，給過往行人們羞辱着。這個奇辱，她柔順地忍受着，使一切有識的人們，都敬重她，可憐她。

二

話說園吏和他妻子撫養王子和公主，看待得和親生子女一般。他們長大了，個個都氣宇非凡，不失皇家子女的風度。園吏和妻子用皇族中的名字，題給他們——最長的，叫巴門，次叫貝維，公主叫貝里若德。

這些王子和公主都受有高深的教育，於書籍之外，又注重身體的運動，如騎馬，射箭。那妹妹也並不肯示弱，常

and, bending the bow. The sister, unwilling to be outdone, often outdid her brothers in various *contests* of skill. The keeper of the gardens, delighted to find all the expense in the training of his adopted children so well repaid, resolved to do still more for them. He had been content with his *lodge*[2] at the entrance of the garden, but now *purchased*[3] a *country-seat*[4] near the city, furnished it in the richest manner, and stocked its park with deer, that the Princes and Princess might *divert*[5] themselves with hunting when they chose.

To this place, in view of his advancing years, the Emperor permitted him to retire. His wife had been dead for some time, and he himself had not lived in his new abode more than six months, when he was surprised by so sudden a death that he had not time to give the Princes Bahman and Perviz and the Princess Perie-zadeh the least account of the manner in which he had saved them from *destruction*.[6] They had known no other father, and *mourned*[7] him as such, with all the honor which love and *filial*[8] gratitude could prompt. Satisfied with the large fortune he had left them, they lived together in perfect *union*,[9] free from desire for greatness at court, or places of honor, which they might easily have had.

One day when the two Princes were hunting and the Princess had remained at home, an old *devout*[10] woman came to the gate at the hour for prayers, and

---

【註】 1. 比賽. 2. 宿所. 3. 購買. 4. 別墅. 5. 娛樂. 6. 滅亡.
7. 哀弔. 8. 孝順的. 9. 一致. 10. 虔敬的.

和他哥哥們作種種技術上的比賽。園吏見他的養子養女，對
於他一番心血，並非白化的，願意給他們再受更高深的教
育。他本來很滿足地住在園門口的，但現在卻於近城處，買
了一所別墅，裝璜得非常華麗，園子裏且養了一隻鹿，給
王子和公主們，用着行獵。

因爲園吏年老了，得邀皇帝允許，告老在這去處。他
妻子先時已死掉了，他自己住在這新屋裏，也不到六個月，
一天忽然這般快的死去，他甚至要想告訴打救王子巴門和
貝維，及公主貝里若德的情形，給他們知道，一點兒都求
不及說得，便死了。他們並不知道，尚有別的父親，喪禮
上竭盡他們的孝思。他遺給他們的財產很大，他們都很滿
足；兄妹三個一塊兒居住着，雖然他們很容易得到顯貴的地
位，但他們卻是不想。

有一天，兩個王子都出去打獵了，公主留在家中，恰
當祈禱的時候，有個老尼走來，要求進來借一處地方祈禱。

asked leave to go in and say hers. The Princess ordered the servants to show her into the *oratory*,[1] and when her prayers were done, the woman was brought before Perie-zadeh in a great hall, more beautiful and rich than any other part of the house. When they had talked a little while, the Princess asked her what she thought of the house, and how she liked it.

"Madam," answered the devout woman, "if I may speak my mind freely, it lacks but three things to make it complete and beyond compare. The first of these is the speaking-bird, so strange a creature that it *draws*[2] round it all the singing-birds near by, which come to accompany its song. The second is the singing-tree, the leaves of which are so many mouths, which form an *harmonious concert*[3] of different voices, and never cease. The third is the yellow-water, of a gold color, a single drop of which being poured into a vessel properly prepared, increases so as to fill it at once, and rises up in the middle like a fountain, which always plays, and yet the *bas n*[4] never *overflows*.[5]"

"Ah, my good mother," cried the Princess, "how much I thank you for the knowledge of these *marvels*,[6] of which I have never heard! Surely you know where they are to be found, and will do me the favor to tell me."

【註】 1. 禮堂. 2. 吸引. 3. 和諧的音調. 4. 盆. 5. 溢出. 6. 奇事.

公主命僕人引她到禮堂去，一忽兒，她祈禱完了，給帶到貝里若德的廳子裏，這廳是屋子裏最齊整和華麗的一間房間。她們略談幾句後，公主便問她這屋子如何，她歡喜不歡喜。

那尼姑說道：『姑娘，據我想來，如要這屋子華美無比尚缺三件東西，第一，是一隻會說話的鳥兒，這鳥兒能引攏一切會唱歌的鳥，伴着牠唱歌。第二，是一棵能唱歌的樹，這樹葉永遠不會凋謝，能作出各種和諧的音調。第三，是一種黃水，有黃金般的色彩，滴一點在盆裏，那水便會漲起像滿盆的樣子，中部且如泉水般的噴湧起來，但盆內的水是永不會溢出的。』

公主大聲說：『呵，我的好媽媽，這些奇物，倒虧你知道，我卻聽也不曾聽過！那末，你定然知道他們是在何處的了，請告訴我，當感激不盡。』

"Madam," replied the good woman, "I am glad to tell you that they are all to be met with in the same spot on the borders of the kingdom, towards India. The road lies before your house, and whoever you send needs but to follow it for twenty days, and on the twentieth let him ask the first person he meets where the speaking bird, the singing tree, and the yellow water are, and he will be *informed*."[1] After saying this, she departed.

When the Princes returned from hunting they found the Princess Perie-zadeh so silent and *pensive*[2] that they thought she must be ill. It was some time before she would answer their questions at all, and then she said:

"I always believed that this house, which our father built us, lacked nothing. But this day I have learned that it wants three *rarities*,[3]—the speaking bird, the singing tree, and the yellow water. If it had these no countryseat in the world could be compared with it." Then she told them what these things were, and asked her brothers to send some trusted person in search of them.

"Sister," replied Prince Bahman, "it is enough that you wish these rarities; I will go for them myself, and *set out*[4] to-morrow. You, brother, shall stay at home with our sister. I commend her to your care."

Prince Bahman began at once to prepare for the journey, and learned from his sister the directions

---

【註】　1. 告知.　2. 納悶.　3. 奇物.　4. 出發.

女尼答道：『姑娘！我很歡喜告訴給你，牠們都在向印度去的本國邊境一個地方。這路途由你屋子前，一直走去，你無論派遣什麼人去，只須走了二十日，在第二十日這一天所遇見的第一個人，問他會說話的鳥兒，唱歌的樹兒，和黃水在那兒，就可知道了。』說畢，告別而去。

王子們打獵回來，瞧見公主貝里若德這般沉靜，納悶，他們想她定然病了。她見問，有好一會沒有開口，已而說道：

『我常想，我們父親爲我們建造這座美麗屋子，什麼都完備無缺了。今天我才知道如要使這座別墅，在天下無比。倘缺三件異物——會說話的鳥兒，唱歌的樹兒，和黃水。』她就訴說一遍，這些是什麼東西，求哥哥們差一可信的人去搜尋牠們。

王子巴門答道：『妹妹！倘你定要這些異物；我當自己去取，明天動身。弟弟，你可和妹妹在家。我教她好好地服侍着你。』

王子巴門立時預備出發，照女尼所示的路徑，第二天

which the devout woman had left her. The next morning he mounted his horse, and Perviz and the Princess began *to bid him farewell.*[1]

"Brother," said the Princess, thinking for the first time of the *perils*[2] that might lie before him, "who knows whether I shall ever see you again! *Alight,*[3] I *beseech*[4] you, and give up this journey. I would rather never behold nor possess the speaking-bird, singing-tree, and yellow-water than run the risk of never seeing you more."

"Sister," replied Bahman, "my will is *fixed,*[5] and you must let me go. Yet, as I may fail, all I can do is to leave you this knife. If, when you pull it out of the *sheath,*[6] it is clean as it is now, it will be a sign that I am alive; but if you find it *stained*[7] with blood, then you may believe me to be dead."

Then he bade *adieu*[8] to her and Prince Perviz for the last time, and rode away.

III

When Prince Bahman got into the road, he never turned to the right hand nor to the left, but went directly forward towards India. The twentieth day he saw on the roadside a very singular old man, who sat under a tree near a *thatched*[9] house.

His *eyebrows*[10] and his beard, which grew over his mouth and reached down to his feet, were as white as

【註】 1. 告別. 2. 危險. 3. 下來. 4. 請求. 5. 打定. 6. 鞘. 7. 沾污. 8. 告別. 9. 茅草的. 10. 眉毛.

他跨上了馬，貝維和公主都送他起行。

公主在這時候，才想到恐有不測的危險，說道：『哥哥！誰知道我定能再瞧見你呵！我求你下馬來不要去罷！我寧願不要什麼撈什子——會說話的鳥兒，唱歌的樹兒，和黃水要使你冒這樣大的危險！』

巴門答說：『妹妹，我已打定主意，你須讓我去吧。不過，我當然或有不測的，如今可把這刀留下給你。你可時時把牠拔出鞘來看，倘這刀仍然如現在一般白亮的，我便是活着；如果你見刀上污有血跡，你當相信我死啦。』

他便和她及王子貝維，鄭重辭別，上馬去了。

三

王子巴門上了路，他不轉向右方，也不折向左方，直向印度那方向朝前走去。在行滿二十天這一天，他瞧見路旁一個古怪的老頭兒，坐在一棵靠近一間茅舍的樹下。

他的鬚眉雪一般的皓白，從嘴上罩過，一直拖到足下。

snow. The *nails*[1] of his hands and feet were grown to an immense length; a flat, broad umbrella covered his head. He wore no clothes, but only a *mat*[2] thrown round his body. The old man was a Dervis, long retired from the world.

Prince Bahman had been expecting all that morning to meet some one who would tell him the way to the place he sought, and saluted the Dervis with pleasant words. But the answer could not be understood, and Prince Bahman saw that the trouble arose from the hair hanging over the old man's mouth. As he was unwilling to go any farther without the *instructions*[3] he wanted, he got off his horse, pulled out a pair of *scissors*,[4] and said:—

"Good Dervish, I want some talk with you, but your hair prevents my hearing what you say. If you will consent, I will cut off some part of it, and of your eyebrows, which make you look more like a *bear*[5] than a man."

The Dervish did not oppose the offer, and smiled when the Prince said to him at last: "You are now a man, but before nobody could tell what you were."

"Sir," said the Dervish, "I am ready to show my gratitude, in any way. Tell me how I may serve you."

Then Prince Bahman asked him the way to find the speaking bird, the singing tree, and the yellow water. While he spoke, the old man's face became

---

【註】 1. 指甲，爪. 2. 布巾. 3. 指導. 4. 剪刀. 5. 熊.

他的手甲和脚甲長得極長；頭上覆着一把平闊的傘。赤裸裸地沒穿衣服，腰間只圍着一條布巾。那老人原是一個回教隱士，遁跡多時，和世界不聞不問了。

那天早上，王子巴門切心地盼望遇見一人，指點他所要去的去處，乃非常和悅，用尊敬的話兒，向隱士致禮。但是那人的回話都是不能懂得，王子巴門知道這是由於鬍眉覆着老人的嘴巴的緣故。因爲他不願胡亂地奔跑，遂下了馬，拿出一把剪刀來，說道：

『好隱士呵，我要和你說幾句話，但你的長鬍使我聽不見你的囘答。如果你願意，我將給你剪掉一部分的鬍眉。這茸茸地罩滿了你的臉，好像一隻熊呢。』

隱士也不反對，當王子最後對他說：『你如今可像一個人了，以前都沒有誰認識你啦。』這時候，他笑了。

隱士說：『先生，我很感謝你，請你告訴我，我怎樣可以爲你效勞。』

王子問他去找會說話的鳥兒，唱歌的樹兒，和黃水的途徑，打從那兒去。當他說時，那老人的臉兒沉下來了，

grave,[1] and at first he made no answer. But Prince Bahman *urged*[2] him to speak, and at last he said:

"Sir, I know the way you ask of me, but the dangers are greater than you suppose. Many gentlemen as brave as yourself have asked me this question, and not one of them has come back. Therefore, if you would not *perish*,[3] take my advice. Go no farther, but return home."

"Nothing shall turn me back," said Prince Bahman in reply; "whoever attacks me, I am brave and well armed."

"But your foes will be unseen," said the Dervish, "and how can you defend yourself from such?"

"No matter," said the Prince: "since you know the way, tell it me."

When the Dervish found that he could not move Prince Bahman from his purpose, he took a *bowl*[4] out of a bag that lay by him, and said:

"Since you will not be led by my advice, take this bowl; when you have mounted your horse, throw it before you, and follow it to the foot of the mountain. When the bowl stops there, alight, leave your horse with the *bridle*[5] over his neck, and he will stand in the same place till you return. As you *ascend*,[6] you will see about you a great number of large black stones, and will hear on all sides many voices, uttering a thousand *threats*[7] to keep you

---

【註】 1. 嚴肅的. 2. 催促. 3. 死亡. 4. 碗.　　馬勒. 6 登慌.
7. 恐懼.

好一會兒，沒有作聲。但王子巴門再三催問着，末了他才說：

『先生，你問我那條路兒，我是知道的，但是危險得很呢。許多紳士，和你一般勇敢，來問我這話兒，但沒有一個人得囘來。所以，要如你不要自蹈危險，該聽我的忠告。不要再去，囘家罷。』

王子巴門答說：『我不能囘家，任憑誰來攻擊我，我很勇武，又有軍器抵敵着。』

那隱士說：『那些敵人們，都是肉眼所不能瞧見的呢！這樣的敵人，你怎能抵禦？』

王子說：『不管牠，因爲你知道那路徑的，便請告訴我罷。』

隱士見他主意堅定，不能說動他，只得從袋裏掏出一隻碗兒來，遞給他道：

『因爲你不聽我的忠告，也罷，拿這碗兒去；在你上馬的時候，把這碗丟在馬前，跟着牠，就可到山脚下。碗兒停的時候，你便下馬，把馬繫好在那兒，等你囘來。你走上山的時候，滿眼都是些黑色大石塊兒，耳朵裏聽得喊聲無數，都說着些恐嚇的話兒，阻止你上山。你且不必驚

from reaching the top of the mountain. Be not afraid; but above all things, do not turn your head to look behind you, for in that instant you will be changed into such a black stone as those you see, which are all youths who have failed in this quest. If you escape this danger, of which I give you but a *faint*[1] idea, and get to the top of the mountain, you will see a *cage*,[2] and in that cage is the bird you seek; ask him which are the singing-tree and the yellow-water, and he will tell you. I have nothing more to say, except to beg you once more to turn back."

After these words, the Prince mounted his horse and threw the bowl before him. It rolled away so swiftly that he had to put his horse to a *gallop*[3] to keep it in sight, and when it had reached the foot of the mountain it stopped. The Prince alighted, laid the bridle on his horse's neck, saw the black stones of which the Dervis had told him, and began to ascend. He had not gone four steps before he heard voices, though he could see nobody. Some said, "Where is he going?" "What would he have?" "Do not let him pass;" others, "Stop him!" "Catch him!" "Kill him!" and others, with a voice like thunder, "Thief!" "*Murderer*[4]!" Others, in a *gibing tone*,[5] cried: "No, no; do not hurt him; let the pretty fellow pass; the cage and bird are kept for him."

In spite of[6] all these voices, Prince Bahman went on with courage for some time, but *at length*[7] there

<hr>

【註】 1. 模糊的. 2. 鳥籠. 3. 馳跑. 4. 謀殺者. 5. 嘲笑犀. 6. 不管. 7. 終於.

怕；但最最要緊的，　你切不可囘頭向後看，　因爲一囘頭，那時候，你就要變成一塊黑色大石了。你眼前所見的那些黑石，其實就是許多在這上面,失敗的少年們變成的啦。我所說的這些危險，還不足盡其萬一，要如你能逃過到了山頂，就可看見一隻鳥籠，那籠裏就是你所尋的鳥兒；你問他唱歌的樹兒，和黃水在那兒，他會告訴你的。以外，我沒有什麽要說的了，除非再勸你一句話，還是囘去的好。』

王子聽了這些話以後，便勒馬前行，把那碗兒抛在面前。碗兒滾的極快，他竭盡馬力追趕，僅能追到，滾到山脚下，牠便停下了。王子下騎，把馬鞍取下掛在馬兒頸上，他看見許多黑色大石，有如隱士所告訴他的，他走上去了。沒有走上四步的光景，便聽見有許多人聲，可是一個人影也瞧不見。有些說：『他到那兒去呢?』『他要取什麽東西?』『不要讓他走;』有些說：『阻止他!』『捉止他!』『殺掉他!』又有些卻如雷聲一般：『賊!』『謀殺者!』又有些嘲笑的聲音：『不，不；不要傷害他；讓這漂亮傢伙過去罷；那鳥籠兒在山上，等候他呢。』

王子巴門，絲毫不爲這些聲音所動，鼓着勇氣，向前

wa: so loud a *din*[1] near him, behind, before, and on all sides, that he was seized with dread, his legs trembled under him, he staggered, and, finding that his strength failed him, he forgot the Dervish's advice, turned about to run down the hill, and that instant was changed into a black stone. At the same moment his horse was changed likewise.

From the time Prince Bahman left home the Princess Perie-zadeh always wore the knife and sheath in her girdle, and pulled it out several times a day, to know whether her brother were yet alive. She found that he was in perfect health, and talked of him often with Prince Perviz.

On the twentieth day, as they were talking thus, the Prince asked his sister to pull out the knife to know how their brother did. When she saw the blood run down the point, she was seized with horror and threw it down.

"Ah, my poor brother," cried she, "*woe*[2] is me! I have caused your death, and shall never see you more! Why did I tell you of the speaking bird, the singing tree, and yellow water, or why did I listen to the idle tales of a *silly*[3] old woman?"

IV

Prince Perviz was as much distressed as the Princess at their brother's death, but he knew how greatly she still desired to possess the speaking bird,

---

【註】 1. 喧鬧. 2. 悲痛. 3. 糊塗的.

走了多時，忽聽得前後左右有大聲咆哮不止，他忽然害怕起來，兩條腿禁不住發着顫抖，於是心裏躊躇，腳步兒打着幌，他頓忘隱士的忠告，掉頭要望山下奔逃，在這當兒，他驀地變成一塊黑石了。同時候，他的馬兒也變成和他一樣的東西。

公主貝里若德，自王子巴門去後，便把那刀佩在腰間，每天總拿出來，看驗幾次。她發見他是好好的。常和王子貝維說着。

在這第二十天上，當兄妹二個談到他們的哥哥，王子教妹妹把刀抽出鞘來看看，她抽出刀來，見刀上帶有血跡，這時候，她唬的把刀落在地上。

大聲說：『呵！我可憐的哥哥啊！我是多麼悲痛。這是我使你死於非命，將永遠不能再看見你了！我爲什麼要告訴你，要會說話的鳥兒，唱歌的樹兒，和黃水呢？我要聽那無聊的老婆子的傻話，做什麼呢？』

四

王子貝維對於哥哥的死，和公主同樣的哀痛，不過他知道她，對於那會說話的鳥兒，唱歌的樹兒，和黃水，仍

the singing tree, and the golden water, and resolved to set out on the morrow to obtain them.

The Princess did what she could to *dissuade* him, but in vain. Before he went, he left her a *string*[2] of a hundred pearls, telling her that if they would not run when she should count them upon the st ing, but remain fixed, that would be a certain sign that, he had met the fate of their brother, but that, he hope , would never be.

On the twentieth day he met the Dervis and asked the same question as his brother, Bahman. Th old man told him that a young gentleman, who looked very like him had gone b a short time before, and had not yet returned. He warned Prince Perviz, as he had warned his brother, of all the dangers that must be met, and begged him to turn ba k But at last, when he saw that the young man could not be moved, he gave him a bowl with the same nstructions he had given Prince Bahman, and so let him depart.

The bowl stopped as before at the foot of the mountain, and Prince Perviz began to walk up, with his mind *resolved*[3] to reach the *summit.*[4] But before he had gone above six steps he heard a voice which seemed to be near, as of a man behind, saying in a ton of *insult*[5]: "Stay, youth, that I may punish you for your *rashness.*[6]"

Then the Prince forgot the Dervis's advice, *clapped*[7] his hand upon his sword, and turned about

---

【註】 1. 勸阻. 2. 一串. 3. 決定. 4. 山巔. 5. 侮辱. 6. 魯莽. 7. 提.

是念念不忘，所以他打定主意，明天去求得牠們囘來。

　　公主雖是竭力勸阻他，卻是無效。在他動身前，他留給她一百粒珍珠的一串珠子，告訴她道，當她在串子上數牠們的時候，要如這些珠子，都固定在一起不動，這便是一種符號，是他已遇着和哥哥同樣的命運了，但是，他希望那些珠子將永不會固定着。

　　第二十日的這天，他遇到那隱士，仍和他哥哥巴門一樣地問着他。那老人告訴他，在不多時以前，有個少年紳士，模樣和他相仿，去了沒有囘來。他警戒他，有許多必須經過的危險，和警告他哥哥一樣的勸他囘去。末了，見他終不爲動，纔給他一隻碗兒，又吩咐和王子巴門一樣的幾句話讓他去了。

　　那碗兒滾到山腳下停住。王子貝維上山去，他決定非走到山巓不可。不過他走了五六步光景；卻聽得有個人的聲音，似乎在他的後邊很近的樣子，用一種侮辱似的聲調說：『停住，少年！你的魯莽，我必把你殺掉。』

　　這時候，王子怒不可遏，頓時忘了隱士的警告，拔出劍

to *revenge*[1] himself; and he and his horse were changed at once into black stones.

Day after day the Princess Perie-zadeh had counted her pearls, and on the twentieth, instead of moving as they had done, all at once they became firmly fixed, and the *token*[2] told her surely that the Prince her brother was dead. She had made up her mind what to do if this should happen, and set about the carrying out of her plan at once. She disguised herself in her brother's robes, told her servants that she would return in two or three days, and, well armed and *equipped*,[3] mounted her horse the next morning, and took the same road as her brothers.

On the twentieth day she met the Dervish, who urged her, as strongly as he had urged her brothers, to turn back, and told her of the dangers in store for her.

"By what I understand," she said to him when he had finished speaking, "the two difficulties are, first, to reach the *cage*[4] without being frightened at the terrible *din*[5] of voices I shall hear; and, second, not to look behind me. For this last *caution*,[6] I hope I shall be mistress enough of myself to heed it. As for the first, if it is permitted, I will stop my ears with *cotton*,[7] that the voices, however loud and terrible, may not cause me to lose the use of my reason."

【註】 1. 復讎. 2. 信號. 3. 武裝. 4. 鳥籠. 5. 喧聲. 6. 警告.
7 棉花.

來，轉身便想復讎。這時候，他的人和馬驀地裏，變成兩塊黑石頭了。

公主貝里若德每天數着珠子，到了第二十日，珠子忽然不動。這光景，她決定她的哥哥，又是死啦。她原早已想定，倘這次再遭失敗後，她立卽應運用如何方法，出去使其成功。她穿了她哥哥的衣服，準備着應用軍器，囑咐僕人二三天後，方始囘家，第二天早上一早騎上馬走了。那路程是和她哥哥一樣的。

第二十天上，遇見這隱士，他照例切心地勸告，教她囘去，並告訴她怎樣的危險。

當他說完時，她向他說道：『你所講的，我都已懂得。我知道有兩種困難，第一，要到鳥籠那兒去，切勿要被四處種種怕人的巨聲嚇倒；第二，萬勿囘頭看望。關於第二點，我想能夠辦得到，不致有失。不過對於第一點，如果可以的，我得把綿絮塞緊了耳朵，那末，聲音無論多麼可怕和嘈雜，也就不能誤我的事情。』

The Dervish did not object to this plan, and the Princess, throwing down the bowl he gave her, followed it to the foot of the mountain.

Here she alighted, and stopped her ears with cotton. After she had looked well at the path leading to the summit, she began at a *moderate pace*,[1] and walked on without fear. She heard the voices, and perceived the great service the cotton was to her. The higher she went, the louder and more numerous the voices seemed, but they could make no *impression*[2] upon her. At the *insulting*[3] speeches which she did hear, she only laughed. At last she saw the cage and the bird, and at the same moment the clamor and thunders of the voices greatly increased.

The Princess, rejoicing to see the object of her search, doubled her speed, and soon gained the summit of the mountain, where the ground was *level*.[4] Then, running directly to the cage, and clapping her hand upon it, she cried: "Bird, I have you, and you shall not *escape* me." At this moment the voices ceased.

While Perie-zadeh was pulling the cotton out of her ears, the bird said to her: "Heroic Princess, since I am *destined*[6] to be a slave, I would rather be yours than any other person's, since you have obtained me so bravely. From this instant I obey all your commands. I know who you are, for you are not what you seem, and I will one day tell you:

【註】 1. 大路步. 2. 印象. 3. 侮辱. 4. 平坦的. 5. 逃掉. 6. 派定.

隱士沒有反對這計策，所以，公主丟下隱士給她的疋兒在馬前，跟着到了山脚。

這兒她下了馬，把綿絮塞緊了耳朵。她仔細地望好山路，乃大踏步向前，沒有一點兒驚慌。她聽見種種聲音，卻聽不清楚是什麼，方知綿絮對她有這等的妙用。她愈走上去，那些聲音似乎愈高，愈多了，但牠們對她並沒有一點兒印像。那些侮辱聲音，她雖是聽得，不過一笑罷了。末後，她瞧見那籠兒和鳥兒了，同時，那些喧鬧和雷一般的聲音，愈加增多，增高。

公主瞧見了她所求的目的物，快活非凡，飛步向前，早就到了山頂，那兒是很平坦的一塊平地。她直衝到鳥籠那兒，抓了牠在手裏，大聲說道：『鳥兒，我得到你啦，你不要逃掉呵！』這時候，這些聲音驀地寂靜。

當貝里若德把綿絮從耳朵裏取出時這鳥兒對她說道：『勇敢的公主啦，今後我配定做你的僕人了，我十分願意做你的僕人，爲的你是這般勇敢地得了我去。自後，我當事事服從你命令。我知道你是誰，這連你自己還沒有知道得，

more. In the mean time, say what you desire, and I
am ready to obey you.''

"Bird," said Perie-zadeh, "I have been told that
there is not far off a golden-water, which is very
wonderful. Before all things, I ask you to tell me
where it is."

The bird showed her the place, which was just
by, and she went and filled a litt'e silver *flagon*[1]
which she had brought with her. Then she returned
to the bird and said:—

"Bird, this is not enough; I want also the
singing-tree. Tell me where it is."

"Turn about," said the bird, "and you will see
behind you a wood, where you will find this tree.
Break off a branch, and plant it in your garden; it
will take root as soon as it is put into the earth, and
in a little time will grow to a fine tree."

The Princess went into the wood, and by the
sweet concert she heard soon found the singing-tree.
When she had taken one of its branches, she returned
again to the bird and said:-

"Bird, this is not yet enough. My two brothers,
in *search*[2] for thee, have been changed into black
stones on the side of the mountain. Tell me how I
may *restore*[3] them to life."

The bird would say nothing at first, but when
the Princess *threatened*[4] to take its life, it bade her
sprinkle[5] every stone on her way down the mountain
with a little water from the golden fountain. As she

【註】 1. 甕.　2. 尋求.　3. 恢復.　4. 恐嚇. 5 灑.

過後一天，我再告訴你罷。現在，你要什麼，說罷，我預備服從你。』

貝里若德說：『鳥兒！我聽說，離此很近有一種金水，是很奇罕的。別的且慢，你便先告訴我這水在那兒罷。』

那鳥兒告訴她，這水是在靠近一邊的所在。她走去盛滿一小銀罐，這銀罐她是帶在身邊的。她囘來。又對鳥兒道：

『鳥兒，還不止這個啦！我還要那唱歌的樹兒。告訴我，那棵樹在那兒呢？』

鳥兒說：『轉過身來，你可看見你身後有一個林子，那林子中你便尋得這樹。折一個椏枝兒，插在你的園子裏；一著上，這樹兒卽會生根，霎時候，便長成一棵美好的樹了。』

公主走進林子裏去，聽見非常悅耳和諧的音調，她就發見那唱歌的樹兒。她折了一個椏枝兒，囘到鳥兒那裏說：

『鳥兒，這還不殼呢。我的兩個哥哥，爲來尋求你，都變成黑石，在這座山上。告訴我，我怎樣可以恢復他們的生命。』

鳥兒初時不肯直說，但在公主恐嚇牠，要殺死牠的時候，牠纔囑公主在下山的當兒，用金水灑在每塊石頭上。她把金水灑下，果然見每塊石頭驀地變成雄糾糾氣昂昂的

did this, each stone became a man on a horse, fully *equipped*.[1] Among these men were her brothers, Bahman and Perviz, who exchanged with her the most loving embraces. When she had told them and the band of noble youths how she had brought them back to life, she bade them follow her to the old Dervish, to thank him for his good advice, which they had all found to be *sincere*.[2] But he was dead, whether from old age, or because he was no longer needed. The procession, headed by Perie-zadeh, went on, growing smaller in numbers day by day as the youts who had started with it departed by the roads leading to their various countries.

As soon as the Princess reached home, she placed the cage in the garden; and the bird no sooner began to *warble*[3] than he was surrounded by *nightingales*,[4] *larks*,[5] *linnets*,[6] *goldfinches*,[7] and every sort of bird in the country. The branch of the tree was no sooner planted than it took root, and in a short time became a large tree, the leaves of which gave as sweet a concert as those of the tree from which it was gathered. A large basin of beautiful marble was placed in the garden; and when the Princess poured into it all the yellow water from the flagon, it reached at once to the edges of the basin, and afterwards formed in the middle a fountain twenty feet high, which fell again into the basin without ever running over.

【註】 1. 武裝. 2. 誠篤. 3. 囀鳴. 4. 夜鶯. 5. 百靈鳥. 6. 紅雀.
7. 金翅雀.

騎馬男子。在這些人裏邊，她看見她哥哥巴門和貝維，他

們驚喜極了，交換地親抱着她。她乃告訴那兩個哥哥，和一

羣高貴的少年們，是怎樣地把他們救活的，並囑他們同到那

老隱士那兒去，道謝他的忠告。但是他因年老還不知沒用，

已經死了。於是由貝里若德領頭，一大隊人馬前進，到了

分路口，那些少年們各自囘國去了。

公主一到家中，就把鳥籠兒放在園子裏；這鳥兒張口

一鳴，立時被夜鶯，百靈，紅雀，金翅雀兒，以及各式各

樣的鳥兒圍繞在中間。那橇枝兒纔栽到地上，便生根發芽，

立時長成一棵華美青葱的大樹，那些樹葉奏出一種和諧的

音調，差不多和原樹一樣好聽。園子裏放着一個美麗大理

石的大盆兒；公主把銀罐裏的黃水纔倒下盆去，立時漲滿

了一盆，後來盆中又湧起一道噴泉，足有二丈來高，但噴

下的水花，從不溢出盆外。

V

The report of these wonders soon spread abroad, and many persons came to see and admire them. The two Princes soon took up their old way of living, and one day, when they were hunting two or three *leagues*[1] from the house, they chanced to meet with the Emperor of Persia. The respect they paid him with an easy and graceful air, their handsome *mien*,[2] and the knowledge, which he soon gained from them, that they were the sons of the former keeper of his gardens, won them his favor at once. This was increased by the skill *displayed*,[3] at his request, in the chase, and by their bearing when they came a few days later to his court. They were *loath*[4] to make this visit when the Emperor first demanded it. But when they asked their sister's advice about it, she said: "Let us consult the speaking-bird;" and the bird said: "The Princes, your brothers, must yield to the Emperor's pleasure, and in their turn invite him to come and see your house."

So the visit to the court was paid. As the Princes entered the city, many of the people wished that the Emperor had two such handsome sons; and the Emperor himself was so pleased with their wit and good judgment that he said: "Were they my own children, and suitably educated, they could not have been better trained." When they left the court, they begged the Emperor that he would visit them

【註】 1. 里洛 (約三哩). 2. 風采. 3. 表現. 4. 厭惡的.

五

這些奇物很快的就傳揚開去，許多人都來觀賞牠們，大家稱美不止。兩個王子仍繼續他們舊時的生活。有一天，當他們在離家很遠的郊外，打獵的時候，他們偶然遇到波斯皇帝。 他們向皇帝行禮時， 那禮貌的合度， 人物的俊秀，談吐的聰明和雅馴，而且又是前園吏的兒子，馬上就得到皇帝的寵愛。 他們的技術尤為皇帝所賞悅， 皇帝命他們，在幾天以後，到宮廷裏去見他。但他們心裏似乎很不願意。因此囘去和公主商量着，她說：『讓我們同鳥兒去商量這事情罷。』那鳥兒說道：『公主，你的兩位哥哥，定然要承迎着皇帝的歡心，同樣地，須請他駕幸你們的家裏來。』

因此決意到宮廷裏去拜望。當王子們進城的時候，許多人民希望皇帝有這樣的兩個俊美的兒子；皇帝自己聽見這樣的話兒，也十分歡喜，他說道：『便是他們是我自己的兒子， 適合地教育他們， 也不能把他們訓練得更好了。』當他們要拜別的時候，他們懇求皇帝能夠看望他們和他們

and their sister, of whom they had already told him, when next the hunt should bring him near them.

"Our house," they said, "is not worthy your presence; but monarchs sometimes have taken shelter[1] in a cottage."

"My c ildren," he answered, "your house cannot be oth r tl an beautiful, and worthy of its owners. My pleasure in seeing it will be the greater for having for my hosts[2] you and your sister, who is already dear to me from what you have said of her. Meet me to-morrow morning at the place where I first saw you."

The Princes returned home and told their sister of the favor with which they had been received, and of the visit that was to be paid them in the morning.

"Then we must think," said the Princess, "of prepa ing a repast[3] fit for his majesty. Let us consult[4] the speaking bird, he will tell us, perhaps, what meats the Emperor likes best."

When the bird was asked this question, his answer was:

"Good mistress, you have excellent cooks; let them do the best they can; but, above all things, let them prepare a dish of cucumbers[5] stuffed[6] full of pearls, which must be set before the Emperor in the first course before all the other dishes."

"Cucumbers stuffed full of pearls!" cried Princess Perie-zadeh amazed. "It is an unheard-of[7]

【註】 1. 處身. 2. 主人. 3. 酒席. 4. 商量. 5. 胡瓜. 6. 裝填. 7. 罕聞的.

的妹妹，這妹妹他們早經告訴給他了，當下次行獵的時候，他們要把她帶來和他叩見。

他們說道：『我們的家裏，原不值得皇上駕幸的；但皇帝有時也許不嫌茅舍哩。』

他答道：『我的孩子們，你們的家有你們這樣的主人自然再好也沒有了。我很歡喜有你們和你們的妹妹，做我的主人，你的妹妹，據你們所說，我已很歡喜啦。明天早上，可在我初見你們的那個地方，會見我罷。』

王子們囘到家裏，告訴他們的妹子，皇帝如何寵愛他們，並且說，明天早上皇帝要駕幸到他們的家裏來。

公主說：『那末，我們必須考慮一下，要設備些適合的酒席，以迎接聖駕。讓我們和會說話的鳥兒商量去，他可以告訴我們，什麼肴饌為皇帝所最喜歡的。』

當鳥兒見問的時候，牠答道：

『好女主人，你有手段很高的廚夫，讓他們為你盡力罷。不過最緊要，在給皇帝上第一道菜的時候，須教他們辦下一碟兒，由珍珠串成的胡瓜。』

公主貝里若德吃驚地說：『珍珠串成的胡瓜！這眞是

dish! Besides, all the pearls I possess would not be enough."

Then the bird told her where the pearls would be found, by digging under a certain tree in the park early the next morning. Here, indeed, she found plenty of pearls for the purpose, and took them to the head cook, for she and her brothers had agreed that the bird's advice must be closely followed. The cook was as much amazed at his order as the Princess had been, but took the pearls, and in the morning everything was ready for the Emperor.'s coming.

The next morning the Princes met him early in the forest, and when the heat of the day *obliged*[1] them to leave off the *chase*,[2] they made their way to the house, where the Princess Perie-zadeh was waiting to receive them. She threw herself at the Emperor's feet, but he stooped to raise her, and gazing for some time at her beauty, said:—

"The brothers are worthy of the sister, and she is worthy of them. I hope to know you better, my daughter, when I have seen the house."

Then the Emperor was led through the rooms. "My daughter," said he, "do you call this a country-house? The finest and largest cities would soon be *deserted*[3] if all country-houses were like yours. I do not wonder that you despise the town. Now let me see the garden."

Here he was first amazed by the concert which

【註】 1. 逼迫. 2. 行獵. 3. 抛棄.

上所罕聞的菜，就是我所有的珍珠也不夠呢。』

鳥兒便告訴她，這些珠子在那兒可以得到，教她明天一早可向園子裏第幾棵樹根下，掘着就得。這兒她果然得了很多的珍珠，就交給他們的廚夫，因爲她們兄妹間早就商量好，鳥兒的忠告一定要聽從的。廚夫見說，和公主一般的吃驚，不過他取了珠子，到第二天早上肴菜都預備好，只待皇帝駕臨。

第二天早上。王子們一早就出去，到林子裏去會他，等到日光的炎熱逼迫他們不能再行獵了，他們乃引着路還家，那兒公主貝里若德早已準備接駕。她跪伏在他面前，皇帝親手扶她起來，對她的美麗仔細看了好一會，說道：

『有這哥哥們方不枉有這妹子，可是她也不枉有他們。我希望多多的認識你，我的女兒，你們的屋子我也瞧了。』

於是皇帝被引進屋子的時候，他說：『我的女兒，你說這屋子是一所村舍嗎？要如一切的村舍都像你的一樣，那末，最富麗和最大的市城，都要變做荒郊了。我無怪你們要看不起市城呢。現在，且引我到園子裏去罷。』

在園子裏，他驚奇着耳邊的音樂，使他讚美的話都說不

he heard, without being able to see any players. "It is the singing-tree," said Perie-zadeh; "it came to me at the same time with the yellw-water and the speaking-bird, which your majesty may see after you have rested yourself."

When he had looked more closely at the singing-tree, and in his surprise asked many questions about it, he could not rest without seeing the yellow-water and the speaking-bird. The beauty and wonder of the fountain, rising from a basin of one entire stone, *fed*[1] by no spring, but formed, as the princess told him, from the contents of one small flagon, held him as if *spell-bound*.[2] "I must come often and see this," he said at last: "but now let us go and see the speaking-bird."

Its cage was hung in one of the windows of the hall, and, when they drew near to the place, the Emperor asked why the trees near by were all filled with warbling birds, yet none were in the other trees of the garden. The Princess answered:

"They come from all parts to *accompany*[3] the song of the speaking bird. If you attend, you will hear that his notes are sweeter than those of any of the other birds, even the nightingale's."

The Emperor entered the hall; and, as the bird continued singing, the Princess *raised*[4] her voice, and said: "My slave, here is the Emperor; pay your *compliments*[5] to him."

【註】 1. 供給. 2. 着了魔. 3. 陪伴. 4. 提高. 5. 致敬.

出口了，貝里著德說：『這是唱歌的樹兒啦。這樹兒和黃水及會說話的鳥兒，是一起得來的，其餘兩種，陛下息一會兒可以去瞧。』

當他仔細賞覽那唱歌的樹兒，他的好奇心使他發出許多關於這樹的問話，他再也不能遲待着，去瞧黃水和會說話的鳥兒。這泉水的瑰麗和奇異，從一個純粹大理石的盆中噴出，卻沒有泉源，公主告訴他，這泉水僅為一小銀罐兒，這時候，他幾乎詫異得好像著了魔似的。說道：『我定然要常來，賞看這泉水；但現在讓我去瞧會說話的鳥兒罷。』

鳥籠掛在大廳的窗口，當他們走來的時候，皇帝問她，為什麼靠近這窗口的樹上，有這麼多的歌唱着的鳥兒，而園子裏別些樹上，卻一隻不見呢？公主答道：

『他們都是來陪伴這會說話的鳥兒的。 倘你留心聽，牠唱叫的聲音，便可聽出牠的音調比任何的鳥兒，都來得和諧好聽，就是黃鶯兒也遠不及牠呢。』

皇帝走進廳裏，鳥兒正在繼續在唱歌，公主高聲說道：『我的僕人，這兒是皇帝；你來行禮罷。』

The bird left off singing that instant, when all the other birds ceased also; then it said: "God save the Emperor. May he long live!" The repast was served at the sofa near the window where the bird was placed, and the Emperor replied, as he was taking his seat: "Bird, I thank you, and am rejoiced to find in you the sultan and king of birds."

As soon as the Emperor saw the dish of cucumbers before him, he reached out his hand, and took one; but when he had cut it was in *extreme*[1] surprise to find it stuffed with pearls.

"What *novelty*[2] is this?" he said; "and why were these cucumbers stuffed thus with pearls, since pearls are not to be eaten?"

He looked at the two Princes and Princess to ask them the meaning, when the bird, breaking in, said:

"Can your majesty be so greatly surprised at cucumbers stuffed with pearls, which you see with your own eyes, and yet so easily believe that the Queen your wife was the mother of a dog, a cat, and a piece of wood?"

"I believed these things," replied the Emperor, "because the *nurses*[3] *assured*[4] me of the facts."

"Those nurses, sire," replied the bird, "were the Queen's two sisters, *envious*[5] of the honors you bestowed upon her, and burning for revenge. If

【註】 1. 極端的.　2. 古怪.　3. 保姆.　4. 使確信.　5. 嫉妒的.

那鳥兒這時候，停止唱歌，一切的鳥兒們都隨着停止了；牠乃啓口道：『上帝祝福皇上。願皇上萬歲，萬萬歲！』酒席設在大廳裏，是靠近鳥兒的所在，皇帝入了席，口裏說道：『鳥兒，我感謝你好意，你是百鳥中的王和蘇丹。』

那皇帝一瞧見碟兒裏，有着胡瓜，便伸手取了一個；但當他用刀來切的時候，一看乃是珍珠串成的。倒大吃一驚。

他說：『多古怪的菜呀！你用珍珠串成這樣的胡瓜嗎，但是珍珠可以吃嗎？』

他看着兩王子和公主，問是何意，但鳥兒插口說道：

『陛下親眼瞧見珍珠串成胡瓜的樣子，便這般吃驚，但你聽著說皇后產下一隻狗，一隻貓，一片木塊卻爲什麼很容易的信任呢？』

皇帝答說：『我相信，是因爲那保母對我說的。』

鳥兒答道：『這保母們，是皇后的兩個姊姊，她們着着你給皇后的光榮很是嫉妒，於是暗中設計報復她。你若

you examine them, they will confess their crime.
The two brothers and the sister whom you see
before you are your own children, *exposed*[1] by them,
and saved by the keeper of your gardens, who
adopted and brought up the children as his own."

"Bird," cried the Emperor, "I believe the truth
which you reveal to me. The feeling which drew
me to them told me plainly that they must be my
own kin. Come, then, my sons, come, my daughter,
let me embrace you, and give you the first marks
of a father's tender love."

Weeping tears of joy they embraced one another.
The Emperor finished his meal in haste, and said;
"My children, to-morrow I will bring the Queen
your mother; therefore make ready to receive
her."

He set out at once for the city, where the first
thing he did was to order the Queen's two sisters
to be put to death. Then, followed by many lord
of his court, he went to the great mosque, and
called forth the Queen from the shed where she
had *languished*[2] so many years, and, embracing her
in her *wretches plight*[3] before all the people, told
her with tears in his eyes how he had been deceived,
and legged forgiveness for the wrong he had done
her. "Soon," he said, "you shall see the Princes
and the Princess, our lovely children. Come, and
take your former rank, with all the honors which
are your due."

___

【註】 1. 遺棄. 2. 焦思.

把她們審問起來，她們必定認罪直說。眼前你看見的，這兩個哥兒和一個姐兒，乃是你自己的孩子們，他們被棄以後，幸虧園吏救了撫養他們。長大起來，便把他們認做自己子女的。』

皇帝說道：『鳥兒呀，你說的話兒，使我十分可信。我一接近他們就感想，他們像是我自己的血肉一樣。來，我兒，來，我女，讓我擁抱你，初次給你們為父親的溫存罷。』

他們相互地擁抱着，快活的流淚。皇帝慌忙食畢，說道：『我的孩兒們，明天我可帶你們的母親來，你們預備接見她罷。』

他馬上囘宮，第一件事，就命把皇后的兩個姊姊，一併處死。隨後，他就率領百官朝臣，到那個大寺院裏，命令把皇后從茅舍裏放出，那兒她已住有許多年了，就在衆臣的面前，他不管她穿着襤褸的衣服，親手抱住她，淚流滿面地告訴她，他怎般地受了欺矇，並求她恕他無意的過失。他說：『你就可瞧見我們可愛的孩子了。恢復你的原位，受你應有的光榮。』

The glad news spread quickly through the city, and early the next morning the Emperor and the Queen, whose *mournful*[1] dress had been changed for rich robes, set out with all their court for the house of the Princes Bahman and Perviz and the Princess Perie-zadeh.

"These, much *injured*[2] wife," said the Emperor, "are our children. Embrace them tenderly, since they are worthy both of me and of you."

When they had all finished the splendid repast prepared for them, and had marveled at the singing tree and the yellow fountain, and, most of all, at the speaking bird, the entire company returned to the city in joyful procession. Crowds of people came out to meet them with cries of joy. All eyes were fixed not only upon the Queen, the two Princes and the Princess, but also upon the bird, which the Princess carried before her in a cage; and every one admired his sweet notes which had drawn all the other birds to follow him, flying from tree to tree in the country, and from one *housetop*[3] to another in the city.

With this *pomp*[4] the Princes Bahman and Perviz and the Princess Perie-zadeh were brought at length to the palace, and nothing was heard all that night but rejoicings, both in the palace and in the utmost parts of the city, and these lasted many days, and extended throughout the empire of Persia.

【註】　1. 襤褸的.　2. 損毀的.　3. 屋頂.　4. 光榮.

　　這快樂的消息立刻傳遍全城，在第二天早上皇帝和皇后，穿了華麗的衣服，率領衆大臣，同到王子巴門，貝維與公主貝里若德的家中。

　　皇帝對着皇后說：『這些便是我們的孩子們啦。你溫存地抱住他們罷，他們眞不愧爲我和你的子女哩。』

　　當他們用畢陳設精美肴饌時，大家驚奇着唱歌的樹兒，和黄的泉水，對於會說話的鳥兒，尤其表示驚嘆，全隊人馬歡聲動地囘到城中。百姓們也都出來，歡呼口號，迎接他們。每個人的眼睛，不但看着皇后，看着王子們，和公主，還要爭先恐後的看那鳥兒，這鳥兒是放在公主面前的籠中；每個人對於他甜密的歌聲，嘆賞不止，許多珍禽歌鳥都跟着他，經過鄉村的時候，他們從這棵樹兒飛到那棵樹兒，走到城裏的時候，他們又從這屋頂飛到那屋頂。

　　這般的光榮，王子巴門和貝維及公主貝里若德，終於囘到宮裏，城外城內，眞是一片歡聲，通宵達旦，過了數天，就傳遍全波斯國境。

11. The Story of Sindbad the Sailor

In the reign of the same Caliph, Haroun Al Raschid, of whom we have already heard, there lived at Bagdad a poor *porter*[1] called Hindbad. One day, when the weather was very hot, he was employed to carry a heavy burden from one end of the town to the other. Being much *fatigued*[2], he took off his load, and sat upon it, near a large *mansion*[3].

He was much pleased that he stopped at this place, for the air was completely filled with the pleasant *scent*[4] of *wood of aloes*[5] and *rose-water*[6], *wafted*[7] from the house. Besides, he heard from within a concert of sweet music, mixed with the notes of nightingales and other birds. There was also the smell of several sorts of *savory dishes*[8], and Hindbad was sure there must be a great feast within. He knew not to whom the mansion belonged, and asked one of the servants standing by the gate in rich apparel.

"How," replied the servant, "do you live in Bagdad, and know not that this is the house of Sindbad the Sailor, the famous voyager who has sailed around the world?"

The porter lifted up his eyes to heaven, and said, loud enough to be heard.—

"*Almighty Creator*[9] of all things, consider the difference between Sindbad and me! Every day I

【註】 1. 脚夫. 2. 疲乏. 3. 大廈. 4. 香氣. 5. 沉香. 6. 玫瑰水. 7. 吹出. 8. 香美食品. 9. 萬能的造物主.

十一　航 海 家 孫 柏 達 的 故 事

話說哈龍亞爾拉西德凱　　夫在位的時代，那時候巴革達德有個窮腳夫，叫做辛巴德。一天，天氣十分炎熱，他被人僱挑一擔重擔，從市鎮的這一頭到另一頭去。因為疲極，他就落下肩來，坐在靠近一所大莊院的地方。

他在這處歇腳，非常快活，因為那屋子裏吹出沉香和玫瑰水一種快人的香氣，並且聽到一種甜蜜的樂聲，夾着黃鶯兒和別種鳥兒的啼唱。又有幾種香美食品的氣息，據辛巴德猜想，院子裏定是大張筵席在宴客吧。他不知道這是誰家的莊院，遂問站在門首的，一個衣服鮮麗的僕人。

那僕人答說：『什麼？你住在巴革達德，難道不知道這是水手孫柏達的家裏嗎？這著名的航海家曾航行了全球的。』

這腳夫把眼睛望着天上，大聲地嘆說，聲音很足使人聽見。——

『萬能的造物主宰呵，想着孫柏達和我的不同罷！我

suffer fatigue and distress, and can scarce get *coarse*
barley bread for myself and my family, whilst happy
Sindbad freely spends vast riches, and leads a life of
unbroken pleasure. What has he done to obtain
from Thee a lot so agreeable? And what have I d...e
to deserve one so wretched?"

While the porter was speaking thus, a servant
came out of the house, and, taking him by the arm,
made him *enter*,[2] for Sindbad, his master, wanted to
speak to him. He was led into a great hall, where
many people sat round a table covered with all sorts
of savory dishes. At the upper end sat a *comely*,[3]
venerable[4] gentleman, with a long white beard, and
behind him stood a number of officers and servants,
all ready to attend his pleasure. This person was
Sindbad. Hindbad was much *abashed*,[5] and saluted the
company trembling. But Sindbad seated him at his
right hand and served him himself with excellent wine.

Now Sindbad had heard the porter's complaint
through the window, and this it was that led him to
send for Hindbad. When the feast was over, Sindbad
addressed him, asking his name and employment,
and said: "I wish to hear from your own mouth what
you said just now in the street."

Hindbad hung his head in shame, and answered:

"My lord, I *confess*[6] that my fatigue put me out
of humor, and, for the *rash*[7] words I *uttered*,[8] I beg
your pardon."

【註】 1. 下品. 2. 進去. 3. 溫雅的. 4. 可敬的. 5. 羞慚. 6. 懺悔.
7. 鹵莽的. 8. 說出.

每天挑擔，壓得精疲力竭，所得還不足餬一家之口，快活的孫柏達却自由自在地，享樂他巨大的財產，只愁享用不盡。他為什麼從你得到這般的幸運？而我為什麼你却給我這般愁苦的命運啊？』

當挑夫正是這般不平地說的時候，一個僕人從屋子裏走來，挽了他的臂，教他進去，因為他的主人，孫柏達，要同他說話哩。他被引進一間大廳裏，那裏許多人圍坐着，桌上擺着各種美味的碟兒。上首端坐一位溫雅，可敬的老紳士，白鬚拂胸，後邊站着許多僕人，侍候他。這人卽是孫柏達。辛巴德十分羞慚，惶悚地對衆人行禮。但孫柏達却教他坐在他的右邊，用好酒款待他。

原來孫柏達從窗口裏，聽到那腳夫的怨言，所以命人把辛巴德喚來的。當酒席吃完時，孫柏達卽和他談話，問了他名字和職業，說道：『我願聽你方纔在街上說的是什麼？』

辛巴德含羞垂着頭，答道：

『我主，我因為疲困極了，始不平地胡說了幾句，至於我所說的粗話，還要請你原諒！』

"Do not think me so unjust," said Sindbad, "as to resent them. But I must set you right about myself. You think, no doubt, that I gained without labor or trouble the ease I now enjoy. Do not mistake; before attaining this estate I suffered for several years more trouble of body and mind than can well be imagined. Yes, gentlemen," he added, turning to the whole company, "what I have endured would cure the greatest *miser*[1] of his love of riches; and with your leave I will relate to you the dangers I have met."

The First Voyage of Sindbad the Sailor.

My father was a rich merchant of good *fame*[2]. He left me a large estate, which I wasted in *riotous living*[3]. I quickly saw my error, especially in misspending my time, which is of all things the most valuable. I remembered the saying of the great Solomon, which I had often heard from my father: "A good name is better than precious *ointment*;[4]" and again: "Wisdom is good with an *inheritance*.[5]" I resolved to walk in my father's ways, and *embarked*[6] with some merchants on board a ship, we had fitted out together.

We *steered*[7] our course towards the Indies. At first I was troubled with sea-sickness, but speedily regained my health. In our voyage we touched at

---

【註】 1. 守財奴. 2. 名譽. 3. 遊蕩生活 4. 油. 5. 遺產. 6. 乘船. 7. 取道.

孫柏達說：『不要想我這般不公平，教你怒恨他們。但我要爲自己辨白，使你不致誤會。你疑心我豐衣足食是不勞而獲的嗎！你錯想了，我創成這樣的基業，所受身心的苦楚，眞不是語言所能形容呢。』他又向衆客人說：『諸位先生，我所受的困難苦楚，遠足使一般愛財如命的人們，望而卻步；現在我爲你敍述我所經歷的種種危險吧。』

孫柏達第一次的航海

我的父親是個有名的富商。他遺給我一份大產業，因我終日遊蕩，給我胡亂化完了。我立刻覺到我的錯誤，尤其是在虛耗我的光陰，這是人生一切中最寶貴的。我記起了大沙羅門的格言，這些格言是我常聞父親所說的：『令名尤勝於名貴之油；』又說：『有財產者，宜有智慧。』我決定學法先人，遂同幾個商人，登在一隻船上，預備起行。

我們所定的航程，是向印度羣島的。我初時不免受着暈船的痛苦，但很快就恢復健康了。在我們的航程中　幾

several islands, where we sold or exchanged our goods. One day, *whilst*[1] under sail, we were *becalmed*[2] near a small island rising but little above the level of the water and resembling a green *meadow*.[3] The captain permitted such persons as were so inclined to land; of this number I was one. But whilst we were eating and drinking, and resting from the fatigue of the sea, the island of a sudden trembled and shook us terribly.

The trembling of the island was soon noticed on board the ship, and we were called to *reembark*[4] quickly, or we should all be lost; for what we took to be an island proved to be the back of a *sea-monster*.[5] The *nimblest*[6] got into the *sloop*[7]; others *betook*[8] themselves to swimming; as for me, I was still upon the island when it sank into the sea, and I had only time to catch hold of a piece of wood that we brought from the ship to make a fire. Meanwhile the captain, having taken the others on board, resolved to make the most of the favoring *gale*[9] that had just risen, and sailed away.

Thus was I left to the mercy of the waves for the rest of the day and the night that followed. By this time I found my strength gone, and was despairing of my life, when happily a wave threw me against an island. The bank was high and *rugged*,[10] but some roots of trees helped me to get up. When the sun arose, I was very *feeble*,[11] but

---

【註】 1. while. 2. 傍泊. 3. 草地. 4. 回船. 5. 海怪. 6. 最敏捷的. 7. 單桅帆船. 8. 委（身）. 9. 風. 10. 峻險. 11. 疲憊.

次遇見海島，都上岸做我們的賣買。有一天，在我們航行中，忽發見有一小島，升起水面，島上好像有綠草的樣子。這時候，風平浪靜，船遂椗泊在島邊。因得到船長的允許，許多人都到島上去。我也是其中的一個。但我們正在吃喝高興的當兒，想把數日海行的疲勞，來舒暢一下，那海島忽然震動簸搖起來，使我們嚇得要死。

這島的震動，船上的人立刻瞧見了，一片聲響聲呼我們趕快上船，不然我們難免一死了，因為我們所認為海島的，乃是一個海怪的背啦。最敏捷的搶到小船上；還有些人跳入海裏游去；但我呢，在這東西沉入海中的時候，卻還留在島上，我只搶得一片板木在手，這些板木是從船上帶來生火的。這時候，海上發着順風，船長等到那些人上船，遂決意趁風開航了。

這樣地，我被拋棄在海浪中，有一晝夜。這時候，我真精疲力竭，但正在和我性命掙扎的當兒，幸而一個大浪把我打到一個海島邊。那海岸是十分峻險，幸虧拉着幾個樹根，始爬上海岸。太陽已升起了，我仍是憊困，無力起

managed to find some *herbs*[1] that were fit to eat, and a spring of good water. Thus refreshed, I advanced farther into the island, and reached a fine plain, where I saw some horses feeding. As I went towards them, I heard the voice of a man who appeared and asked me who I was. When I had told him my adventure, he led me by the hand into a cave, where there were several other people, no less amazed to see me than I was to see them.

I partook of some food which they gave me, and then learned that they were *grooms*[2] belonging to the *sovereign*[3] of the island, where they brought the king's horses every year for *pasturage*.[4] They were to return home on the morrow, and had I been one day later I must have *perished*,[5] because the inhabited part of the island was far off, and I could never have reached it without a guide.

The next morning they took me to the capital of the island, and presented me to the sovereign. When at his request I told him of my misfortune, he was much concerned, and gave orders that I should want for nothing; and his commands were carefully *fulfilled*.[6]

As a merchant I met with many men of my own profession, and sought news from Bagdad and the opportunity to return; for the capital of the island has a fine harbor, where ships arrive daily from many quarters of the world. I took delight also in hearing the talk of learned Indians, and *withal*[7] paid

---

【註】 1. 草. 2. 馬夫. 3. 霸主. 4. 放牧. 5. 死亡. 6. 奉行. 7. 又.

行。於是設法找些可以吃的草和泉水，充了飢渴，精神方見恢復一點。我向這島中走去，到得一塊很好的平原，見有若干馬匹養在那裏。當我向馬兒走去的當兒，我聽得一個人聲，問我是誰。我把我的遇險事情告訴給他，他就挽着我手引我到一山洞去，那洞裏有很多人，見我去，和我瞧見他們一般的驚奇。

我吃了他們給我的一些東西，知道他們是那島王的馬夫，每年他們要把島王的馬兒，帶來放青。他們明天卽要回家去，要如我再遲一天，我定然要死在島上，因島上的居民若遷遠了，如果沒有一個引導者，我是永不能尋見他們了。

第二天他們帶我到島上的城子裏去。　引我朝見島王。島王問我，我把遭難的事情告訴他，他很關心，傳命使我所需要的一切，均由他供給。他的命令由他臣屬很謹慎地奉行了。

我操商業，因此遇見同行中的許多人，時常從他們打聽巴革達德的音息，和囘家去的機會；原來那島的京城有條良港，　天天有船隻，　從世界各處駛來的。　我聽得博學的印度人談話，　非常快活，　他們都是島王的臣子，　又遇

my court to the sovereign, and met with the governors
and *petty kings*[1] that were subject to him, telling
and learning much.

There belongs to this king an island named
Cassel, where the *mariners*[2] said that every night
the noise of *drums*[3] might be heard. This wonderful
place I visited, and on the way thither saw fishes
of one hundred and two hundred *cubits*[4] in length,
that occasion more fear than hurt; for they are so
timid[5] that they will fly upon the *rattling*[6] of two
sticks or boards. I saw likewise other fishes, about
a cubit in length, that had heads like *owls*.[7]

One day, as I was at the port after this visit,
the ship arrived in which I had embarked at
Bussorah. I knew the captain at once, and went
and asked him for my *bales*.[8] "I am Sindbad," said
I, "and those bales marked with his name are
mine."

"Heavens!" he exclaimed, "whom can we trust
in these times? I saw Sindbad perish with my own
eyes, and now you tell this tale to possess yourself of
what does not belong to you."

But at length he was persuaded that I was no
cheat,[9] for there came people from his ship who knew
me, and expressed much joy at seeing me alive.
"Heaven be praised," said he at last, "for your
happy escape! There are your goods; take and do
with them as you please."

【註】 1. 諸侯. 2. 航海家. 3. 鼓. 4. 長度名，約合十八吋. 5. 膽怯.
6. 連續不斷聲. 7. 貓頭鷹. 8. 貨囊. 9. 冒騙.

到好些臣服島王的總督和諸侯們，從他們增進了不少的見識。

　　屬於這島王的島，名叫加西爾島，據航海家說，終夜可以聞到鼕鼕的鼓聲。這個異島，現在我身歷其境，想探求奇異的原因，結果看見二三百呎長的大魚兒，初看時覺得可怕，但牠並不害人；原來牠們很膽怯，聽　杖擊聲或船碰聲，就嚇得驚逃了哩。我又瞧見別些魚兒，約莫十八英吋長，魚頭好像貓頭鷹一般。

　　有一天，我正在港口眺望的時候，有一隻船向前駛來。我前去一看，卻是我以前乘赴波沙拉去的那隻船。我一眼便認得那船長，就走去向他索我的貨物。我說：『我是孫柏達，這些標着名字的貨包，乃是我的。』

　　他大聲說：『上帝！這時候，我們能信任着誰呢？我親眼瞧見孫柏達沉在海中死了，你現在卻來冒認別人家的貨物。』

　　但是最後他終於信任我不是冒騙了，因爲在他船上有許多人和我認識的，現在見我活着，都走來向我道賀。於是他說：『你能逃免大禍！眞是可喜。你的貨物都在，請你拿去罷。』

What was of greatest worth in them I presented to the sovereign, who was much pleased to hear of my good fortune, and gave me in return a gift of still greater value. Then I took leave of him, and went aboard the same ship after I had exchanged my goods for products of that country. I carried with me wood of aloes, *sandals*,[1] *camphire*,[2] *nutmegs*,[3] *cloves*,[4] *pepper*,[5] and *ginger*.[6] We passed by several islands, and at last arrived at Bussorah, whence I came to this city with great wealth.

Here Sindbad stopped, and gave Hindbad a purse of money, bidding him return the next day, and hear the story of the next voyage. This was repeated each day, till all the voyages were described.

The Second Voyage of Sindbad the Sailor

After my first voyage, I meant to spend the rest of my days at Bagdad, but I soon grew *weary*[7] of an idle life, and put to sea a second time, with merchants of known honesty. We embarked on board a good ship, and, after committing ourselves to God, set sail. We traded from island to island with great profit. One day we landed on an island where we could see neither man nor animal. There were many fruits and flowers, and whilst some were gathering them, I took my wine and food, and sat down near a stream *betwixt*[8] two high trees, which formed a thick shade. I made a good meal, and

【註】1. 檀香. 2. 樟腦. 3. 豆蔻. 4. 丁香. 5. 胡椒. 6. 薑. 7. 無聊. 8. 介于.

　　我隨選取我貨件中最貴重的東西，獻給島王，他聽到
我有這樣好的幸運，十分歡喜，賜我價值更高的禮物，來
作為酬報。我告別了他，和士民交換些土產，便搭了同一的
船起行。　我置辦的貨物中，有沉香，檀香，樟腦，豆蔻，
丁香，胡椒，和薑。　我們駛過了數島，終於到得波沙拉
島，那里我這些貨物，無不利市十倍，我就賺了很多的錢
囘來。

　　說到這裏，孫柏達住了口，給辛巴德一個錢袋兒，教
他明天再來，聽第二次航行的故事。

孫柏達第二次的航行

　　在我第一次航海後，我在巴革達德閒住了幾時，就感
到游閒生活的無聊，於是又作第二次的航行，同伴都是著
名忠實的商人，我們搭乘一隻堅固的船，把自己交給上帝
之後，遂開始航行了。從一個島轉到另一個島，賣買上都
得到很大的利益。一天，我們航行到一個島，這島上旣沒
有人煙，也沒有獸跡。島上倒有好多的菓兒和花草，有些
人採摘牠們。這時候，我獨自拿了酒食，到臨河兩棵高樹

afterwards fell asleep. I cannot tell how long I slept, but when I awoke the ship was gone.

In this sad *plight*,[1] I was ready to die with grief. I cried out in *agony*,[2] I beat my head and breast, and threw myself upon the ground, where I lay some time in despair. Why was I not content with the produce of my first voyage, which would have kept me in comfort all my life? But it was too late to repent. At last I resigned myself to the will of God. Not knowing what to do, I climbed to the top of a lofty tree, where I could look about on all sides for signs of hope. Towards the sea there was nothing but sky and water. Looking over the land, I saw something white, and, coming down, took some of the food I had left, and went towards it, not knowing at the great distance what it was.

As I drew near, I thought it to be a white *dome*[3] of enormous size; and when I touched it I found it to be very smooth. There was no opening on any side, and there was no climbing to the top over the smooth surface. It was at least fifty paces round.

By this time the sun was about to set, and all of a sudden the sky became as dark as if it had been covered with a thick cloud. I was amazed at this sudden darkness, but much more when I found it was caused by a bird of *monstrous*[4] size, that came flying towards me. I remembered that I had often heard mariners speak of a *marvelous*[5] bird called the *roc*,[6] and felt sure that the great dome by which I stood

【註】 1. 環境. 2. 苦痛. 3. 圓屋頂. 4. 怪大的. 5. 奇異的. 6. 大鵬鳥.

蔭下，坐着吃喝。我吃得很爽快，便倒頭睡着了。我不知我睡有多久，但醒時那船早已開行。

在這悲慘的環境中，我端的憂忿待死。我驚怕狂叫，搥胸探脚，躺倒在地，足有好一卮兒失神落魄。爲甚我還不知滿足呢？我第一次海行所得，不是很夠供給我一生受用嗎？但懊悔已經來不及了。到後來，只得委生死於天命。茫然地，攀上一棵高樹上去，四面張望，看有無得救。在海面上，只見滔滔白浪，水和天打成一片。向陸地上望去，我看見有些白的東西，下了樹，再將吃剩的東西吃完，便向那兒走去，卻不知到底有多少遠。

當我走近的時候，看見卻是白得雪也似的一個巨球。我想這是一所廣大的圓屋頂了；用手去摸，覺得很光滑。各面都沒有洞口，因很平滑，卻又不能攀上頂尖去。這東西至少有五十步渾圓。

這時候，太陽差不多漸漸西沉了。但一忽兒，天上忽然烏黑了，好像給一塊濃厚烏雲掩住的一般。我正驚惶這突如其來的黑暗，不過天色卻愈變得黑了，我張目一看，原來一隻怪大的鳥兒，撲地飛來。我忽然悟到，這就是航海家說的，一種名叫大鵬鳥兒的異鳥，我所站的這巨大白

must be its egg. *In short*,[1] the bird alighted and sat over the egg. As I saw her coming, I crept close to the egg, so that I had before me one of the legs of the bird, which was as big as the *trunk*[2] of a tree. I tied myself strongly to it with my turban, in hopes that the roc next morning would carry me with her out of this desert island. After having passed the night in this condition, the bird flew away as soon as it was daylight, and carried me so high that I could not see the earth. Then she descended with so much speed that I lost my senses. But when I found myself on the ground, I quickly untied the knot, and had scarcely done so when the roc, having taken up a *serpent*[3] of monstrous length in her *bill*,[4] flew away.

The spot where I was left was surrounded on all sides by mountains, that seemed to reach above the clouds, and so steep that I could not possibly get out of the *valley*.[5] It seemed to me that the place was no better than the desert island from which the roc had brought me.

As I walked through the valley, I found it *strewed*[6] with diamonds of a surprising bigness. But the pleasure of looking at them was soon destroyed by another sight, which filled me with terror, namely, a great number of serpents, so monstrous that the least of them could *swallow*[7] an *elephant*.[8] In the daytime they hid in their *dens*[9] from their enemy, the roc, and came out only in the night.

【註】 1. 一霎眼間. 2. 樹幹. 3. 蛇. 4. 鳥喙. 5. 山谷. 6. 散播. 7. 吞. 8. 象. 9. 洞.

球，定是牠的卵子。一霎眼間，那鳥兒停翅坐在這卵上，我見牠下來的時候，就貼伏在卵上，在我的面前，看見的就是這鳥兒的一隻脚，這隻脚足有樹幹般粗細。我用頭巾把身體緊緊繫在這鳥脚上，希望那鵬鳥，明天可以帶我飛出這個荒島。一夜這樣地過去了，一到東天發白的當兒，鳥兒忽然飛起，把我帶入這般高遠，地面都不能看見。不多時牠降落下來，降落時使我知覺完全失去。當我一發覺近着地面的時候，我連忙鬆下頭巾，還不曾完全鬆掉的時候，那大鵬鳥已啄得一條大蛇在嘴裏，便又飛去了。

我被遺落下的這個地點，四面都是高山，這些山峯高入雲霄，看來無論如何，總爬不出這深谷的。那大鵬鳥將我帶到這地方，據我看，似乎並沒有勝似那個荒島。

我在山谷裏走的時候，卻見那很大的，晶耀奪目的鑽石，徧地都是。不過這喜悅立即消滅了，非但沒有喜悅，且充滿着害怕，原來，看見有好多大蛇，這些蛇至少能張口吞下巨象的。白天牠們躲在洞裏，以躲避大鵬鳥，祇有夜裏出來。

I spent the day in walking about in the valley. When night came I went into a cave where I thought I might rest in safety. I closed the low and narrow entrance with a great stone, to preserve me from the serpents, but did not shut out all the light.　Soon the serpents began *hissing*[1] around me and put me in such extreme fear that I could not sleep.　When day appeared the serpents retired, and I came out of the cave trembling.　I can justly say that I walked upon diamonds without feeling any desire to touch them. At last I sat down, and ate some of my food, and, *in spite of*[2] my fears, fell asleep, for I had not closed my eyes during the night.　Scarcely were they shut when something that fell by me with a great noise awoke me.　This was a large piece of raw meat; and at the same time, I saw several others fall down from the rocks in different places.

I had never believed what I had heard sailors and others tell of the valley of diamonds, and of the means employed by merchants to obtain jewels from it.　But now I found that I had heard the truth.　For the fact is, that merchants come to this valley when the eagles have young ones, and throw great joints of meat into it; the diamonds, upon whose points they fall, *stick*[3] to them; the eagles, which are stronger in this country than anywhere else, *pounce*[4] with great force upon these pieces of meat, and carry them to their nests on the edge of the rocks to feed their young; then the merchants run to their nests, drive

---

【註】　1. 發呼呼聲.　2. 不顧.　3. 黏著.　4. 撲.

我那天在這山谷裏，一直步行到晚。晚上找得一個山洞，以爲安身之計。這洞口又窄又低，我掇塊大石頭，抵住穴口，以防巨蛇的毒害，不過外邊的是看得見的。不多時，那些巨蛇圍着我四周，呼呼地遊動，使我驚慌得一夜不敢閉眼。天亮了，這些巨蛇方始退去，我纔從洞裏抖戰着爬將出來。我可說，我雖然脚脚踏在鑽石上，但絲毫未曾想到要拾取牠們。我終於坐下，吃些兒食物，心裏雖然悲傷，因爲一夜沒睡，實在倦極，也就睡着了。一雙眼兒還不曾合攏，不知是些什麼東西從天上丟下來，險些兒打在我身上，砰的一聲，立時把我驚醒。原來是一大塊肉兒；同時我又看見別處地上，有同樣的東西丟下。

以前曾聽水手們和別些人們說着鑽石山谷，和那些珠寶商人怎樣去取的故事，初聽聽我總是不信。現在我卻不料親歷其境了。原來一般珠寶商人到了這山谷來，因地險無法探取，乃在鷹孳育的時候把大塊的肉片從山上丟下，地上的鑽石卽膠黏在肉上；那處的鷹來得特別強健，能將這大塊的肉啣起，啣到牠們山上面的巢窩裏，用以飼着雛鷹，商人們乃到牠們的巢邊，大聲噪喝，把鷹嚇走，遂拾下那

off the eagles by their shouts, and take away the diamonds that stick to the meat.

In this *device*[1] I saw the means of my escape.

I gathered the largest diamonds I could find, and put them into a leather bag fastened at my waist. Then I took the larges of the pieces of meat, tied it close around me with the cloth of my turban, and laid myself upon the ground, with my face downwards. I had scarcely placed myself thus when one of the eagles bore me, with the piece of meat to which I was fastened, to his nest on the top of the mountain. The merchants at once began their shooting to frighten the eagles, and when they had driven the birds away, one of them came to the nest where I was. He was much alarmed when he first saw me, but soon began to quarrel, and asked me why I stole his goods.

"Do not be uneasy," said I; "here are diamonds enough for you and me, more than all the others have together. They have to take what chance brings them, but I chose for myself, in the valley, those which you see in this bag."

The other merchants now crowded around in amazement, and led me to their camp. When I showed them the diamonds in my bag, they *confessed*[2] that they had never seen any of such size and beauty. I prayed the merchant who owned the nest to which I was carried (for every merchant had his own) to take for his share as many as he pleased. He

[註] 1. 策略. 2. 承認.

肉片上的鑽石。

在這個策略裏，我瞧見我脫逃的方法了。

我揀着最大的鑽石，拾了許多，放在一隻皮袋中，緊扣在腰間。於是我取了幾片最大的肉，用我的頭巾，把我福裹在肉裏，躺在地上，臉向着下邊。我恰把自己安置好，卻有一隻大鷹將我和肉啣去，飛到山頂牠的窩裏。那些鑽石商立卽發聲大噪，將鳥兒們驚走，有個商人走到我所在的巢邊。他初見我的時候，很覺驚奇，但頓時手鬧起來，責問我爲什麼盜他的鑽石。

我說：『不要吵！這兒有的是鑽石，爲你我所共有的，他人一輩子也取不到這麼多的。他們不過偶然拾得幾粒罷了，我卻自己從這山谷裏揀來的，你看看那袋子裏吧。』

其他商人也圍着過來，大家吃驚不已，遂引我到他們的幕帳去。當我把我袋裏的鑽石，拿給他們瞧時，他們都承認從未見過這般又美，又大的鑽石。我便命那守巢的商人（因爲每個商人各有一個巢守着的，）任意揀取。他但揀

contented himself with one, and that the least of them, and, when I urged him to take more, said:

"No, this will save me the trouble of making any more voyages, and will raise as great a fortune as I desire."

When each of the merchants was satisfied with the diamonds which the eagles brought them, we left the place, and traveled near high mountains, where there were serpents of *prodigious*[1] length, and from these we had the good fortune to escape. We took ship at the first port we reached, and touched at the Isle of Roha, where the trees grow that yield camphire. Here also is found the *rhinoceros*.[2] This animal fights with the elephant, runs his *horn*[3] into his *belly*,[4] and carries him off upon his head; but when the blood and fat of the elephant runs into his eyes, and makes him blind, he falls to the ground; then, strange to relate, the roc comes and carries them both away in her claws, for food for her young ones.

In this island I exchanged my diamonds for merchandise. After trading at various towns, we landed at Bussorah, whence I proceeded to Bagdad. There I gave large presents to the poor, and lived in honor upon the vast riches I had gained with so much fatigue.

The Third Voyage of Sindbad the Sailor

I grew weary soon again of living an idle life, and, hardening myself against the thought of any

【註】 1. 巨大的. 2. 犀牛. 3. 角. 4. 腹.

取一粒頂小的。我教他再取，他說道：

『不，這個已足使我受用不盡，省卻我許多高山遠水的跋涉勞苦了。』

當每個商人將鑽石採取得滿意時，我們便離開那處，打那些有大蛇的高山的近處經過。幸而都逃過了危險。我們一走到海口便上船，航行到盧哈島，那兒有產樟腦的樹，也有一種犀牛，這走獸和象激戰的時候，用他的角刺進象的肚皮裏，舉了便走；但是象血和油質滴進他的眼中，使他瞎了眼，便倒臥在地上；說也奇怪，那大鵬鳥兒會飛來，將牠們一併用爪抓了去，作為牠雛鳥的食物。

在這個島上，我用鑽石交換了些商品。從幾處市城兜賣了後，我們到波沙拉島上岸，轉輾回到巴革達德來。這兒我給許多禮物與貧民，倦遊回來，我所得到巨大的財產，足夠使我安樂受用。

孫柏達第三次的航行

安樂的生活，不久使我又覺得厭煩起來，壯心復萌，

danger, embarked with some merchants on another long voyage. After trading at several ports, we were overtaken one day by a dreadful *tempest*,[1] which drove us from our course. Before it ceased we were brought to the port of an island, which the captain was very unwilling to enter; but we were obliged to cast *anchor*.[2] The captain then told us that in this and some islands near it dwelt *hairy*[3] savages who would soon attack us; and, though they were but *dwarfs*,[4] we must not resist them, for they were more in number than the *locusts*,[5] and, if we happened to kill one, they would all fall upon us and destroy us.

We soon found the captain's words but too true. A great multitude of frightful savages, about two feet high, covered all over with red hair, come swimming towards us, and surrounded the ship. They *chattered*[6] as they came near, but we understood not their language. They climbed up the sides of the ship with surprising quickness. They took down our sails, cut the cable, and, *hauling*[7] the vessel to the shore, made us all get out, and carried the ship into another island, from which they had come. We saw at a distance a vast pile of building, and made towards it. We found it to be a palace, *elegantly*[8] built, and very lofty, with a gate of *ebony*[9] of two leaves, which we opened. Before us was a large room, with a *porch*,[10] having on one side a heap of human bones, and on the other a vast number of

---

【註】 1. 暴風雨. 2. 錨. 3. 多毛的. 4. 矮子. 5. 蝗蟲. 6. 喳喳地說. 7. 拖. 8. 壯麗地. 9. 烏木. 10. 石階.

途不再以危險爲念，我結合幾個商人又去作長途航行。從幾個商埠做過買賣後，一天，遇到可怕的暴風雨，把我們打失了原來的航路，飄到一個島口裏，風雨還兀自不歇，船長原不願入口的，但我們沒法，只得拋下了錨。船長於是告訴我們，在這個及附近幾個島上，都有徧體生毛的野人住着，他們就要來襲擊我們哩；雖然他們都是矮子，我們卻無法敵住他們，因爲他們人數，多得如蝗蟲，要如我們偶然壞了他們中的一個，他們定然成羣地來，要把我們全行撲滅纔罷。

不多時船長的話果眞實現了。我們看見一大羣可怕的野人，約莫二尺高，徧體披着紅毛，泅着水向我們游來將船包圍着，他們來的時候，口裏喳喳地說個不住，可惜我們不懂得他們的語言。他們上船來，異常敏捷。取下了我們的帆，割斷了我們的纜，把船拖到岸邊，將我們盡行驅逐下來。他們原從那另一個島上來的，便把我們的船開往那島去了。在那很遠的地方，我們瞧見有一所大屋宇，向這屋子走去，原來是個大宮院，建築得又壯嚴，又高大，兩扇門是用烏木做的，我們把門推開，一眼就見一間廣大的房間，前面有一石階，在一邊堆積著一大堆人骨，另一邊

roasting-spits.[1] We trembled at this sight, and were seized wih deadly fear, when suddenly the gate of the room opened with a loud *crash*,[2] and there came out the *horrible*[3] figure of a black man, as tall as a lofty palm-tree. He had but one eye, and that in the middle of his forehead, where it blazed bright as a burning coal. His foreteeth were very long and sharp, and stood out of his mouth, which was as deep as that of a horse. His upper lip hung down upon his breast. His ears were like an elephant's and covered his shoulders; and his nails were as long and *crooked*[4] as the *talons*[5] of the greatest birds. At the sight of so frightful a genie, we lost our senses, and lay like dead men.

At last we came to ourselves, and saw him sitting in the porch, looking closely at us. Then he *advanced*,[6] and, laying his hand upon me, took me up by the *nape*[7] of my neck, and turned me round, as a *butcher*[8] would turn a sheep's head. When he saw that I had nothing but skin and bone, he let me go. He took up all the rest one by one, and viewed them in the same manner. As the captain was the fattest, he held him with one hand, as I would a *sparrow*,[9] and thrust a spit through him; he then kindled a great fire, *roasted*,[10] and ate him for his supper. Then he fell asleep, *snoring*[11] louder than thunder. He slept thus till morning As to ourselves, it was not possible for us to enjoy any rest, and we passed the night in the most painful fear. When day

---

【註】 1. 燔肉爐. 2. 震裂聲. 3. 可怕的. 4. 彎曲. 5. 爪. 6. 前進. 7. 頸背. 8. 屠夫. 9. 雀. 10. 烤炙. 11. 發鼾聲.

卻是很多的燔肉爐。我們見了驚駭得發抖，正在惶駭萬分的時候，忽然那房間的門開了，聲音極大，走出來的乃是個形容可怕的黑人，足有一棵高的椶樹兒那麼高大。他只有一隻眼睛，這眼睛是長在他前額的，睛光灼灼，好像一塊燒紅的煤一般。他的嘴足有馬嘴般深大，門牙又長，又犀利的伸出口外。上唇直垂到胸前。耳朵像象的一般，遮沒兩個肩膀；指甲又長又曲，好像最大鳥兒的爪子一樣。一見這般可怕的巨人，我們都駭得失掉知覺，死人似的倒臥在地上了。

　　我們醒來的時候，見他兀自坐在石階上，緊緊地看着我們。見我們伸動，他走來，夾頸子一把，便先把我捉住，翻來覆去，把我前後都察看一遍，好像一個屠手看一頭羊一般。當他瞧見我骨瘦如柴，一點肉也沒有，遂放下把其餘的人們，一個個地，都同樣的看了一遍。因爲那個船長，生得最肥胖，他一手把他抓起，好像抓黃雀兒一般，用叉把他叉了；生起一大爐餤餤的火來，烤炙一回，便把他當做一頓晚餐。吃畢，卽倒便睡，鼾聲響似巨雷。他這樣地一直睡到了天明。至於我們，一夜憂愴悲急，再也不能合眼。

appeared the giant awoke, went out, and left us in the palace.

The next night we revenged ourselves on the *brutish*[1] giant in the following manner. After he had finished his inhuman supper on another of our seamen, he lay down on his back and fell asleep As soon as we heard him snore, nine of the boldest among us, and I, took each of us a spit, and, putting the points of them into the fire till they were burning hot, we thrust them into his eye all at once, and blinded him. The pain made him break ou in a frightful yell; he started up, and stretched out his hands to seize and kill us; but we ran to such places as he could not reach. After having sought for us in vain, he *groped*[2] for the gate, and went out, howling in agony.

We left the palace at once, and came to the shore, where we made some *rafts*[3] each large enough to carry three men. We waited till day before getting on them, for we hoped that by morning the howling, which we still heard, would cease, and that the giant would be dead; and if that happened we meant to stay in the island, and not to risk our lives upon the rafts. But day had scarcely appeared when we saw our cruel enemy, with two other giants, almost o. the same size, leading him; and a gr at number were coming before him at a quick pace.

We waited no longer to take to our rafts, and put to sea with all the speed we could The giants, seeing this, took up great stones, and, running to the

【註】　1. 兇暴的.　2. 摸索.　3. 木排.

早上那巨人醒了，出去，把我們關在宮裏。

　　第二夜，我們在以下的情形裏，用計來報復這兇暴的巨人。在他又吃了我們中另一個伙伴當作晚餐，他仰面睡着了。我們一聽到他的鼾聲，我伙伴中九個最勇敢的人和我，各自拿了一柄叉兒，先向火爐中燒得發紅。立即刺入他的眼睛裏，把他眼睛弄瞎了。這個痛苦使他大聲可怕地，咆哮起來；他跳起亂抓，要想殺死我們；我們即四處躲避，使他不能抓到。抓了一會兒，見抓不到我們，他摸索着門，狂奔出去，大聲痛吼。

　　我們立刻走出宮院，奔到海灘邊，便做了幾個木排，每個木排足容三個人駐足。等到天明纔開將出去，因為我們希望到早上，那猶能隱隱地聽見的巨人吼聲，也許能停歇了，那個巨人也許死了；要如遇到這情形，我們留住在那島上，要比寄身在木排上飄打好得多哩。但是天還沒有發亮，我們就瞧見那兇暴的敵人，同着另兩個同樣高大的巨怪，他們飛步向前，尤如疾風暴雨打來。

　　我們再不能一刻停留了。便慌忙地登上木排，盡力向海裏開行。巨人們瞧見了，拿了大石頭，奔向沙灘，接連

shore, entered the water up to the middle, and threw so exactly that they sank all the rafts but that I was upon; and all my *comrades*,[1] except the two with me, were drowned. We rowed with all our might, and got out of the reach of the giants. The next morning, after a night of fear, we were thrown upon an island, where we landed with much joy, and found good fruit, which *refreshed*[2] us greatly.

At night we went to sleep on the seashore, but were awakened by the noise of a serpent of surprising length and thickness, whose scales made a *rustling*[3] noise as he moved himself along. It *swallowed*[4] up one of my comrades, in spite of his loud cries and his efforts to save himself. *Dashing*[5] him several times against the ground, it crushed him, and we could hear it *gnaw*[6] and tear the poor fellow's bones, though we had fled far off. The next day, to our great terror, we saw the serpent again. "O Heaven, to what dangers are we *exposed!*[7]" I cried. "We escape from a giant and the waves, only to meet with this!"

The next night, having satisfied our hunger with fruit, we mounted a tall tree, hoping to pass the night in safety. But soon the serpent came hissing to its foot, raised itself up against the trunk, and, reaching my comrade, who sat lower than I, swallowed him at once and went off.

In the morning when I came down, I was ready to throw myself into the sea in my despair. But I

【註】　1. 伙伴們.　2. 恢復.　3. 沙沙響.　4. 吞.　5. 投擲.　6. 嚙. 7. 遭受.

向海中擲來，他們投無不中，把這些木排盡行打沉，祇剩下我的一個沒有打中；我的衆伙伴們，除了兩個人和我外，都沉在海中溺死了。我們竭力逃脫，不曾爲巨人捉着。在一夜的驚慌中，第二天早上，我們又被飄流到一個島上，那兒我們登岸，異常歡喜，發見許多好的菓兒，飽食一餐。

晚上我們便躺臥在沙灘上，但是卻被一條十分粗長的巨蛇驚嚇了，牠爬行時鱗甲着地，沙沙作聲。這蛇吞了我的一個伙伴去，不管他怎般狂呼掙扎着，牠昂頭將他渾身上下繞著，不久便吞了下去。我們雖然逃得遠了，還聽到牠嚼這可憐人骨頭的響聲。第二天，給我們驚慌的，仍瞧見那條怪蛇。我驚呼着：『唉！天呀！我們置身在這樣的危險境裏！我們逃過了巨人和險浪，卻又碰到這東西啊！』

第二晚，我們吃飽菓兒後，攀上一棵很高的樹上，希望得平安度過此夜。但那毒蛇很快的嘶嘶地爬來，把頭伸向樹上，伸到坐在我下面的伙伴，立刻把他吞去了。

早上我下樹的當兒，在我的失望中，我預備投身大海

resisted this *impulse*,[1] and collected a great quantity of small wood, *brambles*,[2] and dry *thorns*,[3] and, making them up into *fagots*,[4] made a wide circle with them round the tree, and also tied some of them to the branches over my head. Within this circle I shut myself up when night came, with such satisfaction as I could get from having neglected nothing that could save me. The serpent failed not to come at the usual hour, but was prevented from reaching me by the *rampart*[5] I had made. He lay below me till day, like a cat watching in vain for a mouse that has reached a place of safety. When day appeared he retired, but I dared not to leave my fort until the sun arose.

God took pity on my hopeless state, for, just as I was about to cast myself into the sea, I saw a ship in the distance. I cried aloud and waved the linen of my turban. Then I was seen, and the captain sent his boat for me. When I came on board, the merchants and seamen *flocked*[6] about me to hear how I came into that deserted island, in a region where *cannibal*[7] giants and serpents were known by the oldest sailors to abound. When I stood before the captain in rags, he gave me one of his own suits. Looking *steadfastly*[8] upon him, I knew him to be the person who, in my second voyage, had left me in the island where I fell asleep, and sailed without me or sending to seek for me.

【註】 1. 衝動. 2. 荆棘. 3. 荆棘. 4. 柴把. 5. 防禦物. 6. 羣集. 7. 食人肉的. 8. 不變地.

了。但我突然轉念，卻拾着很多的樹枝兒，有刺的樹枝，和荊棘，束成若干把兒，將大樹的周圍，圍成爲一個大圈兒，在我頂上的樹技上，又細了許多，夜裏我躲藏在裏邊，因爲關於自衞的事情，在佈置上既沒有疏漏，因而也就覺得放心，毒蛇依時到來；可是他爲我所築的防禦所阻住，再也不能爬到我的地方。他好像一隻貓伺着躲洞的老鼠，躺在我下邊，直到天明，方才退去。但我未到太陽升起，還兀自不敢出來哩。

老天憐恤我，在我極度失望要投身入海的時候，我遠處卻瞧見有隻船駛來。我大聲呼救，一壁把我的頭巾揮個不住。我終被牠瞧見了，船長送着小船來。當我到得大船，一羣商人們和水手們都圍住我，要聽我怎地會到那個荒島去的，這附近的地方，盡是爲食人肉的巨人和毒蛇所據，凡最有經驗的水手們大都知道的。當我穿着破衣服，站在船長的面前，他給我一套衣服換了。我向他凝視一會，便認出他是那個船長，當我第二次航行時，我睡着在一個島上，他沒有查找我，把船開去了的。

"Captain," said I, "look at me, and you may know that I am Sindbad, whom you left in that desert island."

"God be praised!" he cried, after he had *scanned*[1] me closely. "I rejoice that fortune has set right my fault. There are your goods, which I always took care to preserve." I took them from him, and thanked him for his care of them.

We remained at sea for some time, touched at several islands, and landed at last at the island of Salabat, where *sandal-wood*[2] is obtained. In another island I furnished myself with *cloves*,[3] *cinnamon*,[4] and other spices. After a long voyage, in the course of which I saw such creatures as a *tortoise*[5] twenty cubits in length and breadth, I arrived at Bussorah, and thence returned to Bagdad, with so much wealth that I knew not its extent. I gave a great deal to the poor, and bought another large estate besides what I had already.

The Fourth Voyage of Sindbad the Sailor

After I had rested from the dangers of my third voyage, my passion for trade and *novelty*[7] soon drove me from home again. When I had settled my affairs and taken a stock of goods for *traffic*,[8] I took the route of Persia, traveled over several provinces, and arrived at a port, where I embarked. It was not long before our ship wrecked. Several of the

---

【註】 1. 熟視. 2. 檀香. 3. 丁香. 4. 肉桂. 5. 龜. 6. 慾望. 7. 好奇. 8. 貿易.

我說：『船長；請瞧我，你也許能認識我，是給你丟下在那荒島上的孫柏達呢。』

他凝視了我一會，驚叫着說：『讚美上帝，我幸喜能補救我的過失。 你的貨件都在這兒， 我小心地爲你保存着。』當下我取着貨物，謝了他爲我小心的保護。

我們在海中又勾留若干時候，經過幾處海島，最後到出檀香的賽拉伯島靠岸。 在另一個島上， 賣完我的丁香，肉桂，和別幾種的香料。在這冗長的海途中，我瞧見一隻十六尺方圓的大龜。我到得波沙拉，囘到巴革達德，所得的金錢，眞是難以計算。我散了大批的錢給窮人，又另置了許多的產業。

孫柏達第四次的航行

第三次的危險方纔驚魂甫定，我那商業慾和好奇慾，很快地又驅我離開家去。 我把事情料理好， 辦得一批商品。打波斯走去，經過了數省地方，纔到一個海口登船。這船不久卽被海浪打破了。幾個商人和水手全被淹死，全船的

merchants and seamen were drowned, and the cargo was lost.

I had the good fortune, with a few others, to get upon some *planks*,[1] and we were carried by the *current*[2] to an island which lay before us. There we found fruit and spring water, which saved our lives. Early the next morning, we explored the island, and saw some houses, which we approached. As soon as we drew near, we were surrounded by a great number of negroes, who seized us, shared us among them, and carried us to their respective *abodes*.[3]

I and five of my comrades were carried to one place; here they made us sit down, and gave us a certain *herb*,[4] which they made signs to us to eat. My comrades did not notice that the blacks took none of it themselves, and ate *greedily*[5] But I, *suspecting*[6] some *trick*,[7] would not so much as taste it, which happened well for me, for in a little time I saw that my comrades had lost their senses, and that when they spoke to me they knew not what they said.

The negroes fed us afterwards with rice to make us fat, for they were *cannibals*[8] and meant to eat us. My comrades, who had lost their senses, ate heartily of it, but I very *sparingly*.[9] They were *devoured*[10] one by one, and I, with my senses entire, as you may readily guess, grew *leaner*[11] every day. The fear of death turned all my food into *poison*.[12] I fell into a sickness which proved my safety, for the negroes,

---

【註】 1. 板. 2. 海浪. 3. 住所. 4. 草. 5. 貪心地. 6. 懷疑. 7. 詭計. 8. 食人者. 9. 缺乏地. 10. 吃去. 11. 較瘦的. 12. 毒藥.

貨品也就覆沒了。

有幾個人和我，都還幸運，抓住了幾塊船板，在海浪中，被飄流到一個島邊。這島上有鮮菓，清泉，得救了我們的生命。第二天早上，我們卽進島內探險，看見有幾所房屋。當我們近前的時候，立卽被一大羣尼格羅人所包圍，將我們捉住了。他們就同伙中，將我們各人分好，帶往各自的屋裏去。

我跟我的五個伙伴做一處，被帶往一個地方。那兒他們教我們坐下，給我們一種草，做手勢教吃，我的伙伴們未曾留心黑人們自己不肯吃那種草，卻貪心地吃着。但我懷疑有甚詭計，一根都不吃，這眞是我的造化，因爲一會兒，我瞧見我的伙伴們都神經昏亂發癡了，當他們對我說話時，他們自己不知道是說些什麽。

尼格羅人隨後便用米飯，飼養我們，使我們發胖，因爲他們都是些吃人的黑人，心想要吃掉我們。我的伙伴們既失了知覺，貪心地吃着，但我卻吃得很少。他們一個個都被黑人吃去，我呢，因爲知覺完善，一天瘦似一天，又看見同伴那樣悽慘的死去，眞令我驚心駭目，心想不如仰毒藥自盡了罷，又未死去，我因此臥病，豈知反因這病而救

having killed and eaten my comrades, and seeing me to be withered, lean, and sick, put off my death.

Meanwhile I had much liberty, and scarcely any notice was taken of what I did. Therefore one day, when no one but an old man was left about the houses, I made my escape. For seven days I traveled, avoiding places which seemed to be inhabited, and living on *coconuts,*[1] which served me both for meat and drink. On the eighth day, I came near the sea, and saw some white people, like myself, gathering *pepper,*[2] of which there was a great plenty in that place. To them I went without fear.

They came to meet me when they saw me, and asked me, in Arabic, who I was and whence I came. I was overjoyed to hear them speak in my own language, and told them of my *shipwreck,*[3] and how I fell into the hands of the negroes.

"These negroes," replied they, "eat man. By what *miracle*[4] did you escape?"

Then I told them what I have just told you, and they were greatly surprised. When they had finished gathering pepper, they took me with them to the island *whence*[5] they had come, and presented me to their King, who was a good prince. He listened with surprise to the story of my adventures, and gave me clothes, and commanded that care be taken of me.

The island was well peopled, and the capital a place of great trade. The Prince treated me with

---

【註】 1. 椰子. 2. 胡椒. 3. 船舶破壞. 4. 異事. 5. 由此.

我一死，因為那些尼格羅人，吃完我的伙伴們，見我又瘦又病，遂把我暫且擱下不吃。

這時候，我得了不少的自由，我的行動也少受他們的監視。有一天，屋子裏沒有人，祇留一個老頭兒在家，我卽逃走出來。為要逃免被黑人們擒捉，盡向無人煙的地方逃奔。獨自個兒在荒郊上奔走七天，天天摘椰子來當飢，療渴維持生命，第八天上，我奔到海灘邊，見有幾個和我相似的白人，在收集着胡椒，這東西在那個地方，本來很多的。對於他們，我是不害怕了。

當他們瞧見我走去的時候，都前來迎接我，操亞拉伯語，問我是甚麼人，從那處來的。我聽見異域上有說本國話的人，大喜過望，遂把海船失事，及怎樣落在尼格羅人手中的情形，一一都講給他們聽了。

他們說：『那些尼格羅人，是吃人的。你能夠逃出來，倒是件異事。』

我又把上面出險的情形，述了一遍，他們深為駭異。當他們採完胡椒，帶我到一個島上，這島是他們居住的，他們有一個很和善的國王，又引我朝見他。他頗驚奇我的冒險，賜我衣服，命手下人好好的款待我。

那島上人煙頗密，京都乃是個商業繁盛的地方。國王招

much kindness, and I, delighted with such a retreat after my misfortunes, was soon looked upon rather as a native than as a *stranger*.[1] I observed one thing which seemed to me very strange. All the people, even the King, rode horses without *bridle*[2] or *stirrups*[3]. One day I found workmen who made, under my directions, a saddle with stirrups and a bit. These I presented to the King, who was so pleased with them that he made me large presents. I made several others for the ministers and chief officers of his household, which gained me great *repute*[4] and regard.

One day the King, to whom I constantly paid court, said:—

"Sindbad, I love thee; I have one thing to demand of thee, which thou must grant. I have a mind thou shouldst marry, that so thou mayst stay with us, and think no more of thy own country."

I *durst*[5] not resist the prince's will, and soon I was married to one of the ladies of his court, noble, beautiful, and rich. We lived together in perfect *harmony*,[6] but I could not forget Bagdad, and planned to make my escape as soon as might be.

At this time the wife of one of my neighbors, with whom I had made a very *strict*[7] friendship, fell sick and died. I went to comfort him in his sorrow, and said as soon as I saw him: "God preserve you and grant you a long life."

【註】 1. 他國人. 2. 馬勒. 3. 馬鐙. 4. 名譽. 5. 敢. 6. 和藹. 7. 深厚的.

待我很是優厚。我呢，在遇難後得到這樣的安樂所在，也很
滿意了。我不久卽被島上的人民看做一個本國人一樣。我隨
發見一件事物，似乎很覺得奇怪的。舉國人民和國王都是
一樣的騎馬，卻沒有馬勒或馬鐙。一天，我找得一個工匠，
在我的指示下，做一副馬鞍，有踏鐙，有坐子。我拿去獻
給國王，國王很是喜說，隨賜給我許多禮物兒。我又做了
幾具，贈給朝裏大臣們，和國王家裏的大官，使我同樣地
受到不少的光寵。

　　我是時常隨朝的，一天，那國王對我說：

　　『孫柏達我很歡喜你，我有一件事情要求你，你可不
能推辭的。我想你應該結婚了，你便長住在本國罷，再不
必囘到你的故國去。』

　　我不敢違抗那島王的意旨，隨後就和他朝裏的一個女
子結婚，這女子又賢，又美，又富，我們倆過得十分和愛，不
過我卻不能忘掉巴革達德，我常時打算，一遇機會，就想逃
囘來的。

　　我有個鄰人，和我交情很深，這時他妻子病死了。我
在他悲哀中，走去安慰他，一見他便說：『上帝保佑你，願
你長壽。』

"Alas!" replied he, "how may that be? I have not above an hour to live, for I must be buried this day with my wife. This is a law in this island. The living husband is buried with the dead wife, and the living wife with the dead husband."

While he was telling me of this barbarous custom, the very account of which *chilled my blood*,[1] his *kindred*,[2] friends, and neighbors came to assist at the funeral. They dressed the *corpse*[3] of the woman in her richest robes and all her jewels, as if it had been her wedding day; then they placed her on an open *bier*,[4] and began their march to the place of burial. The husband walked first, next to the dead body. When they reached a high mountain, they took up a large stone, which formed the mouth of a deep pit, and let down the body with all its apparel and jewels. Then the husband, embracing his kindred and friends, let himself be placed on another bier, with a pot of water, and seven small *loaves*,[5] and was led down in the same manner. The mouth of the pit was again covered with the stone, and the company returned.

I describe all this the more carefully, because I in a few weeks' time was to be the chief actor on a similar occasion. Alas! my own wife fell sick and died. I made every *plea*[6] I could to the King not to expose me, a foreigner, to this inhuman law. I appealed in vain. The King and all his court, with the chief persons of the city, sought to soften my

---

【註】 1. 心膽爲寒. 2. 親族. 3. 屍體. 4. 棺架. 5. 麵包. 6. 辯護.

他答說：『唉！這是怎麼能毀？我最多不過再活一兩點鐘的時間了，因爲我今天必須要殉葬我的妻子呢。這是島上的律例。凡活的丈夫須和死的妻子同葬，活的妻子也須和死的丈夫同葬的。』

這個野蠻的風俗，我聽了，不禁心膽爲寒，當他說話的時候，他的親族，朋友，和鄰里們都來助理喪務。 他們把死了的婦人，穿着最華麗的衣服，和戴上她的一切首飾，好像結婚的日子一樣；乃放在一具屍架上，擡往落葬的去處。那丈夫先時是跟着死屍後邊步行的。當他們到了一座高山，他們揭起一塊大石蓋來，這石蓋是蓋在一個深坑的口上的。他們便把屍體和牠的衣飾放進去。於是那丈夫和他的親戚，朋友們， 都一一擁抱爲禮， 讓自己放倒在另一具屍架上，一壺水，七塊小麵包，在同樣情形裏放了下去。坑口重用石頭蓋好，送喪的人各自囘家。

我細細地描述這個，因爲幾期星後，我就做了這幕活劇裏的同樣的主角啦。不幸，我自己的妻子也病死了。我用各種說辭，辯護我是個外僑，不合受這不人道的律例所支配；但是完全無效，那國王和衆朝臣，及城裏的紳士們，

sorrow by honoring the funeral with their presence: and when the *ceremony*[1] was finished, I was lowered into the pit with a vessel full of water and seven loaves. As I neared the bottom, I saw, by the aid of a little light that came from above, what sort of place it was. It seemed an endless *cavern*,[2] and might be about fifty *fathoms*[3] deep.

I lived for some time upon my bread and water, when one day, just as I was nearly exhausted, I heard something *tread*,[4] and breathing or panting as it moved. I followed the sound. The animal seemed to stop sometimes, but always fled and breathed hard as I approached. I pursued it till at last I saw a light, like a star. I went on, sometimes lost sight of it, but always found it again, and at last discovered that it came through a hole in the rock, which I got through, and found myself, to my great joy, upon the seashore. I fell upon the shore to thank God for his mercy, and shortly afterwards saw a ship making for the place where I was. I made a sign with the linen of my turban, and called to the *crew*[5] as loud as I could. They heard me, and sent a boat to bring me on board. It was fortunate for me that they did not inspect the place where they found me, but bore me away at once.

We passed by several islands,—the Isle of Bells, Serendib, and Kela, where *lead mines*[6] are found, also Indian *canes*[7] and *excellent camphire*.[8] The people of

---

【註】　1. 儀式.　2. 洞穴.　3. 噚（度名，長六呎）　4. 行走.　5. 水手.
6. 鉛鑛.　7. 甘蔗.　8. 最好的樟腦.

爲安慰我起見，特允許我葬的時候，他們都來臨葬；當葬禮已畢，我乃被放落在一個深坑裏，同着一滿盂的水和七個麵包。當我將落到坑底的時候，我借着上面來的細微光線，細瞧這是一個怎樣的洞穴。這似乎是個無底的洞兒。差不多有三百多尺深。

我依賴麵包和水，坑裏住了幾天，一日，我正在精疲力竭的當兒，忽聽得一種東西在行走。在行動時，卻伴着呼吸或喘哮。我跟着這聲音走去。這動物有時似乎停歇着，但是常是奔逃得很快，當我追近時，牠愈覺得氣促了。我一直趕去，趕到一個去處，瞧見一縷光線，好像一顆明星一般。我繼續走去，忽暗忽明，最後看到這是從一個石穴裏透出來的，我從石穴穿將過去，不禁大喜過望，原來我巳爬到沙灘上來哩，我倒身跪在沙灘上，拜謝上帝慈悲，不久便見有船隻駛來。我用頭巾揮舞，口裏嘶聲大喊。水手他們聽見了，放小船來接我到船上。很幸運的，他們並未查問我從那兒來，立卽載我去了。

我們經過幾島，——貝士羣島，殺倫提白羣島，和加拉羣島，那幾處出有鉛鑛，印度甘蔗，和最好的樟腦。島

these places are so barbarous that they still eat *human flesh*.[1] We touched at several other ports, and finished our traffic, and at last I arrived happily at Bagdad. Out of gratitude to God for his mercies, I gave large sums towards the support of several mosques and to the poor, and enjoyed myself with my friends.

The Fifth Voyage of Sindbad the Sailor

All that I had undergone could not cure me of my desire to make new voyages. Therefore I bought goods, departed with them for the best seaport,[2] and that I might have a ship at my own command, waited till one was built for me. As I had not goods enough of my own to load her, I took with me several merchants, of different nations, with their wares.

We sailed with the first fair wind, and the first place we touched at, after some time, was a desert island, where we found an egg of a roc, equal in size to the one I have mentioned already. There was a young roc in it, just ready to be *hatched*,[3] and its *beak*[4] had begun to break the egg.

The merchants who landed with me broke the egg with *latchets*,[5] and made a hole in it, pulled out the young roc *piecemeal*,[6] and *roasted*[7] it. I had begged them in vain not to meddle with the egg.

【註】 1. 人肉. 2. 海口. 3. 孵化. 4. 喙. 5. 手斧. 6. 片片地. 7. 烤炙.

上的士人很是野蠻，他們仍然吃人肉的。我們沿着幾個商埠，把我們的貨物銷了，我終於很快活地囘到巴革達德來。九死一生，終於脫險，我取出許多的錢財，捐助幾所寺院和救濟一般窮人們，很快活地和我的朋友們額手慶賀。

孫柏達第五次的航行

以前航行種種的險惡，都不能摧毀我向海外經商的壯志。我便辦齊貨品，到一最大的海口，因爲我要一隻船兒，由我親自指揮航行，乃特命趕造一隻。我自己的貨品因不能裝滿牠，卻招裝幾個異國的客商，和他們的貨件。

我們的船開行，眞是一路順風，行了幾時，第一次攏岸的，是個荒島，我們在島上發見有個大鵬鳥的卵，大小和我以前說的那個差不多。這卵殼有隻雛鵬，恰經孵化出來，用牠的喙開始啄破卵殼。

幾個和我登岸的商人，用手斧把卵兒劈破，成一個穴洞，從洞裏把那雛鳥拖出，撕成碎片，烤炙吃了。我求他們不要去動那卵兒，全然不聽。

Scarcely had they finished their repast, when there appeared in the air far off two great clouds. The captain of my ship, knowing by experience what they meant, said they were the *male and female parents*[1] of the roc, and urged us to reembark with all speed.

The two rocs approached with a frightful noise, which they *redoubled*[2] when they saw the egg broken and their young one gone. They flew back in the direction they had come, and were gone for some time, while we made all the sail we could, to try to prevent that which unhappily befell us.

They soon returned, and we saw that each of them carried in its *talons*[3] a huge rock. When they came directly over my ship, they *hovered*,[4] and one of them let go his rock; but by the quickness of the *steersman*[5] it missed us, and fell into the sea. The other so exactly hit the middle of the ship as to *split*[6] it into pieces. The seamen and merchants were all crushed to death, or fell into the sea. I myself was of the number of the latter; but, as I came up again, I fortunately caught hold of a piece of the wreck, and swimming, sometimes with one hand and sometimes with the other, but always holding fast to the plank, the wind and the tide favoring me, I came to an island, got safely ashore.

I sat down upon the grass to rest, and then went into the island to explore it. It seemed to be a *delicious*[7] garden. Everywhere I found fruit and

---

【註】 1. 父母. 2. 倍增. 3. 爪. 4. 盤旋. 5. 舵手. 6. 打碎. 7. 美麗的.

　　他們還沒有把鳥肉吃完，天空遠處已瞧見有兩片黑雲起來。我們船長從經驗上得到，曉得牠們就是這小鵬鳥的父母啦，驚告我們趕快登船逃走。

　　那兩隻鵬鳥飛到近處，聲音異常可怕，當他們看見卵兒已壞，他們的雛子沒有了，聲音越發響得怕人。他們又復飛回原來的去處。我們爲要逃脫這不幸的災禍，竭力把船駛去。

　　不多時牠們回來了，我們瞧見每隻鳥的爪裏，喞了一塊大石頭。他們逕飛到我們的船頂上，盤旋空中。一隻鵬鳥兜頭把他的石塊放下，但因掌舵人手脚敏快，沒有打中，卻抛在海裏了。那另一隻卻瞄得這般準確，一下便投中我的船上，正中船艙，把船打成粉碎。那些水手們和客人們，不是在石下壓成肉醬，便是顚入海中。我也給顚入海中，不過在入水後，又復冒起，我抓得一塊破船板，緊緊地抱住，用一隻手交換着。向前泅去，終因風順，助我泅到了一個島邊，安穩地上岸。

　　我坐在草地上小憩一會兒，便入島內探險去。這島好像一個美麗的花園。到處都見有美菓，清溪，和碧澄的水。

streams of fresh, pure water. Of these I ate and drank.

When I had gone a little way into the island, I, saw an old man who appeared very weak and *infirm*.[1] He was sitting on the bank of a stream, and at first I took him to be one who had been shipwrecked like myself. I went towards him and saluted him, but he only slightly bowed his head. I asked him why he, sat so still; but, instead of answering me, he made a sign for me to take him upon my back, and carry him over the *brook*.[2]

I believed him really to stand in need of my help, took him upon my back, and, having carried him over, bade him get down. To that end, I stooped, that he might get off with ease; but instead of doing so—and I laugh every time I think of it—the old man, who to me appeared quite *feeble*,[3] threw his legs, *nimbly*[4] about my neck. He sat *astride*[5] upon my shoulders, and held my throat so *tight*[6] that I thought he would have strangled me, and I fainted away.

In spite of[7] my fainting, the ill-natured old fellow still kept his seat upon my neck. When I got my breath again, he thrust one of his feet against my side, and struck me so rudely with the other, that he forced me to rise up against my will. Then he made me carry him under the trees, and obliged me now and then to stop, that he might gather and eat fruit. He never left his seat all day; and when I lay down

---

【註】 1. 殘廢的. 2. 澗. 3. 衰弱的. 4. 敏捷地. 5. 騎坐地. 6. 緊的. 7. 不顧.

我便吃了個爽快。

當我進島不多的時候，瞧見一個老人，看來很像衰弱羸瘦的樣子。他坐在一條溪邊，初時我認爲他和我一般，是一個遇險的人。我走向前去，向他問好，但他僅把他的頭略爲點一下兒。我問他爲甚麼這般靜靜的坐着；他並不囘答，但示意教我駝他渡過澗去。

我信他眞心需要我幫助的，遂背了他，從澗裏走了過去，教他下來。那時候，我屈傴了背，爲的使他容易落下；不過我弄錯了，說起來眞覺好笑，那個老人我看他很衰弱的，那知非常敏捷，一躍便騎坐在我的肩上。兜頸一夾，把我夾得喘氣不來，好像要將溢死的樣子，於是我昏暈過去了。

不顧我昏去，那怪惡的老人，却仍然坐在我頸上。當我蘇醒的時候，他却用脚踢我，又用一隻脚很命踢我脅下，逼迫我站立起來。他就命我背他到菓樹下邊去，時時教我住步，爲的是他可以探摘菓兒吃。他整天地不肯下肩；晚

to rest at night, he laid himself down with me, holding still fast about my neck. Every morning he *pinched*[1] me to make me awake, and afterwards forced me to get up and walk, and *spurred*[2] me with his feet.

One day I found several dry *gourds*[3] that had fallen from a tree. I took a large one, and, after cleaning it, passed into it some *juice*[4] of *grapes*,[5] which abounded in the island. Having filled the gourd, I put it by, and, going for it some days after, tasted and found the wine so good that it gave me new vigor, and so raised my spirits that I began to sing and dance as I carried my burden.

The old man, noticing the effect of the wine upon me, made me a sign to give him some of it. I handed him the gourd, and, the liquor pleasing his *palate*,[6] he drank it off. As there was some quantity of it, he soon began to sing, and to move from side to side in his seat upon my shoulders, and by degrees to loosen his legs from about me. Finding that he did not press me as before, I threw him upon the ground, where he lay without motion; then I took up a great stone and *slew*[7] him.

I was extremely glad to be thus freed forever from this troublesome fellow. I now walked towards the beach, where I met the crew of a ship that had cast anchor, to take in water. When I told them of my adventure, they said: "You fell into the hands of the Old Man of the Sea, and are the first who ever

【註】 1. 搇. 2. 踢. 3. 葫蘆. 4. 汁. 5. 葡萄. 6. 嗜好. 7. 打死.

上我睡了，他也一塊兒和我躺下，仍緊抱住我的頭頸，使我動彈不得。每天早上，他用手指兒捏醒我，隨後便迫我起行，并用他的兩隻脚不住的踢我。

一天，我見一棵樹下，落下幾個乾的葫蘆。我揀了最大的一個葫蘆兒。把肉去掉洗淨後，擠着許多葡萄汁盛在葫蘆裏，這些葡萄在島上徧地都是。擠滿了一葫蘆，我便把它放在一邊，過了幾天，卻釀成美好的葡萄酒，喝了使我精神大增，我肩膀上雖負了人，還兀自唱歌狂舞哩。

那老人見酒有如此的效力，便做手勢教我取點兒酒給他喝。我把那葫蘆兒遞給他，他嘗了，感到酒味這般可口，一口氣便把酒都喝完。因爲酒能發興的，他開始唱歌了，漸漸地在我肩膀上搖動起來，不能坐穩，因此這兩隻腿兒也就鬆弛下來了。我見有勢可乘，乃用力一掀，將他慣在地上，不能轉動，我就取了一塊大石，把他打死。

我這般地逃脫了這討厭的傢伙，覺得十分歡喜，便向港口行去，卻巧遇到幾個船夫，恰在拋錨，上岸來取水。我把我的冒險事情訴給他們聽，他們都說：『你陷落在海上老人的手裏啦，却是第一個人能儌倖免逃脫的。他捉到一

escaped *strangling*.[1]　He never *quitted*[2] those he had once embraced till he had destroyed them, and many are the men he has *slain*."[3]

Their captain received me with great kindness, and after some day's sail we arrived at the harbor of a great city, the houses of which *overhung*[4] the sea.

With some of the people of this town I went to gather cocoanuts after their own method. When we reached a thick forest of cocoanut trees, we saw a great number of *apes*[5] of several sizes, which fled as soon as they saw us, and climbed to the tops of the trees with amazing swiftness.

The merchants, with whom I was, gathered stones, and threw them at the apes on the trees. I did the same; and the apes, out of revenge, threw cocoanuts at us so fast and with such *gestures*[6] as to show their anger clearly. We gathered up the cocoanuts, and from time to time threw stones to *provoke*[7] the apes. In this way we filled our bags with cocoanuts, and by degrees I got enough to produce me no small sum of money.

We set sail, and traded in various islands, at one of which I hired divers and with other merchants went *a-pearl-fishing*.[8] Some of the pearls they brought me up were very large and pure. Then I returned to Bagdad, and gave a tenth of my gains in *alms*,[9] and rested from my *fatigues*.[10]

【註】 1. 死. 2. 放手. 3. 弄死. 4. 臨近. 5. 無尾猿. 6. 表情. 7. 挑撥. 8. 拓珠. 9. 施捨. 10. 辛勞.

個人的時候，非把他弄死，永不肯放手的。許多人都死在他的手裏。』

他們的船長很厚待我，行過幾天，我們到得一個大商埠，那裏房屋都是臨海的。

我跟從鎮上的幾個人採椰子去。當我們到了一個椰樹林子裏，瞧見成羣的猴子，大小無數，見我們來，趕忙逃上樹去，個個都有驚人的敏捷。

那幾個商人和我，拾集許多小石片，向那些樹上的猴子擲去。我也跟着投；這些猴子忽怒起來，便摘着椰子，向我們還擊，以爲報復，手脚極爲敏快。我們一邊拾取椰子，一邊仍投小石上去以誘猴子。'我們這樣地拾着無數的椰子，逐漸積到了不少的錢。

我們啓椗了。在許多島上做過賣買後，在一個島上我僱了幾個泅水的人，同着別些商人入海探珠。他們採給我有幾顆珠子，極大極美。我於是囘到巴革達德，捐了十分之一的金錢，做善事業，在家休養。

The Sixth Voyage of Sindbad the Sailor

I know, my friends, that you will wish to hear how, after having been shipwrecked and having escaped so many dangers, I could resolve again to tempt fortune, and expose myself to new *hardships*.[1] When I reflect upon it now it seems that I must have been led by *destiny*,[2] from which none can escape. Be this as it may, after a year's rest, I prepared for a sixth voyage, though my kindred and friends did all in their power to dissuade me.

Once more I traveled through several provinces of Persia and the Indies, and arrived at a seaport, where I embarked on a ship bound on a long voyage, in which the captain and the *pilot*[3] lost their course. Suddenly we saw the captain quit his *rudder*,[4] *lamenting*[5] loudly, pulling his beard and beating his head like a madman. In reply to our questions, he answered:

"A rapid current carries the ship along with it, and we shall all *perish*[6] in less than a quarter of an hour. Pray God to deliver us from this *peril*.[7] We cannot escape, if He do not take pity on us."

At these words he ordered the sails to be *lowered*,[8] but the ropes broke, and the current carried the ship to the foot of a mountain, where she struck and went to pieces, but in such a way that we saved our lives, our *provisions*,[12] and the best of our goods.

【註】 1. 困苦. 2. 命運. 3. 引船者. 4. 舵. 5. 哀號. 6. 覆滅. 7. 危險. 8. 落下. 9. 食物.

孫柏達第六次的航行

我的朋友，我知道你們定然要問我，逃過這許多危險，飽經這許多患難，爲什麼還想嘗試命運。再壓困苦呢？我每想到這問題，總以爲是命運註定，誰都不能逃避的。我差不多休息一年光景，決心要作第六次航行，雖然我的親友們千方百計勸阻我，終不能打消我的主意。

我重經行着波斯和印度幾省，到得一個海口登船，航行了許久，船長和引船者忽然迷失了航路。我們驀地瞧見船長拋棄了舵，失聲哀號，扯他的鬚，打他的頭，好像一個瘋子一般。我們問他這是爲什麼？他見問答道：

『一道急流把船帶迷了路，我們眼見一刻光景，就會覆滅。求上帝救我們這危險罷。要如他不可憐我們，我們定然難逃性命啦。』

他說着，便命將船篷落下，但是繩索斷了，那急流箭一般的把船帶到一個山脚下，將牠撞成齏粉，不過我們却救得性命，又帶得些食物，和頂貴重的東西。

The foot of the mountain was covered with wrecks, with a vast number of human bones, and goods and riches of all kinds beyond belief. In all other places it is usual for rivers to run into the sea; but here a river of fresh water runs from the sea into a dark cavern, with a very high and spacious entrance. What is most strange in this place is that the stones of the mountain are of *crystal*,[1] rubies, and other percious stones. Here also are *ambergris*[2] and *wood of aloes*.[3]

It is not possible for ships to get off from this place when once they approach within a certain distance. If the wind is from the sea, this and the current drive them on. If it is a land wind, it is stopped by the height of the mountain, which causes a calm, so that the force of the current carries them ashore. What is worse, it is no more possible to ascend the mountain than to escape by sea. Here we remained in a state of despair, expecting death every day.

When we landed, we divided the food equally, and thus each one lived a longer or shorter time, according to the use he made of his share. I *outlived*[4] my *comrades*,[5] and, when I buried the last of them, had so little food left that I dug a grave for myself. But God once more took pity on me, and put it in my mind to go to the bank of the river which ran into the cavern. I said to myself:—

【註】 1. 水晶. 2. 龍涎香. 3. 檀香. 4. 生存較久于. 5. 伙伴.

那山脚下的破船不少，屍骨堆積累累，至於財寶和貨物，更是不可計算。在別的地方，川水總是注流入海的。但這兒却有一條淡水川，從海邊貫注到一個黑暗的谷中去。那入口又高又闊。這去處更奇怪的，便是那山石都是些水晶，紅寶玉，和別種寶石。這兒也有龍涎香和檀香。

大凡船隻行近到這地方，無論如何總不能脫險的。倘風由海這面吹去，則風和急流把船隻捲入漩渦流去，要如是陸地上的風，風被山阻止，風勢沒有了。而急流的勢力仍把船隻打向岸上去。尤其不幸的，這兒山勢險惡，爬上去並不比飄海容易。於是我們個個心灰意懶，天天但望早死。

當我們上了岸，把食物分配均勻，因此一個人活命的長短，只看他食用的多少了。我的性命比伙伴們都挨得長久些，當我埋完了他們中最後的一個時，我的口糧亦所剩無幾，我只得掘自己的墳墓啦。不過上帝還憫憐我一次，使我忽然想到那條奔注黑暗谷洞去的大川。我看了自言自語道：

"This underground river must somewhere have an *outlet*.[1] If I make a *raft*,[2] and leave myself to the current, it will *convey*[3] me to some inhabited country, or I shall perish. If I be drowned, I only change one kind of death for another."

Out of pieces of *timber*[4] and *cables*[5] from the wrecks, I soon made myself a solid raft. Then I loaded it carefully with some chests of rubies, emeralds, ambergris, rock crystal, and bales of rich stuffs, and went on board with two *oars*[6] that I had made, leaving the raft to the course of the river, and resigning myself to the will of God.

As soon as I entered the cavern, I lost all light, and the stream carried me I knew not whither. Thus I floated on, eating only enough to keep myself alive. But the food was soon spent, and I lost my senses. When I revived, I found myself on the brink of a river, where my raft was tied, amidst a great number of negroes. When I saluted them, they spoke to me, but I did not understand their *tongue*.[7] In my joy I recited aloud the following words in Arabic:

"Call upon the Almighty. He will help thee; shut thine eyes, and while thou art asleep, God will change thy bad fortune into good."

One of the negroes, who understood Arabic, came forward and told me that they had seen my raft, and fastened it until I should awake. Through him I told the others, at their request, of all that had

---

【註】 1. 出口. 2. 浮排. 3. 轉向. 4. 木料. 5. 大氣. 6. 槳. 7. 言語.

『這條懸掛似的大川，一定有個出口的。倘若我造一浮排，投身在這急流中，不是把我帶向有人煙的地方去，便是將我毀滅着。假使我便沉沒了，也不過以死換死罷了。』

取破船上的板木和大繩，我很快的就造了一個堅實的浮排。精揀着好些紅寶石，碧玉，龍涎香，水晶，各打成捆兒，和那些值錢的貨物，都綁好在木排上，又做了兩個槳兒，把木排放入河流中，一聽天命駛去。

當我一入黑谷中，眼前一點兒光亮都沒有，我不知這川流帶我到什麼地方去。我這樣地飄流着，吃了點食物，以免餓死。但是我的食物都吃完了，我便失了知覺。當我醒來的時候，我却見自己是在一條河岸上，我的木排却繫在河邊，在一大羣的黑人中間。當我向他們致禮的時候，他們問我，但是言語不通。我因大喜過望，乃操亞拉伯話大聲說道：

『憑全智全能的上帝。他將會幫助你們；請閉了你們的眼睛，當你們入睡的時候，上帝會變換你們的壞運，成做好運啦。』

內中有一個黑人，聽得懂亞拉伯的話，走前來告訴我說，他們已瞧見你的木排了，將木排繫着以待我蘇醒。由他翻譯，我乃告訴他們我所經歷的一切情形，這是他們所

befallen me. The story was so strange that they said I must tell it to their king myself. Then they mounted me on a horse, and some led the way, and some followed with my raft and *cargo*.[1]

The king received me kindly, and bade me sit by his side while I told him what I have told you. When my bales were opened in his presence, he marveled at what they contained, above all, at the rubies and emeralds, which *surpassed*[2] any in his treasury.

When I saw with what pleasure he viewed them, I fell at his feet and said:

"Sire, not only is my person at your majesty's service, but the cargo of the raft, and I beg of you to *dispose*[3] of it as your own."

But he would take none of my goods, and promised that I should leave his *realm*[4] richer than I came. His officers were charged to serve me at his expense, and every day I paid the King my court, and saw what was most worthy of notice in the city. By way of *devotion*[5] I made a *pilgrimage*[6] to the place where Adam was confined after his *banishment*[7] from Paradise.

Then I prayed the King to allow me to return to my own country, and his permission was most kindly given. He would force a rich present upon me; and at the same time charged me with a letter for the Commander of the Faithful, our sovereign, saying to

---

【註】 1. 貨物. 2. 勝過. 3. 處置. 4. 王國. 5. 敬禮. 6. 朝拜. 7. 遺謫.

要知道的。他們聽了，覺得奇怪，便命我親自告訴他們國王去。就教我坐在一匹馬上，幾個人在前引路，幾個人在後跟着，把我的木排和貨物漱去。

邢國王和藹地接待着我，當我把一切歷險事由像告訴你般地講給他聽的時候，他教我坐在一旁。我將包裹在他面前打開給他看，他瞧見裏邊的貨物，大為驚訝，尤其是這些紅玉和碧玉，每塊都勝過他國庫裏的所有。

我瞧見他喜歡這些東西，便跪在他面前，說道：

『萬歲。不但我個人當為陛下效勞，便是我木排上的貨物，也是陛下的，請陛下自由處置。』

但是他並不取我的貨物，且允許我回國時，要比來時更富。他命衆朝臣陪我，每天我隨衆上朝，留心國內最堪注意的東西。我因出於敬禮，朝拜了一次聖地，這聖地是亞當由樂園遣謫下來而被幽禁着的去處。

朝拜過聖地後，我懇求這國王放我回國，他和善地允許了。他送了一注重禮物給我，同時候，着我帶一封信給我們的教主皇帝，對我說道：『我請你為我幹這個差事，

me: "I pray you give this present for me, and this letter to the Caliph Haroun Al-Raschid, and assure him of my friendship."

The letter from the King of Serendib was written on the skin of a certain animal of great value, very scarce, and of a *yellowish*[1] color. The characters of the letter were of *azure*,[2] and the contents as follows:

"The King of the Indies, before whom march one hundred elephants, who lives in a palace that shines with one hundred thousand rubies, and who has in his treasury twenty thousand crowns enriched with diamonds, to Caliph Haroun Al-Raschid.

"Though the present we send you be slight, receive it as a brother and a friend, in token of the hearty friendship we bear for you, and of which we are willing to give you proof. We desire the same part in your friendship, since we believe it to be our *merit*,[3] for we are both kings. We send you this letter as from one brother to another Farewell."

The present consisted of one ruby made into a cup, about half a foot high, an inch thick, and filled with round pearls of half a *drachm*[4] each; and the skin of a serpent, whose scales were as bright as a piece of gold and preserved from sickness those who lay upon it; besides a vast quantity of the best quality of wood of akes and *camphire*,[5] and a female slave of great beauty, whose robe was covered over with jewels.

[註] 1. 黃色的. 2. 藍色的. 3. 名譽. 4. 格蘭. 5. 樟腦.

把這封國書帶給哈龍亞爾拉西德凱立夫去，並請你爲我好說。』

那賽倫提白國王的信，是寫在一張珍貴，稀罕，黃色的獸皮上。字跡是藍色的，內容如下：

『印度羣島國王謹拜書於哈龍亞爾拉西德凱立夫座前：竊敢國王麾前列大象百匹，宮庭以紅寶玉十萬塊爲裝飾，國庫內嵌鑽石之皇冠，以二十千數。

『今謹具微禮，略表微忱，獻於座前。以此菲物爲盟，與左右結手足之誼，同心相照，忝附邦交，勿忘永好。鑒其愚誠，勿却爲禱。』

那貢禮是紅玉盃一隻，約莫半尺高，一寸寬，盛滿幾種寶珠，每種重半格蘭；蛇皮一張，皮上鱗甲輝煌如金，人臥其上，可以免除百病；又有最好的檀香和樟腦無數，外加一個最美的妃子，她的衣服是用珠寶嵌滿的。

As soon as I reached Bagdad I presented myself before the caliph with the letter and gift. When he had read the letter he asked if the king of Serendib were indeed so rich and *potent*,[1] and, bowing to his feet, I assured him that it was all true, and told him in what state the prince appeared in public, with a throne on the back of an elephant, surrounded by officers and a guard of a thousand men.

"The officer who is before on his elephant," I said, "cries from time to time with a loud voice: 'Behold the great monarch, the mighty Sultan of the Indies, greater than Solomon.' Then the officer behind the throne cries in his turn: 'This monarch, so great and powerful, must die, must die, must die.' And the officer before him replies: 'Praise alone be to Him who liveth forever and ever.'"

The caliph was much pleased with my account, and sent me home with a rich present.

The Seventh and Last Voyage of Sindbad the Sailor

After my sixth voyage I had given up all thoughts of going to sea again, for my age required rest, and I wished to expose myself to no more risks, but to pass the rest of my days in peace. One day, however, an officer from the palace came and said the Caliph must speak to me.

"Sindbad," said he, when I had bowed to the floor before the throne, "I stand in need of your

[註] 1. 強的.

當我一到巴革達德，便把這信和禮物，親自獻給凱立夫。他念完那信，問我這賽倫提白國王果然是這般富強嗎？我向他鞠躬到地，啓奏這一切都屬眞情，且告訴他那王是怎樣臨朝，他的寶座是在一隻大象的背上，朝臣和一千個衞隊圍繞着他。

我說：『他象前有個官員，時時高聲喝唱：「瞧這大皇帝，印度羣島全智全能的蘇丹，比沙羅門更偉大！」於是那寶座後有官應聲唱道：「這樣又富，又強的皇帝，定不免要死啦！一定死啦，一定死啦。」象前官便接口道：「願他萬歲，萬歲，萬萬歲。」』

凱立夫見我描模得這般有趣，十分歡喜，重厚賞賜，送我囘家。

孫柏達第七次卽最末次的航行

在我六次航行以後，我已不想再去航海了。要因爲我年高力衰，但願長此休養，以享淸福，不願更暴身於危難。話雖如此，一天，宮中有個使臣來，稱凱立夫有旨，要召我談話。

我到他殿前，俯伏到地，他說道：『孫柏達我有事命

service; you must carry my answer and present to the King of Serendib."

This command was to me like a *clap*[1] of thunder. Though I had made a vow never to leave Bagdad, I saw that I must obey. The Caliph was well pleased, and ordered me a sum of money *ample*[2] for my needs.

In a few days I departed with the letter and present, and, after a safe voyage, reached the Isle of Serendib.

"Sindbad," said the King, when I was brought before him with great *pomp*,[3] and had bowed to the earth, "you are welcome; I have many times thought of you. I bless the day on which I see you once more."

I thanked him for his kindness, and delivered the gifts from my *august*[4] master. The Caliph's letter was as follows:—

"Greeting, in the name of the Sovereign Guide of the Right Way, from the Servant of God, Haroun Al-Raschid, whom God hath set in the place of vice-regent to his Prophet, after his ancestors of happy memory, to the potent and *esteemed*[5] King of Serendib.

"We received your letter with joy, and send you this from our imperial residence, the garden of superior wits. We hope when you look upon it you will erceive our good will, and be pleased with it. Farewell."

【註】 1. 霹靂. 2. 充足的. 3. 榮華. 4. 尊嚴的. 5. 尊敬的.

你；我要你帶你的囘書和禮物，給賽倫提白國王去。』

　　這命令對我好像青天一個霹靂，雖然我立誓不再離開巴革達德，我却不得不服從。凱立夫很是歡喜，賜下許多金錢，供我使用。

　　過了幾天，我帶信件和禮物，開始航行，一路平安，到得賽倫提白羣島。

　　我立刻帶到國王的面前，對他行過了禮。他說：『琛柏達！我很歡迎你；我掛念你們久了。我如今再看見你、十分歡喜。』

　　我感謝他的好意，便把我尊嚴主人的禮物獻上。凱立夫的信如下；

　　『承最尊無上光明之導師，上帝之僕，哈龍亞爾拉西德，奉天承運，叨祖上蔭庇，謹拜書於光榮強盛之賽倫提白國王座前：

　　『茲接王書，欣喜莫名。謹備禮物數事，皆御宮之所選，上苑之所出也。聊答厚貺，略表微忱，尚乞晒納。不宣。』

The Caliph's persent was a complete suit of cloth of gold, fifty robes of rich stuff, a hundred of white cloth, the finest of Cairo, Suez, and Alexandria; a vessel of *agate*,[1] half a foot wide, on the bottom of which was *carved*[2] a man with one knee on the ground, who held a bow and an arrow, ready to *discharge*[3] at a lion. He sent also a rich *tablet*,[4] which, according to tradition, belonged to the great Solomon.

The king of Serendib was highly pleased. Soon I obtained leave to depart, though not easily. Dismissed with a large present, I sailed at once for Bagdad, but had not the good fortune to arrive there so soon as I had hoped. God ordered it otherwise.

Three or four days after sailing, we were attacked by *pirates*.[5] Some of the crew were killed, and I, with others who did not resist, was taken to a remote island and sold.

I fell into the hands of a rich merchant, who treated me well, and dressed me handsomely as a slave. In a few days he asked me if I knew any trade. I told him I was a merchant, robbed of all I possessed. "Tell me," said he, "can you shoot with a bow?" I said it had been one of the exercises of my youth. Then he gave me a bow and arrow, took me behind him on an elephant, and carried me to a *thick forest*.[6] Stopping before a great tree, he said: "Climb up that, and shoot at the elephants, of which there are many in this forest, as you see them pass

【註】 1. 瑪瑙. 2. 雕刻. 3. 發射. 4. 鉛板. 5. 海盜. 6. 叢林.

　　凱立夫的禮物是一全套的金線織成的衣服，五十件上料宮袍，一百件白衣。俱是開羅，蘇彝士及亞立山大的名貴出品；一隻瑪瑙盆，有半尺來闊，雕的是一個人屈膝在地，引弓發矢，作勢要射一隻獅子的樣子。一塊華美的鉛板，據傳說，是偉大的沙羅門的遺物。

　　那賽倫提白國王接受了，大喜。雖然再三挽留，我不多時便辭回了。他送我一份重禮，我想立卽囘到巴革達德，但是並不如我所預期的那樣迅速。上帝命令我轉入另一途徑。

　　在船開駛了三四天後，我們受到海盜的襲擊。有幾個水手被殺死了，我和別些人不曾反抗他們，乃被載到一個遠島上，被賣了。

　　我落在一個富商家裏，他待遇我還好，給我穿得很好，好像一個富家僕人的樣子。過了幾天，他問我做些什麼事情。我答說，我是個商人，我所有的東西，都被海盜劫去了。他說：『告訴我，你可會射箭嗎？』我就說這是我自小熟練着的玩意兒。他乃給我一張弓和幾枝箭，和我同騎在象上，叫我坐在他的後邊，到一個叢林裏。在一棵大樹前停住了，他說道：『攀上那棵樹去，這林子裏有許多野象，

by, and if any of them fall, come and give me notice." Then he left me, and returned to the town, and I remained upon the tree all night.

In the morning I shot one of the many elephants that passed under the tree, and when the others had left it dead, I went into the town and told my *patron*[1] of my success, which pleased him greatly. Then we returned, and dug a hole for the elephant, in which my patron meant to leave it until it was rotten, when he would take its teeth and trade with them.

For two months I did this service. One morning I was amazed to see that the elephants, instead of passing by, stopped and come towards my tree with a *horrible*[3] noise, in such numbers that the plain was covered, and shook under them. They surrounded the tree, w th their trunks uplifted, and all fixed their eyes upon me. This frightened me so that my bow and arrows fell out of my hand.

My fears were not without cause, for soon on of the largest of the elephants put his trunk round the foot of the tree, *plucked*[4] it up, and threw it on the ground. I fell with the tree, and the elephant, taking me up with his trunk, laid me on his back, where I sat more like one dead than alive. He put himself at the head of the rest, who followed him in line, carried me some distance, then laid me down on the ground, and retired with all the others. When they were gone, I got up, and found that I was upon a

---

【註】 1. 主人. 2. 腐爛. 3. 可恨的. 4. 拔.

來來往往，你瞧見他們來的時候，便射，射倒了象，可來報告。』他乃留下我，獨自囘到市鎮。我終夜守候在樹上。

早上有一羣象從樹下經過，我引弓射箭，射死他們中的一隻，其餘諸象都奔逃而去。我囘鎮告訴我主人，他見我成功，十分歡喜。我們囘到那兒，掘了一個地洞，把象埋下，我的東家原是象牙商，他想把象爛了，單取象牙去賣的。

這樣子我幹了兩個月。一天早起，我吃驚地見有許多象到我樹下，並不過去，只站着駭聲狂叫，象來的很多，把地面站滿，叫聲如天崩地裂一般。他們圍繞着那棵樹兒，把鼻子高高地掀起，一齊定睛望着我。這使我驚惶失措，把弓箭都駭得失落在地。

我不是無原無故的驚慌一忽兒，有一隻最大的象用鼻捲住樹根，用力向上一拔，一下便將那樹連根帶土的拔將起來。我和樹倒了下來，那隻象用鼻子，將我取在他背上，我動彈不得，像死人一般。他駝了我在前行走，其餘的象紛紛地在後跟着。他們帶我到了一個地方，棄下我，走了。

long and broad hill, almost covered with the bones and teeth of elephants. I doubted not but that this was their *burialplace*,[1] and that they carried me thither on purpose to tell me that I should no longer kill them, now that I knew where to get their teeth without doing them harm. I did not stay on the hill, but turned towards the city, and, traveling a day and a night, came to my pattron.

He had believed me dead, for he had found the tree pulled up in the forest, and my bow and arrows on the ground. When he had heard of my escape, we set out for the hill, and brought back as many teeth as an elephant could bear. Then my master told me how many slaves had been killed by the elephants, and blessed me for making him and his whole city rich. "I can treat you no more as a slave," he said, "but as a brother. I give you your liberty *henceforth*.[2] I will also give you riches."

To this I answered that the only reward I wished was leave to return to my own country. "Very well," said he; "the *monsoon*[3] will soon bring ships for *ivory*.[4] Then I will send you home."

While waiting for the monsoon we made many journeys to the hill, and, when my ship sailed, my master loaded half of it with ivory on my account. With this I traded a various ports, gaining vast sums of money. Besides the ivory, my master gave me precious gifts. The last *portion*[5] of my journey I made by land, and when it was done I was happy in

---

【註】 1. 墓地. 2. 以後. 3. 時季風. 4. 象牙. 5. 部分.

他們走去，我便翻身起來，便瞧見是在一個長闊的山中，這山裏堆滿象骨和象牙。我乃知道這是象的墓地，頓悟到他們帶我來的目的，好像告訴我說，這兒有的是象牙，我不該再射殺他們了。我不敢停留在山上，就立卽逃回城去，跑了一天一夜，纔到我主人的家裏。

我主人認我已死了，因爲他發見那樹已拔起倒在林子裏，弓箭都落在地上。當他聽見我告訴他的故事，我們就同到那山中去，把象牙滿滿地裝了一象。我主人因告訴我，許多奴僕曾被象殺死。他祝福我，因我的好運氣得使他和全城都富裕了。他說：『我決不再把你當作奴僕了。我從現在起便給你自由，我當以兄弟來看待你，並且要給你錢財。』

我答說，唯一的心願，只求你送我回返故國。他說：『很好，等時季風起，我的象牙船立卽出發。那時送你回家吧。』

在等時季風的當兒，我們到那山中，又去了多次。當我的船將起行的時候，主人贈我足有半船的象牙，作爲酬勞。我就把這些象牙，到各處海口去發賣，得了無數的錢回來，除象牙外，我主人且贈我許多貴重的禮物。最後一段旅途，我是從陸地上走的，一路快活地暗想，我不怕海

t inking I had nothing more to fear from the seas, from pirates, from serpents or from the other perils to which I had been exposed. Safe at Bagdad, I waited upon the cal ph at once, and told h m how I had f. filled his mission. He loaded me with honors and rich present, and I have ever since *devoted myself*[1] to my family, kindred, and friends.

Sindbad here finished the story of his seventh and las voyage. "Well, friend," he said, turning to Hindba , "did you ever hear of any person that suffered so much as I have done? Is it not just that after all this I should enjoy a quiet and pleasant life?"

Hindbad in answer kissed his hand and said: "Sir, my pains are not to be compared with yours. You not only deserve a quiet life, but are worthy of all the riches you possess, since you make so good a use of them. May you live happily for a long time."

Sindbad ordered another purse of mony to be given him, and told him to give up carrying burdens as a porter, and to eat henceforth at his table; for he wished Hindbad to remember all his life that he had a friend in Sindbad the Sailor.

【註】 1. 委身.

浪，不怕海盜，不怕毒蛇，一切所經歷的危險，我居然一一逃過了。到了巴革達德，我立卽去朝見凱立夫，覆旨稱差事已經辦完。他慰勞着賜我許多寶物，自今以後，我只想和家人，親戚，朋友們相周旋了。

孫柏達到此把他第七次那最末次的航行講完。便掉過頭來，向辛巴德說：『你可曾聽見有像我這樣經歷艱難辛苦的人嗎？你想我經過這樣的患難，現在享受我安樂的生活，公平不公平呢？』

辛巴德乃吻着他的手說：『先生，我受的辛苦決不敢和你相比。 你不但該享受一種安樂的生活，而且一切財富，都該爲你所有，因爲你用得這般得當呢。願你康健。』

孫柏達給他另一袋錢，教他不必再做挑夫，自後可來做他的食客；因爲他願辛巴德一生，記住他曾經是水手孫柏達的一個朋友。

12. The Barmecide Feast

I have now, said the *talkative barber*[1] who had related the strange adventures of his five brothers, only to tell the story of my sixth brother, called Shacabac, with the *harelips*.[2] After beginning his life in comfort, a reverse of fortune brought him to beg his bread. One day as he passed a great house, with many servants standing within its *spacious*[3] court, he went to one of them, and asked him to whom the house belonged.

"Good man," replied the servant, "whence do you come that you ask me such a question? Does not all that you see tell you that it is the palace of a Barmecide?"

My brother, knowing well how generous all the Barmecides were, prayed one of the gate keepers at once to give him an *alms*.[4] "Go in," said the man; "nobody *hinders*[5] you, and speak to the master of the house; he will send you back satisfied."

My brother, who expected no such politeness, thanked the *porter*,[6] and entered the palace. He went on till he came to a richly furnished hall, at the upper end of which he saw an old man, with a long, white beard, sitting on a sofa. He thought it must be the master of the house, and indeed it was the Barmecide himself, who said to my brother,

---

【註】 1. 健談的理髮匠. 2. 缺嘴. 3. 廣大的. 4. 布施. 5. 攔阻. 6. 管門人.

十二、理髮匠第六兄弟的故事

　　健談的理髮匠，談到他五兄弟的奇遇，說道，我現在要講第六兄弟的故事了。我六弟名叫舍加巴克，是個缺嘴。初時景況很好，後來時運不佳，終使他變做乞丐。有一天，他從一所大莊院走過，見院子裏奴僕成羣，便進去問這屋主是誰。

　　一個僕人說：『你從那處來的，要問這樣的話？你看見這一切，難道還不知是巴米賽德的屋子嗎？』

　　巴氏支族很多，我兄弟素來聽得他們慈悲慷慨的，便求着管門人給他一點布施。那個人說：『走進去！沒有誰攔阻着你，你可逕對主人說去；他定會打發你，使你滿意的。』

　　這般的客氣，殊出我兄弟意外，當下他謝過管門人，向院子裏走去。一直走到一間裝璜美麗的大廳，見上首沙發椅上，有個長白鬍鬚的老人坐着。他想這當是主人了，果然正是巴米賽德本人，他對我兄弟，很是歡迎，並非常和

in a very *civil*[1] manner, that he was welcome, and asked him what he wanted.

"My lord," answered my brother, "I am a poor man who needs help. I *swear*[2] to you I have not eaten one bit to-day."

"Is it true," *demanded*[3] the Barmecide, "that you are *fasting*[4] till now? Alas, the poor man is ready to die for hunger! Ho, boy!" cried he, with a loud voice, "bring a basin and water at once, that we may wash our hands."

Though no by appeared, and my brother saw neither water nor basin, the Barmecide fell to rubbing his hands as if one had poured water upon them, and bade my brother come and wash with him. Shacbac caught the spirit of the Barmecide's *jest*,[5] and knowing that the poor must please the rich, if they would have anything from them, came forward and did as he was bidden.

"Come on," said the Barmecide, "bring us something to eat, and do not let us wait." Then, though nothing appeared, he began to eat, *as if*[6] something had been brought him upon a plate, and putting his hand to his mouth, began to eat; and said to my brother:—

"Come, friend, eat as freely as if you were at home; you said you were almost dying of hunger, but you eat as if you had no *appetite*."[7]

"Pardon me, my lord," said Shacabac, who

【註】 1. 和藹的. 2. 賭咒. 3. 詰問. 4. 餓. 5. 玩笑. 6. 好像. 7. 食慾.

藹地問他來意。

我兄弟答說：『我的主人，我是個窮人，需人幫助。我敢對你賭咒，我今天一些兒東西都不曾吃過。』

這巴米賽德說：『眞的嗎？你果眞餓到現在嗎？啊！這可憐的人要餓死了！』他高聲喊說：『噲，侍者！快端一盆水來，給我們洗手。』

雖然並沒有侍者，我兄弟也不見有水或盆兒端來，這巴米賽德居然把他的手，磨擦有聲，好像眞的洗手一樣，他便喚我兄弟同他洗着。舍加巴克心知這巴米賽德是同他開玩笑，但又明知窮人們有事懇求富人，必須百依百順的阿諛他。

巴米賽德說，『來！拿幾碟兒食物來吧，不要讓我們久等。』這時，雖然並沒有食物端來，他却就桌子邊坐下，好像什麼食物放在面前一般，舉手向口，津津有味的吃起來了；向我兄弟說道：

『來，朋友，隨意放量吃。不必客氣；你說，你差不多要餓死了，但是你好像並沒有胃口的。』

我兄弟完全模仿他的舉動，一面說：『主人！恕我，你

perfectly *imitated*[1] what he did. "You see I lose no time, and that I play my part well enough."

"How like you this bread?" said the Barmecide. "Do not you find it very good?"

"O my lord," replied my brother, who saw neither bread nor meat, "I have never eaten anything so white and so fine."

"Eat your fill," said the Parmecide. "I assure you that it cost me five hundred pieces of gold to *purchase*[2] the woman who bakes me this good bread."

Soon the Barmecide called for another dish, and my brother went on eating, only in idea. There was never better *mutton*[3] and *barley broth*,[4] the Barmecide said, and my brother assented. Then there was a goose with sweet *sauce*,[5] and a *lamb*,[6] fed with *nuts*.[7] Of this the Barmecide boasted especially, and of all my brother, who was ready to die with hunger, pretended to eat.

"You honor me by eating so heartily," said the Barmecide. "Ho, boy, bring us more meat."

"No, my lord, if it please you," replied my brother, "for indeed I can eat no more."

"Come, then," said the Barmecide, "and bring the fruit." When he had waited long enough for the servants to appear again, he said to my brother: "Taste these *almonds*.[8] They are good and fresh

【註】1. 模仿. 2. 買. 3. 羊肉. 4. 麥湯. 5. 醬油. 6. 羊肉. 7. 菓兒. 8. 杏仁.

不見我，一刻不停的，儘量地大吃大嚼嗎？』

巴米賽德說：『你想這麵包怎樣？味道不是很好嗎？』

我的兄弟原不見有麵包或食盆，但勉強答道：『呵，我的主人，這樣又白又好的麵包，我從來未曾吃過。』

巴米賽德說：『儘量吃，我老實對你講，替我做這樣好麵包的那個女子，我出五百金買來的哩！』

巴米賽德立刻又另喚了一碟菜，我兄弟繼續在假扮做吃。巴米賽德說：『這羊肉和麥湯沒有比這更出色的了。』我兄弟應和着。於是有用上等醬油煮的鵝肉，腔裏用菓兒實着煮的羊肉，巴米賽德又是大誇而特誇了一回，我那眼見餓死的兄弟，對於這一切，都假做吃着。

巴米賽德說：『你胃口眞不壞，噲，侍者，再端菜來。』

我兄弟答說：『不必客氣，我實在吃得太飽了。』

巴米賽德說：『那末也好，便拿水菓來吧。』他居然等了好一會兒，以待僕人到來，和我兄弟說：『嘗嘗這些杏仁，看怎樣？牠們都是上等新鮮採來的。瞧，這樣有各種的菓

gathered.　Look, here are all sorts of fruits, cakes, and *sweetmeats*.[1]　Take what you like."

Then, stretching out his hand, as if he had reached my brother something, he still bade him eat, and said, *"Methinks*[2] you do not eat as if you had been so hungry as you said you were when you came in."

"My lord," replied Shacabac, whose *jaws*[3] ached[4] with moving and having nothing to eat, "I assure you I am so full that I cannot eat one bit more."

"Well then, friend," the Barmecide went on, "we must drink some wine now, after we have eaten so well."

"I see you will have nothing wanting," said Shacabac, "to make your treat complete; but since I am not used to drinking wine, I am afraid I may not act with the respect that is due to you.　Therefore let me be content with water."

"No, no!" said the Barmecide; "you shall drink wine," and at the same time he commanded some to be brought, as the meat and fruit had been served before.　He made as if he poured out for both, and said, *"Drink my health,*[5] and let us know if you think this wine good."

My brother pretended to take the glass, and looked to see if the color was good, and put it to his nose, to try the *flavor*.[6]　He then made a low bow to the Barmecide, to show that he took the liberty to

【註】　1. 糖果.　2. 我想.　3. 牙牀.　4. 痛.　5. 請飲此爲我壽.　6. 香味.

438

兒，乾餅，和糖果在此。請隨意揀吃！』

　　他乃伸手，好像遞什麼東西給我兄弟似的，仍慇懃地勸他吃着，說道：『你可太客氣了，你來時曾說怎樣餓着，但我看你並沒有吃什麼呢？』

　　舍加巴克沒有東西進口，可是牙牀卻假裝吃食，搬動得疼痛了，便答說：『主人，我是很飽了，一些兒不能多吃了。』

　　巴米賽德接口說：『也罷，朋友，我們既吃的這麼爽快，現在該喝些酒了。』

　　舍加巴克說：『謝你的盛情，勞你這樣欵待，週到無缺；不過我不慣喝酒的，惟恐酒後失德，倒是不便。我們還喝水吧。』

　　巴米賽德說：『不，不！你該喝酒好；』同時他便呼取酒來，食物和水果，好像先時一般的陳設着。他裝做倒兩人的酒的樣子，說道：『請飲此爲我壽，且爲我品品這酒味怎樣？』

　　我兄弟裝做把杯喝着，先看酒色佳不佳，再嗅酒味如何，他乃向巴米賽德打了一大躬，舉杯祝慇的壽，後卽自

drink his health; and then drank with all the signs of a man that drinks with pleasure.

"My lord," said he, "this is very excellent wine, but I think it is not strong enough."

"If you would have stronger," answered the Barmecide, "you need only speak, for I have several sorts in my *cellar*.[1] Try how you like this."

Then he made as if he poured out another glass for himself and one for my brother, and did this so often that Shacabac, *feigning*[2] that the wine had gone to his head, lifted up his hand, like a drunken man, and gave the Barmecide such a box on the ear as made him fall down. He was going to give him another blow; but the Barmecide, holding up his hand to ward it off, cried: "Are you mad?"

Then my brother, making as if he had come to himself again, said, "My lord, you have been so good as to admit your slave into your house, and give him a treat. You should have been content with making me eat, and not have forced me to drink wine; for I told you that it might cause me to fail in my respect to you. I am very sorry for it, and beg you *a thousand pardons*.[3]"

When he had finished these words, the Barmecide, instead of being angry, began to laugh with all his might. "I have been long," said he, "seeking a man of your sort. I not only forgive you the blow you have given me, but I desire that we may be friends from this time forth, and that you take my

---

【註】　1. 酒窖.　2. 假做.　3. 千萬原諒.

由取喝，他乃裝做一個人喝酒的，各種狂樂的樣子。

他說：『這酒果然是再好也沒有了，不過我想，還欠醇烈。』

巴米賽德答說：『如你要醇烈的酒，你只說便了，因為我酒窖裏，各種的酒都有。你且嘗嘗這酒怎樣？』

他便裝做倒另一杯酒給自己，另一杯酒給我兄弟的樣子，且倒且喝，這般頻繁，舍加巴克假做酒醉了，手舞足蹈起來，好像一個醉漢的樣子，便伸手給巴米賽德一掌打去，打得他一個跟蹌。他又伸手要打第二掌時，却被巴米賽德舉手格開了，大叫道：『你瘋了不成？』

我兄弟乃假裝忽然驚醒的樣子，說道：『主人，承你大德，容你的僕人進來，加以厚意的款待。你只該教我吃飽罷了，不必強我喝酒；因為我早經說過，這酒或許使我對你失禮；我十分得罪，千萬請你恕我。』

當他纔說完這話，巴米賽德非但毫無怒意，反哈哈狂笑不止。說道：『像你這樣的一個人，我找得好久了。我不但恕你一切，並願今後我們做個好友，你就住在我的院子

house for you home. You have had the g od nature *to adapt yourself to my humors*,[1] and the patience to keep the jest up to the last. We will now eat in good earnest."

Then he *clapped*[2] his hands and commanded his servants, who appeared at once, to cover the table, and my brother was really treated with all the dishes of which before he had eaten only in *fancy*.[3] Wine and music followed, and the Barmecide's goodness to my brother did not stop there, for finding him to be *a man of wit and sense*,[4] he soon gave him the care of his household, and for twenty years, until the Barmecide's death, Shacabac performed his duties well.

【註】　1. 投合我的風趣. 　2. 拍擊. 　3. 想像. 　4. 才識兼備的人.

裏來。你眞好耐性兒，能投合我的風趣，偏有耐性，把這玩意兒一直做到底。我們現在眞個吃罷。』

　　他逐拍掌，呼喚僕人們，他們立時出現了，鋪上桌布，一道道的菜，果然是先前所想像吃的菜碟，我兄弟如今是眞個吃了。隨後就是酒和音樂，巴米賽德對我兄弟的好意，還不至此，因爲他見我兄弟是個才識兼備的人，便又周濟他的一家，凡二十年。巴米饗德死時，舍加巴克哀哭盡禮。

13. The History of Prince Zeyn Alasnam and the Sultan of the Genii

I

There was a sultan of Bussorah, *prosperous*[1] and beloved. He had only one source of sorrow, that he was childless. He therefore gave large alms to the *dervishes*[2] in his dominions, that they might pray for the birth of a son. Their prayers were granted, and a son was born to him and his queen; the child was named Zeyn Alasnam, which means *"Ornament*[3] of the *Statues.*[4]*"*

All the *astrologers*[5] of the kingdom were called together to foretell the infant's future. They found by their calculations that he would live long, and be very brave; but that all his courage would be little enough to carry him through the misfortunes that threatened him. The sultan was not alarmed, but said: "My son is not to be pitied, since he will be brave; it is fit that princes should have a taste of misfortunes, for thus is their virtue tried, and they are the better prepared to reign."

He rewarded the wise men and dismissed them, and caused Zeyn to be educated with the greatest care. But while the prince was still young, the good Sultan fell sick of an illness which all the skill of his physicians could not cure. Knowing that he must die, he sent for his son, and advised him to try to be

---

【註】 1. 强盛的. 2. 僧衆. 3. 飾品. 4. 祀像. 5. 星卜家.

十三　王子陳亞拉生與魔王的故事

一

從前，波沙拉有個蘇丹，非常強盛，且極受民衆愛戴。他事事滿足，只有一件，使他憂傷不已，便是他尙沒有孩子。他乃大布施境內僧衆，想求得一子。果然皇后卽誕生一子。那孩子名做陳亞拉生，意義是『神像的飾品。』

國內許多星卜家都召來，卜算這嬰孩的命運。據他們推算，他可以長壽，且十分勇敢；不過他將來所遭的風險要更大，常不是他的勇氣所能耐得。蘇丹聽了，並無驚色，但說道：『我兒不必着人憂慮，因爲他是很勇敢；王子們應該親嘗一些兒患難辛苦，然後他們的德性纔能堅定，纔更能適於治國。』

他賞賜術士們去了，却非常小心地教育着陳。但這王子還沒有長大成人，而蘇丹已經染病在牀，一切醫生診治，均無起色，眼看沒有生望了，他乃召兒子到來，囑咐他好

445

loved rather than to be feared, to avoid *flatterers*,[1] and t、be as slow in rewarding as in punishing.

After his father's death, Prince Zeyn soon began to show that he was *unfit*[2] to govern a kingdom. He gave way to all kinds of *dissipation*,[3] *conferred*[4] upon his young but evil mates the chief officers of the land, lost all the respect of his people, and emptied 、、 treasury.

The Queen, his mother, *discreet*[5] and wise, tried to correct his conduct, and warned him that he would lose his crown and life if he did not mend his ways. The people began to murmur, and a general *revolt*[6] would soon have followed, if the Sultan had not taken the advice of his mother. He dismissed his youthful advisers, and gave the government over to aged men, who knew how to control the people.

Zeyn repented sorely that his wealth was spent, and to no good purpose. Nothing could comfort him in his distress. One night in a dream a venerable old man came towards him, and said, with a smiling face, "Know, Zeyn, there is no sorrow that is not followed by *mirth*,[7] no misfortune that does not bring at last some happiness. If you desire to see the end of your affliction, set out for Grand Cairo, where great prosperity awaits you."

The young Sultan was much struck with his dream, and spoke of it very seriously to his mother, who only laughed and said: "My son, would you leave

---

【註】 1. 佞人. 2. 不適. 3. 放蕩 4. 授給. 5 謹慎. 6. 叛亂. 7. 安樂.

生治國，須受人民愛戴，不要給他們怨恨；應該遠避佞人，明慎賞罰！

王子陳從他父親死後，就被看出不善治國。他把一切重要職務，授給一般惡少奸佞掌管，自己却是荒淫無度，弄得民心大失，國庫虛空。

他的母親（皇后，）却是個謹慎聰明的婦人，為改正他的行為，警告他若再不補救過失，和改良行為，他必要失掉他的皇冠和生命。那些百姓早就發生怨望，如果這蘇丹再不聽他母親的忠告，照例要發生叛亂了。他便趕掉那些惡少政治家，把治國的職務，仍交一般老臣，他們知道怎樣管理人民。

國庫早已空虛，國內財政毫無辦法，陳深自悔恨，悶悶不樂。有一天晚上，他夢見一個態度莊重的老人走來，對他笑說道：『陳，你可知道：「安樂足以興悲，艱難可以生樂」的道理嗎？倘你要使苦盡甘來，須走往開羅去，自有大量的財富候着你。』

這少年蘇丹對於這夢，大受感動，他很鄭重的，把這夢兒說給他母親聽，她祇是笑着說道：『我兒，你難道為了夢

your kingdom and go into Egypt on the faith of a dream, which may be a *deceit*?[1]"

"Why not, madam?" answered Zeyn; "do you believe all dreams are false? No, no, some of them are sent from Heaven. My teachers have told me a thousand cases which will not let me doubt of it. The old man who appeared to me had something more than human about his person. If you will have me tell you what I think, I believe it was our great Prophet himself, who, pitying my sorrow, intends to relieve it. I am resolved to follow his advice."

The queen tried to *dissuade*[2] him, but in vain. The sultan begged her to govern the kingdom in his absence, and set out one night privately from his palace, and all alone took the road to Cairo.

After much trouble and *fatigue*[3] he arrived at that famous city. He alighted at the gate of a mosque, where, being spent with weariness, he lay down. No sooner was he fallen asleep than he saw the same old man, who said to him: "I am pleased with you, my son; you have believed me. Now, know I have sent you on this long journey only to try you; I find you have courage and resolution. You *deserve*[4] that I should make you the richest and happiest prince in the world. Return to Bussorah, and you shall find immense wealth in your palace. No king ever possessed so rich a treasure."

Prince Zeyn was not pleased with this dream. "Alas!" thought he to himself when he awoke, "how

---

【註】 1. 虛妄的.　2 勸止.　3. 勞苦　4. 值得.

的緣故，竟離開你的國家，走向埃及去嗎？這夢或許是盧妄的呢。』

陳答道：『母后，爲什麼不去？你道夢是盧妄的嗎？不，不，有些夢是上天給示的。我的師傅們替我講過成千的例子，決不使我有所疑惑的。我所夢的那老人，據我看來，大有意義，倘你要我解釋，我相信那便是我們大預言者的本身，他哀憐我的憂愁，有心特來救着我。我打定主意，聽從他的忠告了。』

皇后想再勸止他，終竟無效。這蘇丹遂把國政，暫託母親代理，當夜私自走出皇宮，獨自個兒迤向匪羅走去。

經過許多勞苦，最後到得那座名城，他在一所囘教寺院門前下馬，因爲途上辛苦了，便躺下歇歇，不覺便自睡着，夢中却又見那同一老人，來對他說道：『我歡喜你，我的孩子，你聽信我的話兒。如今，你該知道，我使你走這樣的長途，不過爲試試你罷了；你果然有勇敢，又有決心。你值得我使你成爲世上最富最快樂的王子了。回波沙拉去，你自見有無數的錢財在你的宮裏。這般富的財物，是從來的國王不曾有過的。』

王子陳對於這夢，好生不快。當他醒來尋思道。『啊唷！我是多麼錯誤！那個老人我認做是我們預言者的，原

much was I mistaken!   That old man, whom I took
for our Prophet, exists only in my disturbed brain.
My fancy was so full of him that it is no wonder I
have seen him again.   I had best return to Bussorah;
what should I do here any longer?   It is fortunate
that only my mother knows why I came hither; my
people, if they knew, would make a jest of me."

He set out at once for his kingdom, and when he
arrived the queen asked him whether he returned
well pleased.   He told her all that had happened,
and the queen, seeing his disappointment, gave him
comfort instead of *reproof*.[1]

"Do not *afflict*[2] yourself, my son," said she; "if
God has appointed you riches, you will have them
without any trouble.   Be contented; be *virtuous*[3]; seek
to give your subjects happiness; thus you will win
your own."

II

Sultan Zeyn vowed that for the future he would
follow his mother's advice, and be directed by the
wise viziers[4] she had chosen to help him in the
government.   But the very night after he returned to
his palace, the old man came to him for the third
time in a dream, and said:—

"The time of your prosperity is come, brave
Zeyn; to-morrow morning, as soon as you are up, take
a little *pickaxe*,[5] and dig in the former Sultan's *closet*[6];
you will find there a rich treasure."

【註】 1. 訓斥. 2. 愁苦. 3. 有德的. 4. 賢臣. 5. 鋤. 6. 退休室.

來是起於我的胡思亂想，我刻刻把他放在心裏，現在再夢見他，自然毫不足怪。我最好便囘波沙拉，還在這兒幹甚？幸而我出宮來，僅母親一人知道；百姓們要如知道了，豈不把這個傳做笑柄嗎？』

他馬上囘國，到的時候，皇后問他怎樣。他把經過的情形告訴給她，皇后見他大爲失望並不怪他，却好好地安慰他。

她說：『我兒不要愁苦，倘上帝賜你財富，你自會得着的，不必枉自辛苦，且自滿足着；你力行德政；加惠百姓；便能使國富民強了。』

二

蘇丹陳立誓，將來一切的事情，要聽從他母親的告誠，他母親替他選用許多賢臣，來輔佐他。但是當他在囘宮的那天晚上，這老人却第三次顯現在他的夢中，說道：

『現在你興盛的日子要到啦。勇敢的陳，明天早上，你一起牀，可取鋤到先前蘇丹的退休室，掘着地上，那裏你可發見豐富的寶藏。』

As soon as the Sultan awoke, he got up, ran to the Queen, and eagerly told her of the new dream.

"Really, my son," said the Queen, smiling, 'this is a very *capricious*[1] old man; but have you a mind to believe him again? At any rate, this new task is not so bad as your long journeys."

"Well, madam," answered the Sultan, "I must own that this third dream has restored my confidence. This night he has exactly pointed out to me the place where these treasures are. I would rather search in vain than blame myself as long as I live for having missed, perhaps, great riches by doubting at the wrong time."

Then he left the Queen, caused a pickaxe to be brought to him, and went alone into his father's closet. He began at once to break up the ground, and took up more than half the square stones with which it was *paved*,[2] but yet saw no sign of what he sought. Resting for a moment, he thought within himself, "I am much afraid my mother had cause enough to laugh at me." But he took heart, and went on with his labor. On a sudden he discovered a white *slab*,[3] which he lifted up, and under it he found a *staircase*[4] of white marble. He lighted a lamp at once, and went down the stairs into a room, the floor of which was laid with *tiles*[5] of *chinaware*,[6] and the roof and the walls were of *crystal*,[7] The room contained four golden tables, on each of which were

---

【註】 1. 變化無常的. 2. 鋪砌. 3. 石板. 4. 扶梯. 5. 花磚. 6. 瓷器 7. 水晶.

蘇丹醒來，立卽奔到皇后的房裏，急切地把這新夢告訴給她。

皇后笑說：『我兒，眞的嗎？這是個變化無常的老頭兒；但你可再相信他嗎？無論怎樣，這工作倒沒有長途奔波般的辛苦呢。』

蘇丹答說！『母后！我虧得有此第三夢，倒把我的信心恢復了。這遭，他明白地給我指出那財富的所在。我寧願去白找一次，省得後來因失去大財，懊喪不及。』

他遂辭別母親，取了一把鋤，獨自走到他父親的退休室去，立時發掘那地面，室中原用方石砌地，他掘了一半的石頭，不見有甚東西。休息了一囘，心裏想道：『我很怕母親、又會耻笑我。』乃振作精神，繼續工作着。忽然掘見一層白石板，把石板揭將起來，見下邊有大理石砌成的一道扶梯，他立卽點了火，從扶梯上走下去，卻到得一間屋子，地面是用瓷磚砌成，屋頂和牆壁却是水晶造成。那屋子裏有四張金桌子，每張桌上有十個美麗的石甕。他

ten *urns*[1] of beautiful stone. He went up to one of these urns, took off the cover, and, with no less joy than surprise, found it full of pieces of gold. He looked into all the forty, one after another, and found them full of the same coin, and, taking out a handful, he carried it to the queen.

His mother was amazed at what he told her. "O my son!" said she, "take *heed*[2] you do not *lavish*[3] away all this wealth foolishly, as you have already wasted the royal treasure. Give not your enemies so much cause to rejoice."

"No, madam," answered Zeyn, "henceforth I will live in such a manner as shall be pleasing to you."

The queen desired to be shown the wonderful room, which her husband had made with such secrecy that she had never heard of it. Zeyn led her to the closet, down the marble stairs, and into the chamber where the urns were. She looked curiously at everything, and in a corner *spied*[4] a little urn of the same sort of stone as the others. The prince had not noticed it before, but opening it found within a golden key.

"My son," said the queen, "this key certainly belongs to some other treasure; let us search well; perhaps we may discover its purpose."

They examined the chamber with the greatest care, and at length found a *keyhole*[5] in one of the *panels*[6] of the wall. Here the key readily opened a door which led into a chamber, in the midst of which

---

【註】 1. 甕. 2. 謹慎. 3. 浪費. 4. 發見. 5. 鑰匙孔. 6. 夾板.

揭開一個甕蓋一瞧，驚喜交集，却見滿甕黃晶晶的，都是金子哩。四十個甕兒，一個個瞧了，個個都盛滿同樣的金錢，他遂抓了一把，帶給皇后瞧去。

他母親見如此說着，驚訝不已。『呵我兒！今後你更格外謹慎，不可和先前一般的恣意，枉自浪費，教你的讎人們歡喜啦。』

陳答道：『母后！今後我當力自檢點，教你歡喜。』

那皇后高興地親自到室中去，原來她丈夫嚴守着祕密，便是她也從不曾聽到一些口風。他引她進了退休室，從石梯上下去，到那有甕兒的房間裏。她把這些東西一一細瞧過去，在屋角中，却見一個同樣的小石甕。王子先前不曾注意到，那甕兒有一把金鑰匙在裏面。

皇后說：『我兒，這鑰匙兒定屬另一寶庫的了；讓我們細瞧，也許能發見出來。』

他們細心地向屋子裏，看驗過去，最後看見有個鑰匙孔在牆的一塊夾板上。用鑰匙向孔中插進，很容易開得，門開處，便是另一房間，裏面有九座赤金打就的神座。那

were nine *pedestals*[1] of *massy gold*.[2]　On eight of them stood as many statues, each of them made of a single diam nd, and from them *darted*[3] such a brightness that the whole room was perfectly light.

"Oh heavens!" cried Zeyn, "where could my father find such *rarities*?[4]" The ninth pedestal surprised him most of all, for it was covered with a piece of white *satin*,[5] on which were written these words:—

"Dear son, is cost me much toil to *procure*[6] these eight statues; but though they are wonderfully beautiful, you must know that there is a ninth in the world, which *surpasses*[7] them all; that alone is worth more than a thousand such as these.　If you desire to be master of it, go to the city of Cairo in Egypt. One of my old slaves, whose name is Mobarec, lives there; you will easily find him.　Visit him, and tell him all that has befallen you.　He will conduct you to the place where that wonderful statue is, and you will obtain it in safety."

Having read these words, the young Sultan said to the Queen: "I will set out for Grand Cairo; nor do I believe, madam, that you will oppose my going."

"No, my son," answered the Queed; "you are certainly under the special care of our great Prophet. He will not suffer you to *perish*.[8]"

【註】 1. 神座. 2. 赤金. 3. 發射. 4. 奇寶. 5. 緞. 6. 獲得. 7. 超過 8. 毀滅.

八個神座上都有神像，這些神像個個都是整個兒的鑽石雕成，端的晶輝奪目，把一室裏照得異常明亮。

陳驚叫道：『我父親從何處覓得這樣的奇寶來？』那第九座神座，尤加引起他的驚奇，因為那座上有一方白緞子，上寫着：

『親愛的兒子，我獲得這八個神像，不比得閑，却費了無窮辛苦。但牠們雖然奇美珍貴，你須知世上尚有第九神像，價值超過這一切神像之上；只要有牠一個，可抵得這些神像成千。你如願意取牠，可往埃及開羅去。我有一老僕，名做莫巴克，是住在那兒；你當容易找到他的。見着他時，說明來由。他自會引你到這奇像的去處，使你平安地得到他的。』

念了這些話兒，這少年蘇丹便對母親說道：『我要上開羅走一遭；母后，我信你必不再阻止我吧。』

皇后答說：『我兒！你旣受神的暗示。他決必不會教你受禍的。』

III

The Prince took with him only a small number of slaves, and, arriving safe at Cairo, inquired for Mobarec. He found him to be one of the wealthiest men of the city, living like a great lord, in a house always open to strangers. Zeyn was shown to it, and knocked at the gate, which was opened by a slave, who demanded: "What do you want, and who are you?"

"I am a stranger," answered the prince, "and, having heard much of the Lord Mobarec's *generosity*,[1] am come to lodge with him."

The slave went to tell his master of the stranger's presence, and soon returned to bid the prince welcome. Zeyn went in, crossed a large court, and entered a hall richly furnished, where Mobarec received him with great *courtesy*,[2] returning thanks for the honor Zeyn did him in lodging at his house. The prince, having answered his *compliment*,[3] said: "I am the son of the late Sultan of Bussorah, and my name is Zeyn Alasnam."

"The Sultan," said Mobarec, "was formerly my master: but, my lord, I never knew of any children that he had; what is your age?"

"I am twenty years old," answered the sultan, "how long is it since you left my father's court?"

"Almost *two-and-twenty*[4] years," replied Mobarec; "but how can you convince me that you are his son?"

【註】 1. 大度. 2. 體儀. 3. 致候. 4. 二十二.

三

王子僅帶少數僕從，一路平安，到了開羅，訪着莫巴克。原來他乃是城中一個最富的人，廣招賓客，好似一個王公大臣，陳到了那裏，叩門，有僕人出來開門，問道：『貴客有何見教，姓甚名誰？』

王子答說：『我是個外客，因仰慕莫巴克爵主大名，特來拜訪的。』

那僕人進去通報，不久即來對王子說主人有請。陳進去，穿過了天井，到一所陳設華麗的賓廳，便見莫巴克早在那裏恭迓他。賓主寒喧已過，王子道：『我是波沙拉前蘇丹的兒子，名字叫做陳亞拉生。』

莫巴克說：『這蘇丹乃是我的從前主人；但是，我的主公，從不曾聽見他有孩子，你多少年紀了？』

蘇丹答說：『我二十歲，你離開我父王多久呢？』

莫巴克答說：『差不多二十二年了，但你怎能使我信你，確是他的兒子。』

"My father," replied Zeyn, "had beneath his closet an underground room, where I have found forty urns full of gold."

"And what more is there?" said Mobarec.

"There are," answered the prince, "nine pedestals of massive gold; on eight of them are as many diamond statues, and on the ninth a piece of white satin, on which my father has written what I must do to procure another statue, more valuable than all the rest together. You know where that statue is; for it is written on the satin that you will conduct me to it."

When he had spoken these words, Mobarec fell down at his feet, and, kissing one of his hands, said:—

"I bless God for having brought you hither. I now know you to be the Sultan of Bussorah's son. If you will go to the place where the wonderful statue is, I will show the way; but you must first rest here a few days. This day I *entertain*[1] the great men of the city. Will you come and be *merry*[2] with us?"

"I shall be very glad," replied Zeyn, "to be admitted to your feast."

"Mobarec led him at once under a *dome*[3] where the company were gathered, seated him at a table, and served him on the knee. The merchants of Cairo whispered to one another: "Who is this stranger, to whom Mobarec pays so much respect?"

When they had *dined*,[4] Mobarec addressed the company: "Know, my friends, that this young stranger is the son of the Sultan of Bussorah, my

【註】 1. 宴會. 2. 樂幸. 3. 圓室. 4. 餐畢.

陳答道：『我父親在他退休室的地窖裏，藏有四十罎金子。』

莫巴克說：『此外可有什麼？』

王子答說：『還有九座赤金打就的神座；八座神座上有鑽石的神像，那第九座上是一塊白緞子，緞子上我父親囑我務須取到那另一個神像，這神像的價值要勝過其餘八個的價值。你該知道這神像在那兒，因為緞子上寫明要你引導我去的。』

當他說着這些話的時候，莫巴克早向他跪下，吻着他手道：

『我謝上帝帶你到此。我如今知道你果然是沙波拉蘇丹的兒子了。倘你要到那異像的地方去，我來引路便是；不過你該休息幾天。今天我正宴會本城的許多大人物，不知你肯否榮幸呢？』

陳答說：『很好，我非常快樂，你准我蒞席。』

莫巴克便引他到一間圓室中，那裏衆賓客均已齊集，請王子坐下，跪着進食。開羅的商人們都暗暗納罕：『這客人是誰，莫巴克對他這般敬重着？』

當衆人餐畢，莫巴克對那些人說道：『你們知道，這少年客人是我主公波沙拉蘇丹的兒子。他父親買了我，到

master. His father *purchased*[1] me, and died without making me free, so that I am still a slave, and all I have belongs of right to this young Prince, his sole *heir*.[2]"

Here Zeyn broke in: "Mobarec, I declare before all these guests, that I make you free from this moment, and that I *renounce*[3] all right to you and all you possess. Consider what you would have me do more for you." Mobarec kissed the ground, and gave the Prince most hearty thanks.

The next day Zeyn said to Mobarec: "I have taken rest enough. I came not to Cairo to take my pleasure. It is time for us to set out in search of the ninth statue."

"Sire," said Mobarec, "I am ready, but you know not what dangers you must face."

"Whatever the danger may be," answered the prince, "I am ready; I will either perish or succeed. All that happens in this world is by God's direction. Do you but bear me company, and let your courage be equal to mine."

Mobarec, finding that Zeyn's mind was made up, called his servants and bade them make ready for the start. When the prince and he had made their own preparations, they set out. After traveling many days they came to a delightful spot, and alighted from their horses. Mobarec then said to the servants: "Do you remain here till we return." Then he said to Zeyn: "Now, sire, let us advance by ourselves.

【註】 1. 買. 2. 唯一的嗣人. 3. 取消.

死尚未還我自由，所以我仍是個奴僕，我所有的一切，都是蘇丹的唯一的嗣人這少年王子的。』

陳接口說：『莫巴克，我在諸位客人前，立時釋你自由，取消我們間主僕關係。你想我還有什麼，應該爲你做的呢。』　莫巴克以吻接地、給王子十二分的感謝。

第二天，陳對莫巴克說道：『我休息夠了。我不是到開羅來玩樂。我們便去找那第九座神像罷。』

莫巴克說：『我早準備好了，但你該知道這有怎樣的危險，必須遇到啦?』

王子答說：『不論如何艱險，我是準備嘗試的；我並不措意於成敗，一切聽天由命。祇顧鼓起你的勇氣，給我做伴便是。』

莫巴克見陳立意旣堅，乃喚他的僕人們，命收拾一切，準備出發。王子和他自己也收拾一番，便出發前去。走了許多天後，到得一個令人愉快的地方，他們跨下馬來。莫巴克乃吩附僕人道:『你們便在這裏，等候我們囘來罷。』

We are near the dreadful place where the ninth statue is kept. You will stand *in need of*[1] all your courage."

They soon came to a vast lake. Mobarec sat down on the *brink*[2] of it, saying to the prince: "We must cross this sea."

"How can we," answered Zeyn, "when we have no boat?"

"In a moment," replied Mobarec, "the *enchanted boat*[3] of the Sultan of the Genii will come for us. But you must not speak to the boatman, though his figure seem strange to you. Whatever you see, say nothing, for I tell you now, that if you *utter*[4] one word when we are *embarked*,[5] the boat will sink."

"I shall take care to be silent," said the Prince; "you need only tell me what I am to do, and I will obey."

Whilst[6] they were talking, he spied on the lake a boat made of red *sandulwood*.[7] It had a mast of fine *amler*,[8] and a blue satin flag. There was only one boatman in it, and he had the head of an elephant and the body of a tiger. When the boat was come to them, the monstrous boatman took them up one after the other with his *trunk*,[9] put them into his boat, and carried them over the lake in a moment. He then took them up with his trunk again, set them ashore, and instantly vanished with his boat.

【註】 1. 需要. 2. 岸邊. 3. 神船. 4. 說出. 5. 乘船. 6. 正當.
檀香紫木. 8. 琥珀. 9. 象鼻.

他又向陳說：『現在，我們便自去罷。那第九神像可怕的地方近了。你須鼓起勇氣來。』

他們走到一個大湖。莫巴克坐在岸邊，向王子說道：『我們須渡海呢。』

陳答說：『沒有船隻，我們如何渡過？』

莫巴克答道：『一會兒，魔神蘇丹的神船，便來迎接我們了。那船夫形狀極怪，你却不能和他說話。無論你見了甚麼，千萬不能開口，現在我告訴你，如登船時一說話，那船立刻就沉沒了。』

王子說：『我當留心靜默着，你囑我怎樣，我必服從。』

他們正當說話的時候，便見湖遠處有一隻檀香紫木的船兒飛來。豎着一根上好琥珀做成的桅，上面懸着一面藍緞的旗。船上只是一個船夫，這人象頭虎身。船到時，那怪船夫用他的鼻，依次把他們捲了，放在他的船裏，端的霎眼時間，把湖渡過了。他又掀鼻將他們一一捲上了岸，忽然間，連船連人都不見了。

"Now we may talk," said Mobarec; "the island we are in belongs to the King of the Genii. Look round you, Prince; behold the beautiful fields and trees; hear the songs of a thousand birds unknown in other countries."

Zeyn could not enough admire the beauties around him, and still found something new, as he advanced *farther*[1] into the island. At length they came before a palace built of *emeralds*,[2] surrounded by a wide moat, on the banks of which grew such tall trees that they shaded the whole palace. The gate was of massive gold, and was approached by a bridge formed of one single *shell*[3] of a fish, at least six *fathoms*[4] long and three in breadth. At the head of the bridge stood a company of very tall genii, who guarded the entrance into the castle with great clubs of steel.

"Let us go no farther at present," said Mobarec; "these genii will destroy us unless we perform a magical *rite*."[5] Then Mobarec laid on the ground two large *mats*,[6] on the edges whereof he scattered some precious stones, *musk*,[7] and amber. Afterwards he sat down on one of the mats, and Zeyn on the other, and Mobarec said to the Prince:—

"I shall now, sire, *conjure*[8] the Sultan of the Genii, who lives in this palace. If our coming into this island pleases him not, he will appear in the shape of a dreadful monster; if it pleases him, he will

---

【註】 1. 碧玉. 2. 城楪. 3. 殼. 4. 噚 (度名, 長六呎). 5. 禮節. 6. 蓆, 7. 麝香. 8. 祈請.

莫巴克說：『現在我們可以說話了，我們所在的這座島，是屬魔國的國王的。你瞧，這四處的風景，美田佳樹，是多麼秀麗；你聽，這百鳥的歌聲，是別處從不曾聽見過的。』

陳舉目四望，賞覽景色的美麗，不勝稱羨，而且每到一處，必有一處異常的景緻，眞是仙宮梵宇，觀賞不盡。他們最後到一座宮院的而前，都是碧玉造成的，一條闊大的城濠，濠邊高樹參天，足以蔭覆宮院。那城門是赤金的，靠近門處，便有一橋，是一尾魚殼造成的，至少有三十六尺來長，十八尺來闊，橋塊有一隊很高的魔神站着，他們各持着大鐵棒，守衛那城子的。

莫巴克說：『我們現在且停步吧！我們急須行一種魔國的禮節，不然，這些魔兵便要弄死我們。』莫巴克乃鋪下二條大蓆，每條邊上都散滿着幾種寶石，麝香，和琥珀。他自己坐着一條，教陳坐着一條，向王子說道：

『我現在要祈請那魔神蘇丹了，他便住在這宮院裏。倘我們到這島上，他不歡喜時，卽現出怕人的怪物來；倘他

show himself in the shape of a handsome man. You must rise at once and salute him without going off your mat; for you would certainly perish should you stir[1] from it. You must say to him, 'Lord of the Genii, I wish your majesty may protect me, as you always protected my father; and I most humbly beg of you to give me the ninth statue!' "

Then Mobarec began his magic rite. Instantly their eyes were dazzled by a long *flash*[2] of lightning, followed by a *clap*[3] of thunder. The whole island was covered with a thick darkness, a *furious*[4] storm of wind blew, a dreadful cry was heard, the island felt a shock, as of an earthquake, and the Sultan of the Genii appeared in the shape of a very handsome man, yet there was something *terrific*[5] in his air.

When King Zeyn had spoken the words taught him by Mobarec, the Sultan of the Genii, smiling, answered:

"My son, I loved your father, and each time he came to pay me his respects I gave him one of his statues. I have no less kindness for you. Some days before your father died, I made him write the words you read on the white satin. I promised to protect you, and to give you the ninth statue, most beautiful of all. It was I whom you saw in a dream in the shape of an old man; I caused you to open the underground place where you found the urns and the statues. I know what brought you hither, and on certain conditions you shall obtain what you desire.

【註】 1. 離開. 2. 閃光. 3. 瓦霤. 4. 狂暴的. 5. 可怖的.

歡喜時，便顯出一個好看的人形來。你須站着向他致禮，但不要離開坐蓆；倘你離開便要死的。你須對他說：「魔神的主啊，我懇求你保護我，因爲你常保護我父親的；我千萬懇求你，把那第九神像賜給我吧！」』

莫巴克開始行他的魔禮。忽然一道閃電，使他們眼睛眩耀，隨後便是一個巨雷。全島上愁雲密佈，狂風怒號，怪聲突起，好像地震一般，那島震動得簸搖不已，魔蘇丹變成一個十分雅緻的人形出現，但是看他的態度間，還露出有些可怕的凶形。

陳照莫巴克的話兒，說了一遍，於是魔蘇丹笑答道：

『我的孩子，我愛你的父親，當他每次來拜謁我的時候，我便給他一個神像。我對你，也是一般的慈悲。你父親臨死以前的幾天，我教他寫這些字句在白緞上，留給你的。我允許保護你，把那最美的第九神像給你。夢中的老人就是我；命你發掘地室，得見那些甕兒和神像的，也就是我。我知道你來的動機，但你必須履行了某種條件，纔能得到

You must return with Mobarec, and you must swear to come again to me, and to bring with you a young maiden who has reached her fifteenth year, and has never wished to be married. She must be perfectly beautiful, and you so much master of yourself as not even to wish to marry her as you are bringing her hither. I will give you a lo king- lass,[1] which will clearly *reflect*[2] no other image than that of the young maiden you seek. Now swear that you will observe these terms, and keep your oath; otherwise I will take away your life, in spite of the kindness I feel toward you."

Zeyn Alasnam swore that he would faithfully keep his word, and the Sultan of the Genii handed him a looking-glass, saying: "My son, you may return when you please; there is the glass you are to use."

Zeyn and Mobarec then took leave of the Sultan of the Genii, and went towards the lake, over which the boatman with the elephant's head *ferried*[3] them as he had done before. They joined their servants, and returned with them to Cairo.

IV

When they had rested a few days, Mobarec told Zeyn that he knew a very *shrewd*[4] old woman who would help them. Thus a number of beautiful maidens of fifteen years of age were brought before King Zeyn; but when he had viewed them and tested

【註】 1. 鏡子. 2. 反照. 3. 渡載. 4. 聰明的.

我的寶物。你且同莫巴克囘去，須給我立誓要重來，來時
要帶一個十五歲妙齡的女郎同來，她是永不曾想要結婚的，
她必須絕色全美；　但你把她帶來的時候，　必要克制自己，
好像並不想要和她結婚的那樣才行。我給你那把鏡子，你
選擇的時候，只把這鏡子一照。若見鏡中有一個明淨的少
女，這女孩兒就是的了。現在你給我宣誓記着這些話，務
須遵誓；否則我便取你的性命，決不絲毫憐憫的。』

　　陳亞拉生宣誓必忠守誓言，魔蘇丹乃給他一面鏡子，
道：『我的孩子：你且囘去；這便是有用的鏡子。』

　　陳和莫巴克拜別魔蘇丹，向湖上走去，湖上那個船子，
仍和先前一樣的渡載他們。他們會集了僕人們，囘開羅去
了。

<h2 style="text-align:center">四</h2>

　　當他們休息幾天後，莫巴克對陳說，他認識一個聰明
的老婆子，足以幫助他們行事。於是許多十五歲妙齡的美
女，帶到陳的跟前來了；但是當他用鏡子照察時，個個女

them with the glass, it always became clouded. After finding that there were no maidens in Cairo who did not wish to be married, Zeyn and Mobarec went to Bagdad, where they *hired*[1] a great palace, and soon made *acquaintance*[2] with the chief people of the city.

At this time there lived at Bagdad an imaun named Boubekir Muezin, famous for his *charity*.[3] To him Mobarec went and offered a purse of five hundred gold pieces, in the name of Prince Zeyn, to be given to the poor. The next day Boubekir Muezin waited on Prince Zeyn to return to him his thanks, and, on hearing the purpose of his visit to Bagdad, told him of a young maiden, the daughter of a former vizier of the Sultan of Bagdad, of whom he felt sure that she would fulfill the required terms. He offered to ask her from her father as the wife of the prince, if he would go with him to her father's *mansion*.[4] As soon as the vizier learned the prince's birth and purpose, he called his daughter, and made her take off her *veil*.[5] Never had the young Sultan of Bussorah beheld such a perfect and *striking*[6] beauty. He stood amazed and taking out his glass at once, found that it remained bright and clear.

When he knew that he had at last found such a person as he sought, he begged the vizier to grant her to him. The cauzee was sent for at once, the contract signed, and the marriage prayer said. Then Zeyn conducted the vizier to his house, where

---

【註】 1. 租借. 2. 熟識. 3. 慈善事業. 4. 邸. 5. 面幕. 6. 觸目的

子的影兒，都是烏雲似的。陳和莫巴克既見開羅沒有選得中的女子，逐到巴革達德去，租了一所大莊院，交識一般重要的人物，不久就和他們廝混熟了。

這時候巴革達德，有一個回教徒，名做卜伯墟，墨任，是一個著名的專做慈善事業的人。莫巴克取五百金洋給他，用王子陳的名義，捐助窮民。第二天，卜伯墟。墨任為向王子陳道謝的緣故，特意招待他，並聽到他來巴革達德的目的。他告訴他們有一個少女，是巴革達德蘇丹前臣的女兒，據他想來，定能適合這個條件。他和他們同到那前臣家中去，他願意替王子做媒，向她父親說項。那大臣知道王子的來意和身世，便喚女兒近前，命她揭去面幕。這般十全十美絕色的女郎，波沙拉蘇丹永沒有瞧見過。他心裏暗暗喝彩，取出鏡子來一照，但見鏡影十分清明。

當他知道他終于尋着了他所需求的人，就求那大臣允許他的婚事。於是立刻請了回教牧師，訂立婚書，關於結婚上的祈禱，也如儀做了。陳乃引導那大臣到他的屋子裏，

he gave him a feast and valuable presents. The next day he sent a vast quantity of jewels by Mobarec, who led the bride home, where the wedding was kept with all the *pomp*[1] that became Zeyn's rank and *dignity*.[2] When all the company was dismissed, Mobarec said to his master:

"Let us begone, sire; let us not stay any longer at Bagdad, but return to Cairo. Remember the promise you made the Sultan of the Genii."

"Let us go," answered the prince. "I must take care to keep my word; yet I must confess, my dear Mobarec, the *damsel*[3] is so charming that I am *tempted*[4] to carry her to Bussorah, and place her on the throne."

"Alas! sire," answered Mobarec, "take *heed*[5] how you give way to that thought. Whatever it costs you, be as good as your word to the Sultan of the Genii."

"Well, then, Mobarec," said the Prince, "do you take care to *conceal*[6] the lovely maid from me; let her never appear in my sight—perhaps I have already seen too much of her."

When Mobarec had made all things ready for their journey, that returned to Cairo, and thence set out for the island of the Sultan of the Genii. When they were arrived, the maid, who had journeyed all the way in a litter, unseen by the Prince ever since the marriage, said to Mobarec:—

【註】 1. 榮華. 2. 高貴. 3. 姑娘　4 誘惑. 5. 注意. 6. 隔離.

給他重價的聘禮，并用酒筵款待他。第二天，由莫巴克送了許多珠玉飾物去，便引着新娘囘來，當晚舉行婚禮，一切合於陳的莊嚴和身分。當親友們散去時，莫巴克對他主子說：

『讓我們去吧，不要再勾留在巴革達德了，向開羅去。記住你對魔蘇丹的誓言。』

王子答說：『讓我們去，我當保守誓言；不過，親愛的莫巴克，我老實告訴你，這姑娘却是太迷人了，我恨不得立刻帶她囘波沙拉去，把她放在皇座上。』

莫巴克答說：『啊呀！趕快斷絕這樣的思想吧，你旣對魔蘇丹宣了誓，若便這樣，你是無益處呢。』

王子說：『是的，那末你可把那尤物和我隔離；讓她不要再現在我的眼裏。——恐怕我已瞧得太多了。』

莫巴克依命辦好，他們便囘開羅去，再從開羅轉到魔蘇丹的島上。沿路那姑娘坐在一頂轎兒裏，從結婚後，她就不給王子瞧見了，及他們到魔島時，她問莫巴克道：

"Where are we?　Shall we soon be in the country of the Prince, my husband?"

"Madam," answered Mobarec, "it is time to tell you the truth.　Prince Zeyn married you only in *order to*[1] get you from your father.　He did not promise to make you Queen of Bussorah, but to bring you to the Sultan of the Genii, who has asked of him a maiden of your loveliness and purity."

At these words, she began to weep *bitterly*,[2] which moved the Prince and Mobarec　"Take pity on me," said she.　"I am a stranger; you will have to answer to God for your *treachery*[3] towards me."

Her tears had no effect, for she was presented to the Sultan of the Genii, who after looking at her closely, said to Zeyn:—

"Prince, I am satisfied with your *conduct*.[4]　The maid you have brought me is beautiful and good, and I am pleased that you have been master of yourself to fulfill your promise to me.　Return to your own land; and when you enter the room where the eight statues are, you shall find the ninth which I promised you."

Zeyn thanked the King of the Genii, and returned with Mobarec to Cairo, and thence with haste homewards to see the ninth statue.　But he could not help thinking often with *regret*[5] of the maiden he had married, and *blamed*[6] himself for her sorrows.

〔註〕1. 爲……起見.　2. 傷心的.　3. 欺騙.　4. 行爲.　5. 惋惜. 6. 謟責.

『我們現到何處了？可曾到我丈夫的國裏沒有？』

莫巴克答說：『夫人，我如今老實對你說罷。王子娶你，他的目的，不過使你離開你的父親啊。他不許你做波沙拉皇后，但帶你到魔島上來，那魔蘇丹曾問他要一個女郎，須像你那樣的端好。』

她聽了這些話兒，開始痛哭起來，使王子和莫巴克也覺得可憐。她說：『可憐我吧！我是個孤身女，你若欺騙我，上帝也不能容你的！』

她的流淚並沒有效驗，因爲她已經帶到魔蘇丹這裏了，他細瞧了她一回，對陳說道：

『王子，你的行爲使我很滿意。你所帶來這女子，美好無比，你却謹守誓言，保住自身，尤其使我歡喜。你便回國去，當你到了那八個神像的屋裏，我所許給你的，這第九神像就可看見了。』

陳謝過魔王，急急回到開羅，再轉道回家，以看那第九神像。不過他對於那結婚的姑娘老是念念不忘，爲了她的緣故，又深自悔恨。

"Alas!" said he to himself, "I have taken her from a *tender_father*,[1] to sacrifice her to a genie. O, *matchless beauty*![2] you deserve a better fate."

V

Troubled with these thoughts, Sultan Zeyn at last reached Bussorah, to the great joy of his subjects. He went at once to give an account of his journey to his mother, who was in a *rapture*[3] to hear that he had obtained the ninth statue.

"Let us go, my son," said she; "let us go and see it, for it is certainly in the underground chambers, since the Sultan of the Genii said you should find it there."

The young sultan and his mother, both impatient to see the wonderful statue, went down into the room but how great was their surprise, when, instead of a statue of diamonds, they beheld in the ninth statue a most beautiful maiden, whom the prince knew to be the one he had *conducted*[4] into the island of the Genii!

"Prince," said the young maid, "you are surprised to see me here. You expected to find something more precious, and I doubt not that you now repent having taken so much trouble. You expected a better reward."

"Madam," answered Zeyn, "Heaven is my w tness that more than once I nearly broke my word with the Sultan of the Genii to keep you to myself. Whatever be the value of a diamond statue, is it

---

【註】 1. 慈父. 2. 絕色無雙. 3. 大喜. 4. 護送.

他自己說道：『唉！我把她從她慈父手裏收了來，却給與魔王，白犧牲了。啊！絕色無雙的姑娘你該受一更好的命運支配呢！』

五

蘇丹陳一路胡思亂想，終於回到波沙拉，臣民皆大歡喜。他立刻把事情對母親講了，她聽說他得了這第九座神像，自是喜不自勝。

她說：『便讓我們去到那地室裏去，瞧這神像，因爲那魔蘇丹許你在那裏發見這神像呢？』

少年蘇丹和他的母親，都焦急着要去看一看奇像，便同入地室去；但是他們瞧見的，並不是神像，却是一個天姿國色的美女，坐在第九神座上，這美女，王子一看便認識是他送將魔島上去的，大家吃了一驚！

那姑娘說：『王子，你在這裏瞧見我，要駭異吧。你本希望要得更貴重的東西，如今我想你要懊悔白走一遭了。

陳答說：『姑娘！有天爲證，我帶你到魔蘇丹那裏去的時候，險些兒要破誓。無論一個鑽石神像的價值怎樣，

worth as much as your being mine? I love you above all the diamonds and wealth in the world."

Just as he finished speaking, a clap of thunder was heard, and the place shook. Zeyn's mother was *alarmed,*[1] but the Sultan of the Genii appeared at once, and drove away her fear.

"Madam," said he to her, "I protect and love your son. I had a mind to try whether, at his age, he was master of himself. This is the ninth statue I designed for him. It is more rare and precious than the others. Sir," said he, turning to the young Prince, "live happy, Zeyn, with this your wife; and if you would have her true and *constant*[2] to you, love her always, and love her only."

With these words the Sultan of the Genii *vanished,*[3] and Zeyn, enchanted with the young lady, caused her that very day to be *proclaimed*[4] Queen of Bussorah, over which they reigned together in happiness for many years.

【註】 1. 驚慌. 2. 恆久的. 3. 不見. 4. 擁立.

怎能及得你這美人？我愛你，勝過世上一切的鑽石和財物呢。』

當他說話完畢，忽然哄的一聲雷鳴，震得滿屋亂幌，陳母正自驚慌，那魔蘇丹早就顯現出來，安慰她。說道：

『夫人！我是保護和愛好你的兒子的。我有心要試驗他，看在他的年齡上，有沒有克制的功夫，這便是我許他第九神像的原由。這是希世之珍，價值遠過以前的幾個。』他回頭對少年王子說道：『先生！你可和妻子兩口兒，好生快活地住着；倘你要她對你永效忠貞，你須永遠地，專心愛她就是。』

那魔蘇丹說了這幾句話後，就不見了。王子陳重得佳婦，心坎裏喜歡得了不得，當日便冊立她爲波沙拉皇后，他們快樂地共同治理波沙拉，有許多年代。

書名：天方夜談（英漢對照）
系列：漢英對照經典英文文學文庫
主編：潘國森、陳劍聰
原作者:佚名
漢譯:佚名

出版：心一堂有限公司
地址：香港九龍旺角彌敦道610號
　　　荷李活商業中心18樓1805-06室
電話號碼：(852) 6715-0840
網址：www.sunyata.cc
　　　publish.sunyata.cc
電郵：sunyatabook@gmail.com
心一堂讀者論壇：http://bbs.sunyata.cc
網上書店：http://book.sunyata.cc

香港發行：香港聯合書刊物流有限公司
香港新界大埔汀麗路36號中華商務印刷
大廈3樓
電話號碼：(852)2150-2100
傳真號碼：(852)2407-3062
電郵：info@suplogistics.com.hk

台灣發行：秀威資訊科技股份有限公司
地址：台灣台北市內湖區瑞光路七十六巷
　　　六十五號一樓
電話號碼：+886-2-2796-3638
傳真號碼：+886-2-2796-1377
網絡書店：www.bodbooks.com.tw
心一堂台灣國家書店讀者服務中心：
地址：台灣台北市中山區松江路二〇九號1樓
電話號碼：+886-2-2518-0207
傳真號碼：+886-2-2518-0778
網址：www.govbooks.com.tw

中國大陸發行 零售：
　　　　深圳心一堂文化传播有限公司
深圳：中國深圳羅湖立新路六號東門
　　　博雅負一層零零八號
電話號碼：(86)0755-82224934
北京：中國北京東城區雍和宮大街四十號
心一堂官方淘寶流通處：
http://sunyatacc.taobao.com/

版次：2019年4月初版

　　　HKD 188
定價：NT　698

國際書號　978-988-8582-61-7

Title: Stories From Arabian Nights
　(with Chinese translation)
Series: Classic English Literature
Collections with Chinese Translation
Editor: POON, Kwok-Sum(MCIoL,
DipTranCIoL), CHEN, Kim
by Anonymous
Translated and Annotated (in Chinese)
by Anonymous

Published in Hong Kong by Sunyata Ltd
Address: Unit 1805-06, 18/F, Hollywood Plaza,61(
Nathan Road, Mong Kok, Kowloon, Hong Kong
Tel: (852) 6715-0840
Website: publish.sunyata.cc
Email: sunyatabook@fmail.com
Online bookstore: http://book.sunyata.cc

Distributed in Hong Kong by:
SUP PUBLISHING LOGISTICS(HK)
LIMITED
Address： 3/F, C & C Buliding,
36 Ting Lai Road, Tai Po, N.T.,
Hong Kong
Tel： (852) 2150-2100
Fax： (852) 2407-3062
E-mail： info@suplogistics.com.hk

Distributed in Taiwan by:
Showwe Information Co. Ltd.
Address: 1/F, No.65, Lane 76, Rueiguang
Road, Neihu District, Taipei, Taiwan
Website: www.bodbooks.com.tw

First Edition April 2019
HKD 188
NT 698

ISBN: 978-988-8582-61-7